LOOSE NUKES

By Bill Griffeth

Bill Griffeth

With gratitude to my wife Nancy for encouraging me to undertake this project

Acknowledgments

This book owes its creation not only to the family, teachers, and friends who have influenced me, but also to the multitude of writers whose works have inspired me. In particular I want to thank New School teachers Sidney Offit, John Reed, and Katia Lief and their students; the Lamas of Halton (Karen Jackson, Jane Petrovich, Mark Offer, Will Leskevich, and Peter Blake); and early readers Nancy Griffeth, Lesley Greyling, Zinnia Maravell, Rebecca Knack, and Berenike Schlüren. The insights contained in the comments of all of these people have made *Loose Nukes* a much better book than it would otherwise have been. Many writers have inspired me to join their ranks. Special thanks to John Irving, J.K. Rowling, and Ian McEwan, whose characters came to life for me and whose styles set a high standard of elegance and power. All remaining deficiencies in content and style are my responsibility.

Contents

CHAPTER 1

The Widower

Coot Jenkins stepped warily into the dark room, alert for the slightest sound or motion, fearful of making a costly mistake. He paused a few seconds for his eyes to adjust to the dim light, then crept forward. Seeing a sudden movement out of the corner of his eye, Coot spun to his left, aimed his 9mm Glock at the shadowy figure, and fired twice. Three more threats, three more targets dispatched. A fifth shadow moved, but Coot was too slow. This time he heard a sharp crack and knew that, had this been a real gunfight, he would have been a dead man. Instead, the lights came on and Justin, his 20-something tactical combat instructor, joined him in the small room.

"Not bad for an old dude, Mr. Jenkins."

Coot frowned at the younger man's backhanded compliment. He was just a little slower than he had been as an Army Ranger toward the end of the Vietnam War. So what if his hair had turned gray in the intervening years? He was still trim and fit.

"Old dude?"

Justin turned red beneath his tan. "Sorry, Mr. Jenkins. I just meant to congratulate you." Justin extended his left hand.

Coot glanced at Justin's empty right sleeve. His frown faded, momentary annoyance replaced by appreciation for Justin's sacrifice. Coot shook the young veteran's hand, as he realized once more how lucky he was to have come home from Vietnam in one piece.

The two men left the close-quarters shooting range and returned to the main desk of Potomac Tactical Training. Coot returned the Glock and magazines that he had used in the four-hour individualized course.

"Thanks for your help today," he said. "I've kept up my marksmanship skills by shooting at static targets, but your training course is much more realistic."

"We get a lot of Nam vets coming to us," said Justin. "Especially if they've been laid off."

"Aren't you worried a guy might use his enhanced skills to waste a bunch of people at a school or movie theater?"

"We don't train anyone we suspect might cause trouble." Justin pointed to a bulletin board covered with photos of men and a few women who had taken P.T.T. courses. "See how many of our students get jobs with private security services?" He turned back toward Coot. "What sort of work do you do, Mr. Jenkins?"

"I'm on the staff of Scientists Against Future Extinction."

"That's some sort of anti-war group, right?" Justin looked away, then back at Coot. "Kind of an odd job for a vet, isn't it?"

"My job is to prevent nuclear war." He smiled at Justin. "What better job for a vet?"

Justin still looked puzzled. "So why are you taking a tactical combat course?"

"We've had some break-ins in my neighborhood recently," said Coot. "I want to be better prepared."

"You should be confident," said Justin. "You improved quickly as the session went on."

"I just hope I don't need to use my new skills."

* * *

On his way home through Washington after the tactical combat training session, Coot passed the cemetery where his late wife Frannie was buried. On impulse, he turned his blue Camry around and returned to the memorial garden's main entrance. He drove along the narrow roads that led through well-kept plots to Frannie's grave. He parked and climbed out of his car. The clear blue sky and chill air reminded Coot of the day he had buried Frannie. A piece of polished granite marked the spot under the great golden maple tree where he had said goodbye to her for the last time. Tears came to his eyes. He brushed them away as quickly as they had come.

He wished he had thought to bring flowers. Frannie was always delighted when he brought her flowers. Later, as she lay dying at home, he made sure to keep fresh flowers in her room. Frannie's favorites were from her own garden: soft white and buttery yellow daffodils, deep red and purple irises, peach-colored roses. Without her magic touch, the garden was now a poor reminder of the beauty she had brought into his life. He could hardly bear to look out the kitchen window at the plots that she had so carefully tended.

In her final weeks, Frannie had become weaker and weaker, her deteriorating condition reflected in the hospice nurses' growing pessimism and Coot's own increasing dread of losing the only woman he had ever loved. Oddly, he could not remember Frannie's actual death, but he could not forget the pitiless lowering of her coffin into that awful, empty pit, now filled with dirt and covered with grass at his feet.

A large American car came slowly along the road. The driver parked just behind the Camry and a woman got out of the rear seat. Jill Meecham, chief of staff of the National Security Council, spoke to her driver, then walked toward Coot.

Coot and Jill had known each other for two decades, both having been active in the arms control community. Coot recommended Jill for her position at the N.S.C. when the new administration came into office. Jill and her husband Jay were two of Coot and Frannie's closest friends. Jill often brought them food during Frannie's final, difficult weeks, and Jay contributed his excellent homemade preserves for Coot and Frannie's last breakfasts together. Coot had never needed such good friends more.

"I came to visit my father's grave." She pointed. "Just over there. But you look like you might need some company." Jill put her hand on Coot's arm. "Losing Frannie has been awfully hard on you."

Jill's support freed Coot to face the full force of his longing for Frannie. Coot bowed his head, tears once more welling up in his eyes. "Yes," he murmured. "Awfully hard."

Jill patted Coot on the back. "I wish there were some way that Jay and I could comfort you."

"You two have been terrific." Coot wiped his eyes on his shirtsleeve. "I just have to be stronger."

"You were plenty strong in arguing for the abolition of nuclear weapons, when all the 'serious' people said it was too late." Jill squeezed Coot's arm. "You made it respectable to be an abolitionist."

"Frannie urged me to go public." Coot sighed, looked down at the granite marker. "I couldn't have done it without her encouragement."

"Still, you were the one who took the risk."

"I suppose."

"Did you and Frannie talk about what you would do after she was gone?"

"Some." Coot smoothed the grass around Frannie's marker with his right shoe. "I didn't want to think about it. I still don't."

"Maybe you should." Jill smiled gently at Coot. "Frannie told me the last time I saw her that she hoped you would find someone else to share your life with."

Coot sobbed in a great convulsion of grief, regained control, looked at Jill, with red-rimmed eyes. "There'll never be another Frannie."

"Of course not. But there could be someone else, remarkable in her own way." Jill patted Coot on the back one final time, wished him well, and walked back to her car.

Coot lingered at Frannie's grave for a few more minutes. Could Jill be right? So far he had not met anyone remotely as appealing as Frannie. He could not imagine that he ever would.

CHAPTER 2

The Deal

Peering between antique pots through the front window of The Kyrgyzstan Emporium in central Osh, near the bazaar, Abai watched a stranger struggling toward him against the cold, wet wind that had plagued the city for the past few days. Could this be the man that Abai hoped would make his family both richer and safer?

As he stepped away from the window and prepared to welcome the fellow, Abai looked around his shop at the great variety of objects for sale: ancient gold coins, Russian Orthodox icons, a Leica camera from 1929, memorabilia from the Great Patriotic War, a large bronze bust of Lenin. Abai's collection included many pieces of jewelry, including cholpu, the heavy metal decorations that Kyrgyz women traditionally hung from their hair. Abai had begun as a rug merchant, and he still had the best collection of Persian rugs in Osh. But selling even high-quality antiques and carpets had not made Abai such a wealthy man. He owed his fortune to another line of business.

The stranger finally reached the shop, opened the door, entered, and quickly shut the door against the chilling wind. In his jeans, black turtleneck, and worn black leather jacket, the new arrival looked like the fellows that Abai had seen protesting globalization on satellite television. The man removed his glasses and wiped them dry, then put them back on and looked around. Abai met his gaze.

"Welcome, my friend," said Abai. "How are you, this blustery morning?" He was proud of his English, which he had learned from the BBC, American TV, and the Internet — his saviors from the isolation he felt, even in Kyrgyzstan's second-largest city.

"My name's Smith," said the man, in an American accent. "Mr. Anthony said you would be expecting me."

"Yes, yes, excellent!"

Abai had let a few people in the trade know he had "several unusual Soviet devices." At last a Mr. Anthony contacted him to find out the nature of the merchandise. After a few minutes of negotiating the price, Anthony agreed to purchase all five of the things. By the next afternoon, Anthony had arranged payment through hawala. He told Abai that "Mr. Smith" would come to inspect the devices, and here he was. If they passed Smith's examination, the hawala broker would release the funds: five million U.S. dollars. Soon Abai would be rid of several very dangerous items — and even wealthier in the bargain.

Abai stroked his gray beard while he poured chai for himself and his new customer.

"Before we have a deal," said the American, sipping the hot beverage, "I must see the devices. All of them."

The lips of the Kyrgyz tightened briefly. His eyes narrowed. "Of course, my friend, of course. Come." He put down his chai and took his jacket and old kalpak from a hook on the wall. Using two hands in the traditional way, he pulled the white wool hat down over his ears. Feeling slightly less nervous, though he did not really believe in the protective powers of the kalpak, he locked the front door of the shop and led the American out a back door into an alley littered with old tires, a couple of abandoned cars, and a blood-stained mattress.

Thirty yards along the alley they entered a garage housing a late-model Mercedes. Inside the building, Abai's driver put down the magazine he had been reading, rose from his chair, and opened the left rear door of the car. Abai gestured for the American to get in, then followed him. The driver closed the car door behind his boss and got into the front seat. Abai gave instructions to his man in rapid Kyrgyz, sure that the American could not understand. The fellow must not find out the location of Abai's secret warehouse.

Abai turned to the American. Pulling a dark piece of cloth from his pocket, he said, "I must blindfold you."

Raising his hand and leaning back as if to fend off the Kyrgyz, the American said, "What for?"

Abai's lips widened in a thin smile. "Even five million U.S. dollars is not enough to buy all my secrets."

Abai tied the rolled cloth around the American's head, blocking his vision. The garage door opened. The car accelerated, lurching into the street.

"It is too bad that you arrived on such a miserable day, Mr. Smith," said Abai. "Usually we have a nice view of Sulayman Mountain."

"Yeah, well, with this blindfold on," said the American, "it would be hard to appreciate."

"For that I am sorry, but...."

"It doesn't matter," interrupted the American. "I'm not here to see the sights."

For half an hour the men rode in a silence broken only by Abai's occasional directions to the driver. Abai hoped the frequent turns would confuse the American as to where they were going.

The Mercedes made one final turn into a warehouse and stopped. Abai removed the blindfold, allowing the American to look around at walls lined with shelf after shelf of various war-surplus items. When the disintegration of the Soviet Union caused a deluge of military equipment of all kinds, Abai and his brother had bought a lot at good prices.

"Come this way," Abai instructed. The two men got out of the Mercedes, walked through an adjoining room, and halted in front of a door secured by a combination lock and two padlocks. Abai unlocked the two padlocks with keys from his pocket, then moved so that the American could not see the digits he entered into the combination lock. He opened the door, revealing a small room with no windows.

Against the far wall were five large backpacks. Abai had no idea how Jyrgal had acquired them. Certainly not through official sales of surplus equipment. Abai should never have agreed to help his brother's widow sell weapons that could kill tens of thousands of people in one blast. How unfortunate that Jyrgal had not sold the things to al-Qaeda before his fatal accident. His brother had feuded with Zawahiri during the first Afghan war and swore he would never again sell anything to "that Egyptian bastard," as Jyrgal called the man who had been bin Laden's lieutenant back then.

Soon Abai would no longer have to worry about the devices being discovered. He was already thinking about how he could make even more money by mentioning this sale to one of those curious fellows who kept offering to pay him for information about weapons purchasers. He had always believed that twice the profit was to be had from double dealing.

* * *

George Boyd entered the room that the old Kyrgyz had unlocked. He immediately noticed five backpacks against the far wall: the Soviet equivalent to the H-912 carrier for the old U.S. Mk-54 Special Atomic Demolition Munition. A Russian contact had told him that, like the Mk-54, the Soviet A.D.M.s could be set to yield between ten tons and one kiloton of TNT — enough to destroy a large bridge or skyscraper or even to level dozens of city blocks. Crucially, they were light enough, at 150 pounds, for a strong man — or woman — to carry. George had grand plans for these devices. He crossed the room and bent over one of the backpacks. The Kyrgyz was close behind him.

"I need to check inside the carriers," said George. "Do you mind?"

"Help yourself, but be careful," said the Kyrgyz. "I do not fancy being vaporized."

George loosened the straps that held the carrier's top closed. The soft sides of the carrier slid down the cylindrical device, revealing a small door behind which he quickly found the control panel. Everything looked just as his Russian contact had described. If the device were not fake, the long-lived plutonium inside would be emitting alpha particles. He turned on his Geiger counter and passed its wand over the surface of the old device. The digital readout indicated the faint level of alpha particle radiation that the Russian had described.

"This one looks good," said George.

"But of course," said the Kyrgyz. "Did you think I would cheat you?"

George ignored the question. His excitement was rising at the thought of possessing such weapons. These five devices, though small, were sufficient to cause a panic in ruling classes around the world. These five devices represented the ultimate in asymmetrical warfare against those who, in their arrogance, sought to dominate the rest of mankind.

George re-fastened the straps of the carrier, then methodically performed the same procedure on the other four devices. All were genuine, as far as he could tell.

George used his cell phone to call the number that Michael Anthony had given him. He said, "Five easy pieces of bacon" and disconnected. He assured the Kyrgyz that the funds would be deposited in the hawala system immediately.

Indeed, Anthony should at that moment have been making a payment to a hawala broker, or *hawaladar*. The funds would be held in escrow until disbursed. George had used hawala before in his travels, especially in the Middle East. Since September 11, 2001, governments around the world had tried unsuccessfully to restrict hawala. Terrorist groups still used it to transfer funds without actually moving money.

"As soon as I've arranged for shipment, I'll call Anthony again and he'll release your payment."

"Let me crate them for you," said the Kyrgyz. "My men will make them look like shipments of pottery."

"Fine," said George. He waited while several fellows were summoned and began to load the carriers onto a dolly. "But I want to watch the whole process."

"No problem," said the old man. "We will follow them."

The workmen wheeled the dolly full of lethal weapons into another area of the warehouse where shipping containers and materials of various sorts were stacked. Two of the men lifted one of the carriers from the dolly and the others began to build a shipping crate around it.

When the weapons were all protected for shipment and effectively disguised, the Kyrgyz offered to deliver them wherever George wanted. Since Anthony did not want the shipper to know the actual contents of the crates, George had already arranged with another smuggler to transport the crates to their various destinations.

When George informed the Kyrgyz of his plan, the old man grimaced. "So, you do not trust me after all."

"Mr. Anthony requires another shipper," said George.

The Kyrgyz accepted this statement without comment, and soon the crates were safely aboard an old truck in a nearby loading bay.

George gave the Kyrgyz the address of the other smuggler. "I'd like to ride with them, then," said George. "Without being blindfolded." At least he would have a chance of defending himself if he could see an attack coming.

"As you wish, my friend — but it will be dark inside the truck."

George climbed into the rear of the truck. The doors closed behind him. From inside his steel box he could see nothing.

The ride was very bumpy in the ancient vehicle, but it was not long. The truck stopped. George's eyes took a moment to adjust to the light as the truck's rear doors opened. The smuggler who thought he was handling ancient pottery was waiting for him.

"Ah, Mr. Smith! Back already, and with Abai? I didn't know he required, shall we say, special services for the shipment of his pottery."

"There's a lot you don't know," said the Kyrgyz arms dealer.

As the five crates were moved from the truck to the dock, George took out his cell phone and once again dialed the number that Anthony had given him. He spoke the words they had agreed on: "The five little piggies are snug in their blankets." Anthony would now authorize his hawala broker, or *hawaladar*, to release the funds to Abai through his counterpart in Kyrgyzstan.

Abai's cell phone rang. He answered it, then smiled. "The pottery is all yours, Mr. Smith."

Now the devices just had to get to their destinations. Despite the many border checkpoints that freight trucks had to pass through on their way from the Caucasus, George and Anthony had agreed that the safest shipping method for four of the devices was by truck. Bribery of border guards was standard practice on the routes the trucks would be taking. Once at a Mediterranean port, the devices bound for the U.S. were to go by ship to Canada. Teams would receive the shipments and take the crated weapons to staging areas. The shipping crates' precious contents, disguised as ancient pottery destined for collectors, had better arrive safely. If even one of the devices did not get to the team responsible for its deployment, the consequences for George personally would be severe. Anthony had made that much clear.

The fifth device was destined for Indian-controlled Kashmir. Although Osh was only 450 miles by air from the heart of Kashmir, the long conflict in Afghanistan and the always-tense relationship between India and Pakistan made air freight too expensive and uncertain an option. NATO might turn back any aircraft attempting to cross Afghan territory, so George had arranged for the fifth crate to be smuggled by truck and donkey from Kyrgyzstan through Tajikistan and Afghanistan into Pakistan, where a team would be waiting to take it to its final destination. The trip through the mountains would be long and difficult. He was glad that he was not going along. The long trip home would be arduous enough.

* * *

"Nuclear weapons on the black market?" Coot Jenkins threw up his arms, ripping off the headset that he was using to talk with his old friend Sergey Bychkov. "Damn!" He leaned his tall frame over and picked up the headset, then straightened up and put it back on. A life-long runner, he normally had a slow pulse and low blood pressure, but Sergey's report had raised both. He calmed himself by sipping hot herbal tea from his favorite New York Mets mug, then leaned back in the chair in his spartan office and probed Sergey for more information. "What evidence do you have?"

Now head of the nonproliferation policy group at Scientists Against Future Extinction, Coot had heard enough false rumors of loose nukes over the years to be skeptical of any such news. Still, Sergey, an analyst at the Russian Academy of Sciences' Institute for U.S. and Canadian Studies, had reliable sources in all the former Soviet republics, so Coot waited for the other man's response.

"Only third-hand reports so far."

"Well, then, it's just another rumor."

Coot asked who the source was.

"An arms dealer somewhere in Central Asia told somebody who told somebody that a few tactical weapons had become available."

"Nothing more specific?"

"Not so far."

Having met years earlier at the U.N.'s Conference on Disarmament in Geneva, Coot and Sergey kept in touch through frequent encrypted conversations over the Internet. Each man had written several books and numerous journal articles on arms control and disarmament during his quarter-century career. Despite his respect for Sergey, Coot remained skeptical. "Don't you believe that all the nukes were transported back to Russia after the Soviet Union broke apart?"

"I'm no longer so sure. There were tens of thousands of them," said Sergey. "Times were hard. People needed money."

Coot raised both hands, carefully this time, though Sergey could not see this sign of his frustration.

"Nunn-Lugar funded retraining and jobs for those people," said Coot defensively, recalling his own testimony in favor of the legislation.

"Your government should have provided more support for those programs," said Sergey, reiterating his frequent complaint.

The two men had long lamented the unwillingness of the American congress and president to increase funding for efforts to prevent knowledge, materials, and especially weapons from getting onto the black market. Anyone with enough money could get almost anything he wanted there, no matter the consequences for the rest of humanity. Until now, nuclear weapons had been an important exception.

"Let me know immediately if you get more information, Sergey." The call concluded, Coot removed his headset and stood up. Before Sergey had called, Coot was working on the keynote speech he would be giving in a few weeks at the Arms Control Association's annual meeting. Now, concerned by Sergey's news, he put aside the speech and thought about the reported weapons. Few groups could afford such devices. One possibility: Islamic extremists backed by Saudi oil money. Another: a criminal gang bent on extorting money from fearful governments. Most disturbing: A shadowy group with a bizarre ideology and resources to match their sinister ambitions.

The intelligence agencies could track only so many people. That was one reason that Jill Meecham had begun an informal group of non-governmental experts to advise the National Security Council on various issues. Of course she had asked him to join the group, since he was widely regarded as one of the most knowledgeable people in the country on nonproliferation policy. The next meeting of the group was scheduled for 3 o'clock that afternoon at the Executive Office Building, across West Executive Avenue from the White House. Should he share Sergey's rumor with the group? It would not be welcome news. A leak could trigger a panic. Better to tell Jill in private first, and perhaps contact a few members of the group later.

The S.A.F.E. offices were just a block and a half west of the E.O.B. on Pennsylvania Avenue, so Coot left for the meeting at a quarter to three. He felt energetic, so he bypassed the sometimes balky elevators and hurried down several flights of stairs to the ground floor. Once outside, he walked southeast under blue May skies toward the gray granite building that Mark Twain had called "the ugliest building in America." Jill had given her outside experts credentials that enabled them to pass relatively quickly through security at the E.O.B. and the White House.

Coot found a seat at the large oval conference table in the conference room moments before Jill walked in, accompanied by another woman whom he had not met but who somehow looked familiar. To Coot's left was Beau Pepys from the Council on Foreign Relations. Beau, always an elegant dresser, was a descendant of Samuel Pepys, the 17th Century English diarist. Coot and Beau joked that they were chosen because Jill had a warped sense of humor about names. On Coot's right was corpulent and clever John Samuels from the Heritage Foundation, a man whose opposition to arms control treaties had brought him into conflict with Coot on several occasions. Directly across the table were Hank Morgan from the Nonproliferation Policy Education Center, Jill, and the new woman. Coot respected Hank's independent, pragmatic approach to nonproliferation issues. Coot was less familiar with the other members of the group, since they were not involved in nonproliferation work.

"Let's begin," said Jill. The chatter ceased. "First, I want to welcome Diana Munson, who has joined my staff as Cyber Security Coordinator. Diana earned her doctorate in computer science at Carnegie-Mellon and was recently a consultant in computer security at BBN in Boston. I am delighted to have her on board."

Diana Munson smiled slightly, intensifying Coot's sense of having seen her before. He studied her face, framed by medium-length golden brown hair. Now that he thought of it, Diana Munson's hair had a similar color to Frannie's in those summers long ago. He hoped Ms. Munson would say something later.

Half an hour into the meeting, Jill invited her new colleague to describe her plans for improving cyber security. This was not an area that Coot knew much about, but the woman's presentation was compelling.

"And so," she concluded, "cyber warfare, like other forms of modern terrorism, is asymmetrical. A few people with a small amount of equipment can do enormous damage to institutions and infrastructure. Countering their efforts requires many people and a lot of powerful hardware and software. My group at the N.S.C. is working to understand our nation's vulnerabilities in this area and to develop plans for their remediation."

She spoke in an earnest and precise way, like...like Frannie. No wonder Diana Munson had triggered such a strong reaction in him.

When the meeting was over, Coot walked around the table and stood next to Jill, who was finishing a conversation with Hank. He cast furtive glances at Diana Munson, trying not to act like a creep intrigued by a much younger woman. As Hank walked away, Coot got Jill's attention and said, "I've heard a report, a rumor, really, that I need to share with you in private. Do you have a couple of minutes?"

"A couple. No point in making you go through security at the White House." Jill turned to her colleague. "May we use your office, Diana?"

"Of course. I'll unlock it for you. I'm still unpacking boxes, so don't expect it to be organized. You'll be lucky if you can find space enough to sit." She laughed, as if marveling at her own tendency to procrastinate. Frannie had laughed like that. Spooky.

Coot nodded and smiled at her, but she did not appear to notice. He followed the two women to Diana Munson's office. Boxes were indeed stacked around the edges of the little room, obscuring the government green paint on the walls. With the tight federal budget, Jill apparently had not given her new employee a redecorating allowance.

Coot and Jill, now alone, sat in the only two chairs in the cramped office. Coot repeated the report that Sergey had given him.

"How seriously do you take this?" Jill asked.

"Seriously enough to follow up on. Has anyone in C.I.A., N.S.A., or D.I.A. picked up similar hints?"

Gathering information from the various intelligence agencies was easier than it used to be. If anything good had come out of the 9/11 attacks, it was that. Coot and Jill both understood that, if the rumor could be substantiated, the weapons must be found and secured. Even tactical nuclear devices could cause enormous damage, especially if detonated in a city.

"I'll personally follow up on this as soon as I get back to my office," said Jill.

With seventeen federal intelligence agencies to rely on, Jill had plenty of resources for investigating the rumor, so Coot simply said he would keep in touch with Sergey and relay any more information the Russian might provide.

Coot left the E.O.B. and walked back to the S.A.F.E. offices. Jill, he knew, would be taking the tunnel that connected the E.O.B. to the White House. Was it good news or bad news that she had received no report that corroborated the rumor? Good, if that made it more likely the rumor was false. Bad, if the rumor were true and the intelligence community had no information about the weapons.

* * *

Exhausted from his thirty-four-hour trip from Osh back to Berkeley and sweating in his leather jacket, George Boyd tramped up the stairs to his third-floor walk-up apartment, pulling his luggage, which thump-thump-thumped against the steps as he climbed.

"Keep it down out there, will ya?" Carl's familiar but muffled voice called out as George reached the second-floor landing. He ignored the demand. Carl had no idea that George had just completed the most important deal in history. One day soon, Carl and everyone else would respect George as the man who triggered the insurrections that ended capitalist tyranny forever.

In front of his own door at last, he fumbled for his key in the right pocket of his well-worn jeans. His glasses were fogged after the exertion of his climb, his eyes so tired he could hardly focus. He unlocked the door, entered the small apartment, and kicked the door shut. He rolled the suitcase into his bedroom, lifted it onto the still-unmade bed, and took out a bottle of maksym, a fizzy, non-alcoholic drink that he had first enjoyed while between flights in Bishkek. He grabbed a bottle opener from a drawer in his cramped kitchen and opened the maksym, then retreated into the living room, where he flopped onto the shabby sofa he had rescued from the curb out front. He sipped the maksym, enjoying how its bubbles exploded on his tongue.

How well he remembered struggling to move that sofa up to his apartment. No one in his building had offered to help. Why was he even bothering to attack the corporate and governmental structures that kept those people down? He knew the answer: his own experiences with oppressive organizations and their leaders. Nevertheless, George sometimes wondered whether the whole anarchist scene was just a futile protest against all-powerful corporate and governmental forces. He always came to the same conclusion: someone has to fight back.

George finished the maksym, lay back on the sofa, and closed his eyes.

The rain came in sheets, creating puddles in all the low places. The sheets became drops, the drops a mist, the mist a memory, but the puddles remained, soaking slowly into the saturated ground, into the fungal mycelium that lay everywhere beneath. Night fell. Primordial fruits that had been forming for days began to draw water from the mycelium, swelling quickly, bursting forth from the wet soil. When the sun appeared through hazy clouds in the morning, the stalks stood like little soldiers with their caps, rank upon rank of them, as far as the eye could see. Mushrooms.

Suddenly awake again, George knew what to name his small group of insurrectionists, the first rebels to spring from the soil of complacency and oppression, the first to challenge and defeat the institutions that exploit the many for the benefit of the few. He and his friends would be the first Mushrooms.

George was not entirely happy with the name. It reminded him too much of bean sprouts and tofu. The group had a more serious purpose than the vegetarianism so fashionable in Berkeley. Their goal was the radical transformation of human society. In the group's "mushroom model" of social change, lots of things were going on underground, preparing for the day when conditions were right and multiple insurrections would simultaneously erupt. He had to admit, though, that the name evoked not only the spontaneous appearance of thousands of mushrooms after a soaking rain but also the specter of mushroom clouds. The Mushrooms' detonation of nuclear devices around the world would show the impotence of corrupt governments to protect their people and would also provide a threat, forcing people to choose sides.

But which side would they choose, the status quo or a new way? Mushrooms could not control the outcome, only provide the conditions. Nor, as anarchists, *should* Mushrooms control the outcome. George accepted this principle. Still, it was hard to live with. He knew what people should do to defend their own interests: rise up, throw off their oppressors, and build new, more limited institutions. Why did so many people fail to understand the logic that led to insurrection? Why were they stuck in their petty lives, worrying about their petty problems, watching their stupid soap operas, reality shows, and ball games? The only way to begin the insurrection was to shake people out of their complacency, give them a real problem to think about.

George shifted his body in the old sofa, trying to get comfortable after his long journey. The sofa was not cooperating.

Mushrooms had an ally in fostering insurrection: the hacker group VI. People argued about the meaning of its name. Some claimed it stood for Viral Infection, since launching computer viruses was one of its members' favorite techniques. Others said it was simply a reference to the old Unix text editor, vi. A few even held that the name was just the Roman numeral for six, but they never explained why this made any sense at all. Some people were just idiots.

VI was crucial to stimulating insurrections around the world because they could get Mushrooms' message out to billions of people by hacking into media websites. If Fox News could promote the 2009 Tea Party uprising to such great effect in the U.S., then a sustained hack into media websites worldwide could potentially stimulate so many people to action that true insurrections were possible. Besides, the insurrections need not be massive, just ubiquitous: present and active in many of the oppressive institutions in the world. Who liked working for a giant corporation, anyhow? Didn't the people trapped in them realize that corporate leaders were only concerned about their own careers and the acquisition of wealth at the expense of the workers?

"Aaaarrrrggghhhh!" Tired as he was, George bolted from the sofa and rushed to his small, cluttered desk.. He wanted to tell the other Mushrooms about his success in buying the weapons. He booted his computer and started VI's communications program. He first contacted Jamie, who had trained to use atomic demolition munitions in the Army. How lucky he was to have found her!

George: *You there?*

He waited. No response. He stood up, walked around, came back.

Jamie: *Yes*

George: *ADMs are on their way.*

Jamie: *Good*

George: *That all you have to say?*

Jamie: *Sorry. Sabrina and I had a fight.*

George: *Don't get distracted from our mission by personal stuff.*

Jamie: *Easy for you to say. You've never been close to anyone.*

George: *Feelings are irrelevant to our mission. Focus, Jamie!*

George: *I gotta tell the others.*

George ended the session with Jamie. She had not even

congratulated him for acquiring the A.D.M.s. He had taken a great risk by agreeing to purchase and deliver the weapons, especially since Michael Anthony refused to tell him who was actually financing the purchase. Worse, his life could be forfeit if Mushrooms failed to get the five devices to their targets. What did he have to do to impress people? His frustration made it impossible to sit still. He resumed pacing around his tiny living room.

George recalled his experiences as a student at The University of Chicago. He had had a fellowship in the Committee on Security Studies, but the faculty were not receptive to his ideas about measures to prevent the proliferation of nuclear weapons and his fellowship was not renewed. Damn them! A bunch of fucking egotists! Especially Professor Edwards. His only concerns were obtaining grants, getting tenure, and becoming known as a Great Man. His family showed the effects of living with such a person. His scrawny, nervous wife with her whiney voice seemed always on the verge of a nervous breakdown. His kids were freaks, the boy making odd noises, the girl always spaced out. Edwards was the worst, but all the professors thought the students were there to assist them in their projects, not to develop themselves into independent researchers with their own ideas and agendas. None of the professors recognized his potential greatness. Or, maybe they did, and were envious that he was the one who would be known by future generations.

While still a student, George had been an observer at the U.N.'s Conference on Disarmament in Geneva. That was a more satisfying experience only because someone had at last paid attention to his ideas and seemed to value his insights. What was the guy's name? Something odd. Codger? No. Coot? That was it. Coot Jenkins, from the Brookhaven National Lab. Nevertheless, back in Chicago, everything had fallen apart and George had never returned to Geneva. Well, he'd show them a thing or two about nuclear security — or the lack of it.

George returned to his keyboard. Doug would appreciate his success in Osh.

George: *You there?*

Doug: *Yeah.*

George: *I got 'em.*
Doug: *All 5?*
George: *Yeah. They're on their way.*
Doug: *We get 2?*
George: *Right.*
Doug: *You did great!*

Like George, Doug had witnessed self-serving leaders and was bitter at their exploitation of the people under them.

George: *We're gonna inspire world-wide insurrection with those weapons.*

Doug: *Especially since the economy still sucks. People want change.*

George: *You still looking for a job?*
Doug: *Yeah.*

The job market in science and engineering was not good in many countries. College and university graduates' unemployment rates were at depression levels. Experienced people were leaving the military but having trouble finding work commensurate with their skills. People with jobs suffered wage stagnation.

Such smart, ambitious, and frustrated people would form the vanguard of insurrection. Others beyond George's group were probably already thinking of how to attack their particular oppressors. When the time came to act, they would be ready. They would become Mushrooms too. Like Doug.

George's optimism returned. He sent cryptic updates to Bennie and Mitch, then went into his bedroom, moved his suitcase from the bed to the floor, stripped to his underwear and lay down, hoping to dream of mushroom clouds this time.

CHAPTER 3
Networking

"Good job!" Jill's whispered praise after Diana's presentation to the advisory committee earlier that day echoed in Diana's memory, eliciting a smile as she set her briefcase down beside the desk in her small apartment on Connecticut Avenue. When she recalled the "Well done"s from a couple of the security mavens, she could not help grinning. How proud her father would have been to see her associating with — and impressing — such people. Tears came quickly into her eyes and a sob caught in her throat at the unbidden thought of his sudden death.

Regaining her composure, Diana kicked off her shoes, which had been pinching her feet all day, and padded into her bedroom. She took off her jacket, slipped out of her skirt, and removed her blouse, carefully hanging each item in her closet. She pulled on a faded pair of jeans and an old Red Sox sweat shirt, rubbed her sore feet, and slid them into the moccasins that she used as slippers. Diana stretched her arms over her head, then let them fall to her sides, feeling the day's tension ebb from her body.

To complete her escape from the enormous responsibility she felt at the N.S.C., Diana went to the liquor cabinet in her living room, found the bottle of Harveys Bristol Cream, and poured herself a glass. She sat down at the rented upright piano that stood against the opposite wall. What better way to celebrate her success and escape the burdens of her new job than to play? Too bad she had had to put her own grand piano into storage when she moved from Boston to Washington. Her new apartment was too small for it.

Diana's neighbors complained if she played even the little upright at night. She had considered getting an electronic keyboard but had been too busy to pick one out. She was careful to restrict her playing to the weekends and early evenings. No one was likely to complain if she played Bach and Chopin for an hour now. Mrs. Gates downstairs might even call to thank her.

The next morning, Diana woke early and went for her usual long run in Rock Creek Park, then returned to her apartment to shower and dress for the day. She went for breakfast to a neighborhood diner she had discovered. The proprietor, whom everyone called "Snuffy," now recognized her whenever she came in.

"Good morning, Miss," Snuffy said, beaming at her. "Would you like to sit by the window this fine spring day?"

"Sure," Diana replied. "That would be lovely." Slowly she was beginning to feel at home in her new city.

The first thing Diana always did each day when she got to her office was to study the daily intelligence briefing. Moments after she finished, Jill called.

"Did you read about the murder in India?" Jill asked.

"Yes, just now." A man had been killed when he inserted his card key into an electronic lock at his Mumbai apartment building, triggering an explosion.

"Then you're aware the victim was an informant against the hacker group VI," continued Jill. "What do you know about them?"

"The Indian government arrested several members of VI for attacking computer systems in Internal Security," said Diana. "Since the arrests, several informants against VI have been beaten."

"And now one has been killed," said Jill. "These guys mean business. See what else you can find out about them."

"I'm already on it," said Diana. She underlined the note she had made to follow up with contacts at the C.I.A. and N.S.A.

Diana respected the breadth and depth of Jill's understanding of national security issues. She knew how all the pieces interacted on the global chess board. She saw common interests and the alliances that might arise from them. Diana was learning to think like Jill. She worried that some of the groups that she was reading and hearing about in briefings might make alliances of convenience to support their agendas. Hackers were the bad guys' new best friends, that much was clear. This fact made Diana's work all the more important.

"How's recruiting going?" Jill asked.

"It's my top priority." Diana had resolved from her first day on the job to get her team up to speed before a group like VI attacked closer to home.

After the conversation with Jill, Diana called her friend, Professor Eugene Stafford at M.I.T.

"Hi, Gene. It's Diana Munson. Have you thought of any candidates for the openings we discussed last week?"

"Good news, Diana," the professor said. "One of our best post-docs, Avi Shopiro, is interested. He's Israeli but a long-time permanent resident of the U.S."

"My group is restricted to U.S. citizens," said Diana. "I hope you understand."

Hiring anyone whose loyalties might not lie entirely with the U.S. for such a sensitive position was asking for trouble, and not just from a Congressman looking to make a name for himself. Independent hacker groups like VI were not the only ones getting ready for cyber conflict. Other countries, such as Russia, China, Iran, Britain, and Israel, were preparing for cyber war. These countries had begun to enlist their native hacker groups in national cyber warfare efforts.

"I have another candidate for you," said Professor Stafford. "Herman Resnik. He studies infrastructure vulnerabilities — and, having grown up on a farm in Iowa, he's as American as anyone can be."

"Great," said Diana. "Please have him send me his resume."

After saying goodbye to the professor, she relaxed a bit, but only a bit. Many essential systems were vulnerable to cyber attack in the U.S. Not enough had been done to protect the power grid, for example. Commercial and government websites were constantly probed. Sometimes attacks succeeded, occasionally spectacularly, with thousands of customer accounts compromised or classified documents revealed. It seemed like just a matter of time before ambitious hackers brought down a system on which millions of people depended in daily life. Herman Resnik might well be the kind of person she needed.

A beep signaled the arrival of an e-mail message. This one was from Rob Jacovich. "How about lunch today?" New in D.C. and busy at work, Diana had no social life. Several male colleagues, like Rob, had asked her to join them for lunch, but she always declined. Her resolve to avoid another romantic entanglement was holding firm. She replied to Rob with "Sorry. Too busy recruiting my team."

Diana accepted loneliness as the price she had to pay to prevent future calamities, both public and private.

* * *

Jamie Saunders was sitting at her computer when a window popped up, announcing an incoming secure call from George Boyd. Good — she much preferred talking to texting. She quickly put her headset on and clicked Accept, but she knew George well enough not to expect an apology for his insensitivity to her feelings when they had last communicated.

"I want to make sure I can rely on you." George's tone had not changed since their texting session.

"Of course you can."

"Good. The two weapons for our team will get to Canada in two weeks to a month."

"Why so long?" Jamie was eager to see whether the devices were similar to the ones she had trained on. Maybe they were even copies of the Army's atomic demolition munitions. How ironic it would be if Russian spies facilitated the work of American anarchists.

"Transportation by truck and boat takes a long time," said George. "Anyway, you should know that, with your expertise in A.D.M.s, you'll be the key person in Mushrooms-inspired insurrections around the world."

"I won't let you down." Jamie was determined to use her knowledge against the system that had ruined her life.

"By the way," said George, "we now have a name."

"Oh? What?"

"Mushrooms." George told Jamie about his dream.

"Cool." Visions of mushroom clouds danced in her head.

After the call was over, Jamie got up from her computer, wandered into her kitchen, and got a Coors Light from the fridge. As she sipped the cold and tingly beer, she thought about the implications of attacking major landmarks around the world with nuclear weapons. Of course the immediate targets would be destroyed. No structure could withstand even a relatively small nuclear explosion. However, she was troubled that the high cost in civilian lives might turn people against Mushrooms instead of proving that ordinary people could do extraordinary things, like acquiring and detonating nuclear weapons. Like defeating giant corporations and corrupt governments.

She had long understood the inevitability of collateral damage when attacking an enemy. Now her enemy was the structure of society as a whole, a society in which a dominant minority exploits everyone else. Having seen first-hand the conditions in the Third World, she also realized that the developed countries had organized world commerce to their own advantage, at the expense of people in the developing world.

Jamie wandered into her living room and sat in her favorite overstuffed chair, which creaked as she lowered her massive body into its comforting cushions. She looked at the bottle in her hand and wondered about the company that made the beer. For whose benefit was it run? She sighed and took another sip.

Jamie had seen the destructive effects of the current social and political systems in her own family: her father committed suicide when his role in a Ponzi scheme had been discovered. He was not able to cope with the twin shames of having knuckled under to the demands of his boss and having cost thousands of innocent investors their life savings. Jamie's mother turned to drink to numb the pain of humiliation and the sorrow of abandonment. Their family's financial assets were seized and their home taken by foreclosure. Jamie had to leave her college, whose financial aid department had felt more sympathy with her father's victims than with his daughter's plight — not least because the college's endowment was one of those victims.

Jamie was angry with her father for his cowardice, with her mother for her weakness, and with her college for its failure to see that Jamie herself was a victim. She spent only a few weeks in the bog of self-pity before her natural resilience enabled her to consider her alternatives with a clear mind. An Army recruiting advertisement resonated with her: "Be All That You Can Be." At last she felt hopeful again. She enlisted.

Jamie's eye caught sight of her old Army scrapbook, where she kept souvenirs of her time in the service. She put the bottle down and walked over to the shelf where the scrapbook lay under some other books. She slid the book of memories out from under the stack and retreated to her chair. She opened the book to its first page and recalled how she had felt when she first joined up.

The Army became her refuge. Her imposing size and physical strength gave her an advantage over the other women recruits, not to mention many of the men. She did well in all aspects of her training, and eventually became one of the first women to work with the Special Forces. She especially enjoyed learning how to "blow things up" and became an expert in demolition, including the use of atomic demolition munitions, or A.D.M.s. Unfortunately, she and another woman soldier were discovered during an amorous encounter in a base stockroom one night. Both of them were given dishonorable discharges for sodomy. Jamie was furious with the Army for its homophobic handling of their cases, despite the repeal of Don't Ask, Don't Tell.

She slammed the scrapbook shut and tossed it back toward the bookcase. "Fuck the Army!"

On her own again and unemployed, Jamie had begun to seek revenge on the social order that had destroyed her parents and wrecked her own life. She found that anarchist literature expressed her attitudes toward society and offered ways to change that society. By chance she met George Boyd at an anarchist demonstration in Seattle. When the police attacked the crowd, they fled together. When George sprained his ankle, Jamie gave him a piggyback ride to safety. It was good practice for carrying an A.D.M. To complete their escape from the police, she and George ducked into a bar, where they ate burgers, had a few beers, and groused about the corruption of society. She liked George for his idealism and his wit.

Afterwards, Jamie took George back to her apartment and taped up his ankle so that he could walk on it. She enjoyed taking care of George. Her temporary jobs did not provide such opportunities. Unfortunately, George seemed to hope for more than nursing care from Jamie, until she made her sexual preference clear to him. George accepted her rebuff without complaint, even sharing with her that his brother was gay. From then on, they were comfortable with each other.

George stayed with Jamie for a few days, sleeping on her couch. She told him about her Army experience and her expertise with atomic demolition munitions. They talked about what they would do if they ever got hold of an A.D.M.

George complained that his job required him to travel a lot but seemed glad that it gave him opportunities to connect with other anarchists and to build up a network of people he could trust. Jamie hoped that his judgment of people was sound.

After George returned to Berkeley, they kept in touch by using VI's communication software. Now Jamie had to decide whether she was prepared to go through with the plan that she, George, and the other Mushrooms had agreed on. If she had to cause massive casualties, she could at least make sure that her girlfriend Sabrina would be safe.

Ah, Sabrina! Jamie once again found a scrapbook in her bookcase. This one, on top of a stack, had pictures of Sabrina and her during the past few months. She liked looking at pictures of Sabrina, who was always smiling and amazingly photogenic.

Jamie had met Sabrina one night at a bar frequented by Seattle lesbians. Jamie, being massive, had always favored pretty, slender girls like Sabrina. When they danced, Jamie would pick Sabrina up and twirl her like a baton, to the amazement of the crowd. Sabrina, a cheerleader in college, told Jamie that she was used to being manhandled during routines on the field but had never before been tossed around by anyone so strong. Jamie wondered if that was because Sabrina had made sure the football team knew of her sexual preference.

Jamie liked everything about Sabrina, including her rich mahogany skin and the springiness of her kinky hair. Her body was just the most obvious attraction. Sabrina was also funny, bright, and unconventional. After college, she had become a software developer, earning the respect of her peers and her managers for producing elegant, efficient code — most amazingly, on time. Sabrina showed Jamie some of the performance awards that she had received. Jamie hoped that Sabrina's success had not depended on her doing a little cocaine from time to time. Jamie got her to agree to stop using drugs but suspected that Sabrina was still snorting when Jamie was not around.

For Jamie's last birthday Sabrina surprised and delighted her by giving her a new smart phone with a bunch of useful apps already loaded and ready for use. She had not had time to try all of them out but did enjoy playing the games. Jamie liked having a nerd for a girlfriend, since her own technical expertise did not extend beyond guns and bombs.

The Mushrooms had considered bringing Sabrina into the group, but Mitch Chambers in particular was opposed to doing so. Mitch told the group that Sabrina was a drug addict who might compromise their security in order to support her habit. Jamie argued in favor of Sabrina, but to no avail. She'd almost left Mushrooms because of that dispute. The group's plan to incite insurrection was too important to abandon for mere personal reasons, so Jamie soldiered on. Soon she would be the most important member of the team, for she was the only one who really knew A.D.M.s.

Jamie looked at Sabrina's face, smiling up at her from picture after picture. Sabrina at the Space Needle. Sabrina in an alpine meadow full of flowers at Mount Ranier. What if she knew what Jamie and the other Mushrooms were planning? Would she understand? Jamie resolved to keep the A.D.M. stuff secret from Sabrina, but she did not like having to do so. One day Sabrina would see the necessity of insurrection, but until then the Mushrooms' plot was one thing they could not share.

* * *

Sabrina Jones had a problem. Her girlfriend of a few months, Jamie Saunders, was always going places, and Sabrina worried when she hadn't heard from Jamie for a few hours. For her part, Jamie told Sabrina that she didn't want to have to keep stopping what she was doing to call her. A tough Army vet, she teased Sabrina for being a wuss. Not wanting to annoy Jamie, Sabrina resisted her frequent urges to call Jamie to make sure she was okay.

Being technically sophisticated, Sabrina soon thought of a solution. For Jamie's last birthday Sabrina gave her a smart phone with many applications, including a tracker app. Sabrina had activated the tracker app before putting the phone back into its box and wrapping it.

The app worked even while the phone was off. Periodically it would wake up the phone and its GPS, then report its location to a tracker program running on Sabrina's computer. Sabrina checked the tracker app whenever she hadn't heard from Jamie and wanted to make sure she was okay. At least she could tell whether Jamie was able to move around.

Sabrina decided not to tell Jamie that her new phone was reporting her location every hour, or at least she put off telling her. She didn't think Jamie would like being tracked, but Sabrina herself needed the reassurance that the tracker app was providing. Telling Jamie could wait until Sabrina felt more secure.

Jamie worked out several days a week to maintain the excellent condition she was in when she left the Army. Whenever they slept together, Sabrina felt completely safe. Pity the midnight intruder who assaulted them in bed. He'd have his genitals stuffed down his throat and his body flung into the street.

The only thing about Jamie that bothered Sabrina was her talk about the need to overthrow the established world order. Maybe Sabrina was a wuss, but she didn't think that the way the world worked was bad enough to justify the violent solutions that Jamie favored.

Sabrina assumed that Jamie's anger was the result of her father's suicide and her own dishonorable discharge from the Army. Jamie was understandably bitter about both events and blamed "the system" for both. Fortunately, Jamie was always gentle with Sabrina and never expressed anger toward her, so it was easy for Sabrina to love and trust Jamie in return.

* * *

Coot Jenkins resolved to verify or debunk the loose nukes rumor by contacting people in his own extensive network, but he did not want to duplicate the efforts inside the government. He needed to talk with people who had contacts outside the arms control community, even outside the legal economy. A couple of people came to mind: Bernard Goldfarb, a journalist who had written extensively on the international arms trade, and Myron Pepsey, an entrepreneur with many diverse business interests. Goldfarb had interviewed Coot for one of his books, and Pepsey was a member of S.A.F.E.'s Board of Directors.

Goldfarb agreed to meet Coot on Tuesday evening at Goldfarb's apartment on Connecticut Avenue, not far from Coot's home on Rodman Street. Having to wait even one day, given the seriousness of the matter, was disturbing, but Goldfarb had another appointment already scheduled for Monday night. Since Pepsey's main office was in Atlanta, he was harder to meet with. He visited D.C. only for a couple of days once a month, and his next visit was not until the following week. He agreed to see Coot for half an hour, at 8:30 A.M. on Wednesday.

Tuesday evening was mild enough for Coot to walk from his home to Goldfarb's. The journalist welcomed him cordially, ushering him into a living room decorated with memorabilia from a lifetime of foreign travel. Coot sat on an Italian leather sofa opposite the entrance, Goldfarb on a wing-back chair across from Coot. A hand-knotted Persian carpet lay between them. A coffee table bearing a pot of tea and two mugs occupied the center of the carpet.

"Bernie, you've been studying the global arms trade ever since the '70s," Coot began. "Why has there never been a substantiated report of the theft of a nuclear weapon?"

"It's not for lack of demand," said Goldfarb. "Al-Qaeda has always been interested in W.M.D."

"Right," said Coot. "So, the reason must be on the supply side."

"Yes," said Goldfarb. "The nuclear powers want their club to remain exclusive."

"But that's at the policy level," said Coot. "What about theft by someone with access to weapons?"

"That's always been a concern," said Goldfarb, "so the nuclear nations have maintained tight security around their weapons from the beginning."

"I understand how things are *supposed* to work," said Coot. Indeed he did, having been involved in numerous policy discussions, but he needed a more practical perspective. "What I want to know is how things have *actually* worked, especially during chaotic times."

"Oh, you mean like at the end of the Soviet Union or currently in Pakistan?" asked Goldfarb.

"Right," said Coot.

Goldfarb's eyes narrowed. "Is there any particular reason for your concern?" he asked.

Coot was not good at deceiving people, especially not someone like Goldfarb who had made a career of reading between the lines and listening for words unspoken. He did not answer right away, but studied the pattern in the rug at his feet. He did not want to risk divulging something to a journalist that might appear in the papers the next day. After an uncomfortable silence, he raised his eyes to meet Goldfarb's and said, "Some things are better left unsaid."

"Of course," said Goldfarb.

"But let me ask you a question," said Coot. "Have you heard anything recently that increases your concern about the security of nuclear weapons?"

"I could respond as you did," said Goldfarb, "but I won't."

Coot leaned forward on the couch, hoping for a revelation.

"I could simply say 'No' and be done with it," continued Goldfarb, "but I know you well enough to be sure you're not simply curious."

"Right," said Coot.

"I don't know how useful this information will be to you, but this is what I've heard within the past week."

"I'm all ears," said Coot, sitting up straighter but still leaning forward a bit.

"Years ago, as the Soviet Union was splitting up, there were rumors that some tactical nuclear weapons had been stolen while being shipped from Kyrgyzstan back to Russia. I tried to find out more about them but without success."

"All of those weapons were accounted for," said Coot.

"That was the official line, of course," said Goldfarb, "but not the truth, according to rumor."

"Have you heard more about them, then?" asked Coot.

"Unfortunately, yes, just today. A Kyrgyz arms dealer named Jyrgal recently died. Word got around that there were some old Soviet-era A.D.M.s in his warehouse. I don't know where they are now, though. Maybe another dealer has them."

"Or *had* them," said Coot. "This is disturbing news. Oh, man!" Atomic demolition munitions were highly portable. Their explosive power could be as much as a thousand tons of TNT. The Soviet A.D.M.s were probably designed, like their American counterparts, to be deployed by men working in pairs in the field, with minimal safeguards against unauthorized use.

Coot stood up and paced around the room, his eyes on the floor, no longer noticing the exquisite carpet.

"Have you told anyone else about this?" asked Coot.

Goldfarb also got to his feet. "No. I was debating whether to tell my contacts in the C.I.A. when you asked to meet. What do you think I should do?"

"Whatever you do, don't publicize it."

"Of course not," said Goldfarb.

"It's important that the *right* intel guys get this lead," said Coot. "Not just anybody in the Agency."

"Yes," agreed Goldfarb,

"I have a contact in the N.S.C. She knows who the right people are and would put you in touch with them."

"Good. Can I expect someone to contact me?"

"Yes. I'll suggest they ask to speak with you about *Jyrgal's toys*," said Coot.

The two men continued chatting for a while longer, but Coot had already gotten what he had come for: confirmation of loose nukes.

* * *

The possibility that terrorists could acquire nuclear weapons on the black market profoundly worried Coot Jenkins. In the days following his conversation with Jill, he spent hours contacting old friends in the arms control and intelligence communities, hoping that his careful probing would not arouse suspicions about his true concerns but would turn up enough scraps of information that he could determine whether dangerous groups were pursuing the weapons that Sergey and Bernie had told him about. He was not even going out for lunch. One day he was eating a sandwich by himself in the break room when a woman approached his table. She appeared to be in her mid-forties, casually but nicely dressed, with a lot of nervous energy.

"You're Coot Jenkins, aren't you?" she asked.

"That's right. Are you new here?"

"Very. I joined S.A.F.E. just last week. I'm Emily Taggert, by the way. Mind if I sit down?"

"Not at all, Emily. Please do." In fact, Coot had hoped she would not interrupt his thinking about a matter that he could not discuss with anyone at S.A.F.E. Too late to escape now.

"Thanks," she said, taking the seat opposite Coot and unwrapping her own sandwich. "I heard your presentation on proliferation threats in Geneva last year."

"Oh? I hope you found it useful."

"Yes, I did. Very insightful. Especially the theme of improving the odds."

"What group are you in?" Coot asked.

"Fissile Materials. How about you?"

"Nonproliferation Policy."

"What projects?" asked Emily.

"Helping Russia secure its nuclear facilities. Facilitating confidence-building dialogues between regional rivals. Building support for the Comprehensive Test Ban Treaty. The elimination of nuclear weapons." He could not tell her about trying to find loose nukes. Not even S.A.F.E. president Ben Barker knew about that activity.

"That sounds challenging, even for someone with your experience." Was she subtly pointing out how much older he was than she?

"Well, I do know a lot of people in arms control circles."

"From what I've heard, your success is built by earning people's trust."

Coot was flattered. Was she coming on to him? "You're too kind," he finally said.

"I don't think so."

"There's not much I can do unless the parties are already determined to find solutions to the problems between them, and then it's not so hard to help them reach consensus."

"Well, I think you're too modest. When I told my friends I might join S.A.F.E., they all mentioned you were on the staff. They said you were a tremendous resource."

Coot felt his face redden. It wasn't often that someone praised him to his face. Frannie had always told him that he was special, but he never really believed her. He knew his own weaknesses. It had never occurred to him that she had a better notion of his strengths. He was older now, but still tall, lean, rumpled, and apparently preoccupied with matters of no interest to ordinary folk — like a professor, although he had never worked toward a doctorate.

Coot and Emily talked at length about S.A.F.E. in general and their own work in particular, until they had finished their lunches.

"I've enjoyed our conversation, but work beckons," said Coot.

"Same here," said Emily.

"I hope you'll like working here."

"I'm sure I will. It was good to meet you, Coot."

Coot went back to his desk and began to read the e-mail messages that had come in while he was at lunch. He could not keep his thoughts from drifting toward Emily. This was unusual. Since Frannie died, he had not had a social life. He viewed the idea of replacing Frannie as disrespectful at best and treacherous at worst. Still, lately, occasionally, he had begun to notice women, like Diana Munson at Jill's meeting. He was slowly coming back to life.

Why not send Emily an e-mail invitation to dinner? Nah, that would seem too eager.

Two days later Coot gave in to the temptation and sent Emily a message suggesting dinner after work sometime. An hour later her reply came: "Thanks. Good idea. Next week?" Coot clicked "Reply" and typed "Wednesday?" Soon Emily's acceptance had Coot's imagination working overtime. Intelligent conversation was a given. How would they get along in other ways?

Coot saw Emily in the office corridors several times in the next few days, but she always seemed too busy to stop and talk. Had she just sucked up to him in the break room because she was new and insecure? Was she worried about going out with someone from work? Was she unable to make up her mind? Despite Emily's apparent ambivalence, they agreed via e-mail that they'd have dinner at 6:30 at Mobius on Connecticut Avenue, a few blocks from Coot's home. Mobius, whose slogan was "Good food with a twist," was one of Coot's favorite restaurants in Washington. He made a reservation for two.

* * *

Hackers make great allies. George Boyd had thought so since the geniuses of VI had supplied him with software for communicating so securely over the Internet that even the U.S. National Security Agency could not break into their conversations. The software created a botnet from poorly-protected computers around the world and kept changing the path along which each conversation was routed, even more than normal IP packet routing. All conversations were encrypted with a triple DES block cipher.

Of course VI had wanted something in return: striking a target in India in the Mushrooms' debut attack. They didn't have a clue that Mushrooms was planning a series of nuclear strikes. George could not make such an important concession, not least because the weapons had been paid for by someone else. This person had given the Mushrooms a list of targets around the world. Fortunately, one of the targets was in India, so Mushrooms was able to accommodate both its allies.

George did not actually know who Mushrooms' benefactor was. The man had always dealt with the Mushrooms through an intermediary, a fellow who said his name was "Michael Anthony." George looked up the name on the Internet and learned that this was the name of the executive secretary of John Beresford Tipton, the reclusive multi-millionaire of the 1950s TV series *The Millionaire,* who gave away a million dollars anonymously every week for five years. The Mushrooms began to refer to their benefactor as "Tipton." The Mushrooms needed money, a lot of money, to buy nuclear devices on the black market. They had few resources themselves, so they accepted Tipton's money and his target list. The targets were spectacular, George had to agree, although it would be difficult to get the weapons to them. Given the presence of radiation detectors at border crossings and airports, deploying a nuclear weapon would be particularly challenging.

George had never learned how Anthony and Tipton had found them. The Mushrooms had stayed under the radar of the world's intelligence agencies since they had gotten together at anarchist gatherings and in transient Internet Relay Chat groups and had continued communicating with VI's comm software. Perhaps Anthony and Tipton had identified them through their own source at such a gathering or group. Anthony would not say.

The Mushrooms used the VI software to discuss the progress of the atomic demolition munitions toward their staging areas. During one conversation on the weapon going into India, George was still in Berkeley, A.D.M. expert Jamie Saunders in Seattle, and team leader Munir Sharif in Sakwar, a town in the part of Kashmir controlled by Pakistan. George had recruited Munir for Mushrooms at the suggestion of Munir's cousin Pervez, a computer hacker working with VI. Munir had put together the rest of his Mushrooms team.

"Where is the A.D.M. now?" Jamie asked.

"In Khorog, Tajikistan," said George, "waiting for smugglers with a four-wheel-drive vehicle."

"Only gravel roads and trails connect Khorog and Sakwar," said Munir.

"The chance of interception is less," said George. "At least that's what a Kyrgyz smuggler told me."

"Right," said Munir. "Stay away from the main roads when crossing borders."

"Is your team ready to go?" asked George.

"All set," said Munir.

"Who's going to arm the A.D.M.?" Jamie's tone suggested skepticism that Pakistanis could manage such a device.

"Faroud," said Munir.

"What does he know about Soviet A.D.M.s?" Jamie continued to press Munir to justify his optimism.

"You're forgetting that Faroud worked for A.Q. Khan," said Munir, referring to the Pakistani nuclear scientist and proliferator.

"He'll need specific information on the device," said Jamie. "I'll send you instructions."

A few minutes later Munir acknowledged receipt of a file from Jamie.

"How are you guys planning to get past the Indian border guards?" asked George.

"We'll shoot our way across, if we have to," said Munir. "Our guys would like to waste a few infidels."

George worried about the kind of recruits Munir had found, but it was too late to change team members now.

"Don't be so trigger-happy," said Jamie. "You'll draw attention to yourselves."

"Right," said George. "On the other hand, we mustn't lose the A.D.M. at the border. Tipton would be pissed, and that would be very bad for all of us."

"Of course we'll try to get the trucks through as ordinary commercial vehicles," said Munir, "but if they try to inspect the crate, we'll have to fight."

"Can't you cross by leaving the main road?" asked Jamie.

"No. There's a fence, and the Indian side is mined," Munir responded.

"Alright," said George. "Cross on the road. Just make sure the crate and your weapons are well-hidden in the trucks."

"Of course," the Pakistani said. "You can count on me."

"One last thing," said Coot. "We're calling ourselves 'Mushrooms' here."

"I like it," said Munir. "Boom!"

The call ended. George wished he were more confident in the ability of Munir and his team to carry out the first operation, but there was little he could do to improve the chances of success now.

Tomorrow he would have a similar call with the team that was to carry an A.D.M. into the U.K. He hoped they would be more aware of the need to be inconspicuous in their trip through the Chunnel. The team that was charged with getting a device into South Korea had the most difficult task of all.

* * *

The sun never set on Myron Pepsey's empire. Late nights and early mornings were inevitable. At least a dozen reports from his business interests around the world awaited him every morning, whether he was in his Atlanta office or traveling, like today in D.C. He had to read them and make any decisions required before the damned meetings began. This Wednesday morning was no different, but that was fine with him. He liked to be in control of events. He always charged ahead, taking advantage of circumstances that might not be repeated. Pepsey, long a supporter of classical theatre, often recited to himself the words of Shakespeare's Brutus:

> *There is a tide in the affairs of men*
> *Which taken at the flood, leads on to fortune;*
> *Omitted, all the voyage of their life*
> *Is bound in shallows and in miseries.*

Myron Pepsey did not intend to be bound in any way.

Pepsey arrived at his opulent D.C. office at 7 A.M., dressed in a pinstriped blue suit with a tie patterned on a Paul Klee painting at the Guggenheim Museum. The huge plants, the plush carpet, the paintings and sculptures, the solid mahogany furniture all helped create an impression of good taste and worldly success. How nice that it was all tax-deductible. The government did well by its corporate citizens, providing a complex and reliable infrastructure, a stable world order, and until recently a political system that functioned smoothly. How ironic that liberals identified valid long-term problems but were unable to convert that into political success. Instead, the federal government was completely hamstrung by small-government conservatives intent on reducing the tax burden of the people whose campaign contributions they needed.

Pepsey, like most extremely wealthy men, preferred low taxes to high, but he was realistic enough to know that a government role was essential in solving long-term problems that the public had not yet focused on. Ideally, the federal government would fund private enterprise to come up with solutions for such problems, rather than providing solutions itself. With the opposition of the low-tax crowd to any federal expenditures, wise or foolish, gaining support for dealing with potential disasters was getting more difficult. The public needed to be convinced that a problem was real and serious before they would support using tax money to deal with it.

Take climate change. Most Republicans and Libertarians were simply wrong on the issue of whether human activity was causing the planet to get warmer. They were also wrong on what the effects of global warming would be. Of course the massive increase in carbon dioxide and methane in the atmosphere was due to the burning of fossil fuels. Climate scientists were largely agreed on that point.

Trusting the scientific community, Pepsey had invested in several "green technology" companies. When growing political opposition to renewable energy programs threatened the value of his investments, Pepsey had joined S.A.F.E.'s Board of Directors in order to support its efforts to draw attention to potentially catastrophic dangers, including not just global warming, but also asteroid impact and nuclear annihilation. The more people became convinced of such dangers, the greater the market for solutions, both public and private. He intended to profit either way.

Pepsey also saw the potential for huge profits as people lost confidence in the various levels of government and relied increasingly on private services. Several Pepsey businesses were involved already in providing security and information services. Diversification was the key to success.

Myron Pepsey was not all business, however. Being a Southern boy, he enjoyed a good laugh. On his wall he had hung a framed photo of himself and John Belushi, in costume, on the *Saturday Night Live* set for the Olympia Cafe. His beard was dark then. Now it was still full but graying. Below the picture was a plaque that read

"No Koch! Pepsey!", a reference both to Belushi's famous line "No Coke! Pepsi!" and to the wealthy and conservative brothers Charles and David Koch, who were as active on the right as Pepsey was on the left.

Pepsey noticed on his calendar that he was to meet with Coot Jenkins from S.A.F.E. that morning. Why had he agree to a meeting whose real purpose Jenkins seemed to be hiding? Jenkins was not getting rich at S.A.F.E. Maybe he wanted in on a Pepsey deal. Jenkins had always made clear, insightful presentations to the S.A.F.E. board. Maybe he would learn something useful from the man.

After 90 minutes of reading reports and issuing instructions, Pepsey was ready for a change of pace when his assistant announced that Coot Jenkins was waiting to see him.

"Mr. Jenkins! So good to see you again!" His greeting was always calibrated to win over a person. How stupid, to make enemies unnecessarily. Better to keep alive the chance of making an ally. Making friends was not the point.

"Thanks for meeting with me, Mr. Pepsey." Jenkins took the seat suggested by a subtle motion of Pepsey's hand. When Pepsey was at his best, most people functioned almost like extensions of him.

"You didn't say exactly why you wanted to chat," Pepsey said. His expression was neutral, giving no clue as to whether he was pleased or annoyed.

"I didn't want to discuss it over the phone," said Jenkins. "Recently I've gotten interested in the economics of nuclear proliferation. I need to know how that part of the world economy actually works."

"Why should I know anything about that?" asked Pepsey.

"I expect that a man in your position has had offers from many businessmen, not all of whom have the same respect for the law that you do."

"I have turned down a few deals that didn't smell quite right to me," said Pepsey.

"Did any involve weapons?" asked Jenkins. "I don't mean guns, but more dangerous weapons."

"Tanks?"

"W.M.D.s."

Pepsey was, of course, familiar with the acronym for "Weapons of Mass Destruction."

"Don't you think I would have reported weapons that could harm so many people, Mr. Jenkins?"

"Reported them? Of course, but not to me."

"So you want me to tell you anything I would have told the authorities?" Pepsey raised a questioning eyebrow.

"I want to understand what chemical, biological, and nuclear weapons have been available on the black market and where they came from."

"And you think I would know? Hardly. I'm not your man, Mr. Jenkins."

"Can you point me to someone who might help me, then?"

"No, sorry. I *am* working on something else that may interest you, though. A play with a disarmament theme. By a young fella down in Chapel Hill. Smart kid. Writes well."

Jenkins looked confused at the sudden change of subject. "That's great, Mr. Pepsey," he said. "Are you directing it?"

"Hell, no! Just producing it. I'm strictly a business guy, not a creative type."

Jenkins laughed. "You must have a creative streak to be such a successful businessman."

"Just a Southern boy's good nose for opportunities."

Something in the way he raised his head or moved his arm must have given Jenkins a clue that the meeting was over, for he said, "All right, then, Mr. Pepsey. Thanks for your time. I really should be going," and stood up. Pepsey escorted Jenkins to the door.

What had Jenkins known that caused him to ask for the meeting? Did he suspect there were W.M.D.s on the black market? A man who could learn about such things outside the government's intelligence apparatus might be useful. On the other hand, by reputation Jenkins was high-minded, intellectual, idealistic. Not the sort of man to cooperate enthusiastically in the profit-oriented, pragmatic world in which Pepsey moved. Like Shakespeare's Cassius, Jenkins had a lean and hungry look and certainly thought a lot. He could be dangerous. Someday they might find themselves on opposite sides of an important controversy. Pepsey resolved to keep an eye on Jenkins.

* * *

Coot left Pepsey's office disappointed that he had not learned anything useful. Perhaps the black market for W.M.D.s was better hidden than he had realized. A journalist like Bernie Goldfarb might be tipped off when such weapons turned up, but a legitimate business man like Myron Pepsey? Maybe not.

During his cab ride back to S.A.F.E. headquarters, Coot brooded over the fact that he had spent the past week trying to learn about the black market for W.M.D.s, but only Bernie had given him new information. The government spooks had better be doing better than he, or there was going to be a catastrophe somewhere in the world. Maybe more than one.

Late Wednesday afternoon, Coot received a message from Emily suggesting they meet at the restaurant. Evidently she didn't want to be seen leaving work with him. Coot walked a few blocks to the Farragut North Metro station. It was just three stops on the Red Line to the Cleveland Park station near Mobius. He got to the restaurant a little before 6:30 and went inside. Frannie had always enjoyed the simple elegance of the place settings and the unusual art displayed on the walls.

"Hello, Mr. Jenkins. Welcome back to Mobius," the hostess greeted Coot. "I saw your name on the reservation list. It's been a while, hasn't it?"

Coot smiled at her. Evidently she recognized him from when he and Frannie used to eat there. "Yes, it has been a while."

"Will Mrs. Jenkins be joining you? You two always seemed to have such a good time together."

"Frannie, uh..." Coot couldn't speak for a moment. This was embarrassing. He regained his composure enough to say, "Frannie passed away a couple of years ago."

"Oh, I'm so sorry! Please forgive me for asking."

"That's all right. You couldn't have known." He paused, then said, "Actually, I'm meeting a colleague from work for dinner. She should be here soon."

How embarrassing, to admit such disloyalty to his deceased

wife! Maybe meeting Emily here was not such a good idea after all.

"May I show you to your table?" the hostess asked. "You'll be able to see her when she gets here."

"Sure."

Coot had to wait just a few minutes before Emily arrived. He waved to get her attention and stood up as she approached the table.

"Hi, Coot. Great suggestion — this is a nice place!"

"I thought you'd like it. Everything I've had here has been delicious."

They studied their menus. Coot decided on the pan-roasted skate wing and Emily the Alaskan halibut.

Coot said, "The wine list is excellent. Would you like to share a bottle?"

"How about a half bottle? Tomorrow is a work day, after all."

After the waiter had taken their orders, Coot said, "So, Emily, how did you wind up at S.A.F.E.?"

"I worked on nonproliferation issues in the State Department. The last reorg reduced resources for nonproliferation work, so I made up my mind to leave as soon as the right opportunity came along."

"I don't blame you," said Coot. "The funding cuts have been disastrous."

"Fortunately, I found out that S.A.F.E. was hiring, so I applied for the job."

"How do you like it so far?"

"It's great! Interesting work, interesting colleagues. What's *not* to like?"

"Not much. S.A.F.E.'s a terrific organization."

"So, tell me about *your* career," said Emily.

"After high school I enlisted in the Army, went to Ranger School, then Vietnam."

"That must have been a tough time for you."

"It was no picnic. Anyway, after the Army I went to college and then grad school in International Relations at Johns Hopkins. My first job after school was at Brookhaven. Having both military experience and academic expertise gave me an advantage there."

"Makes sense."

"When I finally realized that nuclear nonproliferation requires complete nuclear disarmament, I decided to take a more active and public role in advocating the abolition of nuclear weapons. I thought I would have more freedom at S.A.F.E. than at a national lab. We moved to D.C. about ten years ago."

"We?"

"My wife Frannie and I."

"I can't help noticing you're not wearing your wedding ring."

"Frannie died a couple of years ago. Cancer."

"That's terrible! How are you coping?"

"All right, I suppose. Listen, I'd rather not talk about it."

"Sorry. After my divorce I was such a mess. I *needed* to talk about what had happened. I thought maybe you did too."

"There's not much to say. Frannie's gone, and that's that." Didn't people realize he didn't want to be reminded of losing Frannie?

Coot and Emily spent the rest of their meal swapping stories from the long and troubled history of arms control. After they had finished eating their lemon-ginger crème brûlées and drinking their coffees, their waiter brought the check. Coot reached for it, but Emily said, "I'd feel more comfortable if we split this."

They each put a credit card on the silver tray with the check. Soon the waiter was back with charge slips for them to sign. In another minute they were standing on the sidewalk outside the restaurant in the cool evening air.

"Why didn't you want me to pay for dinner?" Coot asked. "I thought that, since you're new at S.A.F.E., dinner would be on me, as a sort of 'Welcome aboard!' treat."

"Because we're colleagues. I want to make sure our friendship stays just that — a friendship. Besides, you don't seem ready for more than that."

"Really? Why do you say that?"

"Because you don't want to talk about what's bothering you."

"I'm a pretty private person. We hardly know each other."

"True, but I do know that you lost your wife. That must have caused you considerable pain. Unless you're able to talk with someone about it, you're most likely coping with it through denial."

Just what he needed — an amateur therapist. "I'm not denying anything."

"See?"

"You're amazing, Emily. In a single evening you've learned things about me that I don't even know myself."

"Sorry if I offended you, Coot. It's just that I got the same sort of push-back from my ex whenever I tried to discuss anything involving *his* feelings. I can understand your not wanting to talk with *me* about it. I just hope you can talk with *someone*."

This was obviously not the time to invite her over to his place. "Well, I can't deny that it's getting late."

"Me neither. Fortunately my car's right here. Thanks for suggesting dinner. I enjoyed chatting with you, and the restaurant was excellent."

"I had a good time, too. See you at the office."

As Emily drove off, Coot began walking north on Connecticut. He brooded all along the several blocks to Rodman. Denial? Did she expect him to dwell on Frannie's death every day for two years? Enough's enough. He wanted to get on with his life.

As he turned west onto Rodman, Coot suddenly felt a tingling sensation all over his body. His knees almost gave way. He stopped walking. What was the matter? His heart was racing. Sweat broke out on his forehead. He sat down on the steps leading into an apartment building, wiped the sweat off with his sleeve, and took a couple of deep breaths. He cradled his face in his hands. The tingling and rapid heart beat continued. Could he be having a heart attack? Should he call 911? Coot got out his cell phone. He gave it another minute. The symptoms persisted. Coot dialed 911. The dispatcher answered almost immediately.

"My name is Coot Jenkins. I'm afraid I'm having a heart attack. My heart's racing and I'm tingling all over."

The dispatcher asked for his location.

"Rodman, just west of Connecticut. Near the fire house." Coot turned around and read the number on the apartment building to the dispatcher, who promised to send the paramedics.

Coot did not have to wait long. An ambulance with lights flashing arrived within a minute of his call. Two men jumped out and ran toward Coot.

"You Mr. Jenkins? We're paramedics. We're here to help you," said one of the men, "Fabrini," according to his name tag.

"Yes. Am I ever glad to see you!" Coot started to stand, but Fabrini told him to stay put.

"You called 911?"

"Yes. I'm afraid I may be having a heart attack."

"Any chest pain? Pain in your arms, shoulders, back?"

"No."

"That's good. Can you breathe okay?

"Yes."

"Any fatigue, weakness, dizziness, nausea?"

"No."

"How's your vision?"

"Normal."

"Good. Now let me take your pulse."

Fabrini held Coot's wrist and looked at his watch.

"Wow, only 80. If that's racing, you must be in terrific shape, Mr. Jenkins!"

"I'm a runner."

"That explains it. Now please roll up your sleeve so that I can take your blood pressure."

Fabrini got a blood pressure cuff and a stethoscope out of the bag he was carrying. He inflated the cuff around Coot's left arm and listened as the pressure in the cuff dropped.

"130 over 80. A little high for a runner, but then you must've had quite a scare." He wrote some things on the clipboard that he had taken from his bag. "I need to listen to your heart, okay?"

"Sure."

Fabrini listened through his stethoscope at several places on Coot's chest and back. "Your heart sounds normal. How are you feeling now?"

"Much better than I did five minutes ago."

"Very good. What were you doing when the symptoms first appeared?"

"I was walking home after having dinner with a friend. Suddenly my whole body was tingling. I felt weak in the knees. I had to sit down. I noticed my heart was beating fast and I was sweating."

"How long did the symptoms go on before you called 911?"

"Just a minute." Coot was feeling ridiculous for calling 911 at all. "Maybe I should just go on home."

Fabrini shook his head. "Just a few more questions, Mr. Jenkins. We want to make sure you're okay." He then asked about Coot's medications, his cholesterol levels, and his family history of heart attack and sudden death.

"Do you really have to go into all this?" Already back to normal, Coot was eager to continue on his way.

"Yes." Fabrini looked up from his clipboard. "The doctor on call will want a complete report. He proceeded to ask about smoking, drugs, and alcohol, to which Coot answered, "Never, not lately, and moderate."

Finally Fabrini got to the mental health part of his routine. "We ask all our patients this. Have you ever suffered from depression or anxiety?"

Coot squirmed in his seat on the steps, then answered, "Not until today."

"You probably just had a panic attack, Mr. Jenkins, but I need to verify that." Fabrini pulled a mobile radio from his belt and began reporting his observations and recommendations. He hung the radio back on his belt and turned to Coot. "Yep, the cardiologist agrees you probably just had an anxiety attack."

Coot stood up. "I'm feeling back to normal now. Sorry for the false alarm."

"You did the right thing. We don't want folks to worry about calling us. It's better for everyone if it's not as bad as they feared."

"Yeah. Thanks for responding so quickly."

"No problem. Glad you're all right. See your personal physician in the next few days, just to make sure."

The two paramedics climbed back into their ambulance, turned off the vehicle's flashing lights, and drove away. Coot resumed his walk home. When he reached his house further up Rodman, he went inside and collapsed into his favorite chair, an old black Barcalounger.

Did his conversation with Emily have something to do with the panic attack? Was he cracking up? He decided to call his personal doctor, Jeff Ford, the next day for advice.

Having a plan of action helped Coot remain calm the rest of the evening, despite recurring thoughts of how certain Emily had been that he was in denial. Insensitive to other people's feelings. In denial about his own. Anxious as hell. How did he get into such a state?

In the morning, Coot called Dr. Ford, who had given him his last four annual physicals. Dr. Ford wanted to see him later that day, in case something serious was wrong. So, Coot took off from work late that afternoon and went to Dr. Ford's office.

After a giving Coot a thorough exam, including an EKG, the internist said, "Everything's normal, Coot, the same as at your last physical."

"That's good, but what caused my symptoms?"

"You most likely had a panic attack. I'm going to refer you to Dr. Lou Rosen, a psychiatrist. He may be able to help you get to the bottom of the attack — and prevent another one."

"I'm not crazy, Jeff. Can't you just prescribe something in case I have another episode?"

"Of course you're not crazy," said the doctor, "but I'm not a specialist in anxiety disorders. Dr. Rosen is. Give him a chance to help you."

"Alright," said Coot. "I guess one visit to a shrink won't cause me to lose my Top Secret security clearance."

"If I were handing out clearances," said Dr. Ford, "I'd be more worried about people who refuse to get the help they need."

Coot was reluctant to see Dr. Rosen, despite Jeff Ford's recommendation, but he called that afternoon to make an appointment anyway. As a preventive measure. Dr. Rosen had just had a cancellation for a Friday morning appointment, so at least Coot would not have to wait long.

* * *

After planning the first attack with Munir, George began to focus again on how to use the attack to foment insurrection. He and

Jamie had talked about what they would do with the kinds of weapons she was trained on — if they could ever get their hands on any — but they had never developed any concrete plans.

Then Tipton had sent Michael Anthony to offer George a deal: Tipton would finance the purchase of several Soviet-era tactical nuclear weapons that had become available on the black market if George would travel to Kyrgyzstan to buy them and then arrange for their deployment to targets that Tipton would specify. Anthony claimed not to know why Tipton had chosen George for his partner. George worried that Anthony was part of an F.B.I. sting, but the opportunity seemed too good to pass up. He accepted the offer.

Tipton's target list included some spectacular sites. Multiple attacks on such places would surely prove to potential allies around the world that Mushrooms was a serious group and that insurrection was possible. People already knew that they were oppressed by the many institutions in their lives. Mushrooms just needed to convince them that they could successfully rise up against those institutions, whether governmental or corporate. If a few people could acquire and use nuclear weapons, other small groups of people would realize they could do previously unimaginable things. Like taking over and breaking up corporations. Like changing corporate governance so that companies did not abuse their workers, pollute the environment, or provide cushy lifestyles for their executives. Like downsizing government, so that it did not suck up so many resources, interfere in individuals' private lives, or intervene on behalf of corporations in numerous places around the globe.

In case potential insurrectionists failed to see their opportunities to defeat their oppressors, George, Jamie, and their fellow Mushrooms had decided to ask the hacker group VI to produce a video with Mushrooms message to the world — and to run the video on the hacked home pages of prominent news websites around the globe. VI's price for doing this work was that Mushroom's first attack would be on an Indian target — in revenge for the imprisonment of several VI members by the Indian government. Fortunately for the Mushrooms, Tipton's list included a target in Indian-controlled Kashmir.

George just had to provide VI with the text in order to get Mushrooms' message seen by billions of people. VI graphics gurus had written software to convert such text into synthesized words spoken by a computer-generated figure. In order not to jeopardize the secrecy of the operation, George could wait until after the first attack to send VI the message for the video. VI members would quickly generate the video from the message and upload it to hundreds of websites on which VI had already installed backdoors.

The Mushrooms had in fact already agreed on the text for the video. Now they just had to wait for Munir's team to attack.

* * *

"What's in this big crate, Omar?" asked Burhanuddin, as they lifted the heavy load into their old Toyota Land Cruiser.

"Old pots," said Omar, irritated that the younger man had reminded him of his ignorance of what they were actually transporting. Why would anyone send ancient pottery by such a tortuous route? Omar did not believe that was what they were carrying. Still, they were making good money. Omar had known better than to raise questions before they were paid the rest of their fee in Sakwar.

Smuggling anything from Tajikistan through the Hindu Kush into Pakistan was not an easy task. The first part of the trip was over an unsurfaced road, which was bad enough, but at Qala Panja the route deteriorated into just a trail. They would have to switch the load from the Land Cruiser to pack animals. Omar needed the money for his youngest daughter's dowry, or he would never have agreed to do it.

The crate loaded, the two men set off for the Afghan border on the old road from Khorog to Ishkashim. The vehicle stirred up clouds of dust as they drove through the arid landscape. The heat was brutal, but they kept the windows up to keep the dust out.

"Fuck, man," said Burhanduddin. "Why don't you get the air conditioner fixed?"

Omar flinched at the profanity, an English phrase that Burha had apparently picked up from watching obscene American shows on satellite TV. Too bad the air conditioning had failed years earlier.

"Clean up your language, Burha, or I'll throw you out right here," he told his young companion. "You can feed the vultures."

It was after noon when they reached Ishkashim. In the heat there were no soldiers guarding the Afghan border at the edge of the neighboring town of Eshkashem. Omar and Burha drove into Afghanistan without stopping. Well before nightfall they arrived at Qala Panja, where they arranged for a porter and pack animals and spent the night, taking turns guarding the Land Cruiser and its mysterious cargo.

The porter, Jala, showed up just after sunrise the next morning. He had four donkeys in tow. One of the beasts was carrying Jala's food and camping equipment. Two donkeys had empty saddle bags. The fourth animal was pulling a little cart.

Omar picked an unburdened donkey for his mount. He and Burha loaded into the saddle bags the supplies and equipment they would need for the journey to Sakwar and back. They lifted the crate into the cart, and Jala secured the crate with ropes.

"Make sure it's not gonna fall out if the donkey stumbles," said Omar. "Those old pots are delicate."

"Old pots?" asked Jala, a mixture of incredulity and surprise on his tanned, leathery face. "Who would haul old pots through the Hindu Kush?"

"Better not to ask questions," said Omar. "Just get us to Sakwar and back, and you'll collect your money."

"A third up front," said Jala.

"Why?" Omar did not like demanding porters.

"Food for the donkeys."

Omar got the required payment from his money belt and handed it to Jala.

The three men mounted their donkeys and set out on the trail to Baroghil, where they planned to cross through the pass into Pakistan. The donkeys seemed sure-footed on the narrow trail, which in the mountainous terrain often threaded its way between rocky cliffs and steep embankments. Still, Omar worried that the donkey with the crate would stumble, causing the crate to slip to one side, overbalancing the donkey cart and making it fall off the trail into a ravine. Jala's donkey, in the lead, slipped once, but caught itself before going over the edge, Jala cursing in Tajik all the while.

Omar marveled at the valleys and gorges through which they passed, and of course the snow-capped mountains were spectacular. The trails, long blocked by ice and snow, had become passable again for a few months. The trip was arduous but a pleasure in some ways. In late spring the alpine meadows were covered in explosions of wildflowers, village fruit trees were in bloom, and the rivers ran fast with water from melting glaciers. The Hindu Kush was a beautiful if dangerous place, and bandits augmented the threats so generously provided by nature.

Days after traversing the Baroghil Pass, the little caravan reached Sakwar, in the Gilgit-Baltistan region of Pakistan. Omar had no trouble finding the recipient of the supposed precious pottery. Munir Sharif turned out to be notorious in tiny Sakwar. A man with grandiose ambitions, people said, but little real accomplishment. A dreamer. Still, he had the money that Omar needed for his return trip — and for his daughter's dowry.

Omar, Burha, and Jala removed the crate from the donkey cart. Munir inspected the crate for damage, then nodded to one of his friends, saying, "Faroud, check it."

Faroud passed some kind of instrument over the crate's surface and seemed satisfied with the results. At any rate, Munir paid Omar the agreed-upon price for the delivery of the pottery. Omar wondered why Munir did not open the crate and inspect the pottery for damage, but he was happy not to have to pass that test. The trip had been difficult, and he had no idea what condition the "pottery" had been in when he received the crate in Khorog.

Omar watched as Munir, Faroud, and a couple of other fellows loaded the crate into an old truck and secured it with ropes. Leaving the other two men in the rear of the truck, Munir and Faroud climbed into the front seat and drove away.

Omar paid Jala another installment of the price they had agreed on. Tomorrow he and Burha would need his help to get back to Qala Panja, where Omar hoped his Land Cruiser would be waiting for them.

* * *

Embarrassed to be seeing a psychiatrist, Coot Jenkins arrived for his appointment with Dr. Louis Rosen just a minute before his scheduled time. As he opened the door to the waiting room, a woman stumbled out, her right hand slipping off the inside knob.

"Excuse me," said Coot. "I didn't expect anyone to be leaving."

The woman, whose left hand contained a crumpled and wet tissue, looked too upset to respond. She hurried into the hall and disappeared around a corner. Across the waiting room, his hand holding another door open, stood a tall, pleasant-looking man.

"Hello, Mr. Jenkins. I'm Dr. Rosen. Please come in and have a seat."

Dr. Rosen was dressed in a sport coat and tie. He appeared to be in his mid forties. His glasses made his eyes look abnormally large. He ushered Coot into his office and indicated one of two chairs facing each other along one side of the room. Both men sat down. Coot looked around the office, noticing a desk, another chair, two large bookcases, three pieces of art, and several framed diplomas on the wall behind the desk.

"You mentioned on the phone last week that you had had a panic attack. Please tell me about it."

Coot recounted his experience after the dinner with Emily as Dr. Rosen sat listening.

"Do you recall what you were thinking about just before the attack?" asked the doctor.

"I was annoyed that people kept asking me about Frannie. My wife. She died a couple of years ago. I was thinking that I wanted to get on with my life."

"Get on with your life?"

"Yeah — have a normal social life again."

"Is something preventing you from having a normal social life?"

Coot squirmed in his chair, then said, "I guess I still feel some loyalty to Frannie."

"I'd be surprised if you didn't. Do you think Frannie would have wanted you not to see other women after she was gone?"

"No. Near the end she even said she hoped I'd... I'd...". Coot choked back a sob, then finished, "find someone else." *What the hell?* Coot thought. This session could be embarrassing.

"Let's talk more about your encounter with Emily. Was she

interesting?"

The slight change of subject helped Coot regain his composure. "Yes, of course. We work in the same field. We had lots to talk about. Plus, she's attractive."

"Did you consider having sex with Emily?"

"The thought crossed my mind."

"Why didn't you?"

"She wanted to nip any possibility of an office romance in the bud. Plus, she didn't think I was ready for a relationship."

"Did Emily explain why she thought you weren't ready?"

"Oh, yes. She said I was in denial."

"Denial about what?"

"About what's bothering me."

"What *is* bothering you?"

"*You're* beginning to bother me, Dr. Rosen," Coot said, before he could stop himself.

"Let me rephrase the question, then. What did Emily *think* was bothering you?"

"Losing Frannie."

"Was she right?"

"Like I told Emily, Frannie's gone and that's that."

"Do you miss Frannie?"

"Like I said before, I just want to get on with my life." He was beginning to feel anxious again. He gazed around Rosen's office, admiring the art and the furnishings. Despite his efforts to distract himself, the anxiety increased.

"Do you think about Frannie much?" Dr. Rosen continued.

"Uh, doc, I'm feeling really uncomfortable. Can we talk about something else?"

"Do you think you can tolerate the anxiety until it dissipates?"

"I guess I can stand it. Why is this happening to me?"

"That's what we were beginning to discuss when the panic attack hit you. Can you tell me a bit about Frannie? What was she like?"

"I'll try. Boy, anxiety is no fun."

"No, it's not. Now, what about Frannie?"

"Right. Well. We met while in grad school. She was very pretty, very vivacious. Everybody enjoyed being around her. She was really smart, too. Sometimes she tried to hide it, like she'd say, 'This may be a silly idea, but...' and then share some tremendous insight she'd had. She was really funny, in a sly way. She wasn't much for puns, but occasionally she'd come up with one that was absolutely dead-on, a clever play on words that went beyond the obvious joke to say something perceptive about the larger context."

"She sounds like an impressive person. How did you two get along?"

"Great, right from the start. She appreciated my sense of humor, which can be a little weird sometimes. I was a nerdy kid and socially insecure. She made me feel like I was the best part of her life. I never understood why. We got married while still in school but waited until we'd finished our degrees before having kids. She was a wonderful mother to our son and daughter. We had been married for 25 years when she was diagnosed with metastatic melanoma. She was very brave, right to the end. I'm not sure that I appreciated just how special she was until...until she was gone."

Coot started to sob. He sat in his chair in front of Dr. Rosen and shook with grief. Dr. Rosen handed him a box of tissues. "I know this is hard for you."

"If I'd broken down like this when I was in the Army, I'd have never heard the end of it." Coot wiped his eyes.

"Therapy isn't like the Army, Mr. Jenkins. It requires a different kind of courage."

"Now that you've lanced the abscess, maybe the pus will drain and the wound will heal."

"I wouldn't put it quite that way."

Coot and Dr. Rosen continued talking about Coot's life before, during, and after his marriage. When their time was up, Dr. Rosen said, "You've had some important insights today."

"Why does facing the truth have to be so painful?"

"Because you are dealing with love and loss."

"I thought I had finished grieving for Frannie, but I guess I was fooling myself."

"We'll take up where we left off the next time I see you."

Coot and Dr. Rosen agreed on a time for Coot's next session. The doctor gave Coot his business card. "Call me if you have another panic attack and it doesn't go away in a few minutes."

In the days after his meeting with Dr. Rosen, Coot winced every time he recalled crying like a baby in front of another man. Coot had just wanted Rosen to explain why he had that first panic attack, and he made him have another one! What kind of doctor would do that? What happened to "First do no harm"?

Coot waited until Sunday night, when he was sure he would get Dr. Rosen's answering service, then canceled his follow-up appointment.

CHAPTER 4

Gathering Clouds

Coot woke a little after seven the Monday after his meeting with Dr. Rosen. Between the loose nukes problem and worrying about having another panic attack, he was feeling a lot of stress. Following a quick breakfast, he decided to go for a walk. Maybe a visit to the gardens on Tilden and International Drive would stimulate him to think of a new way to get information about the black market weapons or help him avoid another anxiety attack.

In a few minutes he was walking east along Tilden Street, past the lovely smoke bushes with their gauzy white plumes. Coot especially liked the small park near the embassies on International Drive. He often walked through the park after breakfast, enjoying the many flowers and interesting plants. Sometimes he encountered people from the embassies, people whom he had met at the many nonproliferation conferences he had attended. They all shared his concern that this beautiful world might be destroyed by the weapons they were committed to eliminating.

He stopped to look at one of his favorite wildflowers — Cow Parsnip. It was a weed, really, but it fascinated him. Each plant looked like a miniature sky palace set on a tall, thin stalk. Each stalk branched near the top into six smaller stalks. At the top of the central stalk was a large dome of tiny flowers. The other five stalks ended in smaller collections of the tiny blooms. It was like a feudal lord's palace surrounded by the less impressive dwellings of his vassals. Upon closer inspection, Coot noticed that the central dome was built of dozens of smaller domes of flowers. Each smaller dome was set on a little stalk that emerged from the top of the central stalk. As Coot leaned over to get a closer look, he noticed that the smaller domes themselves were constructed in the same way: each little stalk branched into a dozen tiny stalks, each topped by a tiny blossom. It was fractal. He wondered whether there were levels of branching too small to see. What an amazing world!

Coot took the stairs up from Tilden, looking to his left at vast swaths of white astilbe climbing up the hill beside him. At last he reached International Drive. He crossed the street and entered the little park. Near the entrance was a small tree, which a nearby plaque said was an apple tree under whose ancestor Isaac Newton conceived his theory of universal gravitation. What would Newton have thought of the uses to which humanity has put its knowledge of physics? Despite Newton's fascination with the Book of Revelation, would he have approved a defensive strategy that could result in the wholesale destruction of the human race in a thermonuclear war?

Coot wandered along the brick paths, checking which flowers had bloomed since his last visit. He found only a few yellow flowers of the sort he had often noticed growing wild along rural highways. Groundsel, were they?

He left the little park and walked north along International Drive. He stopped to inspect some white, globular flowers, each composed of hundreds of tiny blossoms, each at the end of a tiny stalk, like exploding fireworks.

"Coot! Hey, Coot!"

Coot looked up. The short, rotund man hurrying toward him was waving energetically. Coot recognized the fellow as Saeed Mustafa, a Pakistani whom he had first met in Geneva years earlier at the U.N.'s Conference on Disarmament. Coot suspected that he was a member of Pakistan's Inter-Services Intelligence organization, or I.S.I. "Saeed! How good to see you again!"

"Listen, Coot, I need your advice. It's urgent." The man's whispered plea was barely audible. Despite the cool air, he was sweating profusely. "I phoned you at home yesterday and this morning but you didn't answer. And just when I'd given up and gone for a walk, Allah be praised, I found you!"

"What's the problem?" Coot responded in a similarly low voice.

"'Problem' hardly describes the situation. 'Calamity' would be more apt. We believe several old Soviet tactical nukes have been acquired by terrorists and one is now somewhere in Gilgit-Baltistan."

The black market weapons that Sergey had warned Coot about, in northern Pakistan and maybe elsewhere!

"How sure are you?" Coot needed some estimate of reliability before forwarding this information to Jill Meecham at the N.S.C.

"We have two sources, one in Pakistan and one in Kyrgyzstan."

"How many weapons were involved? What kind?"

"At least the one in Pakistan and as many as five others," said Saeed. "Atomic demolition munitions. We don't know whether the one in Pakistan was among the five reported in Kyrgyzstan."

"Loose portable nukes are bad news." Coot understood all too well that A.D.M.s' minimal safeguards might enable terrorists to activate them. "Do you know anything about these terrorists?"

"Only that the report from Pakistan mentioned mushrooms. We don't know if this is the name of the terrorists or maybe a description of the cloud created if they succeed in exploding a nuclear device."

"That's not much to go on."

"Coot, I'm really worried. If India is attacked and Pakistan is blamed, the situation could spiral out of control."

"I understand your concern, Saeed, but why are you telling me about this? I'm not at Brookhaven anymore, you know, much less in the Administration."

Both men fell silent while another early-morning walker strode past them. The man stared at Coot for a moment as he passed.

"Coot, I've always been impressed with your honesty and the way people trust you. Help me convince the Indians that the government of Pakistan has nothing to do with these terrorists and that we are doing all we can to capture them and secure the weapons."

"I appreciate your confidence in me, Saeed, but I don't think I can overcome the deep mistrust between India and Pakistan."

"We need to build trust, Coot, and we need to do it in a hurry.

Can you arrange a contact?"

"I suppose J.K. Ramanujan would be a good choice. He did a Ph.D. in International Relations at Johns Hopkins. His advisor was a Pakistani. He's now a special assistant to India's ambassador to the U.S."

"How soon can you set up a meeting?"

Coot promised to contact J.K. as soon as he returned home but could not say whether or when a meeting would take place. Saeed asked Coot to call him as soon as he knew something.

Having passed on his grim intelligence, Saeed hurried off toward his embassy. Coot headed for the stairs down to Tilden. What a mess! How could Saeed expect him to get the Indians and Pakistanis to trust each other enough to defuse a genuine nuclear crisis?

When Coot got home, he called J.K.'s number at the embassy. After a couple of rings J.K. answered.

"Hello? J.K. Ramanujan here."

"J.K., this is Coot Jenkins. I need to talk with you privately as soon as possible, preferably this morning. Do you have an hour to spare?"

"What's this about, Coot?"

"I can't tell you over the phone. Can I pick you up at the embassy in half an hour?"

"Make it 45 minutes. I'll meet you in front of the Science Wing on Mass Ave."

"Great! I'll be driving a blue Camry. See you then."

Coot phoned Saeed with news of the arrangements. They agreed that Coot and J.K. would pick up Saeed at the southeast corner of Reno and Van Ness in an hour, which would give Coot enough time to brief J.K. on the situation.

Traffic on 34th Street was not too bad for a Monday morning. Coot swung the Camry onto Massachusetts Avenue at Observatory Circle, cruised through Montrose Park, and soon spotted the tall, slender Indian waiting for him. Coot eased the car to a halt and J.K. climbed into the passenger's seat. Coot resumed his drive down

Massachusetts Avenue, heading for the turnaround at Sheridan Circle.

"So, Coot, what urgent business do you have with me this morning?"

"You're not going to like this news, J.K. It seems that there are some loose nukes, including one in Pakistan. Old Soviet-era atomic demolition munitions, to be precise. In the hands of some terrorist outfit. The Pakistanis are doing their best to hunt down these guys and secure the weapons."

"How many devices are involved?"

"A source in Pakistan reported a single device there, but a source in Kyrgyzstan claimed five devices."

"How did you find out about this?"

"I was out for a walk this morning. A couple of blocks from the Pakistani embassy I was hailed by Saeed Mustafa, a fellow I met years ago through the Conference on Disarmament. I think Saeed may work for the I.S.I. Anyhow, he told me that not all of the Soviets' tactical nuclear weapons in Kyrgyzstan were actually returned to Russia. A few have recently been acquired by terrorists. One may be in Pakistan. Saeed seemed most concerned about their being used against India, which might then retaliate against Pakistan."

"A reasonable concern, given the state of relations between our two countries since the Mumbai incident. But, Coot, doesn't it strike you as odd that you're out for a walk, an I.S.I. guy happens to spot you, and then he drops a bombshell like this on you? Why wasn't Saeed in his office, working the phones, meeting with his people to discuss the situation? Why would he even tell you about it, rather than handling it through channels? Surely the I.S.I. has some contacts in Indian intelligence."

"You can ask him these questions yourself, if you're willing to meet him. We're supposed to pick him up in about five minutes."

"Now you tell me! I suppose I've got no choice at this point but to find out as much as I can from Saeed."

Saeed was waiting for them when they got to Reno and Van Ness. He quickly got into the back seat and shut the door. Coot introduced the two men, who shook hands. Coot resumed driving east on Van Ness.

"J.K., I'm so glad you were willing to meet with me," said Saeed. "I assume Coot has told you all about the situation."

"Yes, but before we discuss this further, I need to understand how and why you involved Coot in the matter. Why didn't you work through I.S.I.'s contacts at the C.I.A.?"

"If I were in your position I would be wondering the same thing myself. The explanation, however, is simple. We have known about the weapons for two days already. We have had extensive discussions internally as to how to respond. The I.S.I. is pursuing every possible means to find the terrorists. But what if we don't find them before they detonate the device now in Pakistan? What if, Allah forbid, they use it against your country? What would India's response be, we asked ourselves.

"Since the Pakistani and Indian governments are not on such good terms at the moment, we decided that we needed to make contact through the Americans. To deal with such an urgent problem, establishing trust quickly is essential. We needed an American contact trusted by both sides, ideally someone with expertise on nuclear issues. I thought of Coot right away but was unable to contact him.

"Last night I didn't sleep very well. This morning I was beginning to panic, so I decided to take a walk to clear my head, to calm myself. Allah be praised, I found Coot walking in the gardens along International Drive."

"All right, Saeed. I accept your explanation of Coot's involvement, at least for now. What about these terrorists? Have I.S.I. supported them in the past, as with several other terrorist groups in the tribal areas and Kashmir?"

"No, no, J.K.! Believe me, we had never heard of them until we got reports about their acquiring a Soviet nuclear weapon."

"What are I.S.I. doing to find these guys?"

"Everything possible! Rounding up and interrogating known radical sympathizers. Offering rewards for any information about terrorist activities. We have to be careful, of course, not to set off a panic by announcing the grave nature of the threat."

"What do you want me to do?"

"Report the situation to your government, emphasizing my government's absolute commitment to capturing the terrorists before they can use their weapon. Also, urge your government to take all possible measures to prevent infiltration of the terrorists into India. We must cooperate in every way we can to defeat our common enemy."

"Would your government cooperate in a temporary closing of the border, including the line of control in Kashmir?"

"Under the circumstances, I think so, but I can't promise that."

"What about allowing officers of our Research and Analysis Wing to work alongside I.S.I. officers inside Pakistan for the duration of this crisis?"

"I can propose that to my superiors and let you know."

"All right, Saeed. Meanwhile, I must alert my government. You and I should stay in touch."

The Pakistani and the Indian exchanged contact information.

"Coot, I need to get back to my office."

"Sure thing, Saeed."

Coot drove past Connecticut, turned around, and headed west on Van Ness. He stopped at Reno and let Saeed out, then turned south.

"What do you think about Saeed's story now?" Coot asked his passenger.

"At least he *thinks* he's telling the truth. I'm inclined to believe him. We'll have to see how cooperative his government is."

In a few minutes they were back at the Science Wing.

"Thanks for introducing me to Saeed," said J.K. as he prepared to get out of the car. "If he's telling the truth, both our governments have a lot of work to do to prevent a catastrophe."

"Good luck in convincing your people that the problem is real. Who knows what the consequences may be?"

Coot watched as J.K. headed back to his office. He had listened to the two men's conversation with intense interest. What if some of those weapons were intended for use in Europe or the U.S.? He had to tell Jill Meecham about this development. In her position at the National Security Council she would be responsible for coordinating the Administration's response to the crisis. Coot dialed Jill's number at the N.S.C. Her assistant answered. He identified himself and asked for Jill, then waited for her to pick up.

"Hi, Jill. Listen, I have to meet you as soon as possible on an urgent matter that I can't discuss on the phone. When can I come over? ... 11 would be fine. See you then."

Coot drove to his office, parked, hurried into the lobby, and stepped into the waiting elevator. After a quick trip to the 7th floor, he would head to the N.S.C. Good, just one other passenger. Coot pushed the elevator's Close button a couple of times. Nothing happened. How annoying. A moment later the doors did close and the elevator began its ascent.

With nothing else to do, Coot looked at the other passenger. Diana Munson was returning his stare.

"Hello, Mr. Jenkins," she said. "I wondered whether I would see you here today."

Coot felt his face flush. She had not seemed to pay any attention to him at Jill's meeting or afterwards, even when taking Jill and him to her office.

"Oh, hi, Ms. Munson."

"Please, call me 'Diana.'"

Now she was smiling at him, not flirtatiously but in a friendly, interested way. He tried to respond similarly, but quickly looked away and then back again. He remembered feeling shy and awkward like this when he first met Frannie. He cleared his throat.

"Okay, Diana, and you can call me 'Coot'. Everyone else does."

His long-time nickname suddenly seemed ridiculous to him, and he wished he could just be "Bob."

"What brings you here today?"

"A meeting with Ben Barker."

"About S.A.F.E.'s new cyber security group, I bet."

"Right. Jill and I are delighted to see S.A.F.E. taking this initiative."

Coot watched the progress of the elevator on the green digits above the door. 2...3...4...5... The smooth ascent of the elevator suddenly became jerky.

"Oh, no! I can't believe this," Diana moaned, as the elevator clanked to a halt between floors 5 and 6.

"Don't panic," Coot reassured the young woman. He had plenty of reason himself to freak out, but he had to stay calm and get them rescued. He lifted the handset of the emergency phone and waited for it to connect automatically to building security. Nothing happened. "Rats!" he said. "The phone isn't working. I'll call S.A.F.E.'s office manager. Security will have us out of here in no time." He wished he felt sure that was true.

Coot pulled out his cell phone and placed the call. The office manager promised to alert building security to their predicament and to tell Ben that Diana would be late. Coot relayed this news to his fellow passenger.

"That's a relief," she said. "Thanks."

Coot nodded, as he dialed Jill Meecham's number again. This time Jill herself answered.

"Hi, Jill. This is Coot again. Would you believe it? Diana Munson and I are stuck in an elevator at my office. I don't know how long we'll be in here. I'll call you as soon as we're out."

Coot put his cell phone back into his pocket. He inhaled deeply, then sighed. Why was he not having a panic attack when there was reason to panic? Coot looked at Diana again. He had to act as if nothing were wrong.

"Jill said you went to Carnegie-Mellon."

"That's right. My advisor at Stanford suggested its program in computer security."

"He did?"

"She."

"Sorry! I just assumed your advisor was male. A sign of impending geezerhood, I guess. Maybe the neighborhood kids are right to call me 'Old Coot'." Ouch! Why did he have to say that?

"How *did* you get your nickname?" she said.

"After agreeing to lend my baseball glove to another kid, I made the mistake of telling him not to get cooties on it. He said, 'At least I don't look like a cootie.' From then on, all the boys called me 'Cootie.' My first baseball coach cut it down to 'Coot', and the name stuck. It could have been worse, I suppose. At least I wasn't known as 'Scarface' or 'Cockroach.'"

Diana laughed, that hearty Frannie-like laugh that he had noticed in the E.O.B. Coot grew more uneasy about their similarities. He tried to continue the conversation — and to diminish the age issue. "The 'Old' part was added later by children who thought that anyone over forty had one foot in the grave."

Diana's smile faded a bit.

Had he messed up again? Everything was going wrong at once. He had to inform Jill of the loose nuke in Pakistan.

"Some of the alternatives are definitely worse," she replied at last.

"What?" Her delayed reply brought him back to the present. "Oh, right."

Coot's cell phone rang. He took the call, then closed the phone, returned it to his pocket, and turned to face Diana again.

"The building manager has called the service department at Otis. They're sending someone, but it may be an hour before they can rescue us. We'll just have to wait."

"We'll have to find something unclassified to talk about," Diana said.

Unfortunately there was only one thing on Coot's mind, and he couldn't talk about it. Casting about for something else to say, Coot had a moment of inspiration. "Elevators should at least be equipped with camp stools for such occasions, don't you think?" he asked her.

"Or an inflatable couch," she suggested, her eyes twinkling.

"Too bad we can't just conjure up an entire living room," he said, warming to the subject. "We could play cards or watch TV." This fantasy was better than worrying about terrorists with nuclear weapons loose in the world. He sighed again and shifted his weight.

"Oh, like the tent in *Harry Potter and the Goblet of Fire*?" Diana said. "Wasn't that a wonderful scene!"

"Yes, even to an old coot. It's no surprise that children are disappointed when they realize they won't be going to Hogwarts."

"I haven't given up hope yet. There's adult-onset diabetes and early-onset Alzheimer's. Why shouldn't something *good* happen at an unexpected time?"

Frannie had had a similar childlike delight in wondrous possibilities. Why did Diana keep reminding him of Frannie? Weird. Coot tried to reorient himself to the present. To the actual person with whom he was sharing the elevator for the next hour. To his need to get out of the elevator and meet Jill. Perhaps these disturbing thoughts would go away if he could find out some interesting non-Frannie-like facts about her.

"So, Diana, tell me about yourself. Where did you grow up? Where did you go to college? What's your job like?"

"I was born in White Plains but my family moved around a lot. My dad worked at IBM. We called it 'I've Been Moved'. By the time I was in high school we were in San Jose and everybody was into computers. I guess that's how I got interested in software."

Coot nodded at her and tried to pay attention, but thoughts of the nuclear weapon somewhere in Pakistan kept intruding.

"I got a B.S. in computer science at Stanford and a Ph.D. at Carnegie-Mellon, then worked as a computer security consultant for a couple of companies on the West Coast. "

"Impressive."

Diana fell silent for a moment, continuing to look at Coot, then said, "You seem distracted. Am I boring you?"

She had detected his preoccupation. Acting normal was harder than he had thought. He tried to pay attention to his breathing. Inhale.

"No, not at all. Please go on."

"The next part is pretty sad. My dad died and I decided to move back home with my mom. Losing Dad was rough on both of us."

"I know how tough it is to lose someone who's been a big part of your life."

"You do?" Diana's eyes widened..

"Yes. My wife Frannie died about two years ago. From cancer. An aggressive form, even for melanoma. By the time we found it, it had spread into her lungs and bones. She didn't have a chance." The old anger and sadness threatened to overwhelm him. For a moment he couldn't speak.

"How awful! I'm so sorry for you," Diana said, touching his forearm.

It was if Frannie was reaching out to comfort him through Diana. Memories of Frannie's illness rushed back into Coot's mind. He struggled to maintain his composure. "When Frannie got sick I tried to be strong for her, to look for the tiniest silver linings in increasingly dark clouds. When she died, I felt empty, alone, depressed."

"Oh, Coot, you poor man."

Diana's concern made it easier for Coot to continue talking. He had never told anyone except Dr. Rosen so much about his feelings after Frannie's death.

"I quit going to places that reminded me of Frannie. I made excuses when our friends invited me for dinner." He hadn't meant to blurt out the whole sad story of his difficulty in coping with the loss of his wife. "I'm sorry. That's probably more than you wanted to know."

Coot shifted his gaze from Diana to the faux wood paneling of the elevator. Frannie had always made fun of anything faux, false, or phony. How he missed her! His eyes began to tear up. "I don't talk about it much," he croaked.

"Maybe that's why you needed to tell somebody how you felt."

Another amateur therapist? Moved by Diana's obvious sincerity, Coot suppressed that negative reaction, cleared his throat, and swallowed. "I appreciate your understanding," he said. "You're very kind." Despite her reassurance, he felt uncomfortable at having revealed so much of himself to someone he barely knew, so he said, "Let's get back to your story. You eventually left California and came back east?"

A puzzled look flashed across Diana's face. She said, "Yes. I applied for a job at BBN in Boston. Leaving Mom was difficult for both of us, but I felt I needed a new challenge."

"How's your mom doing?"

"Much better. My older brother and his wife and new baby live nearby, so she spends a lot of time helping them. The little one has rejuvenated her."

"I'm not surprised. Since Frannie died, seeing little children has always been a comfort to me. They prove that life goes on, despite pain and loss."

Diana looked away from Coot, sighed deeply, and straightened her shoulders. "I didn't realize how lonely I would feel, moving east, away from my family and friends."

"It does take time to make new friends. Everyone is so busy these days."

"Especially when you have to travel as much as I do to coordinate with government agencies and private groups. I'm gone much of the work week, and on the weekends I have to shop and do laundry and clean my apartment and prepare for the next week's meetings."

"I know what you mean. I have to do all the things that Frannie took care of for years. It's hard to find the energy and make the time for doing other things."

"When you feel so constrained by circumstances, it's easy to slip into a mind-numbing routine. My mom and dad had sacrificed a lot for Dad's career. I just expected to have to do the same."

"How are you feeling about your decision now?"

"Ambivalent. I've been successful, I make good money, and I enjoy my colleagues. Still, there's a part of me that just wants to find a kindred spirit, a friend or ..." Diana paused, looking wistful, then brightened. "But enough about me. What about you?"

"I spent most of my career at Brookhaven National Laboratory, working on nuclear nonproliferation."

"Now it's my turn to be impressed."

"Eventually I realized that it would be impossible to convince other countries not to seek nuclear weapons as long as the nuclear powers like the U.S. possessed large numbers of them. So, years before Frannie got her diagnosis I decided to take early retirement, move to D.C., and join the staff of Scientists Against Future Extinction to work on the elimination of all nuclear weapons and the means of producing them." He hoped it was not too late.

"That's a noble goal."

"It's a goal that we *must* achieve, or eventually an insane leader or a fanatical terrorist will get his hands on one or more weapons and actually use them." Like now.

"What do you do for S.A.F.E.?" She seemed genuinely interested. What a refreshing change from most people he met socially.

"Work on nonproliferation policy. Write newspaper and journal articles. Appear on TV programs as a sort of expert guest. Occasionally I get to testify before Congress."

"You're a celebrity!"

"Hardly, but I do what I can to nudge public opinion in the right direction."

Suddenly the elevator began to move again. It was going down. An unexpectedly magical moment was coming to an end.

Coot and Diana got out of the elevator in the lobby and took another one to the S.A.F.E. offices. Coot introduced Diana to Ben Barker, then said, "It's been a pleasure getting to know you, Diana."

"You, too, Coot."

Diana, like Dr. Rosen, had stirred emotions that he had tried to avoid for years. Grief. Longing. Even hope. Yet, her reminding him of Frannie in so many ways was unnerving. What was he getting into?

Back in his own office, Coot closed the door and sank into his chair. He tried to relax for just a moment, but thoughts of a distant weapon and and a nearby woman performed a dance of fear and longing in his mind. He called Jill to let her know that he and Diana were out of the elevator. He checked his e-mail and phone messages, but there was no new information about the device in Pakistan or the other black market nukes.

Time to get going. He jumped to his feet, checked that he had his White House credentials, and decided to risk another elevator trip for the sake of speed. He left the S.A.F.E. offices and headed down Pennsylvania Avenue toward the White House. He thought of using his race-walking technique to get there faster, but too many tourists were crowding the sidewalks as he neared his destination

After passing through security with his new credentials, he entered the West Wing and was soon alone with Jill in her office. Numerous pictures adorned the walls: Jill with the president, Jill with the vice-president, Jill with the Secretaries of State and Defense, Jill with various Congressional leaders. On the credenza behind her desk Coot noticed a picture of Jill and her husband Jay. Lucky Jill, that she still had her spouse.

Jill invited Coot to sit on the brown leather sofa across the office from her desk. She picked up a couple of mugs and a coffee pot from her credenza and set them on the table in front of the sofa. After they were seated, she poured coffee for both of them.

"Sulawesi Kalosi Taraja. It's organic and fair traded."

Coot could smell its strong, pleasant odor as he took the mug she offered him. He turned to face her and took a sip, but the flavor of a fine coffee took second place in his mind. "Have you ever heard of a group that calls itself 'Mushrooms'?" he asked.

"No, that's a new one on me."

"I found out this morning from Saeed Mustafa, who I suspect is in Pakistani intelligence, that the group has acquired between one and six Soviet-made atomic demolition munitions."

"The ones that were rumored to be on the black market?"

"Maybe."

"Where are the devices now?"

"At least one is in Pakistan, they think."

"Who knows about this?"

"The I.S.I. learned about them two days ago. I put Saeed in touch with J.K. Ramanujan from the Indian Embassy this morning."

"What was J.K.'s reaction?"

"Skepticism at first, but I think he's now assuming the threat is serious. He asked Saeed about closing the border, including the line of control in Kashmir. That's really all I know."

"Why didn't you call me sooner?" Jill's voice signaled irritation.

Coot was startled that Jill would ask such a question. Surely the answer was obvious. "It was vital to get the Paks and the Indians talking immediately." He could only imagine how India would react if someone set off a nuclear weapon on their soil. They'd immediately suspect Pakistan, the I.S.I. in particular. That could quickly lead to retaliation.

"Diplomacy is the government's job, not yours."

Jill's criticism disturbed Coot. He sat up straighter, put down his coffee mug, and raised his hands, palms facing Jill. "I was facilitating, not negotiating."

"Working with other countries is the function of the State Department."

"I'm sure you remember how important back-channel communication was in resolving the Cuban Missile Crisis."

"Of course, but it shouldn't be the first option."

"I called you to arrange a meeting as soon as I left Saeed and J.K.

We couldn't have met much sooner than we did, anyway."

"I suppose it's just as well that you waited," said Jill. "I've been pretty busy dealing with the new threats from North Korea."

She did indeed looked stressed to Coot, who had known her for many years. Maybe that was why she was chiding him for his involvement with the Indians and Pakistanis. With that realization, he felt less defensive.

"Anything beyond their usual bluster?" he asked.

"As you know, they've been testing nuclear weapons again." Jill sighed. "And their long-range missiles are now able to reach the West Coast."

"Yeah." Coot echoed Jill's sigh. "What a world. I'm glad you're the one dealing with it, and not some trigger-happy neocon."

"I've met with North Korean officials," said Jill. "They are very isolated and consequently unrealistic in their understanding of how the world works."

"Such people are prone to miscalculation," said Coot. "I know you're trying to make our red lines absolutely clear to them."

"Of course. Thank God we now have those ballistic missile interceptors in California and Alaska." Jill grinned. "That'll make them less likely to think they can frighten us into not protecting our allies in the South."

Jill's phone rang, cutting short the conversation. She answered it, listened briefly, then hung up.

"An F.B.I. agent is waiting at the security checkpoint to speak with you right now."

"Did they say why?"

"No. I'll walk you back to security now. Let me know if you find out anything else from your contacts."

"Sure."

"Meanwhile, I'll coordinate the Administration's response to the situation in Pakistan."

When Coot and Jill reached the checkpoint, a man in a dark suit rose and walked toward them.

"I'll leave you here, Coot," said Jill. She turned and left.

"Mr. Jenkins?" the man said.

"Yes."

"I'm Agent Smalley from the Federal Bureau of Investigation. I need to ask you a few questions."

"What about? This is a busy day for me."

"So I gather. Would you mind coming back to my office? We'll have more privacy there."

Despite his preoccupation with possible loose nukes, Coot answered, "Okay." What choice did he have? The two men left the White House. Agent Smalley directed Coot toward a black sedan parked in the driveway and opened a rear door for him. Coot got in, immediately noticing the heavy wire mesh between the front and back seats. He didn't like being put into a cage.

"This is Agent Zimmerman," said Agent Smalley, indicating the driver of the car. "We work in the Counterintelligence Branch."

"Why do you want to talk with me?" Their interest in him was a complete mystery.

"We'll explain that when we get where we're going."

They proceeded northwest on Pennsylvania Avenue past S.A.F.E. headquarters, until they reached the J. Edgar Hoover building, the headquarters of the F.B.I. Soon they were settled in what looked like a conference room, except for the recording equipment.

"Would you please tell me what this is about, Agent Smalley?" His refusal to explain anything was annoying.

"What do you know about Saeed Mustafa?"

So, his morning meeting had raised suspicions at the Bureau? He would cooperate, up to a point.

"I met Saeed years ago at the U.N. Conference on Disarmament in Geneva. He was in the Pakistani observer delegation to a meeting on the Non-Proliferation Treaty."

"Would you be surprised if I told you he was with Pakistani intelligence?"

"No. I suspected that myself."

"Do you know what his role is in the I.S.I.?"

"Not specifically. He often attends international meetings on nuclear issues."

"Before coming to the U.S. last year he was the I.S.I.'s main contact with the leadership in the tribal areas."

"So?"

"The tribal areas are controlled by the Pakistani Taliban."

"What are you suggesting?"

"Just that you should be careful in dealing with Mr. Mustafa. He may be playing a double game, relaying information to the militants that might aid them in their jihad against the West."

"Thanks for the guidance, Agent Smalley. I'll keep that in mind." Coot hoped that he sounded sincere.

"Good. If you find out anything from Mustafa that we should know, do share it with us. Here's my card."

Coot took the card. "Of course." He would instead be letting Jill handle liaison with the F.B.I. and other federal agencies.

"Thanks for your cooperation, Mr. Jenkins. Agent Zimmerman will take you back to your office now."

As Zimmerman drove Coot back down Pennsylvania Avenue, Coot asked him "Was that fellow who walked past Saeed and me in the garden this morning one of your guys? Zimmerman just smiled.

A message to call Jill was waiting for Coot when he returned to his desk. He picked up the phone, dialed her number, and once again her assistant answered. In a moment Jill was on the line.

"I trust you were discreet with the Bureau."

"Oh, yes. I'm leaving the liaison aspect up to you."

"Good. Any further word from our friends?

"No, not a peep. Shall I follow up?"

"Get me some contacts at the highest levels you can. I want to follow up but I don't want to spill the beans to anyone who isn't already in the know."

"Okay. I'll do my best."

Coot called Saeed and J.K., got the names of a couple of people for Jill to contact, and relayed the information to her. He wanted to do more. Who were these terrorists? How were they organized? Who were their allies? How did they finance such an expensive purchase? He searched the Web for "nuclear jihad" and got results that looked potentially interesting. He watched an old al-Qaeda video that urged jihadis to attack the West without mercy. He found some transcripts entitled "Nuclear jihadi chatter", but the English was garbled and he could not read Arabic.

After an hour of looking at such useless stuff he gave up. No one had heard of a nuclear-oriented terrorist group. Not even the jihadis. The only references to mushrooms were about the edible and poisonous kinds. He checked his e-mail and responded to those requiring an answer. He leaned back in his chair and once again tried to relax.

* * *

Munir Sharif felt alive, really alive. For the first time in his life, he was part of something momentous, something impressive. He would no longer be Munir the Dreamer, Munir the Schemer. He would soon be Munir the Magnificent, Hero of Pakistan. All he had to do was deliver a package to a certain Srinagar address in Indian-controlled Kashmir, wait while his friend Faroud flipped a few switches, and then drive like hell to get away before a huge explosion destroyed everything within miles of that package.

Of course the Indians would not welcome a truckload of Pakistanis with a nuclear weapon, so Munir the Schemer had a plan for how to get past the Indian Army guards at the Line of Control that separated Kashmir into Pakistani and Indian zones. Regardless of what he had told the American, George Boyd, Munir knew the only way to get across the Line of Control was with guns blazing. He was a great admirer of the Americans' Shock and Awe tactics in the Iraq War. He had recruited mujahideen trained in Kashmir by Lashkar-e-Taiba to provide a highly concentrated dose of Pakistani Shock and Awe for the operation.

Munir and Faroud would meet the LeT fighters on the night of the attack in Chakothi, on the Pakistani side of the Line of Control. Munir and Faroud would have the uncrated nuke in their truck. The LeT fighters would have conventional explosives and other weapons in their truck. The fighters would attack India's checkpoint at the Line of Control west of Uri, while Munir and Faroud, with a smaller LeT guard, would take advantage of the confusion to barrel through the checkpoint before additional Indian forces could join the fight.

Once across the Line, Munir, Faroud, and their guard would continue down Highway 1A past Pattan. To throw off any pursuers, they would then take the Hanjiwera Magam Road, dogleg over to the Aerodrome Road, and head for the Sheikh ul Alam Airport, where Faroud would work his magic and they would make their escape.

Munir was proud of his plan. It was sure to work. It was brilliant! Munir the Magnificent would succeed, where the vaunted Pakistani Air Force had failed in 1971 to destroy the Indian Air Force base at Srinagar.

* * *

Coot woke up, alone in his own bed in the house on Rodman Street, as he had done every morning in D.C. since Frannie's death. Two thoughts occurred to him almost simultaneously: terrorists with a nuclear weapon in Pakistan — and Diana Munson. He would check the news from Pakistan online after getting out of bed. Meanwhile, as he gathered himself to face the day ahead, he reviewed his encounter with Diana the previous morning in the elevator. He had enjoyed being with her, enjoyed her directness, her laughter, her whimsy, but it was weird, how she reminded me of Frannie. Would talking with Dr. Rosen again help him sort out his feelings?

Coot got out of bed and headed for the shower. Maybe a blast of hot water and some coffee would make his brain work better. He ran the water until it was hotter than usual and stepped into the pulsating spray. He lathered his body. He looked reasonably trim. Since Frannie's death, he had spent several evenings a week working out at a nearby gym, and of course he went for long runs with his friends Jack and Roger on the weekends. Too bad his workouts had not prevented his hair from turning gray and getting thinner.

After showering and dressing, Coot went into his kitchen. He filled a mug from the automatic coffee maker, which he had loaded the previous night with Hawaiian Kona, his and Frannie's favorite. It had been two lonely years since he last tasted it. On the way home from work the previous evening, he had smelled the strong odor of exotic coffees as he passed a coffee roaster on Connecticut, so he went inside and bought a freshly-ground pound of Kona. He prepared his usual breakfast of fruit and cereal and sat down to eat. He dipped his spoon into the bowl and brought it back out, filled with several blueberries and a shredded wheat square. He looked at the blueberries, their luscious darkness contrasting with the whiteness of the milk. Why had he not noticed before how pretty a spoonful of fruit and cereal could be?

Coot sipped the steaming Kona. There were so many possibilities with Diana, from the ridiculous to the sublime. Maybe he was getting way ahead of himself. Driving past his headlights, as his dad used to say. He should just slow down, take one step at a time, and see what developed with Diana. He needed help in figuring out why she reminded him so strongly of Frannie. He would make another appointment with Dr. Rosen.

That decision made, Coot walked into his home office and sat down at his computer. He checked the various news services for the latest developments in Pakistan. Nothing dramatic was being reported. The threatening weapon was still hidden, like a shark approaching unwary swimmers.

On Wednesday Coot arrived at Dr. Rosen's office. Fortunately the psychiatrist had not found another patient to take the appointment that Coot had canceled. Coot was feeling more comfortable with Dr. Rosen than he had expected. The younger man's calm, reassuring manner took the edge off Coot's embarrassment at seeing a psychiatrist. He told Dr. Rosen about getting stuck in the elevator with Diana, about their conversation, and especially about how much she reminded him of Frannie.

"It's weird, Dr. Rosen. I've never met anyone else who seemed to be channeling Frannie like that."

"The loss of Frannie caused your feelings about her to recede from your consciousness, only to return with unexpected force. First after dinner with Emily, then in my office, and most recently in the elevator with Diana. The more you can accept these feelings, the less they will be manifested as anxiety or as strange associations."

"I hope you're right. But what should I do about Diana? Is my attraction to her a wish to see Frannie again or am I interested in Diana herself, the real Diana?"

"Can't both be true?"

"Maybe so. Whatever the source of my feelings, what about Diana's? Was there a real and mutual chemistry between Diana and me, or am I just a pathetic old man imagining a relationship that can never be?"

"You'll have to work out that answer with Diana, if you decide to pursue her."

"If I don't try to see her again, I'll always wonder if I made a huge mistake. But if I do pursue her, I'm afraid I'll mess up."

"Why might you 'mess up'?"

"I've been giving the impression that I'm not ready for a relationship."

"Because you have not been willing to meet a woman on an emotional level. You seem to have a different attitude toward Diana. You seem to genuinely care for her."

"What little I know of her, I like."

"So what's your next step?"

"I dunno. Maybe meet her for lunch. But she's so busy. Maybe breakfast would be easier."

"Will you make a date with her, then?"

"I'd like to, but I'm old enough to be her father. Maybe I should wait for another chance meeting."

"Are you usually so passive?"

"No. I just feel so creepy about this." Coot broke eye contact with Dr. Rosen, looked down, shifted in his seat.

"Perhaps your Ranger training in reconnaissance will come in handy."

Coot's eyes snapped back up. "I can't stalk her!"

"Don't Rangers have other methods of gathering information?"

"I'll see what I can come up with," said Coot, embarrassed that he had no idea how to proceed.

Later that morning, Coot was sitting at his desk at S.A.F.E., brooding about whether and how to see Diana again, when a news alert popped up on his monitor: "India-Pakistan Border Closed". Coot clicked on the "More" button and learned that the closure was due to "unspecified terrorist threats". Saeed and J.K. had been doing their jobs well.

* * *

The next weekend Coot met his buddies Jack and Roger in Rock Creek Park for their usual Saturday run. Jack Acton, like Coot, had lost his wife, but Jack had remarried after only a year. Roger James was single, having been divorced by his wife after she had caught him in one too many office affairs.

After they had stretched their middle-aged muscles, Coot set off at a slow trot, Roger and Jack following. Even after stretching, Coot needed to warm up before increasing the pace. Age and injury had forced him to be careful. Just as he had to be careful in pursuing Diana.

Coot needed some practical advice, but he wasn't sure he wanted to go into detail about his interest in Diana. Whether it was shame he felt or merely an instinct for privacy, he wasn't sure. As they topped a hill and began a gentle descent, he decided to lower his guard a bit.

"You guys got any ideas how to get to know a woman without appearing too aggressive?"

"You wouldn't have asked me if you'd read my ex's divorce petition," said Roger. "Ask Jack."

"You interested in anybody in particular?" asked Jack.

"You won't believe this," said Coot. "A few days ago I got stuck in an elevator with a woman I'd met briefly at an N.S.C. meeting two weeks earlier. We chatted for an hour until we were rescued. How clichéd is that?"

"Good job!" said Roger. "Did I ever tell you about..."

Jack interrupted Roger's sure-to-be-lurid tale of conquest, saying, "So you like her well enough to want to ask her out?"

"I've been thinking about it," said Coot, picking up the pace, hoping to avoid more questions by forcing his inquisitors to breathe more deeply and more often.

"I thought...you weren't dating", said Roger.

Coot was quiet.

"You know, since Frannie..."

They'd suddenly come, by an unexpected route, to the most significant event of Coot's adult life.

"Since Frannie died,...you mean?"

There, he'd said it. The one topic they were reluctant to bring up with Coot.

"Yeah....You weren't, were you?"

Subtlety was not one of Roger's strengths. What could Coot say?

"Mostly I was...just looking."

"Just looking?" said Jack.

"Or wondering...about being...with someone."

Roger pointed to a young woman running along the trail toward them. "Like her?"

Coot studied the woman as she approached. Her golden brown hair was tied back in a pony tail. White ear buds indicated that she was listening to an MP3 player. Her T-shirt read "Collaboration Software".

It was Diana.

"Hi, Coot," she managed to say between breaths as she neared them.

Coot, stunned, opened his mouth to reply but words failed him. Roger turned his head and stared at Diana as she passed.

"That's her," Coot croaked.

"She's young enough to be..."

"Yeah, I know... My daughter," said Coot, completing Roger's assertion.

"So, how are you...going to...ask her out?" said Jack.

Coot was relieved that Jack had not picked up on the topic of Frannie. He'd always appeared to understand, without being told, that even years later Frannie's death was a difficult subject for Coot. Coot felt more comfortable answering his questions.

"I don't know...how to...approach her," said Coot. "The age difference...makes it so... so awkward."

Uncomfortable with the conversation, Coot looked around as he ran. The green leaves of the shrubs, the overhanging branches of the trees, and the singing of the birds always made him feel isolated from the troubles of the world, including his own. This particular morning he heard several robins and a cardinal or two. Running the rest of the way without further conversation would have been just fine with him.

The men ran on.

"You still...miss Frannie," said Roger.

"Frannie...was special. ... Unique," said Coot.

"Frannie...*was* special," said Jack.

"Very bright....Very funny." Coot's voice trailed off. He could not continue. Even now, talking about Frannie made him relive the grief he had felt just after her death. Coot stumbled, then caught himself. Jack's remark had made him aware of the numbness that had afflicted him since he lost his wife.

"How are you...feeling...these days,...Coot?" Jack asked gently.

"I don't...*feel* much...anymore."

"Maybe you should...talk with...somebody," said Jack.

"Maybe I will." No need to tell Jack and Roger that he was already seeing Dr. Rosen.

Now that Coot knew Diana was sometimes in his own neighborhood, he realized who might help him: Snuffy, proprietor of Snuffy's Diner on Connecticut Avenue. Coot wasted no time, but took his usual shower, shaved, and dressed in a pair of khaki slacks, a maroon polo shirt, and his walking shoes. He rushed out the front door and headed for Snuffy's. The sky was clear and the air cool. A perfect day to walk the five blocks to Snuffy's.

"Hey, Coot! Where've ya been, lad?" said Snuffy as Coot entered the familiar diner. Snuffy looked the same as he always did: wearing an apron, heavy-set, thinning hair, missing a tooth, and grinning broadly.

"Hello, Snuffy. Good to see you."

"Would you like your usual spot, where..." Snuffy lapsed into an awkward silence and began to adjust his apron.

"Where Frannie and I used to sit? Not today, thanks. I have a problem that I think you can help me with."

"Anything for you, Coot."

"I need to contact someone. A woman. A young woman." Coot described Diana in as much detail as he could remember. "Would you give me a call if she comes in here?"

"I can't promise I'll recognize her, Coot. So many people visit the diner every day, I can't remember everyone."

"Just do your best, Snuffy. I'd really appreciate it."

"No problem."

Remembering how Diana was dressed when as she ran past him in the park, he added, "One more thing: she sometimes wears a Collaboration Software T-shirt."

"I bet I know who she is. Comes in for breakfast sometimes. Very pleasant. Nice looking, too. Next time I see her, I'll let you know."

"When was she last in here?"

"A couple of days ago, I think. She and a young fella sat right over there," said Snuffy, pointing to a booth by the windows.

"Oh? Did they seem to be a couple?"

"Hard to tell. They did seem to know each other pretty well."

Oh, shit! She's got a boyfriend, Coot thought. "I see. Well, let me know if you see her again."

"Sure thing, Coot."

Coot gave Snuffy his phone number, left the diner, and walked home.

On the way, he brooded about what Snuffy had said. A boyfriend! A young guy, too. Damn! How could Coot be sure? He would just have to ask her — if he could meet her in private somehow.

He could not help thinking about *Diana as Diana* versus *Diana as Frannie.* Was he nuts to be so interested in her?

He hoped Snuffy called soon. Nothing to do but wait.

Once home, Coot turned on the radio. He didn't eat, in case Diana showed up for her own breakfast at Snuffy's. His stomach growled, as if in displeasure at having to wait for breakfast. Damn borborygmus! He hoped his gut didn't rumble in front of Diana. If he was lucky enough to meet her again.

Coot turned off the radio. He liked NPR, but not enough to listen to the same newscast twice. Of course they had no clue that, at that very moment, several nuclear weapons might be heading inexorably their way.

His stomach gave another growl. Shh! He had gotten up hours earlier to run with Jack and Roger, but he had not eaten anything — clearly a mistake. 9:15, no call. 9:30, no call. At 9:42 the phone rang. Coot raced to the kitchen and picked up the receiver. "Hello?"

"She's here, Coot. By herself this time, but I can't guarantee she's not meeting someone. You better hurry. No telling how long she'll stay."

"Great! Thanks for the call, Snuffy." At last!

Coot left his house and walked briskly along Rodman toward Snuffy's. The crabapple trees were in full bloom. The extended winter had delayed their blossoming this year. He always enjoyed the sequence of colors they produced: first the green leaves, then the red buds, and finally the delicate white flowers. Today all the colors were visible, as some buds had not yet opened. In a few days the ground beneath the trees would be strewn with white petals and the spectacular display would be just a memory. How sad, that the most beautiful things in life were so fleeting.

He continued along Connecticut toward the diner. Another rumble from his stomach made Coot increase his stride.

"Hey, Coot! Good to see you again!" said Snuffy, winking as Coot came in the front door of the diner.

"Hi, Snuffy. What's up?"

Snuffy glanced toward a booth near the windows — the same booth Diana and her companion had used. There she was, still alone, brow furrowed, reading the menu.

Coot smiled slightly at Snuffy, mouthed a thank-you, and turned toward Diana's table. She was reading the menu as intensely as if it were the Dead Sea Scrolls. He stopped himself from thinking *Just like Frannie used to do.* Coot felt the color rising in his face, his heart beating faster. Not another panic attack, please! He looked at Diana for a moment. When she did not look up, he walked toward her. Still no reaction. He stopped a foot from her table. At last she noticed him. Her mouth opened but she had a confused look on her face and said nothing for a moment. He smiled hopefully at her.

"Oh, Coot! Two chance meetings in one day! Are you with anyone? Would you like to sit down?"

"I was going to ask you the same thing. Whether you were with anyone."

"No, not today."

Relieved, Coot sat down opposite Diana. "So, how've you been? How did your meeting with Ben go?" Still feeling shy, he looked out the window at the pedestrians walking up and down Connecticut Avenue. He remembered his manners and put his napkin over his lap. Finally he looked back at Diana, who seemed to be waiting for his attention before replying.

"I've been fine. Busy, of course, with travel and everything. And, yes, the meeting did go well. We made plans for a joint project. How are you?"

"Okay. Still busy trying to save the world from itself, you know." They couldn't talk about the loose nukes there. He was not even sure whether Jill had shared the news with Diana. What about that guy she was with? He had to find out. "Do you come here often?"

"Once a week maybe. A few days ago my brother Bob was in town, so we had breakfast here."

Her brother! Why didn't he think of that possibility? And another Bob. "Did he like it?"

"Very much. He had strawberry crêpes."

"Mmm, tasty." Coot paused. "The way you were studying that menu when I came in, you looked like you were still trying to make up your mind."

"Any suggestions?"

"The Southwestern Omelet is really good."

"Okay, maybe I'll try it. What are you having?"

"My usual, a Belgian waffle."

Snuffy appeared a moment later, beaming at Diana. "So, young lady, you know my old friend Coot?"

"We met just recently," Diana said. "Through work."

"Snuffy, this is my friend Diana," Coot said.

"Pleased to meet you, Diana." Another wink at Coot. "So, what'll it be?"

"Half a grapefruit to start and some coffee. Black." She glanced again at her menu. "Coot recommended the Southwestern Omelet."

"An excellent choice," said Snuffy, grinning. "You can't go wrong listening to old Coot here."

Coot stiffened, felt his face flush. "What's this "Old Coot" business, Snuffy? Only those under 18 are allowed to call me that to my face."

"No offense meant, my friend, no offense." Snuffy looked

genuinely alarmed. "It's just that we go back a long way, you and me, and I haven't seen you in quite a while."

"You're right, Snuffy. Sorry I overreacted. I'll have the Belgian waffle with fresh strawberries and some whipped cream on the side, plus a large orange juice and coffee." Why had he reacted so strongly to Snuffy's innocent remark?

Snuffy hurried off with their orders.

"Snuffy seems very fond of you," said Diana. "Weren't you a little harsh with him?"

"Yeah. Maybe I feel a little uncomfortable with the topic of age, given how much older I am than you." Coot blurted out this confession before he could stop himself.

"Coot, we're just having *breakfast*! What difference does it make, how old we are?"

Her assessment made sense. He resolved not to drive past his headlights again.

The awkward moment was interrupted by Snuffy, returning with Diana's grapefruit, Coot's juice, a pot of coffee, and two mugs.

"Here ya go. Enjoy!"

"Thanks, Snuffy. You're a prince!" Promotion to royalty was the least he owed Snuffy. Coot sipped his orange juice, which, as always, was freshly squeezed.

Diana leaned closer to Coot and whispered, "See that family over there? Five kids! I don't see how they manage. They've been arguing ever since I sat down."

Coot followed Diana's gaze. The parents did seem to be having a dispute of some sort. The mother was leaning across the table, red-faced and talking rapidly. The father was staring at his plate, occasionally grunting in apparent disagreement. The children were looking from one parent to the other, in various degrees of discomfort and embarrassment. All except for the youngest child, a small boy in a high chair. He seemed to be coughing, as if trying to clear his throat, but without success. The little fellow was turning blue. The girl sitting next to his high chair looked at him, then tried to get her parents' attention. The adults both seemed too caught up in their private drama to notice the girl's pleas or the boy's distress.

Coot jumped up and rushed to the choking child. He seized a stringy piece of meat dangling from the boy's mouth and began to pull. Was it possible for a single piece of bacon to yield a foot of indigestible gristle? Yes. There was the proof. The boy took a couple of deep breaths and began to cry.

The parents, momentarily suspending their verbal combat, looked open-mouthed at Coot but didn't say a word. Then the father leaped to his feet and shouted, "What the hell are you doing, you meddlesome old geezer? Keep your hands off my kids!"

Coot stepped back from the table. "Your son was choking. Neither you nor your wife noticed he couldn't breathe. Someone had to act."

"Are you a doctor?"

"No, but..."

"Then why didn't you call for help? You could have made it worse!"

"I didn't, though, did I? I helped him. You didn't. You ought to be ashamed of yourself."

The man, his face red and his fists raised, rushed at Coot, who stepped quickly to the side, tripped the fellow with his left foot and shoved him hard with his right hand. The man fell to the floor, hitting his face. He struggled to his feet, nose bleeding, rage in his eyes, ready to attack Coot again.

"Hold it right there!" The command had come from a police officer who had just entered the diner. He was very solidly built, not the sort of man a rational person would tangle with. Even the enraged father hesitated, looking from Coot to the officer and back.

"I want to report this old buzzard for molesting my son," he said, a malevolent gleam in his eyes.

"That's outrageous! Coot saved your son's life. You should be thanking him," said Diana, now on her feet and advancing toward Coot and his antagonist.

Snuffy had come running over as well. "Officer Williams, I saw the whole thing. The boy was choking. His parents didn't do anything. Mr. Jenkins here went to help the boy. He got something out of his throat so the little fella could breathe."

The boy's mother had also gotten up from the table and was

trying to get her husband to return to his seat. Her face was also red, but she didn't seem angry. She smiled weakly at Coot and mouthed "Thank you" as she coaxed her husband back to his seat.

Coot, still holding the half-eaten bacon strip, returned her smile.

"Lucky you came in for your morning coffee, Officer Williams," Snuffy said.

"Yeah, looks like it," replied the policeman. He and Snuffy went back toward the front of the diner.

Coot and Diana returned to their seats. Coot rolled up the bacon in a napkin and put it aside.

"That was quick thinking on your part," said Diana. "You probably saved that kid's life, and his dad went ballistic on you. Here, have some Purell," she continued, handing Coot a small bottle of hand sanitizer that she had taken from her purse.

"Thanks. What matters is that the boy's okay."

"Well, I'm impressed. Everyone else, including me, just sat watching, but *you* acted."

"It's lucky I didn't have to use the Heimlich maneuver. They might have thought I was trying to kidnap the kid."

Coot became quiet. Meddlesome old geezer! Old buzzard! What must Diana have thought?

"What's the matter? You were so talkative before the choking incident, but now you seem subdued," said Diana.

"Nothing's the matter. I just didn't like how that guy reacted, that's all."

"Well, he was way out of line with that outburst. Don't let him bother you."

"What if he was right? Maybe I should have shouted for a doctor," Coot said, looking down at his hands. Maybe he was a meddlesome old geezer.

"You saw what was happening. No one else was dealing with it, so you did. That's not meddling."

Coot didn't say anything.

"It's the age thing again, isn't it?"

"I suppose so."

"There are plenty of younger men who couldn't or wouldn't have done what you did, Coot. Your age and experience are assets."

"You're very kind."

"Just truthful."

Snuffy arrived with their food. He put his hand on Coot's shoulder and gave it a hearty squeeze. "Thanks, Coot. You saved that toddler. I coulda got sued. I can't thank you enough. The food's on me." Snuffy proceeded to tear up Coot's ticket.

"Thanks, Snuffy, but you don't have to do that. I don't want you to go out of business on my account," said Coot.

"Then come back more often — and bring Diana with you." Snuffy winked at Diana and left them before Coot could reply.

Coot doused his waffle with syrup and ladled some whipped cream onto it as well.

"You like to live dangerously, I see," said Diana.

Coot had noticed that younger people often were more disciplined in their food choices than he was, and Diana seemed a case in point. He tried to defend his old habits. "As long as I'm careful about my saturated fat intake most of the time, an occasional indulgence of my butter and sugar cravings shouldn't do too much harm."

Diana looked skeptical of this strategy but didn't challenge Coot's assertion.

"Looks like you've made a good impression on Snuffy," Coot said, putting a piece of syrup-and-cream-covered waffle and a juicy strawberry into his mouth.

Diana finished swallowing some omelet and looked at Coot. "Only because I'm with you. Did you and Frannie eat here often?"

"Yes. It was our favorite place to have breakfast."

"I hope being here again isn't too difficult for you."

He looked out the window again. "The place does stir up old memories, but I'll manage. Don't let me spoil your breakfast, okay?"

"You're not spoiling my breakfast, Coot." She laid her hand softly on top of his. "It's great to have a friend who helps people in a crisis and is admired in his community."

"I'm glad you feel that way, Diana." He wanted to tell her that she had helped him, too, by opening at least a crack in the shell he'd built around himself since Frannie died.

"So, what sorts of things do you enjoy?" asked Diana.

"Oh, I don't know. Maybe a concert or a jazz performance. How about you?"

"Surprising music. Music that takes me where I've never been before. Really good jazz is like that. One time I was listening to a clarinet and piano duo, and the players were chasing each other like squirrels on a tree. I'd think I knew where they were going, when suddenly one or the other would veer off in an unexpected direction melodically or harmonically and the other would quickly follow, perhaps with a variation of his own. It was amazing! How about you?"

"It sounds trite, but I like beautiful music. Once at the Ravinia Festival I heard the Chicago Symphony Orchestra play Mahler's Third Symphony. The third movement's post horn solo, perhaps the most evocative sound in all of Mahler's works, was played wonderfully by the orchestra's principal trumpet, Adolph Herseth, from a position off stage. The angel Gabriel himself could have taken Herseth's place and no one would have known the difference. I felt privileged to have heard it."

"Transcendent experiences like that are so rare, and so nice to remember."

"Yes. I still remember the first time I heard Schubert's Fantasy in F minor for piano four-hands. I was fascinated by its alternation between quiet beauty and dramatic intensity. Do you like classical music?"

"Oh, yes!" Now Diana was smiling broadly. "In fact, my dad and I used to play the Schubert fantasy on our piano at home."

"Really? That must have been quite an experience. You two had to be pretty good players to bring that off. Do you still play?"

"Whenever I have a chance, which isn't often these days, with all my travel."

"That's a shame."

"My own piano is in storage and the neighbors don't like me to play my rented upright at night."

"Perhaps I can help you there. I have my grandmother's old Mason & Hamlin Model A. I had it restored to pristine condition just before Frannie got sick. She liked to play show tunes on it."

"That would be wonderful! Do you play, too?"

"Only a little. Embarrassingly poorly, really." Coot sat up straighter and stared out the window again.

"I bet you're better than you're willing to admit. I could give you lessons, if you want, in exchange for the chance to play."

Coot looked back at Diana and grinned. "That sounds like too good a deal to pass up. All right, let's do it. When would you like to check out the piano? It's just had its scheduled tuning, so it's sounding its best right now."

Diana clapped her hands. "Wonderful! I'd love to play it." Excitement shone from her eyes. She looked happier than Coot had seen her in their previous encounters. "I have to do some shopping this morning and run some errands in the afternoon. How about four o'clock?"

"That'll be fine. It'll give me a chance to clean up the house a bit."

Coot gave Diana his address and phone number. "By the way, how can I reach you if there's a problem?"

She handed him a card. "This has my cell phone number. I don't have a land line in my apartment."

They got up to leave.

"Shouldn't we offer to pay for breakfast?" Diana asked.

"Oh, right. Good idea." Coot met Snuffy at the register but his old friend again refused to let him pay.

"I tore up the ticket. I got no idea what you had."

Snuffy waved to Coot and Diana as they left.

"Thanks, Snuffy. See you again soon," Coot promised.

Coot and Diana walked west on Connecticut until they reached Rodman.

"I've got to go that way," said Coot, pointing up the hill.

"See you at four," said Diana. "Bye." She smiled briefly at Coot, then resumed her trek home.

As he watched Diana walk away, Coot realized that his house was a total disaster — and he had only four hours to clean it up.

* * *

"You want to see me, boss?" said Paul Henry, as he closed the door of Myron Pepsey's office. Strictly speaking, Henry was not Pepsey's employee, but he did act as Pepsey's representative when the utmost discretion was required. He was very well compensated for negotiating highly profitable deals on Pepsey's behalf.

Paul Henry had always wanted to be an actor, but his father insisted on his getting a law degree instead. The closest he got to the stage now was in the audience for professional and amateur productions — and in his work on various Pepsey projects. His familiarity with the theatre did give him a rich source of aliases to use when in secret negotiation on Pepsey's behalf. His favorite alias was "Henry Higgins," from Shaw's *Pygmalion* and its musical adaptations for stage and screen, *My Fair Lady*. Sometimes people did not know whether to take him seriously or not when he used this name, but he was always serious. Sometimes deadly serious.

"Yes, Paul," replied Pepsey. "Thanks for coming over so quickly. Is the first act of the drama on schedule?"

"Indeed it is," said Henry, relishing Pepsey's metaphor. "Look for it early next week. I think you will be pleased with the performance."

"Very good," said Pepsey. "You know how I enjoy productions that engage the audience on multiple levels."

"Yes, sir," said Henry. "The first act will have everything. Spectacle. Intrigue. A strong message." Henry was proud that he had managed to assemble a cast that could pull off such an event.

"Excellent. Great theatre transforms the public's understanding of itself and the world."

"Very true," said Henry, "and our drama will certainly do that."

"Exactly the result I want," said Pepsey. "Have you got a cooperative crew backstage, as we discussed?"

"The best that money can buy. They may not be the most supportive crew, but they won't interfere with the actors' doing their jobs."

"What are your contingency plans?" asked Pepsey. His voice was calm, as always in Henry's experience, but somehow his expression communicated the gravity of his question.

"Our actors are experienced," said Henry, "and should be able to cope with any eventuality."

"They'd better be able to," said Pepsey. "This is an expensive production. The less left to chance, the better."

"I've done all I can to ensure that the performance achieves the desired effect," said Henry. "We'll know soon whether our plans have succeeded."

* * *

Coot's house was a mess, of course. He'd had to manage it by himself since Frannie got sick. They'd always said that their house would never have gotten cleaned if they had not had visitors. He'd had no one over in months. He should have hired a new housekeeper. Somehow that never seemed as important as limiting the spread of nuclear weapons or, now, finding loose nukes.

Diana would be there in four hours. He changed into some old clothes. He had to work fast. It was like excavating an archeological site. Old magazines and newspapers lay in piles all around. At least they were sorted chronologically. He saved the two latest issues of each periodical and threw the rest into a recycling container.

The phone rang. Coot raced into the kitchen and checked Caller ID. It was another solicitation. He ignored the phone, damning the generosity that exposed him to telephone harassment. He hurried back to the living room with a can of Endust and a rag. Spray. Wipe. Spray. Wipe. He gave this same treatment to every horizontal surface except for the lid of the piano, which he just wiped carefully. He was a man possessed.

Next he attacked the kitchen. He filled the garbage can with old wrappers, boxes, and cans. He didn't have time to tie up the boxes or wash out the cans for recycling. His courage momentarily failed him when he looked at the sink. Too many dishes, too little soaking. How stupid, to leave them like that! Fortunately he had only a finite number of glasses, plates, pans, and utensils, so he had had to clean them occasionally. Otherwise he would have confronted a mountain of dirty dishes that would have made Sisyphus lose heart. He switched the dish washer from "Econo Cycle" to "Pots and Pans" and began to load it with half-scraped derelicts from the sink. One load in and started, two more to go.

On to his bedroom. Coot stuffed all the dirty clothes lying around into the laundry hampers in his bathroom. He could sort them later. Should he change the bed linens? Why the hell would that be necessary? *Remember the headlights, remember the headlights!* he told himself. Nevertheless, he changed the sheets and pillow cases, threw the spread over the queen-sized bed, taking care to tuck the spread under the pillows. He left the room, making sure to leave the door open enough so that Diana could see he wasn't a total slob.

Three hours to go. Coot ran the vacuum cleaner in the living room, dining room, family room and his bedroom. He loaded the dishwasher again. He swept the kitchen and the hallway. The other bedrooms had not been used in years. Whatever was in them could continue to lurk behind closed doors.

Two hours to go. Oh, God, the bathrooms! He had forgot the bathrooms! What if she sees the stains in the sink and toilet in the guest bathroom? He began there, sprinkling Comet on the vanity and squirting Lysol around the toilet bowl, then going back to scrub and wipe, scrub and wipe. He sprayed a deodorizer into the air for good measure.

On to his bathroom. He surveyed the vanity and the shower. A hairy orange mold was growing around the toilet, looking like something that had escaped from a biological warfare lab. He got a screwdriver and pried it away from the floor tiles and the toilet. It came up in big chunks, which he cast into the little trash can—the right place for any organism that had chosen to live at the base of a toilet. He sprayed Clorox all around the toilet, making sure to soak the area where the toilet met the tile. He scrubbed and scrubbed, satisfied that he had finally conquered the Great Orange Toilet Bowl Monster. After that success, he lost no time in using Lysol in the toilet bowl and Comet on the vanity, doing his scrub-and-wipe routine on them as well. Back in the kitchen he put a third load into the dishwasher.

One hour to go. He smelled like a pig! No telling what had lived around that orange mold. Maybe cooties tended the mold, like it was their garden. He stepped into the shower. The hot water felt great on his sweaty body. He worked shampoo and then conditioner into his hair. He made plenty of lather in his wash rag and rubbed it all over himself. He felt as if he had been born again. He got dressed in the same clothes he had worn that morning. Diana would never know about his secret life as Mr. Clean.

In thirty minutes Diana would arrive to try out his piano. What if she wanted to hear him play? How embarrassing! He hadn't touched the keyboard in months. His fingers felt like ten frozen popsicles. He sat down at the piano, the same instrument at which his grandmother had taught generations of students. He felt like an impostor. No, worse, a traitor. Why had he not taken the many opportunities he had had to really learn to play? He wasn't lazy. He had gone to a fine college. He'd earned a master's degree. He'd worked hard all his life. There never seemed to be enough time for everything he wanted to do, and now he was going to pay the price for making some wrong choices, for his lack of preparation, for not being able to see into the future. It didn't seem fair.

Of course, he had seen into the future well enough to anticipate the appearance of nuclear weapons in the hands of terrorists, but that knowledge had been insufficient to prevent it from happening.

Enough whining, he told himself. Better thaw out those popsicles. He began a set of exercises that his only teacher had given him decades ago. Up and down the keyboard he dragged his hands. The popsicles began to soften. They felt more like ten wieners now. Gaining courage, he tried to play a Bach minuet. He could remember most of it, but he got lost in a couple of places. He rummaged through his old music books, looking for his copy of the *Notebook for Anna Magdalena Bach*. He found it under a collection of Beethoven bagatelles. The piece he was looking for was the very first one in the Notebook, the Minuet in F.

With Anna Magdalena's Notebook on the piano's music stand, he began to play again. This was better. He played through the minuet twice more, gaining confidence each time. He was in the middle of playing it again when the doorbell rang. He glanced at his watch. 3:59 P.M. Apparently Diana was very punctual.

Coot got up from the piano and walked toward the door. He hadn't meant for Diana to hear him playing. What did she think? He opened the door.

"You've been practicing." She looked more pleased than appalled, as she stood holding several paper-bound music books. Her hair was again tied back in a pony tail and she was wearing black slacks and a colorful blouse with an abstract floral pattern. She smelled faintly like flowers, too.

"It's been a while since I've played. My fingers are stiff." He hoped this was a good enough alibi, but he glanced away nonetheless.

"I almost didn't ring the bell when I heard you playing."

"Oh?"

"I wanted to listen when you weren't being spooked by having an audience." Her eyes twinkled as she spoke.

"Good idea." He smiled at her.

"But then it seemed like a violation of your privacy." Her eyebrows knotted.

"No problem. You would've soon found out how lousy I play anyway." Coot grimaced.

"You sell yourself short."

"I wish. Come in and see your new studio."

Coot followed Diana into the house.

"Are you sure you live here?" she asked, looking around the living room, bright with afternoon sunlight. "I was expecting to find a big mess. You didn't rent another place with a piano, did you?"

"No! I mean, yes." Now he was stumbling over his own words. "I do live here, although I admit it wasn't this clean four hours ago."

Diana's eyes twinkled again. "You didn't have to go to so much trouble for me."

"I didn't want you to think I lived like a pig, so I did a bit of tidying up."

"A bit?"

"Well, more like a megabit!"

"Cute -- a computer joke! Were you ever in I.T.?"

"Eye Tea? Is that a beverage or a medication?"

She laughed, again reminding Coot of Frannie. "You're teasing me."

"Could be. Would you like something to drink?"

"Later, maybe. Thanks."

Diana walked around the old Mason & Hamlin grand piano that sat in the far corner of the room, its red mahogany veneer gleaming in the sun. "What a beautiful restoration!"

Coot laughed. "Frannie and I asked if they were sure it was ours, it looked so much better when we got it back."

"Why don't you play that minuet for me again?"

Coot sat down at the piano and began to play. When he had finished the piece, Diana said, "Not bad."

"I'm embarrassed that I don't play better. With my grandmother being a piano teacher, I had opportunities to learn that I didn't take advantage of."

"And now you have an opportunity that you *will* take advantage of. Before you play it again, we need to adjust your posture."

He had fallen into a bad habit of slouching over the keys. She made him sit up straight, but with his shoulders relaxed. She adjusted the height of his seat. She showed him how to position his forearms and hands. "You're too tense. Relax. Breathe in deeply. Breathe out. Feel the tension melt away."

Coot smiled. "You sound like a meditation instructor I once had."

"Good. I hope you remember some of what she taught you."

"*He.*"

"Touché. You're not the only one with gender stereotypes, I guess."

Coot was beginning to feel more at ease around Diana. Paying attention to his breathing helped, but no doubt it was also because she occasionally surprised him by acting in un-Frannie-like ways. Frannie had not been as self-confident as Diana appeared to be. Frannie had rarely directed him to do something, as Diana had just done.

"Now that you've relaxed some, try that minuet one more time."

"Okay. I'll play it again, ma'am." He relished his little joke, hoping she would catch it.

"Are you a fan of Woody Allen?"

"Huh?"

Diana looked puzzled. "Weren't you referring to Woody Allen's movie, *Play It Again, Sam*?"

"No, just to a common misquotation of dialog in *Casablanca*."

"A misquotation?"

"In *Casablanca* Ilsa says, 'Play it, Sam. Play 'As Time Goes By'."

"Oh, right."

Was this another indicator of the difference in their ages? Did Diana take it as such?

"Anyway," Diana said, "let's hear the minuet."

Coot settled himself and began to play. Again Diana listened without commenting until he was finished.

"That's better. You seemed more relaxed."

"Yes."

"But you need to play more expressively."

Coot felt his face redden. "You think I play like a robot?"

"Well, your playing does seem rather mechanical."

Coot yielded his seat. "Please show me how *you* would play it."

Diana seated herself at the piano. Her posture was relaxed but erect. She put her hands on the keys. "You replaced the original ivory key tops with plastic."

"The old ones were yellowed and cracked." He remembered now their discussion with the piano technician. "Frannie didn't want to use ivory."

Diana looked up at Coot. "Why not?"

"She hated the poachers who preyed on elephants for their tusks."

"So do I." Diana turned back to the keyboard. "Listen carefully."

She played the same notes as Coot had, but even to his ear they were much more musical, more even, better articulated. Her playing sounded like she was having fun.

"Can I learn to play like that?"

"Of course you can!"

"How?"

"You just have to know the effect you want and work until you achieve it."

"Exactly how can I do that?"

"Maybe it would help if you sang it first."

"I don't sing much anymore. Frannie would play and we would sing together. I haven't felt much like singing lately."

"I understand. After Dad died I didn't play so well for a while."

Coot did his best to sing the piece the way he had heard Diana perform it.

Diana listened while Coot sang, then said, "Now try to create the same musical effect at the keyboard."

Coot took Diana's place at the piano and began to play again.

"You have a ways to go, but you're improving."

They continued to work through the piece in this fashion for another half hour.

"Coot, I'm really pleased with how much progress you've made in a short period of time."

"Thanks. Now it's your turn to perform."

Coot got comfortable on the couch, while Diana arranged her books on the piano.

Diana ran through a few scales and some more complex exercises. Then she began to play music that reminded Coot of his minuet. He waited until she had finished, then asked, "Was that piece also by Bach?"

"Yes. I told you you have a good ear. It was three movements from his French Suite No. 2. One was a minuet. Did you like them?"

Coot relished her praise as much as he enjoyed her playing.

"They were beautiful."

Diana continued to perform, gradually working her way to more complex pieces. Coot especially liked her interpretation of the first movement of Schubert's Sonata in A major. Hearing it always made him feel cheerful.

"Thanks," Coot exclaimed when she had finished the Schubert. "That piece is one of my favorites."

"Mine, too. Schubert wrote so many lovely things for the piano. What a tragedy for music that he died so young. He was only 31."

"Sometimes I think that any age is too young to die. Frannie was certainly too young. She should have had decades more. Before her diagnosis, she expected to live into her eighties."

"She was fortunate to live with that confidence. Not everyone is so lucky."

"I suppose not."

They both fell silent for a moment. Diana perked up first.

"Your piano sounds very nice, but best of all, you're a good audience."

"I learned a lot from listening to you play. Shall we do this again next Saturday at four?"

"Sure. That would be great."

Coot felt his stomach rumble. He glanced at his watch. "Good grief, it's almost six!" Without thinking, he added, "If you don't have plans for dinner, we can whip up something here."

"Okay. What did you have in mind?"

Coot endured a moment of panic. He hadn't planned anything. What did he have in the kitchen?

"Let's go see what I've got in the fridge and the pantry. We may have to get creative."

"Sure. That could be fun."

Diana followed Coot into the kitchen."Hey, nice kitchen! It's almost as neat and clean as my mom's. I like the layout, especially the island and all the counter space around the sink."

"You should have seen it earlier. It looked like a scene from *Cloudy with a Chance of Meatballs!*"

"Ha! You must be an excellent cleaner, then. Maybe I should hire you to clean my place." She paused. "Well, no, then I'd have to show you what it looks like now."

While Diana was marveling at the unexpected tidiness of the kitchen, Coot was busy rummaging around in the refrigerator.

"I found some bell peppers that we can use for a salad or something. The lettuce is pretty gross, though."

"Do you have onions?"

"Just some yellow ones. And, we need some protein. I didn't have a chance to do my grocery shopping today."

"What about dried beans?"

"I think there are some in the pantry."

Coot looked around in the pantry and came back with a plastic bag of soybeans.

"Oh, good," said Diana. "I know a recipe for a tasty soybean stew. We can use the onions and the peppers in it. Okay?"

"Sure. You be the chef. What can I do to help? Chop the peppers and onions?"

"That would be great. Do you have a pressure cooker?"

"There's one somewhere around here." Coot began opening the doors of the kitchen cabinets, searching for the old stainless steel pot. "Got it!" He set the pot on the counter next to the sink.

"I'll need a strainer for washing the beans."

Coot showed her where the strainer and measuring cups were,

got out a chopping board and a knife, and went to work.

"Make sure that the the little weight on the pressure cooker vent keeps rocking," Coot reminded Diana.

Diana washed the beans, put several cups of water into the pressure cooker, added the beans, and turned on the burner. Coot set a timer for 25 minutes.

"Would you like a glass of wine?" Coot asked her. "I have a chardonnay chilled in the fridge and a merlot in the pantry."

"Sure. I'll try the merlot."

Coot poured the wine into a couple of glasses and handed one to Diana. "To your good health," he said, raising his glass.

Coot thought he saw a slight frown appear briefly on Diana's face, but then she smiled and said, "And to yours. Here, let me help you finish the chopping."

Soon they were done with the peppers and onions, so Coot suggested that they wait in the living room for the soybeans to finish cooking.

Diana sat on the sofa, Coot in his old Barcalounger.

Diana said, "You look very comfortable."

"I've had this chair since before I met Frannie. I searched all the furniture stores in town before I found it. It fit me perfectly. I put it in front of the TV and stereo system in my apartment. The remote controls were on a small table next to the chair. The first time Frannie came to the apartment she burst out laughing and said she felt like she was visiting NASA's Mission Control."

"I hope you let her pick a song or a show sometimes."

"Oh, yes. She could always make a good case for watching her favorite programs. She talked me into watching Masterpiece Theater and Monty Python's Flying Circus."

"She had good taste, then."

"The best. I learned a lot from Frannie."

"You said that she liked to play show tunes."

"Yes. When my grandmother died, my family wasn't sure what to do with the piano. Frannie talked me into taking it. By that time we had married and moved into a house, so there was enough room for it. She could play pretty well, mostly popular stuff. She could hear a tune once or twice and reproduce it at the piano. It was amazing."

"Sounds like she had an excellent ear."

They fell silent for a moment. It was too quiet. They looked at each other and then toward the kitchen.

"Oh, no."

Coot jumped up from his lounger and sprinted toward the kitchen, Diana just behind him. As they entered the kitchen there was a loud *Whoosh!* from the pressure cooker and a scalding stream of soybeans erupted toward the ceiling of the kitchen, just missing one of the recessed light fixtures. The soybeans ricocheted off the ceiling and headed for the cabinets and counters, where they found hiding places between canisters of sugar and flour, on the apples in a fruit basket, and in the bowl containing the chopped onions and peppers.

"At least some of them ended up where they belonged," said Diana.

Coot had to laugh, in spite of the fact that his Herculean effort to clean his kitchen had just been undone by a pyroclastic flow of legumes.

"You have soybeans in your hair," Diana observed.

"So do you."

"Why don't you clean off that chair and sit down? I'll pick those giant cootie skins out for you."

Coot laughed again, wiped the escaped soybeans off the chair, and sat. Diana began to pick the bean fragments off Coot's head. When she had finished, they exchanged places. Coot quickly removed the few soybean pieces that had found their way into Diana's hair. She had been lucky to be second into the kitchen. He enjoyed the scent and feel of her hair, which was a luxuriant brown, tinged with gold.

"We must have looked like a couple of chimps grooming each other," he said.

"Grooming is important for us primates."

"It's time to groom the kitchen, I'm afraid. I can do it myself. You don't have to stay. I should have been listening more carefully."

"Nonsense! It was my job to cook the soybeans, and I blew it. Literally."

"Thanks for helping. Cleaning by yourself isn't much fun."

They spent most of the next hour scraping soybeans off the ceiling, cabinets, counters, and floor, and wiping them off the various containers and other items that had been in the line of fire or were hit on the ricochet.

"Whew, I'm glad that's over!" Coot said, drying his hands on a towel. Diana's company had made the tedious job more quickly — and kept thoughts of loose nukes out of his mind.

"Yeah, it was a mess, all right. The second one you've cleaned up today."

"Tell me about it. I'm just not up for another try with the soybeans. Let's go out for dinner. My treat."

"Are you sure? I don't want to monopolize your whole day."

"Are you kidding? I'm having a great time. Except for the cleaning."

"Where should we go for dinner?"

"There's The Maharajah on Connecticut. Maybe they'll even have dosas tonight."

Diana's Prius was blocking Coot's driveway, so Diana drove, with Coot navigating.

The dark restaurant, with a few pith helmets and swords on the walls, looked like a holdover from the British Raj. Coot and Diana settled themselves at their table and studied their menus.

"Do you like samosas?" he asked.

"Love 'em! Let's get the vegetable kind, if you don't mind."

"Okay, that's one decision made. Shall we each pick a meat or a vegetable?"

"Sure. I really like tandoori chicken. What about you?"

"Maybe the bengan bartha. I hope you like eggplant."

They also ordered naan and rice pullao.

While they waited for the appetizer, Diana got Coot to talk about life in D.C. He told her about not just the tourist attractions like the monuments and the zoo, but also about the restaurants and clubs that attracted permanent residents. His information about the latter was dated, since he had not gone out much since Frannie's death, and he was about to run out of material for conversation when the samosas arrived. Coot inhaled the pungent odors, which he had not smelled since he and Frannie had last eaten at The Maharajah.

"Changing the subject, I hear you're for the total elimination of nuclear weapons," said Diana, as she lifted a fork full of the appetizer to her mouth. "Is that possible?"

"Most people seem to think that the knowledge of how to make an atomic bomb is too widespread to thwart a state or even a terrorist organization determined to possess nuclear weapons."

"And you disagree?"

"Yes. The real key to the elimination of nuclear weapons is to prevent the creation of fissile material like highly enriched uranium or plutonium," said Coot. "I believe that international agreements in this area are possible. Of course they would need to be enforceable and fairly intrusive inspections would be required."

"Good luck. It would be wonderful if people didn't have to worry about The Bomb anymore. I don't know if it's realistic to think you can get rid of *all* nuclear weapons, though. So many countries have them now and others want them. With Pakistan and India hostile toward each other since 1947, with Israel afraid of being overrun by Arab armies, with Iran determined to acquire nuclear weapons, and with North Korea so isolated and paranoid, what chance is there of getting everyone to agree?"

"How do you know so much about these issues?"

"Our briefings at the N.S.C. cover a lot of topics. Besides, my dad was in your camp. He was involved with IBM's winning bid to supply computers for U.S. missile defense systems, but he was skeptical that any computer system could react fast enough and accurately enough to distinguish warheads from decoys in a massive attack."

"I wish I could have met him."

"You would have enjoyed each other's company."

Diana was quiet for a moment, then said, "So, when you're not out saving the world or listening to music, what else you do?"

"Not much. I'd like to travel. My kids keep asking me to visit."

"You have children? You've never mentioned them."

"I haven't?"

Diana shook her head.

"Oh. They're both in graduate school. Jeannie is in psychology at Oregon and Brad is studying non-profit management in Colorado. They work very hard. I don't want to intrude."

"Maybe they want you to 'intrude.' I imagine they miss Frannie almost as much as you do, and you're the only parent they have left. I would have been devastated if Mom had withdrawn into herself after Dad died. We needed each other."

The waiter brought the rest of their order. They served themselves plenty of rice and added portions of the chicken and eggplant. Coot made little partitions from the rice "so that the flavors don't run together," as he put it.

"That reminds me of my dad," said Diana, pointing to Coot's plate. "He painted the basement floor to indicate where each of our toys went. He said he was surprised that we cooperated with the new regime. I guess it was because, for once, our appreciation of rational order overcame our preference for chaos."

"I wish I'd thought of a system like that. Our basement was a tangled mess of bicycles, scooters, skateboards, and other equipment."

They continued chatting as they finished their meals.

"Would you like dessert?" Coot asked Diana.

"Maybe some Indian ice cream. What do they call it?"

"Kulfi. I'll go with the gulab jamun myself."

"Those cheesy little balls covered in syrup? Your sweet tooth is going to bite you someday."

"Maybe so, but I'll enjoy myself until then."

The waiter took their dessert orders and returned with their sweets in a few minutes.

"Returning to our dietary debate," Coot said, "I can run an extra mile or two tomorrow morning to burn off the additional calories I've consumed tonight."

"Oh, that's right — you're a runner."

"Serious runners would call me a jogger, I suppose. You looked like a pretty serious runner or jogger or whatever when I saw you in the park."

"I jog every morning when I can fit it into my schedule."

"My buddies and I run about five miles every Saturday morning, weather permitting, I'd invite you to run with us, but I'm afraid you might prefer one of them."

"You don't have to worry about that."

Diana's reply surprised and intrigued Coot.

"Why not? You're a bright and attractive young woman. Many guys would love to get to know a gal like you."

"I'd rather not discuss my personal life here. I hope you understand."

Coot felt his face flush in embarrassment. "I'm sorry, Diana. I should learn to keep my big mouth shut."

"No problem. I'll explain later."

They finished their desserts without further incident. Coot grew increasingly worried that he had seriously damaged a friendship that had hardly begun. At last it was time to go. Coot paid the waiter and they left The Maharajah.

Diana drove back to Coot's house without having to consult her passenger for directions. She pulled the Prius into his driveway and turned off the engine.

"I have to remember to turn off the car when I stop, since it doesn't make any noise when it's not moving."

"Yes. I've taken to looking into every driveway I pass to make sure that there's not a killer hybrid silently making its way toward me."

"Which brings me to our earlier topic."

"Oh?"

"You asked me why you didn't have to worry that I'd prefer one of your buddies to you."

"Right. Well, you don't have to answer that question. I really had no business saying something like that. I'm embarrassed that I revealed so much insecurity."

"Coot, this isn't about you at all. It's about me."

"You?"

"Yes. There's something I need to explain to you, something you need to know."

"I'm all ears, Diana. Would you like to go inside?"

"No. I'd rather sit here in the dark. It'll be easier that way."

"Okay."

"As you know, I accepted Jill Meecham's offer to join the N.S.C. What you don't know is that I decided to leave Boston in order to put some distance between myself and a couple of painful events."

"Oh? I know about the death of your father. Is there something else?" Coot was eager to learn more about Diana's personal history, but he did not want to seem too eager.

"Breaking up with my fiancé."

"That's a lot to be dealing with all at once," said Coot.

"The two events are related. An autopsy revealed that an aneurysm had ruptured in Dad's brain. Further analysis showed that its cause was a rare genetic defect. My brother Bob and I were tested for the defect. Bob's results were negative. I was not so lucky."

"I'm so sorry," whispered Coot. In the darkness he could barely see Diana. He wanted to reach out to comfort her but was afraid she might misinterpret his touch.

"For some unknown reason, the autopsy took many months, and then we had to wait for the pathologist's report. By the time Bob and I could be tested and received our results, I was already in Boston and involved with Keith."

"I understand medical investigations take a long time," said Coot.

"I feared I might pass the defect to my children. I worried that I would die suddenly while my kids were still young. What if it happened while I was driving them somewhere? I felt like a time bomb that could go off at any moment, destroying everyone close to me," said Diana quietly, her voice conveying deep sadness.

"How did you cope with such an awful prognosis?" asked Coot.

"I broke up with Keith. It seemed only fair to him. He very much wanted children."

"So you entered your precarious future alone."

"Completely. I withdrew. I avoided the places Keith and I liked to visit together: The Museum of Science, Harvard's Arnold Arboretum, the Museum of Fine Arts, the Boston Symphony, Fenway Park."

"Boston's a grand city for culture and sports," said Coot.

"I spent hours playing Chopin on my Steinway. I let the music express my anger, my resignation, and sometimes the triumph that I hoped to feel again someday."

"You were fortunate to have your music," said Coot. "It must have been a great comfort."

"Yes. I developed a taste for jazz but listened mostly at home, alone. I especially liked Billy Holiday's 1956 Carnegie Hall performance of 'Lady Sings the Blues.'"

"It sounds like you were gradually reclaiming your life."

"In some ways. I continued my research in network protocols. I went with a friend to an exhibition of M.C. Escher's drawings at M.I.T."

Diana's sigh in the anonymous darkness made Coot yearn to comfort her with a hug, but he resisted the temptation to touch her and waited for her to continue.

"I resolved to live boldly again. I volunteered at a soup kitchen that fed homeless families. I worked the phones in S.A.F.E.'s campaign to support the Comprehensive Test Ban Treaty."

"Good for you!" exclaimed Coot. "That's such an important treaty for ending nuclear arms races."

"I was feeling better, but then Keith's rebound marriage to my friend Alice set my recovery back. I felt as if I were climbing an Escher staircase that led me back to where I'd started. I wanted to escape my past, to leave Boston, with its painful reminders of the dreams I'd had."

"So then you learned about the cyber security group that Jill was forming at the N.S.C., and you applied?" Coot surmised.

"Right," said Diana. "I had a pretty strong publication record and the support of the S.A.F.E. staff in the Boston office, and I got the job. I said my goodbyes, got into my Prius, and left Boston, feeling more optimistic with every mile."

"Please tell me more about your genetic abnormality," said Coot.

"According to the neurologists we consulted, the deformity grows over time and the tissues weaken. So, I'm fine now, but in twenty years or so the diseased tissue will have spread so much that I could die at any time."

"I'm so sorry! You seem so bright, so energetic. I thought you'd be looking forward to the same things most women your age do.

You know, finding and marrying Mr. Right, settling down, having children."

"I did look forward to all that before my diagnosis. Now, well, how can I get involved with a guy who wants to have a healthy wife and healthy children? There's a 50% probability that I'd pass on the abnormality to a child. I can't take that chance."

"I see."

"So, I've decided not to get involved with anyone. I've thrown myself into my job until I think of a better plan."

"That seems like a poor substitute for family intimacy."

"It sure is."

They sat in silence for a while. Coot had no idea what to say to comfort Diana.

"Anyway, I thought you should know."

"Thanks for confiding in me, Diana. Wow. This is a shock. I never imagined you were having to deal with something like this. If it's any consolation, you have a friend with experience in dealing with women facing life-threatening illnesses."

"Coot, you're so sweet. Frannie was lucky to have married you." She paused. "I feel lucky to have met you."

She reached out in the darkness, clasped Coot's hand, and held it.

"Diana..."

"Listen, Coot. You need to think about what I've told you. Take some time. Then we can talk again." She squeezed his hand, then withdrew hers. "I think I'd better go home now. Thanks for a wonderful day. The breakfast was fun, your piano is an excellent instrument, and The Maharajah rules! Now, why don't you go in and put away those onions and peppers until you can figure out what to do with them."

Coot could feel tears welling up in his eyes. He had not felt such sadness since the days after Frannie had died. It was if Frannie had come back to him and then died again.

He opened the car door and turned quickly so that Diana could not see the tears rolling down his cheeks. He climbed out, stood up into the shadow cast by a utility pole, and turned back toward her.

"Diana, you're a lovely person. I wish I could do something to help you."

"You've done a lot already, so don't worry about it."

"Don't worry about it? Are you kidding? But I will think about everything you've said and then we'll talk again, okay?"

"Okay. Goodnight, Coot."

"Goodnight, Diana."

Coot stepped back from the car. Diana backed the Prius out of the driveway. Coot waved to her as she drove away into the night.

As Diana's car disappeared from sight, Coot unlocked his front door, entered his house, and moved without thinking toward the abandoned onions and peppers in the kitchen. Poor Diana -- facing the certain prospect of a life cut short. Coot put the remains of the aborted meal into containers, which he stuck into the refrigerator. He recalled the day Frannie got her diagnosis, which had been a shock for both of them. He turned out the lights in the kitchen.

At least he could decide whether to risk further involvement with Diana. Of course she might have other expectations for her life than to be involved with an aging peacenik. She had held his hand. What was that about? And who knows? He might die first.

Coot got ready for bed. He slid his legs between the clean sheets. He lay awake for what seemed like hours, pondering his dilemma. Risk involvement and pain? Play it safe and remain alone? Long after midnight Coot began to calm down. Once again he was driving past his headlights. The only sensible course was to wait and see what developed with Diana. Maybe he should talk with Dr. Rosen again, although he was feeling less anxious now.

Coot brooded over Diana's condition and his feelings for her for a few days before giving in to his need for expert consultation and making another appointment with, he had to admit, his therapist. On Tuesday morning Coot drove back to the psychiatrist's office.

"So, Dr. Rosen, I have some good news and some bad news."

"Oh?"

"The good news is that I managed to find Diana at breakfast on Saturday. Even better, we spent much of the day together and had a pretty good time. At least I did, and I think she did." Coot described the breakfast, the piano playing, the cooking catastrophe, and the dinner.

"That all sounds very positive. How do you feel about the encounter?"

"Great! We share a love of music. She's knowledgeable about disarmament issues. I really didn't expect that. She doesn't even seem bothered by the difference in our ages. Of course, as she said, we were just having breakfast."

"You said there was bad news."

"Yes." Coot told Dr. Rosen about Diana's genetic abnormality and the neural deformity that might one day take her life.

"How did you react to that news?"

"It reminded me so much of learning about Frannie's diagnosis. I felt very sad, as if Frannie had come back and then left me again."

"But Diana is not Frannie. How do you feel about a future with Diana?"

"I *do* want to keep seeing Diana. I even want to develop a relationship with her. On the other hand, I *don't* want a repetition of the pain that I suffered when Frannie died."

"Knowing what it feels like, are you willing to risk such pain again?"

"That's the question, isn't it? I don't know the answer. That's why I came back to see you."

"All I can do is ask questions and suggest possibilities. You have to supply the answers. Perhaps you're not ready to answer that question yet. Perhaps you need to know Diana better before you can decide."

"You mean, I shouldn't drive past my headlights."

"Exactly."

"But I knew that myself. I didn't need you to tell me."

"Perhaps you needed to have your thought confirmed."

"I guess so." Coot was silent for a moment. "Well, there's one good thing regarding Diana's illness."

"What's that?"

"She and I have roughly the same life expectancy at this point."

"So it's a fair game after all."

Coot thought of something else he wanted to discuss with Dr. Rosen, maybe the most important thing of all. "I wonder how much Diana likes me. Am I just a father figure to her? Does she just feel sorry for me? Will she ever be able to have a romantic interest in me?"

"You know my response, I expect."

"That I'll have to work out the answers with Diana?"

"Correct."

Coot had his rebuttal ready. "But in the elevator she said I was a celebrity. After the choking incident she said she was impressed that I acted to save that little boy and that my age and experience were assets. In the car after dinner she said she was lucky to have met me. After telling me about her diagnosis she even held my hand. Aren't these all signs that she cares about me?"

"They're certainly signs that she admires you and that she doesn't want to hurt you."

"But not that ..."

"Not that she's in love with you?"

"Well, yeah."

"Are you in love with her?"

Coot squirmed in his chair. Now they were getting to the core of the problem. "Well, uh, I don't know. Maybe. I like her a lot, but I've only spent a few hours with her. It's hard to know for sure."

"May she not feel the same uncertainty about you?"

CHAPTER 5

Stormy Weather

"That must be them," said Faroud, as Munir pulled the old Volvo truck into Chakothi on the Srinagar-Muzaffarabad Road, about two miles west of the Line of Control. The light of the quarter moon low in the western sky barely revealed another old truck beside the road. It was almost midnight. Munir parked his truck behind the other one and turned off the engine. Faroud's pulse quickened as half a dozen armed men climbed out of the back of the other truck. One of the men approached Munir's side of the truck.

"Allāhu akbar," said the man.

"Subhanahu wa ta'ala," Munir replied, using the phrase that Faroud knew Munir and his contact in Lashkar-e-Taiba had agreed on.

Faroud got out of the cab, went around to the rear of Munir's truck, and opened the doors. The man motioned for the others to join Faroud. Faroud climbed into the back of Munir's truck, followed by the five jihadis. As soon as their leader took Faroud's place beside Munir in the cab, they would be ready to begin their assault.

"What's this?" one of the fighters asked Faroud, as he stumbled over the A.D.M. in the faint moonlight.

"Just a little surprise for our Indian friends," said Faroud, looking back over his shoulder as he closed the rear doors of the truck. He was enjoying his role as nuclear triggerman. He heard doors slam shut and the LeT truck start up, its tires briefly spinning in the gravel. At last the engine of Munir's truck came to life and the Volvo also began to move.

Faroud and the LeT fighters sat on the floor in darkness and silence. The truck went at high speed on straight stretches of the road, often slowing quickly and turning sharply, throwing Faroud and the others against the sides of their steel box. Faroud hoped Munir could keep up with the jihadis ahead of them. Driving like this in Pakistan was good practice for what lay ahead.

The truck slowed down and stopped. Faroud could hear voices. They must have gotten to the Friendship Bridge at the Line of Control. He hoped that Munir had bribed the right people so that the guards on the Pakistani side of the Line would not interfere with them. The truck lurched forward again and quickly picked up speed. They were not going to stop so politely for the Indian guards.

Gunfire erupted ahead of them. The jihadis talked excitedly among themselves. Faroud could hear them checking their weapons and saying many "Allāhu akbar"s. Faroud heard something that sounded like metal being smashed and torn. The jihadis up front must have breached the barrier at the Line. Munir's truck picked up speed, swerved as if to get around the LeT truck, and veered sharply to the left. They must be off the bridge and onto 1A. With no other vehicle to follow, Munir was on his own. Faroud hoped he was up to the challenge. Were Munir's many expressions of confidence just more empty boasts?

Faroud got up and cracked open a rear door. Nobody was following them! The Lashkar fighters must have taken the Indians by surprise and pinned them down long enough for Munir to drive through the checkpoint and get out of sight. Still, the Indians may have radioed for backup and reported the illegal entry of a second truck. There was nothing to do but drive on. Again and again, for most of an hour, the truck moved at high speed for a while, then slowed quickly and turned, as it proceeded along the winding 1A.

Faroud heard a vehicle overtaking them from behind, so he opened the door a crack and quickly closed it. A dozen bullets slammed into the sheet steel that was their sole protection. One of the jihadis pushed Faroud aside and opened the door a bit wider, while another fighter dropped to his knee and began to fire his weapon at their pursuers. Faroud heard tires screech behind them, then a crash and explosion.

"Allāhu akbar!" said the jihadis.

On they drove, Faroud and the fighters sitting in silent darkness.

When the truck slowed almost to a halt and made a sharp right turn, Faroud knew that they had reached the turn-off for the Hanjiwera Magam Road. Anyone following them would not expect them to have taken this detour. An hour more and they would be at Srinagar Airport and the Indian Air Force station that shared its runway.

The station was India's most sensitive — and secure — Air Force installation, due to its location in disputed Kashmir and its proximity to China. Munir would try to get the truck as close as possible to the station before Faroud deployed the atomic demolition munition. The A.D.M. could be set to explode with as much force as a thousand tons of TNT. Munir wanted to cause the biggest possible explosion, but Faroud had decided secretly to set the A.D.M. to a lower yield if they could get close to the station. Otherwise, they would cause a lot more civilian casualties at the airport and in surrounding areas.

Faroud had always been opposed to the jihadis who willingly slaughtered hundreds of innocent people in shops, restaurants, busses, and trains. Why did he join Munir in this operation? Munir had only said that he needed Faroud's help to set off an atomic bomb at an Indian military base. Faroud assumed this meant that only soldiers would be killed, and he hated and feared the Indian military as much as any other Pakistani. Just days before the operation, Faroud found out that the target was the Srinagar Air Force Station, which was collocated with a civilian airport near a city of more than a million people. It was too late to turn back. Lashkar-e-Taiba had been engaged. The very men beside him in the truck would kill him if he did not perform his assigned task.

The truck rumbled on toward its destination. The road seemed to be straighter, since Munir was maintaining a more even speed and Faroud was being thrown around less. Just as Faroud was relaxing a bit, the truck abruptly screeched to a halt. There were loud, commanding voices outside. Someone banged on the front wall of their compartment, and the jihadis began to move quickly around him.

"Roadblock. Stay here," one of them commanded him. "I will protect you."

One fighter cracked the rear door open. Another scanned the scene, then motioned the others to follow him. Four jihadis jumped from the truck, turned toward the front, and began firing their weapons, including a rocket-propelled grenade launcher. The remaining fighter closed the door. A loud explosion startled Faroud, and the sharp sounds of bullets hitting the steel walls of the truck ceased. A series of bangs came from the rear door. Two fighters had made it back from the fight. There was blood oozing from the right shoulder of the one with the RPG launcher. His comrade helped him into the truck. Faroud's protector banged on the front wall. The truck started up again.

Faroud was trembling. He had survived two firefights in two hours. How long would his luck hold out? The mission had turned out to be a lot more dangerous than Munir had said it would be. Why had he ever listened to Munir the Schemer?

Again the truck was changing speeds frequently and veering first to one side and then the other. Faroud fought waves of nausea. How much closer to the target would Munir be able to get them?

The truck slowed slightly, turned sharply to the left, and sped up. Faroud hoped they had left the road to the airport terminal and were headed for the Air Force station. They drove for several minutes in relative quiet. Gunfire resumed behind them, bullets pinging off the rear doors. A loud explosion came from the front of the truck, which veered hard to the right, tires squealing. Suddenly the truck began to roll over and over. The jihadis' screams showed they were as frightened as he was. Faroud's head hit the wall or the floor or the ceiling — he could not tell which — but he recognized the weight of the A.D.M. when it finally pinned him to the side of the truck. He had a splitting headache and his leg was bent at an odd angle where the A.D.M. had landed on him. He struggled to remain conscious. His moment had arrived at last. He tried to reach the controls of the A.D.M. They were all dead men, whatever happened next.

Faroud set the yield of the A.D.M. to something below the maximum — he could not see the marks in the dark — and the timer to as close to zero as he could get it. He threw the switch marked "Arm" in Russian just before losing consciousness.

* * *

Tuesday morning at eleven Coot, Saeed, and J.K. met outside the White House at the driveway leading to the West Wing. Jill Meecham had asked Coot to arrange a meeting as soon as possible. The guards checked their identification, then one of the guards escorted the three men to the entrance, where they again presented their IDs and passed through a metal detector and then a body scanner. An N.S.C. staffer escorted them to a conference room. A minute later Jill entered, closing the door behind her. Coot introduced her to the two men.

Jill said, "Thanks for meeting with me this morning. I just want to follow up on the reports of loose nukes in Pakistan and Kyrgyzstan. Have you learned anything else?"

J.K. shook his head. Saeed said, "Nothing specific. One informant was to meet with ISI in Peshawar to convey what he called 'important information' but he never showed up. His body was found yesterday."

"That's ominous," said Jill. "Any other peculiar events?"

"There was a fire fight an hour ago at the Line of Control on the Muzaffarabad-Srinagar road," said J.K. "It was pretty chaotic. Several Indian guards were killed. One truck may have entered from Pakistan without being searched."

"Really? Didn't the guards have orders to fire on any vehicles that refused to stop?" Jill asked.

"Of course, but they were under fire themselves," replied J.K. "Army units are searching for the truck now."

"Let's assume the worst case, then: the second truck was carrying an atomic device. What could be its target?" said Jill.

"My guess is the Srinagar Air Force Station," said J.K.

There was a knock on the door of the conference room. Someone motioned for Jill to come out. In a minute she was back, her face ashen.

"J.K., you were right. A U.S. surveillance satellite has detected a nuclear explosion near the air base. What's more, a group calling itself 'Mushrooms' has hacked into a number of news organizations' websites. They've posted a video claiming responsibility for the explosion and threatening similar attacks in the West."

"Damn!" said Coot, banging his fist on the conference table.

"It's good that you warned us, Saeed," said J.K. "Still, some in India will claim that Pakistan allowed this group to cross its territory in order to attack India in Kashmir."

"Gentlemen, let's all remember that there may be as many as five more devices out there somewhere," said Jill. "We need to work together to prevent another catastrophe."

The meeting broke up a few minutes later. As Coot exited the While House grounds, he turned back to look at the impressive building that symbolized executive power in the U.S. It could all be gone in a flash. Similarly for the Capitol and the other structures whose inhabitants kept the federal government humming along. He began walking west along Pennsylvania Avenue, past the Eisenhower Executive Office Building, the Blair House, and the Renwick Gallery. They all looked so sturdy, but one small nuclear device would wreck them completely. He kept walking. The World Bank. So many people depended on the activities in that building, on the relationships among nations that it embodied. What sort of people would want to destroy what it had taken the entire post-war era — more than half a century — to create? What other targets might they have chosen? What other buildings, other cities, citadels of commerce, of learning, of art? What was motivating those people?

* * *

"Hooah!" exclaimed Jamie when CNN announced the atomic bombing of the Indian Air Force station at Srinagar. Hoping to hear from George, she started her VI comm client — just in time to accept his call.

"They're all dead," said George. "Munir. Faroud. The rest of their team."

This was unwelcome news to someone expecting to carry out a similar attack herself in a matter of weeks.

"What happened?" she asked.

"I'm not sure," said George. "Munir reported by sat phone that they crossed the Line of Control, despite losing a truck full of Lashkar-e-Taiba jihadis in a fire fight."

"I warned him not to go looking for trouble," said Jamie, her voice revealing a mixture of exasperation and frustration. "Why were jihadis involved?"

"Munir wanted more muscle than he could get any other way. By the time I found out, the operation was already underway."

"What else did Munir report?" Jamie was in post-mortem mode now, trying to learn from the mistakes of others.

"Apparently the Indians suspected an attack on the air base. Munir's guys fought their way past one roadblock. Munir was approaching the target when the truck came under attack from helicopter gunships."

"Oh, man!"

"I heard an explosion, tires squealing, metal being torn apart, someone screaming, and then...nothing."

"Poor bastards!"

"At least Faroud managed to detonate the A.D.M." Silence. "Wait a sec. Mitch just came online. I'll conference him in." Another pause. "Mitch, you there?"

"Holy shit! The ragheads did it!"

Jamie had no trouble recognizing Mitch's voice and manner.

"What yield did the fuckers get?"

"It was supposed to be the max — one kiloton," Jamie said, reminding Mitch of the agreement with Munir.

"We'll know soon enough," said George. "Seismic monitoring and satellite surveillance make it impossible to conceal the size of a nuclear explosion."

"The VI vid got onto all the networks," said Mitch. "I didn't like it."

"What's the matter with it?" asked George.

"Too calm, too intellectual," said Mitch. "Not urgent enough."

"We didn't want to come across as a bunch of crazies," said Jamie. "That may not matter much to you."

"Like coming across as a couple of queer losers doesn't matter to you and Sabrina?"

"Mitch, you shameless homophobe," said Jamie, her voice quivering with rage.

"C'mon, guys," interjected George. "We've got our own ops to get right."

"What are we waiting on?" said Mitch.

"Just the delivery of the A.D.M.s, moron," said Jamie. "It takes time to cross the Mediterranean and the Atlantic by ship. Remember time equals distance divided by rate from high school algebra?"

"Jamie..." cautioned George.

"Fuck you, Jamie."

"Try it, and I'll make you even less of a man than you already are." How gratifying it would be to emasculate the nasty little freak.

"Stop! Just stop it!" said George. "We'll never inspire others to join the insurrection if we can't work together ourselves."

"Right," said Jamie, taking a deep breath to calm herself. "How's the cell phone detonator coming along, Mitch?"

"It's done," said Mitch, "provided you gave me the right design specs."

"We won't know for sure until we get the A.D.M.s," said Jamie. "I assumed the Soviets simply copied our W54."

"I think that's what happened," said George. "The Soviets never were very good at miniaturization."

"Let's build some time into the schedule for making sure that the detonator works with the device," said Mitch.

"I've done that already," said George. "We'll sync up again when I know for sure when the A.D.M.s are going to arrive in Canada."

With that, the three conspirators ended their call. Once again Jamie had been enraged by an encounter with Mitch. Why did the guy have to be such a prick?

* * *

By the time Coot returned to S.A.F.E. headquarters, the place was buzzing with the chatter of people talking about the event that many of them had spent their professional lives working to prevent. Coot spotted Emily by the water cooler.

"Hey, did you hear the news?" she asked him.

"Yeah. I was in a meeting at the N.S.C. when it happened."

"What are you going to do now?"

"I want to understand the motivations of the Mushrooms group. Have you seen their video?"

"I was just going to look for it."

"Why don't you come into my office? We can watch it together. Unless that would make you uncomfortable."

"No, I'm fine with that."

The two colleagues went into Coot's office. Coot closed the door, noticing the glass on each side of the door. He pulled a second chair closer to his desk. "Have a seat."

Emily sat down, but looked aside as Coot logged into his workstation. Coot typed "Mushrooms video" into his browser's search box and got over fifty million hits, mostly to videos on how to grow or cook mushrooms. He added " -grow -cook" to the search terms but still got over thirty million hits. In desperation he added "news" this time got only about forty thousand hits. Fortunately several of the links pointed to the new video.

"These fellows are clever," Coot said. "They managed to penetrate most of the major news sites. That's a clue in itself."

He clicked on one of the links — to a news site that usually had good performance. The video had been removed from the page itself, but there was a link to it at the side of the page under "Most Viewed". Two more clicks, and they were watching a chilling message of defiance and threat. Its title: *Your World Is Ending*. The background music: Bob Dylan's "The Times They Are A-changin'."

The title was replaced by a head-and-shoulders shot of a slender man in a plain gray sweatshirt. His face was unnaturally smooth. His race and ethnicity were ambiguous.

"An avatar," said Emily.

When the figure spoke, it was in English.

"Do not be alarmed that I am speaking to you today through a computer-generated form. The power of governments to hunt and kill their opponents is very great. Disguise is essential to effectiveness."

The computer-generated voice was well-synchronized with the avatar's lips.

"That's another clue: they're technically adept," said Coot. What intrigued Coot most, though, was the avatar's message.

"Today is the first day of a new era in human history. Today the power of one state, India, has been defeated by the focused power of individuals — people from around the world who have organized themselves into small groups to take power from governments and corporations, and return it to individuals. You have seen the effectiveness of Mushrooms, a cooperative of men and women trained in the physical sciences and engineering but dedicated to creating a new order in the world. Why did Mushrooms attack the Indian airbase at Srinagar? Because India had imprisoned their allies in VI, a group of computer experts who are using their skills to penetrate and disable the systems used to control the people of India and other nations."

Coot clicked the Pause button on the video. "Had you ever heard of Mushrooms or VI? They're technically trained but they intend to use their knowledge to destroy large-scale human organizations, such as corporations and even governments."

"What would you call them?" mused Emily. "Techno-anarchists? Anarchist hackers?"

"Maybe both terms apply. There's more than one group."

"Right, and maybe other groups we haven't heard of yet. He — it — didn't mention biologists. We could be facing trouble on multiple fronts."

"Yes. It's very ominous. Let's hear what else they have to say." Coot clicked Play on the video.

"You may be wondering what Mushrooms wants, what VI's demands are. The answer is *insurrection!* Not just by these groups, but by everyone who believes that the large institutions of the world exist not for the good of the individual but to perpetuate themselves. We do not expect these institutions to change. Such organizations are incapable of changing their basic nature. They will always oppress the individual. The change we want is their destruction."

Again Coot paused the video. "Did you hear that? *Insurrection! Destruction!"*

"And not just by themselves. By lots of people," said Emily. "They're fomenting worldwide rebellion against human society as it is currently structured."

"Right. Are they nihilists, or do they have something in mind to replace the current order? I mean, how do they expect to feed seven billion people without large-scale organization?"

"Good question."

Coot resumed the video.

"Why did earlier attempts at insurrection fail? Because states and corporations used their monopoly on power to brutally suppress the insurrectionists. Now the tables are turned. Mushrooms has more weapons like the one detonated at Srinagar. VI has penetrated computer systems in governments and corporations around the world. These two groups are beginning to act.

"We urge *you* to form *your own* groups, to begin attacking the institutions that oppress *you*. It is up to *you* to join with like-minded individuals to plant the seeds that will grow into structures that serve *your* needs and the needs of those around you. Not permanent structures whose goal would become self-perpetuation, but social structures that accomplish concrete tasks and then fade away.

"Join us in destroying the old world so that a new world can be born!"

The video ended with a cartoon, as the last verse of Dylan's song sounded from Coot's speakers. The cartoon showed green vines emerging from the ground all around a large tree. Their tendrils climbed the tree's trunk, shot along its large branches, and soon hid the tree from view. A moment later the tree collapsed. The vines began to put out flowers as the song ended and the screen went black.

"Whew!" said Coot. "They don't expect much from ordinary people, do they?"

"Their plan is totally impractical, but that doesn't mean they won't do a lot of damage before they're snuffed out," said Emily.

"What worries me most is their claim to have more devices." Coot stood up and began to pace around his small office.

"So what do we do now?" Emily scooted her chair out of Coot's way.

"Rely on our government and its allies to track these guys down before they can detonate more weapons."

"Do you think they'll succeed?"

"I don't know," admitted Coot. "This is the situation we've all worked years to avoid. The nightmare scenario is happening right before our eyes, and we can't do anything about it."

"The only real surprise is the source — a bunch of insurrectionary anarchists no one had ever heard of."

"I wonder whether Mushrooms and VI are the primary actors. How are they funded? Who determines their policies and agendas? There may be more than one layer to this onion," Coot speculated.

"The conspiracy nuts will have fun with the Mushrooms," said Emily.

"I wish there was something we could do to help figure out what's really going on," said Coot. "After a quarter century to prevent the use of nuclear weapons, I don't like being on the sidelines when they're actually being used."

* * *

"The first act went reasonably well." Paul Henry reported to Myron Pepsey as they sat in Pepsey's opulent Atlanta office, which reflected the man's wealth, power, and taste. "The critics panned it, but what do they know? So what if the actors didn't quite make it to their assigned places on stage? They still managed to deliver their lines effectively."

"'Tis pity they're no more," replied Pepsey, playing on the title of a work by the Seventeenth Century English playwright John Ford — a reference that he knew Henry would understand and appreciate. "How are preparations for the second act coming along?"

"It's taking some time to get all the props into position," said Henry. "Everything should be ready for the second act in a couple of weeks."

"Excellent," said Pepsey. "The two scenes will complement each other well."

"Yes," said Henry, "One scene to make a positive point, the other to show the opposite."

"People need to be shown the benefits of private solutions over public ones," said Pepsey, "or rather how a private solution can accomplish a public good."

"That's a better way to put it," agreed Henry.

"And what better way to get the point across than by dramatizing it?" concluded Pepsey.

* * *

Coot was on time for Saturday's run with Jack and Roger.

As they were stretching, Roger, always ready to light Coot's fuse, said, "So, Coot, given what happened in India, are you still trying to convince people that we don't need nukes?"

"Of course I am. The attack on Srinagar proves how important it is to rid the world of nuclear weapons."

"Don't you think it's a bit, uh, risky to be contending so publicly with people whose main interest is guns, lots of guns?"

"Guns? I'm not proposing any changes in the gun laws."

"Larry Limbick said on the radio the other day that..."

"Are you still listening to that faker?" interrupted Coot. "Don't you realize that he says whatever he thinks will keep his ratings up?"

"You can dismiss Limbick if you like, but he does have some valid issues with the way the country is governed, and a lot of people listen to him," Roger replied.

"What I've noticed about Limbick," said Jack, "is that he really tries to control the conversation when people call in. He interrupts them before they can complete their points. He'll even hang up their calls if he strongly disagrees with them."

"Anyway," said Roger, "Limbick was really getting worked up over the Administration's plans to sign a new arms control treaty with Russia. He said the same people who want to take away individuals' guns want to disarm the country."

"The two issues are completely unrelated. I don't think I have to worry about him," said Coot.

"Maybe not," said Jack, "but you ought to think about the reaction of some of Limbick's fans. It would only take one nut to go off the deep end and decide to eliminate anyone Limbick implies is a traitor."

"I haven't been threatened in any way since I went public with my opinion that preventing nuclear proliferation requires nuclear disarmament, so I don't think I have anything to worry about yet," said Coot. "Anyway, most people who listen to Limbick are harmless enough. Even the ones who make threats are often too cowardly to carry them out."

The three men began their ten-mile run. Conversation would soon get more difficult.

"I hope you're right," said Jack.

"Me, too," said Roger.

Coot thought about the cautions his friends had given him. Maybe they were right. Fortunately he was not on Limbick's radar yet.

As they ran, Roger, as curious as ever, asked Coot whether he had gotten up the courage to pursue Diana.

"We're just friends....She gives me piano lessons...in exchange for playing time...on my piano....Frannie and I...used to have...a lot of fun...around the piano....I miss that."

The three men lapsed into silence for a while.

At last Roger blurted out, "Coot, I'm glad...that you're showing... some signs of life again....You haven't...been the same...since Frannie died."

"Yeah....It's been rough....We had...a great life... together....The cancer...put an end...to that."

"The cancer?...Uh, yeah, that sucked," said Jack. "You were great... to be there...for her...those last two years....It's something...no guy wants...to go through."

"Frannie showed...a lot of...courage," said Coot. "She even...felt bad...that she...was going...to leave me....Imagine that....She got the cancer...but she worried...about *me*. "

"Frannie was great," said Roger. "You were lucky...to have found her."

"Yeah," said Coot quietly, tears welling up in his eyes.

The Monday following his run with Jack and Roger, Coot got a call from Rita Swearingen, a producer at public television station WETA. She wanted Coot to debate Global Zero with a representative of the opposition on *Face-to-Face* the next Friday. Discussing the abolition of nuclear weapons on a nationally-televised debate program was too good an opportunity to miss. He asked who his opponent would be, but Rita had not decided who would represent the other side. She did say he could bring a guest. Perhaps Diana would like to go. Would she be in town?

Coot called Diana's office and cell phones but got only her voice mail. Disappointed, he left messages for her to call him back. That evening Diana returned his call.

"What's up, Coot? You sounded excited."

"I guess you've heard of Global Zero, the international campaign to eliminate nuclear weapons throughout the world."

"Sure."

"Anyway, Ben is one its sponsors, along with political, military, and other leaders. I'm going to debate Global Zero on TV on Friday."

"Congratulations! I told you that you were a celebrity."

"I can bring a guest. Would you like to go?"

"I've always wanted to see how a TV show is produced." She checked her calendar. "What time is the debate?"

"2 P.M."

"That works for me. Thanks for the invitation."

In the days before the debate Coot spent his evenings pouring over S.A.F.E. documents, Global Zero press releases, and recent news items. He also reviewed white papers and opinion pieces concerning non-proliferation and nuclear disarmament that he had saved in his files. He even browsed right-wing websites to learn their positions. On Thursday Coot had Diana ask him questions from a list that he had prepared.

After peppering him with questions for half an hour, she said, "Have you found out who your opponent will be?"

"Not yet."

"You have a right to know who you're up against, don't you think?"

"Yes, but I know the issues inside and out. I've been working in this area for twenty-five years."

"But your opponent may raise irrelevant points to distract

attention from those issues. It might help to know his hot buttons."

"I suppose so, but how can I prepare for that? I'll just have to think quickly and deal with whatever he throws at me."

That night, Roger called. "Coot, guess who you'll be debating tomorrow — Larry Limbick! He plugged the debate on his radio show this morning. Apparently the guy they had originally invited declined at the last minute and Limbick agreed to help them out."

"Good grief! What does he know about proliferation issues?"

"Actually, national defense is one of Limbick's core issues, so he deals with proliferation in that context."

"By mouthing the standard right-wing accusations about unilateral disarmament, I suppose."

"Larry's no dummy, whatever you think of his politics or his methods. He talks about the difficulties in verifying compliance and enforcing embargoes, for example. I hope you're ready for a real debate."

"As ready as I'll ever be. Thanks for the heads-up, Roger."

Diana was waiting for Coot in the lobby of WETA when Coot, wearing a blue suit and a tie that his daughter Jeannie had given him, arrived at the studios on Friday afternoon.

"Nervous?" she asked him.

"A little. It's always better to be a bit anxious than over-confident."

"I'm sure you'll do fine. I told the receptionist I would be meeting you. She said that I could watch from a room with a two-way mirror. Afterwards I'll meet you in the green room. I wonder, is it really green?"

"Not this one. It's a light beige. And, did you know that the so-called black boxes on aircraft are actually yellow or orange?"

"Hah! With facts like that at your command, you'll handle Limbick with ease!"

A middle-aged woman wearing black slacks and a colorful blouse came out a door labeled "Private" and walked toward them.

"Hello, Coot," she said. "I'm Rita Swearingen. It's a pleasure to meet you in person."

"Hi, Rita," said Coot. "This is my friend Diana Munson." Turning to Diana, he said, "Rita is the producer of the *Face-to-Face* debate series."

Rita escorted her two guests through the "Private" door. After showing Diana to the viewing room, she took Coot to makeup, where he got his face powdered.

"Last stop, the studio," said Rita, leading Coot into a large room filled with cameras and lights, all pointing toward a U-shaped table with three chairs. Bottled water, note pads, and pencils were at each place. Several technicians wearing headsets were working at various pieces of the equipment. One of the techs approached Rita and Coot. "Before you sit down, Dan here needs to mike you."

Dan quickly placed the little transmitter on Coot's belt, threaded a thin cable under Coot's left arm, and clipped the microphone pair to Coot's left lapel.

"The mike is live but we still need to test it and set the level," said Dan. "Please say something in a normal conversational tone."

Coot complied. After a few seconds, Dan said, "Okay, you're all set."

"Please sit in the chair on the left, Coot," said Rita. "Bill Moore, as usual, will be the host today. He'll be on set in a minute. Our other guest, Larry Limbick, is running a few minutes late. I couldn't tell you who the other participant would be when you called because he had only tentatively agreed to participate. When he finally did decline, Larry did me a favor by accepting on short notice."

"No problem. A friend told me that Larry had announced his appearance on his talk show."

"Yeah, I heard about that."

As a tall, tanned man walked toward them, Rita said, "Oh, here comes Bill now." Coot stood up and Rita performed the introductions.

"Ever been on TV before?" Moore asked Coot.

"Several times. Never on *Face-to-Face*, though."

"As host, I try to stay in the background and let the two guests interact directly."

A large, red-faced man wearing a plaid sport coat and tie hurried onto the set.

"Hey, Rita! Sorry I'm late." It was Limbick. "Unavoidable business.

You know how it is."

"Hi, Larry. Thanks for subbing today. We need to get you miked and then we can begin. Bill and Coot are ready to go."

Limbick turned to look at the two men. "Hello, Bill. Good to see you again. And *you* must be the famous Professor Coot."

"I'm hardly famous, no professor, and 'Coot' is just a nickname. Like 'Larry'."

Limbick's eyes narrowed slightly, then he was back in stride. "Right. Well, where's Dan? I need a mike."

Soon Dan had Limbick wired and tested. All three men took their places. When the director signaled him, Moore began.

"Today's topic could hardly be more timely, given the recent attack on the Indian airbase at Srinagar. We are debating the proposition 'Nuclear Weapons Should Be Abolished', the focus of the Global Zero campaign. Coot Jenkins of Scientists Against Future Extinction will argue *for* the proposition, radio talk show host Larry Limbick will argue *against* it. In the first part of the program Coot will have three minutes to state his case, then Larry will have the same amount of time to present his. Next, each guest will have three minutes for rebuttal. Finally, Coot and Larry will alternate in asking questions of each other. Coot, you're on."

"Thanks, Bill. There are four reasons that nuclear weapons should be abolished. First, nuclear weapons are less necessary and less effective as a deterrent. Second, terrorists are determined to obtain nuclear weapons -- and use them, as the attack on Srinagar has shown. Third, as long as some states possess nuclear weapons, other states will see them as justified and desirable. Fourth, the more states that have nuclear weapons, the greater the likelihood of nuclear war."

Coot paused to let his words sink in. He noticed that Limbick was scribbling furiously on the pad of paper he had been given. "Why are nuclear weapons losing their deterrent value? Two reasons: the Cold War is over and suicidal terrorists cannot be deterred. The United States no longer regards any major nuclear power as an enemy. The Soviet Union is gone, several of the former Soviet Republics have renounced nuclear weapons, and relations with the Russian Federation are relatively good." *Good, Limbick is still scribbling*, Coot thought. *Maybe he'll learn something.* "What about deterring terrorists? How do you deter someone who believes that if he dies as a martyr he will go straight to Paradise? Moreover, of what conceivable use is a nuclear weapon against an enemy with no cities to defend, living in mountain caves and villages?"

Limbick was rolling his eyes and grimacing. Coot sipped from his water bottle, then began explaining his second point. "Of course the terrorists know that nuclear weapons would be very useful against American cities. One successful strike, even with a tactical nuclear device like the one used at Srinagar, would inflict damage to the target city and to the economy that would dwarf the results of the September 11, 2001, attacks. We absolutely must keep all such devices and the material for making them out of the hands of terrorists. The best way to do this is to destroy existing nuclear weapons and control fissile materials like enriched uranium and plutonium. The problem is that there are thousands of nuclear weapons in the world today and thousands of civilian sites, such as power plants and research labs, that have fissile material. Not all of these weapons and sites are sufficiently secured. They make tempting targets for criminal gangs, who steal nuclear materials and even weapons and then sell them to terrorists like Mushrooms."

"Aren't you done yet, Professor?" interjected Limbick, scowling.

Coot stared at Limbick. The guy was rude and a jerk, that was clear.

"Larry, it's Coot's turn to speak," Moore reminded Limbick. "You'll get a chance to respond in a couple of minutes."

Glancing contemptuously at Limbick, Coot resumed his presentation. "The Nuclear Non-Proliferation Treaty obligates the nuclear weapons states to negotiate in good faith on measures relating to nuclear disarmament. If they don't, non-nuclear states may decide that joining the nuclear club is in their national interest and feel justified in withdrawing their commitment to the nonproliferation part of the treaty. Such actions could precipitate regional arms races among countries with poor command and control systems, and thus increase the risk of a nuclear war breaking out somewhere in the world due to misjudgment, accident, or unauthorized launch."

Coot paused again, then concluded, "In summation, the abolition of nuclear weapons would make the world safer for both nuclear and non-nuclear states." Coot looked at Moore and nodded.

"Thanks, Coot. Larry, the floor is yours," said Moore.

"The professor here doesn't seem to be living in the real world. Russia is run by a gang of ex-KGB agents. Just because they sign a treaty to destroy their nuclear weapons doesn't mean they'll do it. C'mon, professor, get real! How about Iran or North Korea?" Gesturing toward Coot while looking into the camera, Limbick asked, "Does *he* even trust the mullahs in Tehran or the nut job in Pyongyang to live up to their treaty commitments? Look at how Iran has reneged on its pledges under the Non-Proliferation Treaty to declare its uranium enrichment program and to permit international inspections. And North Korea? Hah! Those morons also signed the treaty, but then withdrew from it in 2003 and by 2006 were able to test a nuclear device. So, I ask the professor, what good are treaties on abolishing nuclear weapons? There's no way we can trust other countries to live up to their commitments permanently, so it would be foolish for us to give up our nuclear weapons and risk nuclear blackmail. We must prepare for the worst-case scenario, which is that somebody out there will have a secret stash of nuclear weapons, no matter what treaties they have signed."

Coot was the one scribbling on his pad now. Limbick was more knowledgeable than he had thought. Coot would have to get into the whole verification thicket.

Limbick pressed his attack. "Let's face it: only our friends are going to honor a treaty to secure nuclear sites. Our enemies may sign such a treaty, but they can't be trusted to honor it. We have to assume they'll cheat, not only to maintain their own secret arsenals but to have some left over to sell to terrorists. Shoot, these people are so corrupt, they'd even steal from their own facilities to sell to terrorists on the black market. That's probably how the Mushrooms got their weapons."

Coot looked up at Limbick. Could the fellow really have such a cynical view of human nature and be so pessimistic about international agreements?

Limbick continued, "The professor blames the U.S. and other countries that have nukes for the desire of non-nuclear countries to have nuclear weapons. Hell, if I was the tin-pot dictator of some impoverished backwater, I'd want a nuke just to hold over the tin-pot dictator next door. It's human nature. The professor needs a good course in psychology, I guess. Maybe he can talk one of his pointy-headed friends into letting him audit a class."

Coot's eyes widened and he wrinkled his brow in astonishment. Limbick had a primitive outlook on Third-World countries, that was certain, not to mention a lot of hostility toward academics.

Limbick went on, "The attack on Srinagar proves that the nuclear genie is out of the bottle, and there's no way to put it back in. By having nuclear weapons ourselves, we will make other countries afraid to attack us. We and our allies will be fine. So what if Camel Kingdom attacks Raghead Republic with a nuke or two? In a few days the fallout from their puny bombs will disperse and life will go on. Maybe we'll have to wash our lettuce a little more thoroughly and avoid feeding milk to our babies for a while, but otherwise we won't notice the difference -- except that there will be one or two fewer countries in the Third World."

Coot was looking at his notes and planning his rebuttal. Limbick seriously misunderstood the effects of a nuclear war between two small countries.

Limbick continued, "I do agree with one thing the professor said: terrorists like the Mushrooms are determined to get nuclear weapons and use them against us. That's why we've got to find them, wherever they are, and destroy them. I rest my case."

"Thanks, Larry. Coot, it's time for your rebuttal. You have three minutes," said Moore.

Coot took a deep breath and began. "Larry's statements were so far-fetched and outrageous that I hardly know where to start. At the outset I should acknowledge that I am *not* a professor, as I told Larry before the show. His remarks reveal his anti-intellectual bias and hostility toward academia. He should be ashamed of such attitudes, but apparently shame is beyond him. I'll deal with his misunderstanding of the issues in reverse order. First, it's bad enough that Larry has so little regard for human life that he trivializes the loss of whole countries in a nuclear war. He shows he is ignorant as well as callous by minimizing the effects on our country of a nuclear war between two Third-World countries. Because of regional alliances and tribal allegiances there is a serious danger that such a war would not remain limited to the two nations that started it. The more states that were drawn into the conflict and the more of them that had nuclear weapons, the more radioactive fallout would be produced. Winds would carry this fallout around the world, to land on our farms, to be eaten by us and our children. No, a nuclear war anywhere in the world would be a disaster for the entire human race, including Americans."

Limbick had turned red and was glaring at Coot, who took a drink from his water bottle and went on. "Second, Larry talks as if personal ambition would drive a national leader to make the momentous decision to acquire nuclear weapons. In fact, nuclear weapons are very expensive to produce and difficult to deliver. The driving force for a country's going nuclear has always been the knowledge or fear that an adversary had or was seeking such weapons. That's the classic dynamic of an arms race. The best and easiest time to break this vicious circle is before it gets started. That's why the Non-Proliferation Treaty is so important.

"Larry's third error is his assertion that treaties cannot be enforced. In fact, the Non-Proliferation Treaty mandates a system of voluntary disclosures and systematic inspections that has worked remarkably well since the treaty went into force in 1970. No country wants to incur the expense of developing nuclear weapons if it can be secure without them. I concede that Iran's and North Korea's behavior is a major problem, but I contend that the leaders of those countries are so isolated and fearful of being attacked that they accept harsh economic sanctions as the price of acquiring nuclear weapons for deterrence. If their fear were less, they would be less willing to suffer the consequences of defying the international community. We can reduce their fear by working on solutions to the long-term problems in their regions."

Limbick was scribbling rapidly again, grinding his teeth as he wrote. Coot went on with his rebuttal. "Finally, Larry doubts that the Russians will honor any agreement to destroy their nuclear weapons. Today both sides are well under the limits set by the 1991 START treaty. We know this from on-site inspections and extensive satellite surveillance. To think that every administration from Reagan's onward has allowed Russia to violate the treaty is hopelessly paranoid."

Coot folded his hands and waited for Moore, who said, "And now we'll have Larry's rebuttal."

Limbick looked furious. The color had not receded from his face, and his eyes were narrow slits. "Paranoid, eh? You think it's paranoid to mistrust men whose jobs were to spy on the West? You think it's paranoid to believe that there is plenty of room to hide missiles and warheads in a country as vast as Russia? I say it's hopelessly naive to believe otherwise."

The color rose in Coot's cheeks. It was people on both sides like Larry who kept the Cold War going for half a century.

Limbick sneered at Coot. "You say it's fear of being attacked that motivates the leaders of North Korea and Iran. I say it's naked ambition to dominate other countries. If we don't recognize and thwart their plans for regional dominance before it's too late, we'll be in for a rude awakening when Iran closes the Strait of Hormuz, suddenly reducing the world's oil supply by 20%. It will be a lot quicker and easier to force them to back off if we have nukes and they don't."

Continuing to speak directly to Coot, Limbick said, "You think a conflict between two third-rate countries will likely involve other countries. What proof do you have for that idea? Iraq and Iran fought an eight-year war in the 1980s and no other countries joined the fracas. If the war had been nuclear, that would have been all the more reason for their neighbors to stay out of the conflict."

When Limbick did not say anything else for a few seconds, Moore said, "Larry, you still have almost two minutes left for your rebuttal. Are there any other points you want to make before we go to the Q&A portion of the program?"

"No, Bill. I'm looking forward to cross-examining Coot here. Everyone needs to understand the dangerous course he and his fellow lefties are plotting for this country."

"All right, then. Since Larry had time left in his rebuttal, he may ask the first question. Larry?"

"Explain this to me, Coot: How can you be sure that some Russian general would not hide a few nuclear missiles where inspectors do not go and satellites cannot see?"

Coot cleared his throat. "Larry, surely you understand that no strategy for defense of the country is 100% certain of success. We need to do as much as we can to improve the odds. In the case of Russia, we are better off with large reductions in the numbers of missiles and bombers, even if a few escape detection. In fact, in START I each side was permitted to retain several thousand weapons. The Russian generals had more than enough missiles and bombers left to defend their country, so they had very little motivation to cheat and reason to fear prosecution if they were caught cheating."

Limbick countered, "But you want to eliminate *all* Russian missiles and heavy bombers. If there were a treaty to do so, wouldn't a cautious general keep a few of these weapons hidden away, just in case *we* cheated?"

Coot's opinion of Limbick's intelligence was increasing. "Let's suppose you're right about that, Larry. So, instead of hundreds or thousands of missiles pointed at us, we would have maybe a dozen. Wouldn't that be a great improvement?"

Limbick responded, "Of course, but those dozen could wipe out the twelve largest American cities."

"That's right, at least for a while. But don't forget that hardware ages. Eventually those missiles would become unreliable. Where would the cheater find replacements? The plants for making such missiles would be inspected by our people. It would be much harder to hide a construction site for nuclear missiles than to hide the missiles themselves. As time went by, the initial secret cache of missiles would become less and less useful."

"So, Coot, you agree that for a number of years there would be a possibility that the Russians would have, say, a dozen missiles hidden that they could use against us in a crisis?"

"While that situation is possible, I don't think it's probable. The treaty would gradually take effect. Inspections and surveillance would begin at once, so no new missiles or bombers could be constructed without our knowledge. Over several years existing missiles and bombers would be taken out of service and destroyed. By the time all of the known launch vehicles were gone, any that were hidden initially would be nearing the end of their useful lives. Although this strategy is not 100% certain to abolish all strategic nuclear weapons, it does give us a high probability of doing so, and a much safer situation than we have now."

Moore interjected, "Coot, it's your turn to ask Larry a question."

"Larry, what's your plan for keeping nuclear weapons out of the hands of terrorists?" Would Limbick have anything constructive to say on his pet topic?

"Simple: destroy the terrorists. If they're all dead, they can't attack us."

"Surely you recognize the fact that we've been hunting terrorists for decades and have not come close to eliminating all of them. We didn't even have a clue that the Mushrooms terrorists were hidden somewhere in Pakistan. How do we keep guys like them from getting nuclear weapons?"

"We need to surround them with a ring of steel that all their supplies must pass through. We need to lean on the Pakistanis and the Afghans to get with the program or lose billions in U.S. aid."

"But, Larry, don't you realize how expensive such an operation would be? How many hundreds of thousands of troops would be required? How long the effort would have to be sustained? Do you really think that's the most cost-effective strategy? Wouldn't it be easier to control nuclear materials and weapons at their sources, which are largely known?"

"Well, uh, I guess it would be pretty expensive. But that still doesn't mean that we have to give up our nukes to keep terrorists from getting some. We should just lock down all our stuff and get other countries to do the same."

"You're right that all countries need to have tight control of their nuclear weapons and fissile materials. That's very important. However, human nature being what it is, as long as there are nuclear weapons in the world, especially the smaller tactical weapons like artillery shells and land mines, there will always be the possibility of theft. It would be a lot easier for terrorists to use a completed weapon than to make one from scratch. Again, it's a matter of improving the odds of our success."

"Larry, do you have another question for Coot?" Moore inquired.

"I sure do, Bill. Coot, I still want to know how you think the U.S. can protect its national interests if it can't threaten a nuclear attack anymore? For example, how could Iran be forced to re-open the Strait of Hormuz?"

Coot did not hesitate to respond. "Nuclear weapons are good for destroying cities, which most people find morally repugnant, and for attacking hardened missile sites, which is irrelevant in this case. The U.S. has a formidable array of conventional weapons to do the job. Cruise missile strikes alone could cause immense damage to particular military facilities and civilian infrastructure like power plants, without the great loss of life and global radioactive fallout that would result from a nuclear attack. Moreover, diplomatic pressure and economic sanctions could be tried first, thus avoiding military conflict altogether."

"You lefties are so in love with sanctions, aren't you? They never work but you never give up on them, do you?"

"Larry, you sound like a typical chicken hawk -- always ready to spill other people's blood but never risking your own. Most military leaders, with real experience of war, view military action as a last resort, not as some kind of gung-ho ego trip."

"What do you know about war, Coot? You may not be a professor, but you're still an annoying know-it-all."

"I was an Army Ranger in Vietnam, Larry. Where were you in 1973?"

"In college. High draft number. Hey, it's my turn to ask the question."

"I answered your question. Now it's my turn. Did you enlist when you got out of school, then? You must have been eager to join the fun in 'Nam."

"No, I didn't. I, uh, had other priorities at the time."

"I see. Isn't that the same excuse Bill Clinton gave in 1992, for which you have always criticized him?"

"I thought we were discussing the abolition of nuclear weapons."

"Yes, gentlemen, we are," said Moore. "Larry, your question?"

"No, I'm done trying to get the pseudo-professor here to admit the error of his ways."

"Well, then, Coot, do you have a final question for Larry?"

"No, Bill, I think Larry has discredited himself and his position enough for one evening."

Limbick was red in the face again. He glared at Coot but didn't say anything.

"All right. That's it for this edition of *Face-to-Face*, WETA's debate series," said Moore. "Thanks to Coot Jenkins and Larry Limbick for a lively and informative discussion tonight."

The studio lights dimmed. Dan came over and removed Coot's microphone, then went over to Limbick. Rita approached Coot, smiling. "Well, 'Professor,' you two sure gave us an interesting show. I'm looking forward to seeing the audience response when it's aired tonight."

"My pleasure, Rita. Thanks for the opportunity. Nuclear disarmament is such an important topic."

"Diana is waiting for you in the green room. Why don't you go back there now? I need to talk with Larry."

Coot left the set and headed for the green room, where he found Diana waiting for him, a wide smile on her face.

"You were brilliant!" she said, giving him an enthusiastic hug. "Limbick looked a beaten dog at the end. I'm a little surprised that you were so aggressive with him."

"I get so tired of chicken hawks. If they had seen war like I've seen it, they wouldn't be so enthusiastic for more of it."

Just then Limbick burst into the room. Coot reflexively backed away from the red-faced, huffing fellow, until his way was blocked by a chair.

"You fucking shit, Jenkins! You tried to make a fool of me, you arrogant bastard!" Limbick pushed Coot so hard in the chest that Coot fell backwards over the chair behind him.

Diana acted as if by instinct. She hit Limbick with a karate chop to the neck, then followed up with a punch to the gut. Limbick crumpled to the floor, a look of utter astonishment on his face. He was having difficulty catching his breath. He made no move to get up.

"What are you,... Coot's bodyguard,... bitch?," Limbick panted. "Wait till my lawyer ... gets on your case. You'll regret you ever... messed with me."

Coot had sprung to his feet and was about to grab Limbick by the throat when Rita entered the room. "What's going on? We didn't mean to start World War III here in the green room, gentlemen."

"It's her, Coot's slut. She's some kind of frigging martial artist. She attacked me."

"Only after you pushed Coot over that chair," Diana said, her voice shaking with rage.

"That's right, Rita," said Coot. "Larry lost it a bit. It seems he doesn't like losing an argument." Coot offered a hand to Limbick.

"I don't need your help, you prick," muttered Limbick, as he struggled to stand up.

"Coot, let's leave -- before Mr. Limbick here goes nuclear on us again," pleaded Diana.

"Okay. Sorry for the disturbance, Rita. I hope the show is a success. Thanks again for the opportunity," finished Coot, as he and Diana left the green room.

Once outside the studio, Coot stopped and looked at Diana. "Wow, those were some awesome moves you put on Limbick! How were you able to react so quickly?"

"In college I took a course in self-defense for women. The instructor told us to always be prepared for trouble. When Limbick came into the green room and started screaming at you, I kind of expected him to get physical."

"As an ex-Ranger I should have been thinking the same thing. It's been so long since I was in that sort of situation. I couldn't believe the foul-mouthed coward would do such a thing."

"Well, it's over now. Why don't we go get a drink? My treat."

"You're very generous," said Coot, smiling, "but I owe you one for laying out Limbick like that."

On the Saturday morning following the debate, Jack showed up at Coot's house for their usual run. As they waited for Roger to arrive, Jack said, "That was quite a debate you and Larry Limbick had Friday night! You clearly got the better of him."

"Thanks. He would have done better if he had stuck to real issues like verification and not gotten off into paranoid fantasies."

"Yeah, I guess so. What was all that 'professor' stuff about?"

"Oh, he was just trying to get under my skin and appeal to his anti-intellectual fans."

"Well, I was glad to see you call him out on it — although you were a little harsh."

"He deserved it."

Roger pulled up in his Hummer. "Hey, guys! Sorry I'm late."

"No problem, Roger," said Jack. "Coot and I were just talking about his debate with Limbick on Friday."

"Yeah, I saw that. Great job, Coot. Let's get going," said Roger.

The three men set off at an easy pace for the first mile, then accelerated, making talking harder.

"You do talk... like a professor,... Coot," said Roger. "Not that that's bad."

Coot ignored the remark.

"It's just that you sounded...like you knew what you...were talking about...and were lecturing...a particularly...stubborn student."

"Limbick *was*...stubborn!" Coot said.

"He mentioned the debate...on his talk show yesterday."

"What'd he say?"

"Just that you were...an arrogant...intellectual...with dangerous... ideas...that must be...defeated."

"Was that all he said?" asked Coot.

"Uh, no," said Roger. "He said...he was attacked...after the show...by some dyke...who was with you."

"Damn him!" said Coot.

"He even showed...the bruise on his neck....What was that...all about?"

"After the show...I went back...to the green room,...where Diana was...waiting for me....Limbick stormed in... shoved me...over a chair....Diana hit him...with a couple of...karate punches...that knocked him…to the floor.…That's all."

"Listen, Coot," said Roger after another few minutes of silence, "I didn't like…the way Limbick talked…about Diana.…He made it sound…like she was a ball-busting…left-wing pervert.…You'd better tell Diana…to be on her guard."

"Okay, I'll do that," said Coot. "Thanks for the warning."

The three friends finished their run without further conversation about the debate, Frannie, or Diana.

After he got home, Coot phoned Diana. When he got her answering machine, he remembered that she would have left town that morning to fly to California to visit her family before going to a conference in San Francisco. He left a message about Roger's warning and hung up.

* * *

"The puppets are dancing for their masters again, but we will cut their strings and they will fall in a heap." Vice-Chairman Kim Dae-Hyun smiled in pleasure at his clever metaphor. He looked around the polished teak conference table and received the applause he expected. He had not ascended into the leadership of the National Defense Commission of the Democratic People's Republic of Korea by lacking in self-confidence, but to show he was not egotistical he bowed his head. As the clapping ended, he raised his chin and resumed speaking.

"The People's Army has long been able to conquer the puppet army to the south." The men around the large table nodded and whispered their agreement. "But we have not done so." General Kim scanned the faces of the committee members. "Why not? I ask you." Silence filled the room. He knew each of the men feared being blamed, so he quickly went on. "So far we have held ourselves back because the puppet master threatens to attack us if we use our power to reunify our country." He waved away the young women who had come into the room to refill the drinks of the men around the table. The girls scurried away.

"But we have freed ourselves from this threat." Again the nods and whispers of agreement. "We have defied the puppet master and built nuclear weapons." The whispers became murmurs. "We have defied the puppet master and built I.C.B.M.s." The murmurs became shouts. "Inspired by the Supreme Leader, we have put nuclear warheads onto our I.C.B.M.s and programmed them to rain destruction on the puppet master's cities." The shouts became cheers. "The puppet master cannot attack us without bringing ruin to himself. We *will* reunify our country!" To a man, the members leaped to their feet, as their cheers merged into a great roar of patriotic fervor.

Vice-Chairman Kim left the meeting quickly, but not before Vice-Chairman Gong Dong-Min held his arm and whispered, "Aren't you forgetting the American interceptors?" General Kim merely grunted and continued on his way. He knew about the missile defense system that the United States had deployed in California and Alaska, but he also knew that it had failed several tests.

Would the American president retaliate against the D.P.R.K. for attacking the South, knowing that his own country's safety depended on the perfect operation of an imperfect system? General Kim did not think so. Not when the failure to intercept even one incoming nuclear warhead might mean the destruction of Seattle or Los Angeles, Chicago or New York. Of course, he would welcome anything that decreased the confidence the Americans had in their defensive shield. How he wished the terrorists who attacked Srinagar had struck an American interceptor base instead.

One thing was certain: if the Americans did retaliate against the D.P.R.K. for attacking the South, his compatriots in the Strategic Rocket Forces would launch all surviving I.C.B.M.s at the United States, regardless of any defensive shield. At least one would get through and destroy an American city. The honor of the country must be protected.

CHAPTER 6
Lightning Strikes

As the last stars of the short Canadian summer night were fading from view in the brightening sky, Doug Lloyd listened with mounting excitement to the sound of the small boat approaching. He and Bennie Martin had parked their rented van near a small dock in a cove near Matane, Quebec, and were waiting for the smugglers who were bringing crates that they thought contained ancient artifacts. Doug and Bennie knew better, for George Boyd had told them when and where to meet the disguised atomic demolition munitions. George had arranged for the weapons to be carried by truck from Kyrgyzstan to Syria, then loaded onto a freighter bound for the U.S., and finally transferred to a stealthy go-fast boat of the sort used to bring cigarettes tax-free into the U.S.

Doug had met George in a Berkeley bar just weeks after George, his academic career in ruins, had arrived from Chicago. After a few beers and much arguing about the state of the world, George had convinced Doug that freedom and prosperity for ordinary people required using a trick of the ruling class against them: creative destruction. Just as corporations destroyed some jobs and created others in order to enter new markets and thereby increase profits, so the people must eliminate existing institutions and create new ones in order to enhance individual freedom and increase workers' prosperity.

Doug admired George's understanding of "the big picture": institutions always sought to perpetuate themselves at the expense of the people who worked for them. Doug had witnessed such behavior himself in the way graduate teaching assistants were exploited in the physics department at Cal. He knew plenty of other grad students who felt the same way.

When George had first proposed organizing a group to bring down malignant institutions, Doug was excited by the idea but skeptical that a small group could win against such rich and powerful opponents. George had overcome Doug's skepticism by explaining that, as in asymmetric warfare, the weaker power could win if it found a way to exploit the stronger power's weaknesses, such as vulnerable infrastructure.

George's knowledge of nuclear weapons made his arguments more persuasive to Doug, who understood the physics of such devices but not the manner in which they were deployed and protected. According to George, the disintegration of the Soviet Union had reduced the security of their tens of thousands of tactical nuclear weapons. If a small group could obtain just a few such devices on the black market, it could defeat much larger opponents.

Both George and Doug had realized that secrecy was essential for their plan to succeed. They suspected that any anarchist organization known to the authorities would, sooner or later, be infiltrated by informants. They had been very careful in selecting other members of their group, admitting mostly people they had known for years. Even the group's name, Mushrooms, connoted being kept in the dark.

George had never explained how Michael Anthony and Tipton had found the Mushrooms. All Doug knew was that the two remaining devices were now on their way by boat from the Middle East and were due to arrive at the cove in just minutes.

At last the slender boat came into view. Doug counted three men on board. Bennie, dressed in jeans and an old flannel shirt, got out of the van. Doug joined him. One of the smugglers climbed onto the small dock and approached Bennie and Doug.

"We've come for the artifacts," said Doug.

"It's gonna cost ya another five grand," said the smuggler.

"No way," said Doug. "A deal's a deal."

The smuggler raised his right hand, as if to dismiss Doug's

statement. At his signal one of the men on the boat produced an AK-47 that he aimed at the two Mushrooms. Two shots rang out. Not from the boat but from the woods above the dock. The assault rifle clattered onto the deck, as its owner fell lifeless beside it. The third man raised his hands in surrender and backed away from the weapon. A stocky woman in camouflage emerged from the woods carrying a Barrett M82 sniper's rifle.

"Nice shooting, Jamie!" said Bennie. Jamie Saunders joined her fellow Mushrooms by the dock.

"All right, take your goddam crates," said the first smuggler, his hands also signaling surrender.

"Here," said Jamie, handing Doug a pistol. "Watch these guys while I check the crates."

Doug held the weapon with both hands, as he had seen cops do on TV, and pointed it at the first smuggler. "Get over there," he said, motioning to a spot well away from the dock. You," he said to the third smuggler, "get out of the boat and get over there too." The smugglers had no way of knowing Doug was not used to handling guns, so they did as he commanded.

Bennie searched the two men, found a cell phone and two more weapons, and tossed them all far out into the cove. Jamie and Bennie then heaved the crates out of the boat onto the dock. Jamie opened each one out of the smugglers sight, verified that an A.D.M. was inside, and closed the crate.

"These things look just like the U.S. A.D.M.s I trained on," she said. "Except for the Russian writing."

Jamie climbed back into the boat. Doug, keeping his eyes on the smugglers, asked her what she was doing.

"Disabling the boat's radio," she said. "Looking for phones and weapons." Doug heard more splashes.

Jamie returned to shore. "I'll take over guard duty," she said to Doug, who was happy to return Jamie's weapon to her.

While Jamie kept the smugglers well away from the dock and the van, Bennie and Doug moved the crates to the van, installed lead shielding around them, and hid them under some old tarpaulins.

Doug stuck his head out of the van's rear doors. "Let's go!"

Jamie herded the two remaining smugglers back to their boat

and stood on the dock, her rifle ready, as they started the engines and pulled away.

"Come on!" Doug was more insistent now, fearing that somehow the smugglers would try to avenge the dead man.

Jamie ran back to the van and got in the rear.

"Do you think we have enough shielding around those A.D.M.s?" asked Bennie.

"Yeah," said Jamie, but she nevertheless checked them with the Geiger counter that she had earlier put in the van. "Yeah, they're good to go."

The three Mushrooms drove southwest along the Gulf of St. Lawrence, then headed southeast to pick up Route 2. In four hours, they reached Grand Falls, at the U.S.-Canadian border. Near Grand Falls they left the Trans-Canada and made their way on surface roads west toward the U.S. border, where they crossed without being stopped by U.S. Customs.

"Why do you suppose the Border Patrol has left that crossing unguarded?" asked Jamie.

"Stupidity," said Bennie. "Do they think we can't read a map?"

"The across-the-board budget cuts that began a few years back affected Homeland Security's ability to staff all possible crossings," said Doug. "I read that after the attack in Srinagar and the attempt in Britain, they tried to guard every border crossing, but it takes time to mobilize the National Guard."

The Mushrooms drove another four hours through Maine till they reached Augusta. After checking into a motel, they went shopping for backpacks in which they could conceal the A.D.M.s. Packs with conspicuous Russian markings would not do. The second store they visited sold a pack that was both big enough and sturdy enough for a 150-pound load. They bought two packs and returned to the motel for the night.

The next morning the three conspirators grabbed some muffins and apples from their motel's complimentary continental breakfast, then got back into the van. They crossed Massachusetts on Interstate 95, then went on toward New York, following signs for the George Washington Bridge. Bennie was driving as they entered New York.

"Don't miss the exit for for our rendezvous with Mitch and George," said Doug.

"When have I ever missed an exit," said Bennie, "except when you misread the GPS after we got into Maine yesterday?"

"There's the exit we want," said Doug, ignoring Bennie's defensive taunt.

"I can read," said Bennie, as he changed into the exit lane for Leonia.

Bennie's main role in Mushrooms was as driver and mechanic, and Doug thought that he did not feel respected as much as the other members, even though his role was essential.

"Calm down, guys," said Jamie. "Let's focus on getting these devices to the staging areas."

"Yeah. Sorry, Bennie," said Doug, trying to soothe any hurt feelings. "You're doing a great job."

Once in Leonia, Doug began to look for Overbeck Park, where they were to meet George and Mitch in George's van. He hoped they would not meet any police cars patrolling the area and have to revise their plans to hand off an A.D.M.

* * *

George Boyd looked carefully around Leonia's Overbeck Park for signs of other visitors. Being observed by anyone, especially by the police, while he and Mitch Chambers were waiting for Doug, Jamie, and Bennie, would risk the entire mission. Seeing no one, he sighed with relief and got back into the van he had rented that morning. If only the three other Mushrooms would arrive soon, he would feel more confident of success.

After fifteen minutes, George could see headlights entering the park and moving along the same drive that he and Mitch had followed earlier that evening. The headlights of the approaching car flashed in the short-short-long-short pattern that George and Bennie had agreed on.

"It's them," George assured Mitch.

The S.U.V. with Bennie, Doug, and Jamie inside pulled alongside George and Mitch's. The new arrivals got out.

"Got 'em?" asked George.

"You bet," said Doug, "although Jamie had to waste one of the smugglers." Doug explained about the attempted shake-down.

"Let's get one of the A.D.M.s into the van, guys," said George. "We can't risk any awkward questions from the cops."

Jamie and the four men wasted no time in removing the lead shielding from one of the A.D.M.s.

"My Russian contact said that the Soviet A.D.M.s were copies of the U.S. Small Atomic Demolition Munition," said George.

"Then its yield can be anything from ten tons up to one kiloton," said Jamie.

"What did Anthony say about the yield to use?" asked Mitch.

"Nothing," said George. "Maybe he and Tipton didn't realize the yield could vary."

"Then it's up to us," said Doug.

As they discussed the weapon's yield, Jamie and the men transferred the crated device to George's van and replaced the shielding.

"Let's go for the biggest blast we can get," said Mitch, his face alive with malevolence. "We gotta show we're strong, to get people to join the insurrection."

"The more people we kill, the less likely they are to join us," said Jamie, "and the more they'll just want us dead. I've never been comfortable with Tipton's target in Manhattan."

"Maybe he doesn't want an insurrection," said Doug. "What *does* Tipton want, George?"

"Anthony said he just wanted to support us," said George, "as long as he could choose the targets. And, he wanted us to do the New York op first."

"Tipton's targets are terrific," said Mitch. "We should be glad he's financing their destruction."

"Whatever we think of the targets, we're committed to two more ops," said George. "Let's go."

George climbed into his van with Jamie and Mitch, while Bennie and Doug got back into their van and set off on their drive west on I-80 till toward the next staging site.

George and his two comrades got onto U.S. 1 & 9 and drove south. At times the Manhattan skyline loomed impressively to their left. If their plan succeeded, it would soon look diminished. After proceeding east on the Pulaski Skyway and 12th Street in Jersey City, they arrived at an unremarkable building, which had formerly hosted an off-track betting operation. George unlocked the door. Jamie and the two men quickly transferred the A.D.M. into the secure area that had housed the safes. It wouldn't be there long, but they could not risk its being lost to a random burglar. Especially after the incident with the smugglers, George was glad that Jamie was with them. Another reason, of course, was her expertise in atomic demolition munitions.

* * *

That night Coot was lying in bed reading when he heard the sound of breaking glass and saw a flash of light from the living room. He jumped out of bed, grabbed the Glock he had bought after the P.T.T. course, and ran into the hallway. The smoke detector was going off. He could see flames reflected in the broken picture window. He ran into the kitchen, got the fire extinguisher, and rushed into the living room. The piano was alive with flames licking its mahogany legs and case. Oh, God, not the piano! Damn them!

Coot sprayed the fire extinguisher at the base of the flames under the piano. He could see a broken bottle and the remains of a wick now. A sure sign of a Molotov cocktail. The phone was ringing. Probably the alarm company. Coot did not answer, assuming they would call the fire department. He continued to spray the flames on the piano, its beautiful reddish finish now charred. At last the flames were out, but the piano appeared damaged beyond repair. His beloved piano, which his grandmother had played so well, which Frannie had made sing, which Diana had brought back to life, destroyed.

As Coot surveyed the wreckage, the sound of sirens grew louder. Soon a fire engine pulled up in front of the house, followed by a police cruiser. Through the broken window Coot saw firemen dressed in heavy rubber coats running to the front door with large fire extinguishers. He let them in. The firemen confirmed that Coot had managed to put out the fire, then pointed to the remains of the Molotov cocktail.

"Somebody must've had it in for you, sir," said one of the firemen. "Arson. We gotta get a cop in here."

Another fireman returned with a policeman — a detective named 'Davis', according to the man's name tag. Coot told the detective about the debate, Diana's encounter afterwards with Limbick, and Limbick's denunciation of them on his show. "I'm worried that one of these maniacs will try to attack Diana too. Can you give her some protection?"

"Has she been threatened?" asked Davis.

"Not so far as I know. I don't think Limbick even knew her name."

"Well, then, she's probably safe. Let us know if she gets any threats, okay?"

"You bet. I don't want to take any chances with her safety."

"We'll keep an eye on your home tonight, Mr. Jenkins," said the detective, "so that you can get some sleep. You'll have to call someone to repair that window in the morning."

"Right. Thanks for your help, Detective Davis."

After collecting the remains of the Molotov cocktail as evidence, the police and firemen left Coot alone with his smashed window and the charred remains of his piano. It took Coot an hour to wipe the residue left by the fire extinguisher off the furniture in the living room, and a couple of hours more to calm down enough even to think about going to sleep. During that time he left another message for Diana, telling her about the firebomb and the piano and warning her again to watch out for trouble from Limbick's loonies.

"Coot, are you okay?" Diana's call had wakened him from a sound sleep. She apparently was still operating on East Coast time and had thought to check her phone messages.

"Thanks for calling, Diana. Yeah, I'm okay."

"I feel so bad about this. Maybe if I hadn't hit Limbick he wouldn't have gotten so mad and attacked you on his show."

"Don't blame yourself. Limbick did so poorly in the debate that he was bound to accuse me to hide his own failure."

"Are you sure the piano can't be repaired? Shouldn't you have it looked at?"

"I'm pretty sure it's a total loss, but I'll get my technician to check it out. It would be great if it could be fixed, but I'm sure any repair would take a long time. My lesson and your playing are off for now."

"That's sad. I've really enjoyed working with you and playing your piano."

Coot and Diana chatted for a little while longer. Then Coot said, "Listen, I meant what I said last night about being careful. If the crazies find out who knocked their hero to the floor, you'll be in danger."

"You be careful, too. They *know* who you are."

After saying goodbye to Diana, Coot showered, dressed, and had breakfast. Then he called the man he used for projects around the house, asking him to inspect the damage and give him an estimate for the needed repairs. He also called his insurance company and was dismayed to learn that his homeowner's policy had a $1,000 deductible for this kind of claim. He hated those bloodsuckers.

By noon the local TV stations were reporting the fire-bombing of Coot's home. Apparently neighbors had noticed the commotion and informed the media, who sent camera crews and reporters to record the damage and interview Coot.

"Any idea who bombed your house, Mr. Jenkins?"

"No."

"Why would anyone want to harm you, Mr. Jenkins?"

"No idea." He could not allege revenge as a motive without more proof.

"Do you think the attack was in retaliation for your victory in the debate with Larry Limbick, Mr. Jenkins?"

"You should ask Limbick about that."

"Limbick claims he was attacked by a female friend of yours. Who is she?"

"Next question." It was important to keep Diana out of this mess.

Coot was dismayed on Wednesday morning to pick up his *Washington Post* and find the headline "Karate Kid Levels Limbick" and an article reporting that Limbick's mysterious assailant was Diana Munson. Apparently some enterprising reporters had gotten hold of the police report on the fire-bombing.

After he saw the article, Coot went to his computer and Googled

"Diana Munson". He found out that both left-wing and right-wing bloggers had picked up the story. Diana had become a heroine to the left and a harridan to the right. It would not take long now for Diana to hear about her new fame. She would not be pleased.

Coot's phone rang, as if on cue.

"Coot, what the hell is going on? How did I get dragged into this?"

"Diana, I'm so sorry! The detective asked whether I knew of any reason someone would bomb my house. I told him about the debate and what happened in the green room with Limbick. He asked for your name. I was concerned for your safety, so I gave it to him — and asked about getting you some protection. It didn't occur to me that the newspapers would be interested enough to check the police report."

"I see. Well, I suppose you did the right thing, but now I *do* have to worry about my own safety. I'll be returning home Thursday night. Would you mind calling the police and asking for protection again?"

"Sure. Detective Davis said to contact him if you were threatened. I won't wait that long. After all, there was no advance warning that a Molotov cocktail would be served under the piano on Sunday night."

Coot found Detective Davis's business card and called him. Despite Coot's pleas for protection for Diana, Davis did not feel that the situation required a constant police presence at Diana's apartment. He did promise regular passes by a police cruiser.

Throughout Wednesday, the blogosphere featured battles between Diana's defenders and detractors. The debate with Limbick had dropped out of sight, as far as the bloggers were concerned. Even the new media go for the sensational and ignore the important issues. By Thursday the bloggers were losing interest in Diana. None of them had been able to contact Diana. Her two-punch TKO of Limbick was getting to be old news.

That night Diana called Coot to let him know she had returned to her apartment.

"I've only seen a police car twice, about half an hour apart. I guess they think that's enough protection. The second one just came by."

"Okay. Make sure your doors and windows are locked. Don't order out and don't open the door for anyone."

"I've already checked the doors and windows, and I promise not to let anyone in. Coot, I do appreciate your concern, and ..." Her voice dropped to a whisper. "I thought I heard something in the kitchen. It has a window and a door that opens onto the back stairs. Wait..." Her voice rose in alarm. "Somebody's back there, Coot!"

"Run out the front door! Hurry!"

Coot heard a scream and the sound of the phone hitting the floor. He put Diana's call on hold and dialed 911. The operator answered.

"There's an assault in progress!" he stammered. He gave the operator Diana's address and went back to Diana's call. More muffled screams. He shouted into the phone, "I called 911! The police are on their way!"

Coot hung up, jumped into his car, and red-lined its tachometer. Two police cars were already at Diana's apartment, lights flashing, when he got there. He rushed up the steps, hoping that Diana was unharmed.

A policeman, Officer Nicholas, was standing outside the door to Diana's unit. Coot stopped, panting.

""Is she okay, officer?"

"Who's asking?"

"I reported the assault."

"'They were pretty rough on her."

"What do you mean, 'rough'?"

"Better let her tell you about it, Mr. ..."

"Jenkins. Can I see her?"

"I'll check." Officer Nicholas let himself into Diana's apartment. In a moment he was back. "All right, you can go in."

Coot entered the apartment. A floor lamp's shade was crushed, as if the lamp had been knocked over. Diana must have put up a fierce struggle. Coot heard voices coming from another room. He followed the sounds until he saw Diana sitting on a chair in her bedroom, her right eye swollen, her lip bleeding, and her clothes torn. She was crying. He had never seen her cry. What had they done to her?

Diana looked up. "Oh, hello, Coot. I'm glad you came. Officer Denny and Officer Phillips got here about three minutes after you called. The two men who attacked me ran out the back door when the police got here." She sniffed and wiped her eyes.

"Backup caught the attackers as they came down the rear stairs," said Officer Denny, a short but powerfully-built woman in her twenties. "They're being questioned now."

"That's great. Thanks for getting here so quickly!" said Coot.

The officers nodded. "That's our job," said Officer Phillips. "We have a few more questions for Miss Munson, Mr. Jenkins. Please wait in the living room while we finish."

Coot did as instructed. In a few minutes the two officers came out of Diana's room and Coot went back in.

Diana was still red-eyed but she wasn't crying anymore. He went to her, knelt beside her, and looked into her eyes, those green eyes, the first things he noticed about her that were different from Frannie. "How are you?"

"I've been better. Oh, Coot, there were two of them. They were wearing ski masks. They were big and they smelled like booze and sweat."

"What did they do to you?"

"They caught me just before I got to the front door. One of them grabbed my arm as I swung at him. The other one grabbed my leg when I kicked at his crotch. Then they got mean. The first one hit me in the eye. It really hurt! They forced me to the floor. They tore my blouse. I tried to bite one of them, and he hit me in the mouth. He called me 'a fucking dyke' and said he'd show me what I was missing."

"The dirty bastards! It sounds like you put up quite a fight."

"I tried, Coot, but they were too strong for me. They were tearing my clothes off when the police arrived. I tried to kick one of them where it would hurt the most, but I think I missed. I'm sorry you had to see me like this. I must look like a real mess."

"You're beautiful, Diana. I've never seen anyone look so fine."

"Not even Frannie?"

"You don't have to compete with Frannie."

"Thanks, Coot. I needed to hear that." She sniffed again.

Coot stood up, put his arm around Diana's shoulders, pulled her towards him, and stroked her hair. She rested her head against his thigh. A final sob escaped her, and then she was quiet. They stayed in this awkward position for only a minute. Then Coot released her and she sat back in her chair.

"You're a wonderful friend, Coot."

"I'd like to be more than that, Diana."

"Oh, Coot, I was afraid this would happen. You know why I've avoided getting involved with anyone."

"Yes, but ..."

"No, listen. I feel like a ticking time bomb. I don't want to hurt anyone, especially not you. You've been so kind to me." Diana's eyes were filling with tears again.

Coot realized that he should back off a bit. "We need to get you taken care of. Your eye is swollen and your lip is cut. Do you hurt anywhere else?"

"Just on my arms where they were holding me."

"You should take a nice warm bath. Get rid of all traces of your attackers. Then we can take care of your eye and lip. I'll start the water."

Coot went into the bathroom, turned on the water in the bath tub, and adjusted its temperature. "All set."

Diana came into the bathroom, carrying a pair of pajamas and a robe.

"Can you manage this by yourself?" he asked.

"I think so."

Coot left, closing the door behind him.

Fifteen minutes later Diana emerged. "That felt good. I don't feel dirty anymore. I put some antibiotic ointment on my lip." She sat down on her chair again.

"Good. I'll get some ice for your eye. You'll have a black eye for a few days, I'm afraid."

"There's a cold pack in the freezer that I use to ice sore muscles."

Coot went into the kitchen, where he found the cold pack, which was a green gel in a thick plastic bag. "Here you go," he said to Diana, handing it to her.

She pressed the plastic to her swollen eye. "Ouch!"

"That must hurt." said Coot, wincing. "I'm so sorry this happened to you. I feel like it's my fault."

"Why?"

"One of them called you a dyke. That's the same language Larry Limbick used to describe you on his show Saturday. Roger told me about it."

"So?"

"If I hadn't invited you to the debate, none of this would have happened."

"Don't blame yourself, Coot. Blame the men who attacked me. Blame Limbick."

"Believe me, I do! Still, if I hadn't involved you ..."

"You think you could have saved me, just like you probably think you could have saved the air base at Srinagar, if only you'd done more. Go easier on yourself, Coot. You've got a good heart. You try to do the right thing. You need to accept that nobody's perfect, not even Coot Jenkins."

"Now you're sounding like Frannie again."

"All the more reason to listen to what I'm telling you."

Coot smiled at her. "You should get some rest. Would you like me to stay here tonight? On the couch in the living room, I mean."

"Yes. Yes, I would like that. I thought I was safe here. Now I'm not sure I can sleep if I have to be here alone."

"What are your plans, given what's happened tonight?"

"I'll work from home for a few days." Diana stood up. "I'll get you a blanket for the sofa."

They walked slowly toward the living room.

"Coot..."

He turned to face her.

"I wouldn't mind another hug."

He wrapped his arms around her, trying not to squeeze her bruised body too tightly. She pressed against him. He stroked her hair once more, as she rested her cheek against his chest.

Diana lifted her face and looked into his eyes. "You're the best, Coot. Now let's both get some sleep."

Coot released her, despite an intense urge not to. "Goodnight, Diana. We'll talk in the morning."

* * *

Good news arrived at Coot's desk via the Internet on Monday: The British authorities announced the capture of a Mushrooms team that had attempted to enter the country through the Chunnel from France with a portable nuclear device concealed in a truck filled with crates of pomegranates. News sites trumpeted the success with headlines like "Fruitcase Nuke Attack Spoiled".

Emily Taggert came by Coot's office to talk about the discovery. "First Srinagar and now this! What's next?"

"The Brits estimated that the device they found in the truck had a yield of about a kiloton. That's big enough to level two dozen city blocks."

"How did they catch the terrorists?"

"The private security firm EuroSécurité is claiming credit for the capture," said Coot. "The British government recently hired the firm to operate the Chunnel checkpoint. It was part of the Tories' plan to outsource government services. Security is one area in which, worldwide, private companies are taking over functions that used to be performed by governments."

"Fortunately the guards, whoever they worked for, did not believe the men's claim that they had all recently been in France for radiation treatments," said Emily.

"Let's hope we continue to be lucky," said Coot. He remained worried. Three devices were still unaccounted for.

* * *

"George, we gotta figure out how the U.K. op was busted," said Mitch, as he sat on an old green vinyl-covered couch in the warehouse that had been their staging area and living quarters since he, George, and Jamie had taken one of the A.D.M.s from Doug.

"You think we ought to delay the New York op until we know what went wrong?" George said, as he paced back and forth in the small space.

"No way!" said Jamie. "We've already gotten further than the U.K. op. We're so close to the target." She stood in a semi-defiant pose, her hands on her hips.

"I'm with Jamie," said George. "We're so close to having another successful operation."

"Yeah, but suppose somebody tipped off the authorities," said Mitch.

"The failure was at a border crossing," said George. "We've already gotten the A.D.M.s into the U.S. and one of them almost into Manhattan."

"Right," said Jamie.

"The traitor could pick their time," said Mitch, not giving up easily. "And what about the nuke going into North Korea?"

"The Korean team hasn't been in communication with us," said George. "Internet access in the North is not widely available, and the security apparatus has its tentacles everywhere. We just have to wait and see whether they get the weapon into that mall in Seoul."

"I don't like not knowing whether they got into North Korea okay," said Jamie.

"Getting back to the U.K. bust, do you have any specific ideas as to who would or could have betrayed us?" asked George.

"I've been wondering about Sabrina," said Mitch.

"Sabrina? What the hell, Mitch?" said Jamie. "Is your anarchism just a mask for homophobia?"

"Easy, Jamie," said George. Turning to Mitch, he said, "Why do you suspect Sabrina?"

"She's a fucking addict," said Mitch. "She'd do anything to support her habit."

"Okay, so she does a little coke sometimes," admitted Jamie, "but she's worked as a software engineer at the same new media company for five years. Besides, she and I are really tight, you know. She likes me too much to sell me out."

"What does she *like* about you?" asked Mitch, leering at her.

"Damn you, Mitch," snarled Jamie. "Why are you nut toters so fascinated by what lesbians do in bed? Get over it."

"What does Sabrina know about our activities, Jamie?" asked George. "I hope the answer is 'Nothing.'"

"She knows I'm an anarchist and is even sympathetic, but she thinks I've gone to New York for an action on Wall Street."

"Did she ask you about Mushrooms after the Srinagar op?" asked

Mitch.

"She was interested in the animation that VI did for us."

"Did she ask you if you'd heard of Mushrooms?" said George, who had ceased pacing and was staring at Jamie.

"Yeah, of course, but I just told her they were new to me."

"You know," said George, "we talked about bringing Sabrina into Mushrooms to do the sort of work that VI did for us, but we decided that her drug use made her too much of a risk."

"Bullshit, George! You and Doug decided that. You guys blackballed her. She would have worked out just fine. Even Mitch thought so at the time."

"Maybe so," said Mitch, "but now I'm suspicious. I think somebody with inside knowledge tipped off the Brits."

"Nobody else knows where we are right now," said George. "Nobody else knows the exact date we plan to strike. Even if there is a traitor, he — or she — can do little to prevent tomorrow's action. I say we go ahead."

"I agree," said Jamie.

"What about you, Mitch?" asked George. "The longer we wait, the greater the chance we'll be discovered."

"I guess you're right," said Mitch. "Let's do it."

"We still have to decide on the yield," said Jamie. "How big a blast is required?"

"You know what I think," said Mitch.

"How about we use the minimum yield on this op," said George, "but threaten an explosion a hundred times as powerful the next time, unless people join the insurrection?"

"That might make people get off their butts," said Jamie.

"Yeah," said Mitch. "We make them choose sides."

"I'll set the A.D.M. to ten tons, then," said Jamie.

"No!" said Mitch, his face contorted with obvious frustration. "That might not be enough to take out such a huge building."

"What do you know about it?" said Jaime. "Ten tons is enough to destroy a city block."

Mitch scowled but did not challenge Jamie's assertion.

"This is exciting," said George. "We're on the verge of making history."

"Yes!" said Mitch, leaping to his feet. "Making history!"

"What about writing a new message for VI to hack onto media websites?" said Jamie calmly, still seated.

"Why bother?" said Mitch. "What's a message in comparison to an atomic blast?" He seemed impatient, agitated.

"People will instinctively rally behind the government after the attack," said George.

"We have to force them to switch to our side," said Jamie, "by threatening worse consequences if they don't rise up."

"And we have to give them hope that insurrection is possible," said George.

George spent the next few hours writing a script for VI to turn into a video. The result was a brief but eloquent plea for support, if a bit heavy on anarchist theory.

* * *

"Coot, we've got to talk. Can you come over?" Diana sounded stressed.

"Sure. What's the matter?"

"I'll tell you when you get here."

"Nothing serious, I hope."

"Just come over."

Coot did not press her further, but hopped into his car and drove to Diana's apartment. She greeted him at the front door, where just two days earlier they had shared a warm embrace. Coot was looking forward to another one, but Diana just motioned him inside.

"Please sit down." Her voice was flat, as if she were fighting to control it.

"The suspense is killing me, Diana. What's going on?"

"I found out about Frannie."

"What? What do you mean? Found out what?"

"I found out about the accident, Coot."

"What accident?"

"The car accident. When Frannie was killed."

The panic that overwhelmed Coot was far worse than what he had experienced on Rodman five weeks earlier. His heart was pounding. He was trembling. He felt weak all over. His mind was resisting a radical restructuring of his view of the world, his view of himself. Coot looked at Diana, his eyes wide in terror.

"You were driving."

Coot's anxiety grew worse. "Call Dr. Rosen," he croaked.

"Who?"

"Dr. Lou Rosen." Coot handed her his cell phone.

Diana took the phone, looked up "Rosen" in the contact list, and placed the call.

"Hello? Dr. Rosen? This is Diana Munson. I'm ... Yes, Coot's friend. I'm with him right now. He seems to be having an attack of some sort. ... Yes, here he is."

Coot took the phone from Diana. "I feel awful, much worse than before. I feel like I'm going to jump out of my skin. I think I'm cracking up. Can't you do something to help? ... No, I don't have any pills with me. ... Okay, let me check."

Coot turned to Diana. "Can you drive me to Dr. Rosen's office? He can meet us there."

"Of course."

"Dr. Rosen, we can be there in fifteen minutes. Thanks for your help. ... No, about the same. ... Goodbye."

"Coot, I thought you'd been lying to me about Frannie. I had no idea..."

"I can't talk about it right now, Diana. I'm having a hard time just holding myself together." Another wave of anxiety swept over him.

"Okay. Let's just go get in my car, then."

Coot and Diana left her apartment and were soon driving to Dr. Rosen's office. When they got to the office, Dr. Rosen met them at the door. "Come in, Coot. You, too, Miss Munson, if you don't mind." Dr. Rosen sat behind his desk, Coot and Diana in two chairs in front of the desk.

"Coot, how are you feeling now?"

"Still pretty bad. Worse than last time."

"Here, take this." Dr. Rosen handed Coot a small pill and also gave him some water in a paper cup.

Coot took the pill. "Thanks! I hope this works quickly."

"Miss Munson, that eye looks pretty bad. Were you injured tonight?"

"No. I was attacked by two intruders in my apartment a week ago. Coot and I were talking on the phone. He called the police. They arrived quickly, but not before I got this black eye and a split lip."

"I'm sorry. That must have been terrifying. If you need to talk with someone about it, I can provide a referral. Right now, though, I think we'd better concentrate on helping Coot through his crisis." Turning to Coot, Dr. Rosen said, "Please tell me exactly what happened tonight."

"Diana told me that Frannie died in an accident and that I'd been driving. I panicked, worse than ever before. I thought I was going insane. Nothing made sense. I felt desperate for help. I thought of you. Diana called. We came right over."

"Do you have any recollection of the accident now?"

"No."

"Would you mind if Miss Munson explained what she found out?"

"No. Nothing could be worse than what she's already told me. What happened, Diana?"

"I stayed home from work Friday, nursing my eye. I decided to find out what I could about Frannie. Coot had said she died of cancer a couple of years ago. He'd also said I reminded him of her in some ways, so I was curious about her. I searched for her on the Internet and found a number of articles that mentioned her. One article described the automobile accident in which she had been killed. The article said that Coot had been driving and had run a stop sign. Another car had hit their car on Frannie's side. She was pronounced dead at the scene."

Coot had buried his face in his hands. He was sobbing. He had forgot all about the accident. *Frannie, oh, Frannie! I'm so sorry!*

Dr. Rosen gave Coot a box of tissues. "Coot, tell us what you can remember about the day that Frannie died."

Coot wiped his eyes and look out the window. "I'll try. Some memories are coming back to me now. ... Frannie's melanoma was pretty far advanced. It had already gotten into her lungs and bones. I drove her to the hospital for another dose of radiation. She was very weak.

"Do you remember anything about the night she died?" Dr.

Rosen's voice was very gentle.

"We were driving home. It was raining heavily."

Coot paused and looked first at Dr. Rosen and then at Diana. "I got mixed up as to which cross street we were coming to. I thought we had the right-of-way. I didn't see the stop sign."

"What happened next?"

Coot composed himself for another attempt to describe the events he had long suppressed. "Another car got to the intersection at the same time. Frannie screamed. ... It hit our car on Frannie's side. ... Maybe if she hadn't been so weak from the cancer and the radiation she would have survived the accident. ... Instead, ..." Reliving that awful night was so horrible that he couldn't continue.

"Coot, I know this is very difficult for you, but it's best if you get it all out."

"Instead, she died in my arms. ... Her last words were 'Coot, dear Coot...' ... I wanted to kill myself. I want to kill myself right now."

Diana was crying silently. Dr. Rosen handed her another box of tissues.

"I didn't see the stop sign. It was raining and dark, and I just didn't see it. Oh, God, it was my fault, all my fault!"

"Do you remember anything after the accident, Coot?"

"I went with Frannie in the ambulance.... They took her to the morgue in the hospital.... After a while I got a cab and went home.... The house was dark. I left the lights off. I sat in the living room for an hour or two, in shock, numb... I think I was already getting into denial about what had happened. ...The next few days are a blur. Frannie's body was buried intact, as she had requested. 'Nobody wants organs from someone with cancer,' she'd said."

"How did you cope with Frannie's death after that?"

"I threw myself into my work with renewed purpose. I guess it was because I had not been able to protect Frannie that I wanted to protect everyone else from the greatest danger I knew — nuclear annihilation. I had even less patience than before with people who ignored or denied this danger. I wanted to punish them for their failure to protect *their* loved ones."

"You certainly let Limbick have it with both barrels!" said Diana.

"Not to mention that jerk in the diner," said Coot ruefully.

"And now you're talking about punishing yourself," observed Dr. Rosen.

"Yes," said Coot.

"No, Coot, please — think about your kids. Think about ... me." Diana's eyes again filled with tears.

Coot stared at the floor. He felt he didn't deserve to live.

"Coot, you're feeling the pain of what happened to Frannie as if for the first time. You'll need some time to absorb the experience, to adjust to what for you is a new reality."

"I don't think I *can* adjust to this, Dr. Rosen. It's just too awful."

"You may surprise yourself, Coot, with your ability to recover from this shock. It's natural, once you're no longer in denial, to blame yourself. You may also become depressed. Then, slowly, things will get better."

"I feel so guilty about Frannie and so hopeless that I'll ever be able to forgive myself."

"The medicine you've been taking to reduce panic attacks will also help with depression. Eventually you'll be able not only to accept your responsibility for what happened to Frannie but also to develop a renewed sense of purpose in life."

"I wish I could believe that."

"One day you will."

Coot and Diana thanked Dr. Rosen and began the drive back to the apartment.

"I never told you this, Diana, but that day in the elevator I felt as if Frannie were reaching out through you to comfort me."

"Maybe she was. Her last words expressed love, not blame, you know."

"Help me to remember that, will you?"

The next morning Coot went on his regular run with Roger and Jack.

"Why'd you guys...never question me...when I went on about...how Frannie had died...of cancer instead of...the accident?" Coot asked his friends between breaths as they jogged along through the park the morning after Coot's discovery of his own role in Frannie's death.

"The cancer was all...you talked about...afterwards," said Roger. "No mention of...the accident."

"I though the accident...was just too painful...for you to talk about," said Jack.

"Not just to talk about...too painful even...to remember....I didn't have a clue...about it till last night."

Coot told his two friends about how Diana had unwittingly forced him to confront the truth, with help from Dr. Rosen.

"Man, that's weird!" said Roger.

"How are you coping?" asked Jack.

"It's been really hard," said Coot. "I feel so awful...for having caused...the accident."

"Wasn't it raining...really hard that night?" asked Roger. "The police didn't...even charge you...for running the stop sign...because the...visibility...was so poor."

"That's right," said Jack. "Go easier...on yourself....Anybody could've...made the same mistake...under those conditions."

"I suppose so," said Coot, "but I still feel...responsible....If I had only...been more careful...She was so weak."

"Are you *trying*," said Roger, "to make yourself crazy?"

Coot laughed as heartily as he could while running. He felt as if the black clouds making his mental landscape so gloomy had been pierced by bright beams of sunshine. Roger's directness could be very helpful. "Trying to or not...that's exactly what I was doing!"

"You're past the crazy stage," said Jack. "Now you should focus...on living...in the present...with hopes for...the future."

"Right!" said Roger. "Does that future...include Diana?...She seems...more important to you...than you let on."

"She reminded me...of Frannie at first," said Coot. "Kind of weird....The more time...I spend with her...the more unique she seems....I'd like us to be...more than friends."

"How does *she* feel?" asked Jack.

"Hard to say....I'm sure she cares for me....I'm not sure...in exactly what way."

"You mean...romantically...or otherwise?" asked Jack.

"Yes," said Coot. "She wants to avoid...involvement...with anyone."

"Why?" asked Roger.

"I can't discuss it," said Coot. "She told me...in confidence."

"What she wants...intellectually," said Jack, "and what she wants...emotionally...may differ...and may change."

"I can only hope!" said Coot.

After Coot's piano lesson on Saturday afternoon, this time on Diana's rented upright, he and Diana went to Mobius for dinner.

"My treat," said Coot, as they sat down at their table. "I owe you at least a fine meal for setting me on the road to recovery."

"Are you feeling better, then?"

"Somewhat. I talked with Jack and Roger this morning about the accident. It's beginning to seem more like bad luck than bad driving." Coot unfolded his napkin and put it in his lap. "I still feel like I could have prevented the crash if I'd been looking more carefully for road signs."

Diana looked at him, her brow furrowed, her lower lip protruding. "I'm sorry I caused you to relive so much pain."

"You did me a favor."

"I hope so."

"Enough about me. What's new with you?"

"Monday I've got to take the Acela to New York."

"There you go. Not much time for friends."

"I'm meeting with the Macintosh Consulting Group. In the Empire State Building."

"I guess you've been there before."

"Sure, but only as a tourist. Did you know it's been sold?"

"No."

"Billionaire Myron Pepsey sold it to some Saudi investors."

"Really? Pepsey's on the S.A.F.E. board. I met with him recently."

"Cool. What's he like?"

"Very smooth."

"How did he make his billions?"

"He has many irons in the fire. He runs some businesses directly and participates in others through private equity investments, I hear."

"Interesting. I wonder why he sold the building. It's one of the biggest symbols of American wealth and power in the world."

"Yeah. I have no idea."

"Well, anyway, send me your itinerary, would you? In case I need to talk. I promise not to call during your meetings."

"Sure."

Diana put down her fork. "Do you think there are going to be more attacks?"

"You mean by Mushrooms? Yes, I think they'll try again."

"Where?"

"Could be anywhere. They've attacked in South Asia and Europe. I can't help thinking we're next on their list."

"It's reassuring that they've been caught once since Srinagar."

"Yes, but it's no guarantee that they won't learn from their mistakes or get lucky."

Coot and Diana were finishing their desserts when she exclaimed, "Oh, I almost forgot to ask whether your technician thinks he'll be able to repair your piano."

"In short, yes."

"That's wonderful!"

"He said he'd have to replace the sound board and the pin block, but the action is unharmed. Of course he'll also have to replace the mahogany veneer on the sides of the case and legs."

"Have the police found who threw the bomb?"

"Didn't I tell you? Sorry, I've had a lot on my mind lately. It was the same guys who attacked you. What's more, one of them was the maniac who tried to assault me in the diner. They were bragging about it in the lock-up and a snitch overheard them. We'll have to testify if the case goes to trial."

"I could do without reliving that night!"

"That's understandable," said Coot. "You know, I've been wondering whether that guy from the diner would have attacked us if I had not humiliated him in front of his wife and kids."

* * *

6:30 Monday morning. Washington, D.C. Diana, already awake and thinking about the day ahead, shut off her alarm clock before it could shatter the silence in her apartment. She had packed a small bag the night before for her trip to New York, so she just had to get dressed and eat breakfast. She put on a dark gray pinstriped skirt and matching jacket over a pastel blue blouse. The woman in her mirror looked as elegant, professional, and confident as Diana could manage. Breakfast was instant oatmeal and an apple, with coffee to go. There was no time for anything more elaborate. Diana hated to be late. She was determined to catch the 8:00 Acela, as if her life depended on it. She made it to the waiting Acela with fifteen minutes to spare. She loved riding trains. They never got stuck in traffic jams and she could walk around on long trips.

Despite worries that someone would ask her a question she could not answer, Diana usually looked forward to encounters with other experts, like her friends at the Macintosh Group, the country's oldest and most prestigious computer security consultancy. She remembered laughing with them after Apple appropriated the firm's name for its latest computer, and later, when Apple stores opened their Genius Bars. Steve Jobs's chutzpah was breathtaking. Diana knew who the real Macintosh geniuses were. She very much wanted to hire one of them for her new team in Washington. She hoped she would not embarrass herself by failing to understand some subtlety in their work. She had just begun to re-read some of the group's papers on cyber security when the Acela left Union Station — on time

*　*　*

8:30 A.M. Jersey City. Jamie had been awake for hours. For breakfast she had eaten a couple of Egg McMuffins that George had brought back for her. Having gone over in her mind the plan for deploying a small atomic weapon in midtown Manhattan, she was confident it would work — unless they had been betrayed or some aggressive cop decided to inspect her backpack. Even then, if she could arm the A.D.M. quickly enough and Mitch had balls enough to detonate it with his cell phone, they could do a lot of damage. Although their last act would be spectacular, she did not want this to be a suicide mission.

Jamie realized that she, as a big woman with a large backpack, would be even more conspicuous than usual, but she hoped she would be intimidating enough that no one would try to interfere with her. Jamie wished she had had more experience in shopping in women's clothing stores. Would she be able to take the backpack into a dressing room, a rest room, or ideally a private area of the store? That's where the intimidation factor would help. If bullying failed, she and Mitch might have to improvise.

She really did not want to kill civilians face-to-face. Her experience with accidental death in Afghanistan had left her with strongly negative feelings about that sort of thing. The look on a particular dead girl's face was continually in her mind for months after she returned to the States. Besides, the problems with that scenario were obvious. It would take time to lock the store, herd the staff and any customers into a hidden area, and incapacitate them. One of the people might manage to call for help. A passerby might see or hear what was going on inside the store. No, they would have to be more creative. They had scouted out several stores and restaurants in the area, in case the clothing store did not work out.

"Jamie!" said George. "Snap out of it! We've got work to do."

Jamie's thoughts returned to the present. "Relax, George," she said testily. "There's not much left to do, but I'll finish the prep, if that'll make you happy." She lifted her imposing body from her chair and went across the room to the A.D.M.

"You guys still okay with a ten-ton yield?" asked Jamie. "That's enough to bring down the target."

"How can you be sure?" Mitch was once again in challenge mode. "Did you ever actually see one of those weapons in action?"

Jamie thought of a few things she'd like to say to Mitch, but she stifled them. "Of course not. All the tests were underground, years before I got into the Army."

"The target's a quarter of mile high. We'll look pathetic if we can't even blow out the windows on the observation deck with a nuclear weapon."

"Mitch has a good point." George had always tried to stay neutral during Jamie and Mitch's verbal jousts, so his agreement with her prickly comrade made Jamie reconsider her plan.

She set the yield of the A.D.M. to one hundred tons of TNT while Mitch did a final check of the cell-phone detonator.

They loaded the device into one of the large backpacks that Jamie had bought in Maine, then lifted the ensemble into the van.

George drove them to the Newport PATH station in Jersey City, across the Hudson River from Manhattan.

George and Mitch helped Jamie into the 150-pound backpack. Her size and strength training made it easier for her to handle the weight than for short and skinny Mitch. She had carried combat loads that were as heavy as the A.D.M.

"I'll be looking for you back here just after 10:30," George reminded them. "That means you need to catch the 10:17 train at 33rd Street. We need to get out of this area quickly, in case we missed something and someone can link us to the event."

Jamie and Mitch hurried to catch the train to 33rd Street in New York. Their plan required them to be at the store when it opened at 10:00. They had only ten minutes of slack built into their schedule.

* * *

9:25 A.M. Near Philadelphia. Diana looked up from the Macintosh Group papers she had been reading. The Acela was slowing down as it entered the City of Brotherly Love. Diana was having difficulty following some of the reasoning about a proposed authentication protocol in one of the papers. The Macintosh authors claimed to have proved that their new protocol was secure, provided the underlying crypto system was secure. Diana was not sure they had done it. Had she missed something?

Diana's thoughts drifted toward her friend Coot. She had enjoyed his company the past few weeks, especially the musical aspects. The night she was attacked, he was so comforting, like her father or Keith would have been. Yet he said he wanted to be more than friends. Did she? She liked and admired Coot. She looked forward to seeing him. She had long ago decided not to become involved with anyone, yet Coot was not like Keith or other men her age. He had already reared two children. She could imagine outliving him, which itself was a disturbing thought. She was confused, uncertain about how she felt. He obviously cared for her, but why? Was it just because she reminded him of his dead wife? That would be creepy. She did not want to become romantically involved with a man who saw her as the second version of someone else.

* * *

9:27 A.M. Jersey City. The PATH train was late. Jamie fumed. They only had about ten minutes to spare. A woman's voice on the P.A. system announced that the 9:26 train had been disabled. The next train was due at 9:31. When it arrived, it was full of its own passengers and the ones who had been on the earlier train. There was not enough room for an Amazon with a huge backpack. Jamie was getting nervous. She felt conspicuous. She kept glancing at a surveillance camera in the station, although she knew she should not do anything to draw attention to herself. At last the 9:36 train arrived. Jamie and Mitch boarded the somewhat less crowded train, their ten-minute cushion gone. They kept apart from each other and did not speak. The other passengers seemed preoccupied with their paper or electronic entertainment. Except for two PATH policemen, who were looking at Mitch and whispering to each other. Despite his anglicized name, Mitch had the dark complexion of a recent Latin American immigrant. He had been hassled several times by police who suspected he might be undocumented. This was not a good day for another episode of racial profiling. Jamie felt helpless to intervene, as the cops moved over to Mitch and began to quiz him. Finally he took out his wallet and showed them some identification, and they left him alone. Jamie could tell he was furious and hoped that he would not let the incident interfere with their mission.

At the 33rd Street station they climbed the stairs with their fellow passengers, who could not have realized that they were escorting the cause of their own imminent deaths. Jamie did her best not to show the difficulty of carrying the 150-pound backpack up to street level, although she could not help breathing heavily by the time she and Mitch reached the top.

As they reached street level, Jamie said, "Did you see the surveillance cameras in the stations?"

"Yeah," Mitch confirmed. "Nothing we can do about it now."

The two conspirators separated, made their way up 6th Avenue, turned right on 34th Street, and walked until they reached the clothing store they had chosen, just as it opened at 10 AM. Jamie glanced across the street at the entrance to the Empire State Building. She had always wanted to climb to the top and look down on Manhattan. One more dream she would never realize. When they went into the store, the two saleswomen, one in her twenties, the other middle-aged, were talking with each other, seemingly indifferent to their first customers of the day. For once, that was a good thing.

As she got closer to the two women, she heard the older one say, "Well, you may not need coffee, but I sure do." With that, the woman walked out. Without someone else to talk with, the younger saleswoman looked at Jamie, as if seeing her for the first time, and asked, "Can I help you find something?"

"No, thanks, I'm just browsing," said Jamie. The saleswoman smiled thinly and went over to the checkout counter.

Jamie and Mitch walked around the store, moving gradually toward the dressing rooms. Jamie took a moment to look at the clothes on each rack they passed.

"Who knew insurrection could be so much fun?" Jamie whispered to Mitch as she picked out a pair of jeans with spectacular embroidered decorations. Then, more loudly, "I'll go try these on." Her watch read 10:05.

Jamie was about to enter the farthest dressing room, when the young woman called out, "Sorry, but you can't go in there with that backpack."

Jamie froze. "Where can I leave it, then?"

"We usually keep packages and stuff here at the register." The woman was chewing her gum vigorously, as if she was revving herself up for a confrontation with someone twice her size.

"I don't think it will fit," said Jamie.

"Can we put it in the stock room?" asked Mitch, who had been lurking silently until then.

"Customers aren't allowed back there," said the clerk.

"Aw, come on!" said Mitch. "Are you trying to make it impossible for us to shop here?"

The young woman seemed flustered, indecisive.

"You can come with me and make sure no harm's done," said Jamie, in her most big-sisterly manner. Looking the clerk in the eyes was becoming difficult.

"I guess that would be okay," said the girl.

Jamie relaxed a bit at this development. Leaving the backpack in the stock room was preferable to leaving it in a dressing room.

The two women went to the rear of the shop, where a single door led into a smaller room filled with all manner of women's clothing on racks and in boxes. There was no way for Jamie to arm the A.D.M. without the sales girl's seeing her, so she took off the backpack and set it down between two large boxes to the left of the door. She and the clerk went back into the main part of the store, where Mitch was looking at some embroidered blouses. He glanced up as the two women approached.

"I just put it down," Jamie said, hoping that Mitch would understand that the A.D.M. was not yet armed.

"Okay," said Mitch. "Why don't you try on those jeans we were looking at, while I get some help picking out a blouse for my sister?"

Jamie nodded, then took the jeans she had picked out earlier into the dressing room nearest the stock room. Meanwhile, Mitch wandered from rack to rack, drawing the saleswoman further from the stock room. Jamie waited until the woman bent over to pick up a blouse that Mitch had dropped, then crouched low and crept into the stock room. She quickly opened the backpack, armed the A.D.M., closed the backpack, and locked the double zipper that provided access to the A.D.M. She then hid the backpack in a different location, so that the clerk could not quickly find it. After making sure that Mitch had the sales clerk occupied, she snuck back into the dressing room. In a moment she emerged, carrying the jeans.

"These are the biggest they have, and they still don't fit," she announced.

"I haven't found what I was looking for, either," said Mitch. He thanked the girl for her help, then joined Jamie on the way out of the store.

"Wait," said the clerk, "You haven't got your backpack. You can't leave it here."

"You're crazy if you think I'm going to carry that sucker all around Midtown," said Jamie. "It'll be fine where it is."

"No, I mean, we're not supposed to let people leave any packages in the store."

"Bullshit!" said Mitch, his usual manner at last appropriate to the situation.

"That backpack had better be where I left it when I get back, you hear?" said Jamie, as if the younger woman were a new recruit. She and Mitch left the store, separated, and walked quickly northwest along 34rd Street, and turned downtown on 6th Avenue, descending the steps into the PATH station in time to board the train they wanted. Their car was less crowded than on the trip into the city. Without the backpack, Jamie did not feel so conspicuous.

* * *

10:25 A.M. 34th Street, New York City. Julie Sanchez returned to the store with her coffee and a muffin. She knew she should not eat so many sweets. Her husband had mentioned the weight she had gained since she started working at the clothing store, but she did love those chocolate chip muffins at the coffee shop. She knew he would never leave her over a few extra pounds, not loving their boy and girl the way he did. Inside she found the new hire, Amy Schuler, in a panic.

"What's the matter?" she asked the younger woman as she laid a comforting hand on her shoulder.

"That huge woman left her backpack. I told her not to. She just said she wasn't going to carry it around all day."

"That's not good," said Julie. Her instinct was to take this incident seriously. "Where is it?"

"She put it in the stock room while I watched." Amy hesitated, then added, "Now it's gone!"

"Gone? Did she come back for it?"

"No, no. I mean, it's not where she left it," said Amy. "She must have moved it while I was helping her friend."

Julie reached for the phone at the checkout counter and dialed 911. When the police dispatcher answered, Julie explained the situation. The dispatcher seemed to take her report seriously, asking her questions about the size, shape, and weight of the backpack. He promised to send an N.Y.P.D. bomb squad immediately.

"What should we do?" Amy asked Julie.

"One of us should wait for the police," said Julie. "I'm in charge today. I'll wait."

"I'm the only witness," said Amy. "I'll stay. If it's a bomb, well, your kids need you more than my folks need me."

Julie was tempted by the offer, but she was afraid she'd lose her job if she left the store in the hands of a new hire during an emergency.

"You're very brave and thoughtful, Amy. We'll both wait for the police. Meanwhile, let's look for that backpack."

* * *

10:33 A.M. Jersey City. George was waiting for them in the van as they left the Newport station.

"How'd it go?" he asked.

"The A.D.M.'s deployed and armed," said Jamie. After getting into the van, she described where she had left the device.

"What if someone discovers it?" said George.

"The electronics and the A.D.M. are well-hidden, the main compartment is locked, and the store clerks we saw wouldn't be able to move it," said Jamie. "They were even scrawnier than Mitch."

Mitch glared at her. "You forgot to mention that the PATH stations have surveillance cameras."

"Uh-oh," said George. "You two had better get into different clothes."

While Mitch and Jamie took turns changing clothes in the rear of the van, George drove south, picked up I-78, and headed west.

* * *

10:35 A.M. 34th Street, New York City. Julie met the N.Y.P.D. bomb squad when it arrived at the store and ushered them into the stock room. She and Amy had not yet found the backpack. Amy was still looking. The squad members fanned out, tearing apart racks of clothing, ripping open boxes, in a systematic but frantic search for the backpack. Amy was pulled off the search and grilled for a few minutes by another officer, who then radioed descriptions of a large woman and a small man to police headquarters.

Possibly precious minutes were passing, Julie realized. She worried for Amy, who had her whole life ahead of her. She asked Amy's interrogator whether she could send the girl home. The officer agreed to let her go, but gave her his card, in case she remembered any other details about the two suspects. Amy thanked Julie and left.

* * *

10:40 A.M. Amtrak tunnel between New Jersey and New York. Diana always enjoyed her trips to New York. She expected today to be no exception. From the train she had seen the Empire State Building, where the Macintosh Group's offices were located. The Acela had just entered the tunnel under the Hudson River. In just a few minutes it would emerge from the tunnel in Manhattan, cross the open tracks west of the post office, then disappear again before coming to a halt in the bowels of Penn Station. From there Diana would climb the stairs into the station, then walk one block north and two blocks east to her destination on 34th Street. In fact, Diana thought happily, it looked like a nice day for a walk.

* * *

10:44 A.M. 34th Street, New York City. "Sarge, I found something!" shouted Officer Scott McEwan of the N.Y.P.D. bomb squad. "Goddam, it's heavy!" He turned over a box labeled "Playtex®", pulled out a large backpack, and showed it to his converging teammates.

"Open it up!" commanded Sergeant José Vargas. The sergeant was on his sixty-third suspicious package investigation. The most dangerous case till now had been a briefcase full of fireworks with a crude timer that had failed to detonate at a Russian restaurant in Brooklyn. This case felt different somehow. He thought about his wife, Constanza, and their four kids. Would he ever see them again?

Using bolt cutters to get past the lock, McEwan unzipped the main compartment, exposing several knobs and switches, a blinking red light — and a cell phone.

"Oh, Christ," said Vargas. "That looks an awful lot like the control panel for the demolition nukes the Army had years ago." He was fortunate to have had experience with such munitions in the Army. That experience had helped him get into the bomb squad, get promoted, and now recognize the grave danger facing his adopted city. He activated his communications unit and said, "Code Red! Code Red! Sergeant José Vargas here. Possible nuclear device found at 34th and 5th. Evacuate the area! Evacuate the area!"

"You, get out of here!" Vargas shouted to the middle-aged store employee who had been watching the search from just inside the door to the stock room.

"But I have to..." she began.

"Forget the store. Soon there may not *be* a store," he screamed. "Run!"

"Take the subway at Herald Square. Get the hell away from here," Larry Chan, second in command, urged her, as he took her by the arm and led her toward the front of the store.

"The thing may go off if the cell phone's removed," McEwan suggested.

"We gotta risk it," said Vargas. "It may explode any second." He reached for the phone.

* * *

10:46 A.M. I-78 west of Newark-Liberty Airport. Mitch, as planned, got out his cell phone, which had a new SIM card to hide his identity, and pressed a speed-dial button.

"Die, motherfuckers!" he snarled.

* * *

The sound of the incoming cell phone call had reached the ears of Sergeant José Vargas and the nerve endings in his cochlea had signaled the auditory cortex in his brain, but the interpretation of these signals had not reached the sergeant's conscious mind before his body was vaporized by the several tens of million degree heat generated when the much faster electronic signals from that same cell phone call triggered the explosion of an atomic demolition munition with a yield equivalent to a hundred tons of TNT.

A few fragments of the Empire State Building were found hours, days, even weeks later, some as far away as New Jersey, but most of the great building, along with the twenty thousand people who worked there and hundreds of tourists from around the world, was pulverized by the blast or incinerated by the fireball. The other buildings and people in the immediate area fared no better.

The tissues that comprised Julie Sanchez were blown apart by the 5 pounds per square inch overpressure of the blast half a block behind her as she neared the steps down into the Herald Square subway station. The fragments of her body became part of the expanding fireball from the Mushrooms explosion. Her family would never recover a single atom to bury. Thousands of other families endured a similar lack of closure.

Even though the 1 p.s.i overpressure at Madison Square Garden was insufficient to destroy its superstructure, its glass façade was shattered by the blast wave, shredding those unfortunate enough to be in the way of the flying fragments. Paper in the offices inside caught fire, so that people who were not shredded or burned to death died of smoke inhalation. Similar fires burned in thousands of buildings all over midtown Manhattan. Water pressure dropped, due not only to the many fire department activities but also to a multitude of broken pipes. Most fires burned out of control, until they consumed whatever people and property were in their paths.

Amy Schuler was a lucky girl. She had walked quickly to the Herald Square subway station and caught a waiting uptown B train. At 10:46 the train was approaching the Times Square station when she heard a deafening noise and felt her car being driven violently forward. Her head snapped backwards, hitting the thin metal wall of the trainman's compartment behind her, then rebounded, causing what would later be diagnosed as a grade 4 whiplash injury. Amy would also suffer headaches, plus pain in her neck, shoulders, and left arm, but she knew from the moment of the accident that she was lucky to be alive. Many passengers in her car were not moving, not even moaning, while others lay in contorted positions on the floor or were wrapped around poles.

Above ground at Times Square, the great flashing signs that were not shielded by buildings were destroyed by the blast wave, showering fragments of neon tubes and LEDs by the millions onto the unlucky people below. Of course panic infected everyone. People stampeded uptown, away from the blast, trampling the old, the frail, the merely slow, the homeless lying on their cardboard mats or defending their bags of recycled soft drink cans. The air was full of dust, some of it radioactive fallout. Instead of remaining indoors to escape this real danger, people by the tens of thousands poured out of buildings and joined the scared, the panicked, the hurtling masses, yearning to breathe free.

And the Acela Express carrying Diana Munson was just entering the open area west of the large Post Office building when the blast wave hit it.

CHAPTER 7

After the Fall

Coot was returning to his desk from the restroom when the news broke. The S.A.F.E. office was in chaos.

"Oh, God, no!"

"Where, exactly?"

"The Empire State Building? Gone?"

"The fucking bastards!"

Coot hurried to his desk. The computer screen showed 10:52 A.M. Diana was going to New York today. He looked through his e-mail for the itinerary she had promised to send. There it was: 2104 Acela Express, departing Union Station at 8:00 A.M. and arriving in New York Penn Station at 10:46 A.M. Dear God, no!

Coot grabbed his cell phone and called Diana's number. Voice mail. He asked Diana to call him back as soon as she could.

He checked various news sites. The New York Times site was not responding. The Washington Post site was reporting the time of the attack as 10:46. Diana could have been out of the station by the time the bomb went off. He tried to check the train's status at the Amtrak site, but the server was very slow to respond. After several tries for each link, he got to the Train Status page for the 2104, but the actual arrival time for the Acela was not listed. He cursed.

Coot jumped up from his desk and headed for the break room. Most people in the office were crowded around the large flat-screen TV on the wall, watching CNN's coverage. The screen showed an aerial view of Lower Manhattan. The news anchor reported that destruction was total in a large section of Midtown.

The scene could have been from Hiroshima or Nagasaki after they were leveled by atomic bombs in August 1945.

Many of the staff were staring, red-eyed and mute, at the images from CNN's helicopter, which hovered a mile upwind from the spot where the very symbol of New York had stood mere minutes before. Coot noticed that several places he had visited over the years were also gone: the City University Graduate Center and a New York Public Library building. As Coot watched, the image of the devastated area began shrinking — the helicopter was withdrawing, its crew's radiation exposure having reached the recommended limit.

Coot debated calling Jill Meecham, but decided not to, since she was bound to be totally consumed with the government's response to the attack. Especially when Mushrooms was behind the attack and might have two more devices on their way to other targets.

Coot found a seat and watched the coverage of the worst disaster in American history, a catastrophe that may have ended the life of his dear Diana and tens of thousands of other innocent people.

Coot was startled by a sudden announcement on the public address system: "This is Ben. All professional staff should gather immediately in the large conference room to discuss S.A.F.E.'s response to the attack in New York." Coot walked quickly to join his assembling colleagues.

After everyone had found a seat at the large table or at least a place to stand, S.A.F.E. chairman Ben Barker stood up and waited until everyone had stopped talking. "The explosion of a nuclear device in New York this morning is terrible evidence that S.A.F.E. has been right about the need to eliminate nuclear weapons. As great as the devastation was, the tactical nuclear weapon that exploded was much less powerful than a strategic weapon! There are still thousands of tactical nukes in our country, in Russia, and who knows where else. They have gotten much less attention than their strategic big brothers, but as today's attack shows, they can do enormous harm. We must redouble our efforts for the elimination of all nuclear weapons. The question is, how to go about it? I welcome your ideas. Who wants to go first?"

Several hands shot up at once. "Joe, you're up."

Coot looked at the man Barker had chosen to speak first: Joe Giancola, Publicity.

"Ben, the attack raises our issues into public awareness like nothing has ever done before. We must propose a series of actions that the public will perceive as reasonable and practical. The opponents of nuclear disarmament will use this tragedy to argue for the necessity of maintaining a nuclear arsenal indefinitely. We have to play offense and defense at the same time."

"Thanks, Joe. Arlene?"

Coot turned around to see a short, stocky woman standing in the back of the room: Arlene Schmidt, Congressional Liaison.

"The Congress is divided on nuclear disarmament. Who are our allies? Members who want to slash all parts of the military budget, conventional as well as nuclear. Members who want to balance the budget at all costs, even if that means cutting back some defense programs. Members who understand that nuclear weapons make everyone less safe in the long run. My team has a list of members we think can be persuaded to join this last group, and we plan to lobby them hard."

After several other people had spoken, Barker turned to Coot. "I didn't see your hand up, Coot, but given your performance in the debate against Larry Limbick a couple of weeks ago, I want to hear how *you* think we can get the public onto our side."

Several of Coot's colleagues cheered.

"Well, Ben," Coot began, "Maybe you should ask somebody who can make our case without getting firebombed."

A couple of people laughed nervously, but most people waited quietly for Coot to continue.

"Not letting me off the hook, huh? Okay. We need to reach out beyond our usual supporters. We need to write articles for publications that cater to popular music fans, to gun owners, to fashion-conscious women, to guys interested in building stuff. We need to place people for interviews on popular TV and radio shows. Beyond influencing opinion, though, we need to get people to take action. We should hire someone to produce short videos that people can view online and easily share with their friends. We should make it simple for people who visit our website to send letters to their congressional representatives. Finally, we should find a way to help people organize themselves locally into groups that can pressure elected officials. We would need to support these local groups by producing videos that they can show at meetings and distribute to their friends. It would also be useful to develop a roster of knowledgeable people willing to speak at the groups' meetings."

"That's quite a list, Coot," said Barker. "Rather than assigning people to work on your suggestions, I'm asking for volunteers. If anyone is interested, send me an e-mail stating the project you'd most like to work on. We need to move fast on this. That's all for now. Thanks for your ideas, everyone."

"Good plan!" Emily said as she hurried past Coot. "I want to work on the videos."

* * *

"Goddamn, that was sweet!" Mitch enthused, as he, George, and Jamie got back into their van and resumed driving west on Interstate 80 through Pennsylvania.

Each time they had stopped to change drivers, they had taken a few minutes to watch the television coverage of the destruction of the Empire State Building and much of midtown Manhattan. Video from helicopters showed the extent of the devastation. Buildings from Bryant Park south to 27th Street and Madison Avenue had suffered in varying degrees, from light structural damage to complete destruction. Amateur recordings were more graphic: Monster traffic jams, thousands of people fleeing for their lives, fires consuming entire blocks, bodies burned beyond recognition. At U.N. headquarters due east of the blast site, many windows had been blown out and hundreds of staff were being treated for injuries due to flying glass. Japan's ambassador to the United Nations had issued a statement expressing outrage at the attack and sympathy for the victims. Iran's ambassador suggested that the attack was divine retribution against the "Great Satan" for the obliteration of Hiroshima and Nagasaki.

"How'd ya like that old Jap saying it reminded him of walking around Hiroshima after the atom bomb leveled it?" continued

Mitch.

"Give it a rest, will you," demanded Jamie. "We killed a lot of people today. Doesn't that bother you?"

"It's a little late for worrying about the casualties," said Mitch, turning around in the front passenger's seat and glaring at Jamie.

"You like hurting people," said Jamie, her face flushed. "You're the one who demanded a bigger blast, with more deaths."

"Yeah? They were probably useless morons anyway. And besides, some of them could have identified us."

"You're such a callous bastard, you know that?"

"Get off my case, Jamie. You're the expert on killing people."

"I'm an expert on demolition. You just like killing."

"C'mon, guys, it's over," said George, who was driving. "Our goal is to incite insurrection. Let's talk about the next operation."

"I'm sick of her superior attitude," said Mitch, turning around in his seat and staring at the rocky sides of the cut through which their section of I-80 was passing.

Jamie did not respond to Mitch's remark, but also studied the Pennsylvania countryside as they continued their journey west.

George broke the uncomfortable silence. "Doug and Bennie should have gotten the other A.D.M. into the warehouse by now."

"Right," said Jamie. "From there we can deploy a device anywhere in the area. Do we really need to detonate it downtown?"

"We agreed on the target with Tipton," said George. "I don't think we can change it now."

"Getting squeamish, Jamie?" said Mitch.

"I'm just not as bloodthirsty as you."

"I see. You spill blood, but you don't swallow." Mitch smiled lasciviously. "Sabrina okay with that?"

"Back off, Mitch," said Jamie, her face reddening once again. "You're unbelievably crude."

"Better lay off the taunts, Mitch," said George, worried that his team was coming apart just when it needed cohesion the most. "We have important work to do. Let's focus on that."

"So we're still doing the Sears Tower?" said Mitch, "or whatever it's called now?"

"Yes," said George.

"When will the insurrection start?" Mitch asked. "There's no sign of revolt yet."

"It's been just a few hours since the Empire State Building went down," said Jamie. "We should wait at least a few days to see whether people rise up, as our video message urged them to do."

"Judging from people's reactions at the last rest stop, they're not gonna do squat after just one attack," said Mitch. "Did you hear how everyone hooted when the avatar urged them to rise up?"

"Yeah," said Jamie, for once agreeing with Mitch. "We need to show we're serious about insurrection before they'll do anything."

"Don't you think exploding two nuclear bombs showed we're serious?" said George.

"Sure, but having an A.D.M. captured made us look incompetent," said Jamie.

"And we still don't know how the team was busted," added Mitch.

The insurrectionists drove on. Even the pop music radio stations were broadcasting news from New York. One station reported that the New York police were searching for surveillance camera recordings from the area around the blast. The issue seemed to be whether any recordings from just before the blast had been transmitted outside the area that was destroyed.

"What if they spot Mitch and me on the surveillance video from the PATH stations?" said Jamie.

"Yeah," said Mitch, a sly grin spreading across his thin face. "I bet you and your giant backpack would get their attention now."

"We'd better quit going into places with TVs," said George, "in case pictures of you guys turn up."

"Suppose they find video of us getting out of the van," said Mitch. "They might get the van's license number."

"We've got to hope they don't," said George, "or at least not quickly."

"I don't like leaving so much to chance," said Jamie.

"Me neither," said Mitch. "We'd be the most wanted people in the country, if they knew who we were."

George kept glancing into the rear view mirrors, checking for police cars. The others turned around occasionally and scanned the traffic behind them.

"Uh-oh," said Jamie after one such check. "Smoky coming up fast in the left lane."

The Pennsylvania State Police car overtook them, and a trooper looked over at them. The trio stared straight ahead, as if unaware of his interest. George glanced at the speedometer, which had been displaying 70 ever since he set the cruise control. The officer said something he could not hear. Had their license plate been found on video? The car sped past them. Apparently the van had not yet been identified with the attack.

"Cops make me nervous," said Mitch, his eyes still on the patrol car.

"Just stay calm and we'll be fine," said George.

When they reached the Ohio state line, it was almost 7 PM. They were hungry. They would have to drive over six hours without stopping to arrive at their destination by midnight.

"I'm worried about getting to the warehouse late at night," said George. "Someone might see us and get suspicious."

"True," said Jamie, "but the longer we take to get there, the more likely they'll find the van and us on video."

So they drove on, stopping every hour to change drivers but no longer going into restaurants and stores to watch TV. The rolling hills of Ohio gave way to the plains of Indiana, and the sinking summer sun, like a malevolent Star of Bethlehem, led them toward their destination, until it disappeared in the darkening northwestern sky.

* * *

Coot returned to his desk. He kept hitting Refresh on his browser, hoping to get some information about the Acela carrying Diana to Penn Station, but no actual arrival time had yet been posted. He hoped the train was late. He hoped it was still in the tunnel when the bomb went off. He called and called the headquarters number for Amtrak in Washington, but it was always busy.

He was following several streaming video feeds of news from New York. Most of the New York sites were down, so he was relying on Boston, Philadelphia, and Washington news sites for more information. As he was watching a video stream from philly.com, the video stopped playing. He clicked Pause and Play a couple of times but nothing happened, so he refreshed the page. The video player was still there, but now the familiar Mushrooms theme song, Bob Dylan's "The Times They Are A-changin'", was playing. The title of the video: *Your World Has Ended.* A few seconds later the familiar Mushrooms avatar began to speak.

"This morning Mushrooms detonated a second weapon, this time in New York City. We have destroyed the Empire State Building. Its very name was offensive. It symbolized the arrogance of American power. Today's action signals that the American Empire is ending. It is unfortunate that so many people had to suffer and die. We waited a month after Srinagar, hoping that you Americans would begin the destruction of oppressive corporate and governmental institutions yourselves, but you have disappointed us. Do these institutions hold such sway over your minds that you cannot contemplate freedom, cannot act on your own behalf? Apparently so. Therefore, *we* have acted for you and for all the peoples of the world who are oppressed by American economic, political, and military power. Now that we have shown the way, join us. Organize yourselves! Rise up and throw off your oppressors, or more devastation will follow. The next explosion will be ten times more powerful."

Coot did rise up, but not to follow the instructions of the people who had probably harmed and might have killed Diana, not to mention tens of thousands of other innocent people. These people were delusional. So arrogant. Who would follow a group with such callous disregard for people that they would set off a nuclear device in a city? Yet he knew that his own country had done that not once but twice, and with more powerful bombs. Was there a difference between what Mushrooms had done and what America did to end World War II? Did a greater good ever justify a positive evil? Coot was not a theologian or a philosopher. He was just a guy trying to prevent a few people from harming a lot of others, and he had failed. He had failed himself. Worse, he had failed Diana, just as he had failed Frannie years earlier. He sat down again and rested his head in his hands.

He heard a soft knock. The door creaked behind him. A hand

gently touched his shoulder.

"I'm sorry, Coot," said Emily. "We all feel just awful about this. It must be especially hard for you."

"A good friend of mine was on the Acela, due to arrive in New York just minutes before the blast. I can't get through to her." His voice was a monotone, barely audible.

"Oh. I didn't realize — that's horrible. You poor man! Is there anything I can do to help? Make calls? Anything?"

"No, Emily. Thanks, though. I'll just have to tough this out. Suck it up. Try to keep things from going from bad to worse."

"Don't be too hard on yourself. There's only so much one person or even a small group like S.A.F.E. can do."

"Mushrooms managed to do quite a lot with just a few people. Why couldn't we stop them?"

"I don't know. Anyway, I'll be in my office if you need to talk."

She squeezed his shoulder and left the office, closing the door behind her. Coot stared at his monitor through reddened eyes. He didn't want to see any more scenes of devastation. He started his MP3 player. A favorite, Schubert's Fantasy in F minor for piano four hands, emerged from the small speakers to caress his soul. Diana and her dad used to play that piece. He shook with silent grief.

It was over two hours since the attack. New York was in chaos. People were streaming out of Manhattan, many on foot, trying to escape the radioactive dust thrown into the air by the blast, ignoring broadcast warnings to stay indoors. The 33rd Street station on the Lexington Avenue subway, the Herald Square station, and the 33rd Street PATH station serving New Jersey commuters had been destroyed by the explosion. Penn Station had suffered severe damage when Madison Square Garden collapsed over it. The electromagnetic pulse from the bomb also damaged cell towers, cell phones, and computers throughout lower Manhattan, making communication with people in the area almost impossible. Maybe that was why Diana was not answering her phone.

Coot paid particular attention to reports of crews entering Penn Station through the Amtrak and Long Island Railroad tunnels. They were bringing out the wounded passengers with a chance of survival first. It must be a triage nightmare in there. He hated to think of Diana trapped, frightened, bleeding, suffering.

He opened the address book on his computer and searched for "New York". One of the entries he found was for Hector Villa, a reporter for *The New York Times* whom he had met in Geneva. Coot dialed Hector's number.

"Hector, this is Coot Jenkins. I'm calling from Washington. Are you in New York? ... New Jersey, eh? That's good. Listen, Hector, a friend of mine was traveling from Washington to Penn Station on the Acela this morning. It was due in at 10:46 — about the same time as the detonation. The Amtrak website doesn't say whether it ever arrived. Have you heard anything about trains being delayed, damaged in the tunnels, anything? No? Do you know where they're taking the injured? To hospitals outside Manhattan? Okay. Thanks, Hector."

Not knowing what had happened to her was the worst part.

Coot left his office and caught a cab to the Amtrak headquarters. Surely someone there would be able to tell him what happened to the Acela. When he arrived, there was already a line of people trying to get information on friends and family traveling to or from New York Penn Station. He joined the line, which was not moving very fast. Rumors were swarming around the line like horseflies, biting Coot with every mention of the Acela.

After waiting almost an hour, Coot reached the head of the line, which terminated at a table in the lobby.

"Which train was your passenger on?" asked the woman behind the table.

"The Acela Express due into Penn Station at 10:46 this morning."

"That train never reached the station. It was just emerging from the tunnel when the bomb went off. Most of the dead were in the front of the train, where the blast wave hit. The train was pushed back a ways into the tunnel."

There were deaths, but apparently some people survived. "I'm trying to find out whether Diana Munson was among the ... the casualties."

"Are you a member of Miss Munson's family?"

"I'm a friend."

"I'm afraid I can't give out any information about passengers except to family members, sir. We have to make sure the families have been notified before we release information more generally."

"I see. When will the notification be complete?"

"I don't know. People here in the office are trying to contact the families now."

"All right, then. Thanks for your help." How frustrating.

Coot left the Amtrak headquarters and returned to his office. Should he try to contact Diana's mother? What if she doesn't know Diana was on that train? What if she hasn't heard from Diana or from Amtrak?

Coot was eating a very late lunch at his desk when his phone rang. "Hello?"

"Mr. Jenkins?" a female voice asked.

"Yes. Who's calling?"

"This is Helen Munson, Diana's mother. Diana told me about your Saturday piano lessons and mentioned that you worked at S.A.F.E. I hope you don't mind my calling you at your office."

"Mrs. Munson — thank God you called! Have you heard from Diana?"

"Not yet. Amtrak called a few minutes ago to let me know that Diana was rescued from the Acela just outside Penn Station. She's been taken to a hospital in New Jersey."

"Which hospital?"

"Let me see. I wrote it down somewhere. This is all so confusing. ... Here it is. She's at the Meadowlands Hospital in Secaucus."

"What's her condition?"

"They said she's stable."

"What sort of injuries does she have?"

"They didn't say. Mr. Jenkins, I'm so worried! I've tried calling the hospital but the line is always busy."

"I'm worried, too. Will you be coming east to be with Diana?"

"I want to, but the New York airports are closed."

"If you fly into Washington or Baltimore, I can pick you up and we can drive to New Jersey together."

"That sounds perfect."

"In the meantime, I hope you'll keep checking with Meadowlands Hospital. They should be able to give you more details about Diana's condition. If you find out anything more, please let me know."

"Of course."

"Do you have a hotel reservation?"

"Yes, five nights at the Crowne Plaza near the hospital."

"Then I'll try to make a reservation there for myself as well."

"That'll be convenient."

"One last thing: please call me 'Coot'. Everyone else does."

"Okay, Coot — if you'll call me 'Helen'."

"It's a deal."

Coot and Helen exchanged cell phone numbers, and Helen promised to call Coot with her flight information.

After finishing the call, Coot made a reservation at Helen's hotel and then walked over to Ben Barker's office to explain why he needed to be out of the office.

"Ben, Diana Munson from the N.S.C. was on the Acela that didn't quite make it to Penn Station this morning."

"Oh, no! Is she okay?"

"I don't know. 'Stable' is all they told her mom."

"At least she's alive."

"I promised to pick up her mom at the airport and take her to the hospital."

"Always the Good Samaritan, aren't you, Coot? Isn't anyone else available for chauffeur duty? As you know, this is a very important time for S.A.F.E. We need all hands on deck."

"I'm sorry, Ben. I don't think I'd be of much use here, given the situation."

"Really? It's your plan that we're executing here. We need to have you involved."

"I'll have my cell phone and will participate in the meetings remotely."

"What about a laptop?"

"I need to borrow one with cellular connectivity, so that I can work wherever I need to be."

"Sure. Arrange whatever you need to be effective."

"Thanks, Ben."

"And let me know how Diana Munson's doing, okay?"

"Okay — when I find out myself."

Coot arranged to borrow a laptop with a cellular communication card. He hoped he would be able to use it in the hospital.

Emily stopped by his desk. "Mushrooms is claiming they set off the weapon in New York."

"Yes, I know."

"Have you found out anything more about your friend?"

Coot repeated what Helen had told him.

"Well, I hope she'll be okay."

"Yeah, me too. Thanks."

Just after 4 P.M. Coot's office phone rang again.

"Coot, this is Helen again. I've made a reservation for a flight into Baltimore, and I've got some more information on Diana."

"How is she?"

"It could be worse, but she's still not in good shape. She has fractures of her left arm and leg, plus a ruptured spleen. There was internal bleeding but they were able to stop it."

"How did you find out? Did she call?"

"I called the hospital and spoke to a patient representative. They operated to repair her spleen. Apparently the tear in the tissue covering the spleen was small enough to be stitched back together, so they expect a full recovery."

"How long will she be in the hospital?"

"I don't know."

"Helen, I really appreciate your calling me. I guess we'll have to wait until we see her tomorrow to get a better sense of how she's doing and what sort of care she'll need after leaving the hospital."

Helen gave Coot her flight information and they hung up.

* * *

Myron Pepsey and Paul Henry were enjoying a glass of a fine cream sherry in Pepsey's Atlanta office.

"Man, oh man," said Henry, "the conclusion of that second act was a blast, wasn't it?"

Pepsey smiled. "Indeed, but I also enjoyed the subtlety of the act's first scene. What have you been able to tell about the audience's reaction to the first scene?"

"They applauded when the forces of good overcame the forces of evil," said Henry.

"I hope they understood that that triumph was due to the good decisions made earlier by the victors," said Pepsey.

"Yes, some of the critics did note that in their reviews," said Henry. He raised his glass to his lips and tasted the sweet, dark liquid it contained.

"What did they make of the second scene?" Pepsey asked.

"Most people seemed confused about the purpose of all the violence." Henry looked worried, as if he was afraid Pepsey would be displeased.

"That's to be expected," said Pepsey, hoping to reassure his loyal and effective counselor. So far, the production was going about as well as he had thought it would. "The play promotes a simple concept in a radical way." He took another sip of sherry and waited for Henry to continue his report.

"A few people seemed to understand that the violence occurred because entrenched interests would not allow the solution from the first scene to be implemented," said Henry.

Pepsey leaned back in his large leather chair, looked up, smiled again, then returned his gaze to Henry. "The third act should help more people understand the whole point of the play, then."

* * *

Vice-Chairman Kim Dae-Hyun sat behind the large mahogany desk in his office at the National Defense Commission in Pyongyang, reading intelligence reports that had arrived since he had left the N.D.C. the previous day. Each time the large man picked up a new report, he took another sip of *omija cha*, a five-flavor tea made from *Schisandra chinensis* berries. The complexity of the tea always reminded him to look for subtle implications in the material that he read. Sometimes a sour bit of news could turn surprisingly sweet. General Kim reached for another report with his free hand.

Bad news! Three men had successfully smuggled a small bomb

into the country through Hyesan, on the border with China. The guards who let them enter would likely go to prison for such a failure. Posing as students, the smugglers were staying at the Hyemyung Hotel when the device was discovered in their room during a search by the Ministry of People's Security. A lucky break: officers had been routinely inspecting rooms at random ever since the hotel had been at the center of a prostitution scandal. The bomb had been sent to headquarters in Pyongyang for analysis, along with the three men, who were being held *incommunicado* during the investigation.

The general noticed that the report was dated a week earlier. Why did communications from the provinces have to be so slow? Kim envied the South its electronic communication network. He leafed through the rest of the reports, looking for a related report from ministry headquarters. Ah, here was one. He began to read. Device had Russian markings...Radioactivity detected...Device sent to Yongbyon Nuclear Research Center. He leaned back in his chair and closed his eyes, imagining what the device might be. A dirty bomb? An actual nuclear device? He knew the Americans had an atomic demolition munition that small, but the Russians? They were better allies but worse technologists.

Kim opened his eyes, sat up straighter, checked the knot of his tie in the mirror that he kept hidden in a drawer of his desk. He was careful to look like the powerful man he had become, but he did not want to appear vain. He went back to reading the headquarters report. The smugglers were uncooperative at first, but the standard methods soon loosened their tongues. He knew from experience that such an interrogation was not a pleasant affair. All that screaming. Pathetic. The smugglers were supposed to deliver the device to two North Koreans, but the security police thwarted that plan. Instead, they used the smugglers to capture the two accomplices, who were also now in custody.

The report concluded with a description of the accomplices' plan to smuggle the weapon into Seoul aboard a bus taking South Korean workers home from the jointly-run factory park at Kaesong. Once in Seoul, the terrorists would have used the weapon to destroy the COEX Mall.

Such an attack might be useful if it caused the people in the South to lose confidence in the puppet government, but it could be a problem if the D.P.R.K. were blamed. The Korean People's Army would attack on its own schedule. Kim would make sure that the smugglers and the terrorists were held until the N.D.C. could decide whether to let their plot go forward.

The next step was to learn what kind of device the plotters had brought into the country. He would find out for sure during his regular inspection of Yongbyon two days hence, but he thought he already knew, for the terrorists kept repeating one word under torture: "Mushrooms."

* * *

Frantic with worry about her girlfriend, Sabrina Jones rushed into her Seattle apartment, tossed her purse onto the sofa, and sat down at her computer. Since the terrorist attack on the Empire State Building, only one thing had been on her mind, and it was not the application software she had been working on for the past six months. *Is Jamie safe?* Jamie had said she was going to New York for a demonstration. Could she have been sightseeing in midtown when the bomb went off? Why hadn't she called to let Sabrina know she was okay? Why hadn't she even had her phone on, so she could have answered Sabrina's calls?

She had to know where Jamie was, and where she had been, so she opened the tracker program on her computer. What she saw alarmed her. At 7 A.M. Pacific Time Jamie's phone had reported its location: New York, NY. The program also displayed a link to a map giving the phone's precise location. Sabrina clicked on the link. Her browser opened and her fears were confirmed: Jamie had been right across the street from the Empire State Building at 10 A.M. Eastern Time, less than an hour before the explosion. She might even have been near the terrorists. How frightening!

The log did contain some good news, though: later entries, later than the explosion. Sabrina inhaled deeply and heaved a loud sigh of relief. Where was Jamie now? The tracker program showed her progress west through New Jersey and Pennsylvania, then into Ohio. Where was she going? Why hadn't she called? Sabrina called her again, but still there was no answer.

Sabrina got some leftovers out of the refrigerator and put them into the microwave. While they were heating, she began to wonder whether Jamie had seen the terrorists who had set off the bomb. Probably, given her military experience with explosives, she would have recognized the device.

The microwave beeped, signaling that her dinner was ready. The sound also triggered a new question: What would Jamie have done if she'd seen the terrorists? Confronted them? Called the police? Gotten the hell away? Jamie rarely talked specifically about taking violent action, but she did harbor a deep anger at "the system" for the multiple tragedies that had struck her family. Would she have let such an attack just happen? What an awful thought!

Another beep from the microwave, reminding her that dinner was getting cold. Another new — and even more chilling — question: Was it merely a coincidence that Jamie had been near the Empire State Building just before it was destroyed? Could she possibly have been involved herself? The thought was too terrible to contemplate. Sure, Jamie was a very angry woman, but she seemed to have calmed down in the months since she and Sabrina had become lovers. Anyway, where could Jamie have gotten a nuclear weapon, or come up with the money to buy one? Nothing Sabrina knew about Jamie and her friends supported the notion that they had the resources to mount such an attack. No, Jamie couldn't have been involved. Sabrina felt ashamed for even considering such a possibility.

Sabrina got her supper from the microwave, sat back down at her computer, and nibbled at her food while browsing through earlier reports from Jamie's phone. Those reports were beginning to erode her confidence that she knew and could trust Jamie. What had Jamie been doing in Quebec on Sunday? She spent Sunday night in New Jersey, then went into New York City Monday morning, left before the explosion, and was west of Newark by 11 A.M. So much for Jamie's assertion that she was going to New York for a demonstration. Something strange, even sinister, was going on. Sabrina was becoming more and more troubled. Not so much by concerns for Jamie's safety but by fears that Jamie had deceived her. And, worse, that Jamie might be involved in the most heinous atrocity in the country's history.

Jamie's phone continued to report its location. Around 10 P.M. the tracker program showed that the phone was in Elk Grove Village, Illinois. After that the phone seemed not to move. The map showed an industrial area. It was after midnight in Illinois, but there was no lodging shown on the map. How peculiar.

Sabrina left the tracker program running, got ready for bed, and tried to sleep. She woke up several times in the night to check the phone's location, but it had not changed. Jamie's failure to contact her worried her and made her angry. Exhausted, she took a tranquilizer and was finally able to sleep uninterrupted.

* * *

Tuesday morning Coot kept to his usual routine. By 9 A.M. he was at his desk at S.A.F.E. He participated in a meeting to pick publications and topics for articles. There was enough diversity of interests in the staff so that people volunteered to write pieces for a wide range of magazines. The other meeting Coot attended involved the creation of a roster of people willing and able to speak at meetings around the country. With his many years of attending conferences, Coot had a large number of contacts at various universities, national labs, and think tanks. He suggested a couple dozen people for the first round of calls by the staff.

After the meetings, Coot picked up the laptop that I.T. had configured for him and took the stairs down to the parking level. No risking the elevator today. Just before noon he reached Baltimore-Washington Airport and parked in the cell phone lot. Twenty minutes later his phone rang. Helen had already picked up her suitcase, so Coot agreed to meet her outside baggage claim. She would be wearing a red-and-white-striped top and blue slacks, caught up in patriotic fervor like everyone else.

Coot drove slowly past the cars waiting for other passengers. Too much red, white, and blue on display. He dialed Helen's cell. "I think I see you. Raise your hand." Helen located at last, Coot pulled to the curb and got out.

Helen walked toward Coot, smiling warmly. She extended her hand and they shook. Coot noticed the firmness of her grip and wondered if she was the source of Diana's fierceness.

"Thanks for meeting me, Coot." Tall and erect, she didn't look more than five years older than Coot.

"Happy to do it."

"Diana told me how kind you are."

So, Diana has been telling her mom about me? Coot thought with pleasure. Probing Helen about Diana's feeling for him seemed inappropriate, given that Diana might be fighting for her life at that very moment.

Coot loaded Helen's suitcase into his trunk and they began the drive to New Jersey. The traffic was heavier than he remembered, but the weather was good and the driving not stressful. Helen was easy to talk with.

"Did Diana tell you about the debate?"

"A little. She was embarrassed that she'd hit that Limbick fellow."

"She was amazing."

"Diana was never one to tolerate violence toward someone she cared about."

Someone she cared about! Coot smiled.

There was a lot more traffic going south than north. Sometime after 1 P.M., the two travelers were getting hungry, so Coot pulled into the first service area on the New Jersey Turnpike. Coot looked around to see the choices. Diana might not approve, but Coot was hankering for a Whopper. He got into line at the Burger King while Helen went to the restroom. He could hear people all around talking about the disaster in New York.

"They say 20,000 people were killed in the attack."

"I heard 30,000!"

"Nah, it was only 10,000."

"Only? That's three times as many as on 9/11."

"Who knows how many bombs those guys have?"

"Midtown's a wreck."

"You know those huge signs in Times Square? Gone."

"I pity the poor people looking up at them when it happened."

Helen returned from the restroom and joined Coot in line. "I hope they're not out of salads."

Coot turned toward her. "You and Diana are sure into vegetables."

"You should be, too." For an instant she looked stern, like a strict nun or middle school teacher.

"I'm getting better about it. Diana's influence."

At last Coot and Helen got to the head of the line and placed their orders. When their food was ready, they took it to the car and continued the drive north. Helen helped Coot eat his burger and fries. Once she even caught a slurry of ketchup, mustard, and relish that was about to drip onto Coot's shirt.

There were more and more ambulances in the southbound lanes. Of course: the hospitals close to New York had filled up and victims had to be transported further for treatment.

Traffic slowed, the further north they went. Helen wanted to go straight to see Diana. It was past 7 P.M. when Coot pulled his car into Meadowlands Hospital's parking lot. The lot was almost full. He and Helen walked toward the main entrance. People were streaming in and out. Some wiped tears from their eyes. Others merely looked worried. At the information desk Helen asked where Diana was.

"She's in the I.C.U.," said the lady at the desk. She pushed back strands of gray hair that insisted on falling into her face each time she bent over her keyboard or checked a printout. She looked exhausted.

"Oh, no! Why?"

"You'll have to ask Mrs. Webber, the patient representative." The woman reached for her phone. "I'll call her." Her hand again swept back her recalcitrant hair.

"We'd like to see Diana right away." Helen was showing her eat-your-vegetables side again.

"I.C.U. visiting hours are over," said the woman curtly, proving that she could play the stern card too at the end of a long and difficult day. "You'll have to wait until 8 P.M."

Coot and Helen found seats nearby and waited, each minute seeming filled with an hour's worth of worry about Diana, who lay somewhere above them in the hospital. At last a short, plump woman in a bright print dress approached them.

"Hello, Mrs. Munson. I'm Marilyn Webber, the patient representative. We spoke on the phone yesterday."

"Oh, yes, Mrs. Webber." Helen stood up quickly, as did Coot.

"I've just been looking at Diana's chart and I'll try to answer whatever questions you have. Please come with me."

"I want my friend Mr. Jenkins to hear what you have to say also."

"Certainly."

Helen and Coot followed Marilyn Webber to a small conference room off the lobby. After they were all seated, Helen said, "Why is Diana in the I.C.U.? I thought the tear in her spleen was repaired."

"That's correct, but not the whole story. As you can imagine, it took the fire department quite some time to get to Diana yesterday morning. Even though the tear was small, blood kept leaking from it. We're keeping Diana in intensive care until we're sure the situation is under control."

"How long will that take?" asked Coot.

"At least another day."

"Can we see her when visiting hours begin again at eight?" asked Helen.

"Yes, but remember she's on morphine because of the pain from the surgery."

"I see," said Helen. "Is it still possible to get something to eat inside the hospital?"

"Only snacks from vending machines are available after the cafeteria closes at 2 P.M."

"I hate to suggest this, since I had a Whopper for lunch, but while planning the route from the airport up here I noticed a Burger King a little further east along Route 3," said Coot, as his stomach gave an audible rumble. "At least it would be fast."

"The Wendy's on Meadowlands Parkway is much closer," said Ms. Webber. "Just retrace your path from Route 3 and you can't miss it."

"Thanks for the tip. It's almost 7:30 now, Coot." Helen stood up. "Let's just go there."

"It was a pleasure meeting both of you," said Ms. Webber, as she shook hands with Helen and Coot and gave Helen her card. "Please call me if you have any other questions."

Coot and Helen hurried back to Coot's car and drove to the Wendy's. The parking lot was almost full, but Coot found a space near the back.

"If we're quick, we can probably eat here and still be back by 8," said Coot.

"Okay. I don't know where we'd eat otherwise."

Coot and Helen paid for the salad bar and fixed their salads. Coot noticed how green the lettuce looked, how red the tomatoes were, how purple the onions. Maybe there was something to this fascination with vegetables that Diana and Helen shared.

The restaurant was crowded, but they found a table, ate quickly, and left. Soon they were back at the hospital. If anything, the place was busier than when they had left. Ambulances, with lights flashing, continued to pull up to the entrance to the Emergency Department. Paramedics and E.M.T.s hurried to get their patients inside. Coot and Helen re-entered the lobby. Helen got directions to the I.C.U. from the same exhausted woman who had helped them before. She and Coot hurried to the elevators.

"I trust we won't get stuck between floors!" said Helen.

"Better not," said Coot, "or I might go berserk and trash the thing."

"That doesn't sound like you."

Despite their misgivings about taking the elevator, Coot and Helen were soon in the I.C.U.. Doctors, nurses, and others in lab coats, uniforms, and scrubs were going into and out of rooms on the corridors that radiated from the nurses' station. Helen identified herself and asked where Diana was. Coot followed her to Diana's room. Diana appeared to be sleeping. Coot sat in the only chair in the room, while Helen went to Diana's bedside and whispered, "Diana? Can you hear me? It's Mom." Diana opened her eyes halfway.

"Mom? Am I in California?"

"No, honey, we're both in New Jersey. How do you feel?"

"Really dopey. Somebody gave me this button to push if I feet too much pain. I've been using it a lot."

"Do you know what happened?"

"All I know is that my train was entering New York when there was a bright flash of light and a huge noise. I thought that the train must have been struck by lightning. ... My car was in a tunnel. Stuff began to fall on it. Big, heavy things. ... I was crushed under the luggage rack. I felt my left arm and leg snap, and something hit my tummy really hard and then rolled off. It really hurt. ... I remember screaming. Everybody was screaming. It was awful. I was terrified. I thought for sure I was going to die."

"Oh, honey, I'm so sorry. You don't have to talk about it if you don't want to."

"That was the worst of it. It was dark. I felt like I was falling asleep. I think I must have been losing blood. People around me were moaning and crying and praying and cursing. I could feel the outside air coming in through the window above me. At last I heard voices, strong voices. Someone said, 'There're survivors inside the tunnel.' Soon men in bulky suits were shining lights into the car, pulling the broken glass out of the windows, and climbing inside. One of the men shone his flashlight at me. He said, "She's alive. Let's get her immobilized and out of here." He said he needed to give me some medicine so I wouldn't feel so much pain while they worked on me. I felt a needle stick and that's the last I remember until I woke up here."

"You're lucky to be alive, Diana." Coot stood next to Helen and looked at the bruised young woman for whom he now cared so much.

"Coot, is that you?"

"You bet! Your mom called me after Amtrak notified her you were here. I met her in Baltimore and we drove here together."

"Coot has been a big help, sweetie. He's just as nice as you said he was."

"You're making me blush, Helen." In fact, Coot felt as much delight as embarrassment. He was having a hard time not grinning like a teenager being praised in front of the girl he had a crush on.

"Well, you are."

To distract himself, Coot turned to Diana. "Have you heard what happened in New York?"

"No. Did another train hit the Acela?"

"Something much worse. Terrorists set off a nuclear device at the Empire State Building. Central Manhattan is in ruins. Believe it or not, you were one of the more fortunate victims."

"Oh, no! Was it Mushrooms again?"

"They're claiming credit for it."

"How can people be such monsters?" asked Helen. "They have no feeling whatsoever for their fellow human beings."

"Some of the people on our side want us to respond in kind," said Coot, looking at Helen. "In my opinion, they're not much better. As Gandhi said, 'An eye for an eye, and soon the whole world is blind.'"

Diana whimpered. Coot and Helen turned quickly to look at her.

"Don't forget to push your button, honey," said Helen, handing her the device.

Diana pressed the button. A moment later she looked at Coot with a small smile, said, "It's like magic!", and closed her eyes.

"Looks like she'll be out for a while," said Helen, a mother's worried frown on her face.

"I need to check my e-mail to see whether they need me to do something by tomorrow morning," said Coot, "so I'm going to find somewhere I can work. I'll come get you when visiting hours are over at 11 and we'll go to the hotel."

"Okay, Coot, and thanks again for all your help today."

Coot left Diana's room and walked to the nurses' station, where a Nurse Reynolds was on duty.

"I need to find a quiet place to work," said Coot.

"You might try a classroom."

Coot got directions from the woman and was glad to find a quiet place to work amid the turmoil of the hospital. He read the dozens of e-mails from people working on the plan he had suggested. A few required his response, which he gave carefully. Ben Barker would want proof that Coot could still be effective while working remotely. After an hour he had done what he could, so he left his refuge and returned to the I.C.U. At the nurses' station he was about to ask Nurse Reynolds how Diana was doing when a light suddenly went on at the console next to her.

"Excuse me. I've got to see what's wrong with Miss Munson."

Coot followed her back to Diana's room. Helen was standing at Diana's bedside. She grimaced at Coot.

"My leg has started to hurt a lot more," said Diana, her speech slurred from the effects of the morphine.

"Let me see your foot," said the nurse, and she pulled back the covers from the left side of Diana's bed. "You've got some swelling there. That's not good. I'll get an orthopedist up here right away." Nurse Reynolds left and came back a few minutes later with a young man in green scrubs.

"Hello, Miss Munson. I'm Dr. Zeeland. You say your leg is hurting more?"

"Yes! I'm having to press my magic button more and more frequently."

"Well, that's not good, is it? I see your foot is swollen. We'll have to remove that cast and have a look. It could be compartment syndrome. That sometimes happens after an injury like yours."

"What's compartment syndrome?"

"It's when fluid builds up, putting pressure on the blood vessels and nerves in a part of your body."

"No wonder it hurts!"

"If that's the problem, we'll have to fix it right away."

"Will I need another operation?"

"We'll cross that bridge when we come to it. Just in case, I'll get you into an operating room where we've got the tools to handle whatever we find."

The doctor and nurse left the room. Diana cried out in pain again and pressed her button. Soon her eyes closed and she lay still.

"Oh, Coot, I hope she's going to be okay," said Helen.

"Me, too," said Coot. "I hope Dr. Zeeland can find the problem and fix it quickly."

A few minutes later an orderly entered the room, secured the various tubes and bottles suspended around her, unlocked the wheels on Diana's bed, and wheeled her out. Coot and Helen made their way to the waiting room. They took the last two seats.

"I hope you don't mind if I try to get some work done," Coot said to Helen. "I'll stay here with you, but I need to check on some things."

"You go right ahead. It's nice just to have you nearby."

Coot got out his laptop and was soon connected to the Internet. The first thing he did was search for "compartment syndrome". He learned the importance of treating the condition quickly, to prevent the death of muscle and nerve tissue. A doctor must cut into the fascia surrounding the affected group of muscles, nerves, and blood vessels to relieve the pressure. Could this be done on a patient with broken bones?

Coot forced himself to refocus his attention on S.A.F.E.'s response to the attack on New York. There had been a flurry of e-mail messages since he had checked earlier. He did not care whether they contacted *Popular Mechanics* or *Popular Science*, so he wrote back, "Submit a slightly different version to each." Why couldn't Emily and Joe agree about which videos to produce? Coot suggested they flip a coin to determine whether to produce Emily's or Joe's favorite first. Speed was the important thing.

A more important message appeared in Coot's inbox — a request from Rita Swearingen to appear on a panel to discuss the attack. The program was scheduled for 9 P.M. Wednesday night and would be broadcast live. How could he be on the panel and still support Diana and Helen? Coot wrote back that he was in New Jersey and asked whether he could participate from a nearby PBS station.

Coot shut down his laptop and stowed it in its carrying case, then looked at Helen.

"Want to take a walk?" she asked.

"Good idea," said Coot. "I've done all I can do for now."

Helen learned from Nurse Reynolds that Diana would be in surgery or recovery for at least forty-five minutes more. Helen told the nurse that she and Coot would be walking around for no more than half an hour. She gave the nurse her cell phone number in case she needed to contact them.

As they walked along the corridors, Helen said, "Diana has always been so resilient. If she was dribbling a soccer ball as a little girl and was knocked down by a hard tackle, she'd bounce right back up, determined to get the ball back. No whimpering or whining or waiting for the referee to call a foul."

"It must have been fun to watch her play."

"Yes, it was. Her dad and I were so proud of her. Now she seems a lot more fragile. When she was sick as a child, she always complained about having to stay in bed. Back there in the I.C.U. she seemed so listless. Hearing her cry out in pain was hard."

"I know what you mean."

Coot and Helen walked together in silence, while all around them the hospital staff were hurrying about, wheeling patients in and out of rooms. Some of the patients were completely covered in sheets, leading Helen to whisper, "Oh, my!" Coot understood her unspoken thought: *Not Diana! Please, not Diana!* After the fourth such encounter, Helen suggested they return to the I.C.U., and Coot agreed.

They checked at the nurses' station but Diana had still not returned from surgery, so they went back to the waiting room. Helen sat next to a stout, middle-aged woman, whose dark, lined face carried the message that she had seen more than her share of difficulty in life.

"Who are you here with?" Helen asked.

"My son Julio," she said with an accent that indicated she had learned English well into adulthood. "He's my baby. He's only twenty-two. Monday he started a new job in the city. I am so proud of him! He rides the train from Maplewood to Penn Station, with all the other commuters. They say his train arrived at the station just before the bomb went off. Thank God, he's still alive."

"How is Julio doing?"

"He was bleeding inside. The doctors tried to stop it. They said we'll just have to wait and see. He's a strong boy. I keep praying for him."

When Julio's mother finished her sad story, Coot glanced at the others waiting with them. One man was looking back at him. The fellow was wearing a sport shirt with two buttons unfastened and a gold chain around his neck. Tufts of black hair curled out of the shirt. Did he know this guy?

"You look familiar. Have you been on TV recently?" the man asked Coot.

"Just once. In Washington. You probably didn't see the show."

"I think I did. You're that Coot fellow, aren't you, the one who put down Larry Limbick?"

Thinking that Helen was not likely to know karate, Coot tried to calm the guy down. "You're good with faces. Sometimes I don't even recognize myself in the mirror until I've had my coffee."

"I was on the Jersey City police force for twenty years. A cop who can't recognize people quickly is gonna be a dead cop."

"That makes sense."

"So, what do you think about getting rid of our nukes now, eh? My daughter wouldn't be in the I.C.U. now if we'd nuked those bastards a long time ago."

"I'm sorry to hear about your daughter. A friend of mine's also in the I.C.U. I'm angry too. I wish preventing nuclear terrorism were as simple as nuking a cave full of terrorists."

"When I was a cop, I knew who the bad guys were. I couldn't always prove it, but I knew who they were. We should find out who these guys are in Afghanistan or Pakistan or wherever, and take 'em out."

"The hard part is finding them."

Nurse Reynolds appeared in the doorway of the waiting room. "Mrs. Munson, Diana is back in her room."

Coot and Helen stood up, wished their new acquaintances good luck, and followed the nurse.

"How is she doing?" Helen asked.

"Dr. Zeeland is with her now. He'll explain everything to you."

When Coot and Helen entered Diana's room, Dr. Zeeland was standing next to her bed, reading her chart. Diana appeared to be sleeping.

"Hello, Dr. Zeeland. I'm Helen Munson, Diana's mother. How is she?"

"She'll be sore for a while, but she should recover completely. I had to make an incision in the fascia of the anterior compartment of her left calf to relieve the pressure, but I was able to close it up. There'll be a small scar, but a skin graft wasn't necessary."

"That's wonderful news! Is everything else all right now? Is the repair of her spleen holding?"

"According to her chart, Dr. Murray was able to close the tear in the splenic capsule. There shouldn't be any more bleeding. We'll keep an eye on her for another day in the I.C.U. and then she'll be moved to another room for a few days."

"Diana's a runner," said Coot. "How long will her activities be restricted after she leaves the hospital?"

"That depends on a number of factors, Mr. Munson. We'll just have to wait and see how she progresses."

"Oh, I'm sorry, Dr. Zeeland," said Helen. "I should have introduced you. This is our friend, Coot Jenkins."

"My apologies, Mr. Jenkins. I assumed you were Diana's father."

"No problem, Dr. Zeeland." Coot wanted to retort, *I assumed you were an orderly.*

Diana began to stir. A moment later she opened her eyes.

"How are you feeling, honey?" asked Helen.

"Numb."

Dr. Zeeland turned to face Diana. "That's the result of the epidural we gave you, Miss Munson. It will wear off in a few hours. Are you feeling any pain elsewhere?"

"My arm and under my ribs."

"You can manage the pain with morphine like you were doing before your latest adventure in the O.R.."

"Good."

"As I was telling your mom and Mr. Jenkins, you'll be in the I.C.U. for another day and then we'll move you to a room in a quieter area. Since yesterday the I.C.U. has been a very busy place."

"The whole hospital has seemed busy," said Coot.

"I suppose it is," said Dr. Zeeland. "With all the injuries, I've spent most of my time in the O.R., recovery, or the I.C.U."

"Are you getting enough sleep?" asked Helen.

"Not as much as I'd like, but enough to function. We've had patients coming into the Emergency Department non-stop since yesterday morning. Many of them have broken bones, so we orthopedists have been very busy. In fact, I need to check on several other patients here in the I.C.U. before I go back into surgery. Miss Munson, I'll check on you again soon."

Dr. Zeeland left the room.

"He's very nice," said Helen. "I think you're in good hands."

"Yes," said Diana.

"I hope so," said Coot. "The sooner you get out of the hospital, the better, as far as I'm concerned."

Coot and Helen spent the rest of visiting hours talking with

Diana when she was awake and with each other when Diana needed another dose of morphine. The epidural saved her from feeling any more pain in her leg.

At 11 P.M. Coot and Helen left the hospital and drove to the nearby Crowne Plaza, where they checked into their separate rooms.

"It's a good thing you guaranteed your reservations," said the desk clerk. "With so many injuries from the attack being treated at Meadowlands, we're booked solid for the next week."

Coot and Helen agreed to meet for breakfast at 8:30 the next morning. A bellman helped Helen with her luggage, but Coot carried his single suitcase and the laptop himself. Coot bade Helen a good night as the elevator doors opened. He got settled in his room, which had a single queen-sized bed and a desk at which he could work until he and Helen went to the hospital for the 11 A.M. start of visiting hours in the I.C.U.

Coot turned off the lights in his room and opened the curtains. Across a narrow expanse of water he could see the hospital. He hoped with all his heart that Diana would be fine after her ordeal was over.

* * *

Elk Grove Village. The name connotes a pastoral setting, a quiet spot with grazing ruminants and a few small stores, not a place in which a person would expect anarchists to prepare a nuclear attack on a major American landmark. The village actually contained many warehouses quite near O'Hare International Airport, making it a good staging area. But the airport was not the target that George Boyd and the other Mushrooms were planning to attack.

The night after they had brought down the Empire State Building, George, Mitch, and Jamie arrived at the warehouse that Doug had leased for the Mushrooms. George parked the van inside one of the truck bays. Doug was there to meet them.

"Hey, Doug." George gave his teammate a thumbs-up. "This place is much larger and better equipped than our little building in Jersey City."

Doug grinned. "Glad you like it. I figured we might have to lie low for a while, so I laid in lot of provisions. We can take our time getting ready for the next attack."

"it's great that we can park the vans inside." George. "My van may have been caught by a surveillance camera at the Newport station."

Doug gave the new arrivals a tour of the warehouse, taking care to point out the restrooms and the emergency exits.

"I'm exhausted." Jamie yawned and stretched her large arms. "Where do we bunk?"

Doug showed Jamie to a small office, in which he had already set up a cot for her. Doug next took George and Mitch to a larger room that contained four cots, each with a sleeping bag rolled out. Two had already been slept in.

"Bennie pulled guard duty last night," said Doug. "I'll stay up tonight."

George sat down on one of the cots, removed his shoes, put his glasses on the floor next to the shoes, slipped his feet into the bag, and lay back, closing his eyes. "Just resting..."

"Wake up!" George rolled over in his sleeping bag. Had he fallen asleep? Who was shaking him? Why couldn't they leave him alone? He was fatigued from the excitement of the past couple of days. He needed more rest. The shaking continued. He reached for his glasses and put them on.

"Mitch?"

"Yeah. Get up, will you? We need to strike again soon. To get people off their asses and into the insurrection."

"Calm down, Mitch." George was beginning to wake up now.

"Doug and Bennie are already up," said Mitch. "I'll wake up Jamie."

"No, let her sleep," said George, yawning. "We need her to be sharp."

"Yeah, I guess you're right," conceded Mitch. "I'll let her sleep till noon, but then we've got to talk about what to do next."

George got out of his sleeping bag and went to look for Doug and Bennie. He found them in another area of the warehouse, drinking coffee. Coffee! Doug had thought of everything.

"Hey, George," said Doug. "Get enough sleep? We tried to keep

Mitch away from you and Jamie, but he was really eager to get going on the next attack."

"Yeah, he sure was," said George, "but I did get him to let Jamie sleep."

"What *is* the plan?" Bennie looked at George. "How long do we have to wait?"

"Until we see the effect of the New York op."

Mitch wandered in, scowling, and said, "No, no, no! The longer we wait, the greater the risk we'll be discovered."

"What's the point of another attack if people refuse to join the insurrection?" asked Doug.

"But they *will* join, if we show we're strong enough." Mitch smacked his right fist into his left palm.

"If nuking New York didn't convince them of our strength," said George, "nothing will."

Since the Mushrooms could not agree on when or even whether to strike again, George and Doug's desire to wait carried the day. When Jamie woke up later, she joined their consensus. Bennie was not sure whether to attack soon or to wait, so Mitch was alone in wanting to deliver a quick blow in Chicago.

During the afternoon the team hunkered down, keeping up with events in the outside world through their encrypted satellite Internet feed and the little TV that Doug had brought to the warehouse. At Mitch's urging, they kept their cell phones off and even removed the batteries, so that their presence in the warehouse could not be detected.

George carefully monitored a number of websites while Doug constantly switched channels on the TV. George was disappointed that the Mushrooms' calls for insurrection were being ignored in all the media. Didn't they understand that insurrection was the whole point? Or did they understand all too well and were determined to suppress any rebellion against corporate domination?

All the coverage was about the government's effort to find and stop the terrorists responsible for the destruction of a wide swath of New York City. So far, the Mushrooms had covered their tracks well enough to avoid detection. What could they do now, with the media having recovered from the VI attacks, except execute their plan to destroy the tallest building west of New York?

They needed to act soon: How much longer would their luck hold?

CHAPTER 8

Picking Up the Pieces

Helen was already sitting at a table drinking coffee in the hotel restaurant when Coot walked in on Wednesday morning.

"I hope you don't mind that I ordered before you arrived," she said as Coot took a seat opposite her.

"Not at all. This way you can't blame me for recommending something that turns out to be awful."

Coot gave the waiter his order: a cheese omelet, coffee, and a large orange juice.

"Diana said that you give *good* recommendations at restaurants. Like at that diner."

"That was a very pleasant meal, except for the choking incident."

"She said you saved a little boy's life."

"That's not how his dad looked at it. I'm afraid that episode came back to haunt Diana and me after the debate."

"How so?"

"The angry dad was one of the guys who tossed a Molotov cocktail through my living room window and later attacked Diana in her apartment."

"Really! I didn't know that part of the story."

The waiter brought Helen's fruit plate and Coot's coffee, along with a pitcher of cream and a bowl of sugar. Coot automatically added his usual amount of each to the coffee, stirred the liquid, and waited for it to cool before taking a sip.

"I can't help wondering whether the fellow would have been angry enough to commit multiple felonies if I had not humiliated him in front of his wife and kids. I should have tried to calm him down instead of confronting him the way I did."

"Well, it's usually best to defuse a situation, rather than escalating it. In your profession, you must know about conflict resolution."

"That's why I'm a little ashamed of myself for not handling it better. To top it off, when I embarrassed his hero Larry Limbick in the debate, his anger boiled over and he retaliated."

"Diana contributed to the problem with her attack on Limbick."

"Don't blame Diana for any of this. Limbick had assaulted me. She felt she had to defend me."

"Couldn't she have found a more ladylike way of handling the situation?"

"Diana is part of a new generation, Helen, a generation that celebrates the fierceness of women when their families are threatened."

"That's all I need — a grizzly bear for a daughter."

"Just be glad that Diana's strong. She's going to need a lot of strength to overcome the injuries and terror she endured yesterday."

"I *am* glad she's strong, especially now. I just hope she's strong enough."

"You needn't worry about Diana. She'll be fine."

Coot paused to sip his coffee.

"I've got a chance to practice a new approach in the panel discussion tonight."

"I'd forgotten about the panel. Will you be able to do it from New Jersey?"

"I'll let you know when I find out myself."

"Please do. What *is* your new approach?"

"Years ago I heard the economist Milton Friedman arguing with a woman about welfare policy. He thought that his plan would accomplish the goals of his opponent but that her plan would not. He said, 'I'm on your side — *you're not!*'. I need to show how nuclear disarmament will achieve the national security goals of those who argue against it."

Coot's omelet arrived, and he attacked it without regard to the principles of conflict resolution.

After breakfast Coot returned to his room and used his laptop to connect to S.A.F.E.'s internal network. First he checked his messages. Good news: Emily and Joe had picked an initial video project. A new message from Rita appeared in his Inbox, asking whether he could get to the WNJN studio in Newark at 8:15 that night. He confirmed his participation to Rita right away and notified Ben as well. At least his boss would know that he was furthering S.A.F.E.'s mission. From 9:00 till 10:00 Coot dialed into a meeting to discuss how to help supporters organize locally to influence their representatives in Congress. After that he began work on an article on the dangers of nuclear weapons, including basically the same points that he had made in the debate with Limbick.

At 10:45 Coot quit working on his paper, packed up his laptop, and went down to the lobby to meet Helen.

"Good news — I can do the panel from a studio in Newark tonight," he told her as they walked to Coot's car.

"When will you have to leave?"

"After I.C.U. visiting hours end at seven, unless you want to leave a little earlier for supper."

"No, I want to be with Diana as much as they'll allow. You never know when something may go wrong."

"I agree. At least one of us should be with Diana whenever possible."

Coot drove the Camry through aisle after aisle in the hospital's parking lot, looking for an empty space. At last he spotted someone pulling out and took the vacated space.

"It seems more crowded today than yesterday," he said.

"Perhaps it took people a couple of days to find out where injured family members had been taken and to make travel arrangements," said Helen.

The I.C.U. was about as busy as it had been the previous day. The rooms that Coot and Helen passed on their way to Diana's were all occupied. Occasionally someone would cry out in pain. Ahead of them, an orderly was wheeling another sheet-covered body toward the morgue.

When they entered Diana's room, she smiled and said, "I feel better today. Dr. Murray said there's no swelling around my spleen. It looks like the repair was successful."

"How do your arm and leg feel?" asked Helen.

"I'm still numb below the waist. My arm feels about the same as yesterday."

"How was breakfast?" asked Coot.

"Okay. Nothing like at Snuffy's," said Diana.

"We'll have to go there to celebrate your return to D.C.," said Coot.

"I'd like that." Diana's smile was wonderful to see, especially as she lay seriously injured and in pain.

Around noon Diana's lunch arrived. Helen helped her eat it. As Coot watched Diana eat, his stomach gave a characteristic rumble.

"We should let Diana get some rest after lunch," Coot said to Helen, "while we grab a bite to eat in the cafeteria before it closes."

"Maybe one of us should stay here. You go, Coot — it sounds like you're ready for a meal."

"Okay. I'll be back as soon as I can."

Coot found the cafeteria with help from signs in the elevator and corridors. He ate his lunch as quickly as he could, then returned to the I.C.U. As he stepped out of the elevator, he met Julio's mother. Tears streaming down her face, she look up at Coot.

"Julio is gone. My baby. They couldn't stop the bleeding. I dunno how I'm gonna go on living without him."

She bowed her head. Her body shook with grief. Coot put his arms around her. She sobbed into his chest. He patted her on the back and said, "I'm very sorry to hear about Julio."

"Los diablos!" she screamed. "They killed my Julio. What did he do to them? Nada!"

"I know, I know," said Coot. "It doesn't make any sense."

She pulled away from Coot and looked at him once more, her eyes red, blazing with fury.

"We will find them and punish them, won't we? The devils?"

"I hope so."

"We must, or there's no justice in this world."

The door of another elevator opened. It was going down. She stepped inside and vanished behind the closing door.

Coot stared at the door for a moment, then hurried back to Diana's room. When he got there, Dr. Zeeland was standing beside Diana's bed.

"Hello, Dr. Zeeland. How's she doing?" asked Coot.

"Very well, Mr. Jenkins. She's an excellent patient." He looked at Diana and smiled.

Coot clenched his teeth. He was sure Zeeland liked Diana.

"Dr. Zeeland says they can move Diana out of the I.C.U. later today," said Helen.

"That's good," said Coot, "except that visiting hours end at 8 P.M. in the other parts of the hospital."

"We need to make sure our patients receive plenty of rest, so they can get well enough to go home."

Coot almost had to bite his tongue to keep from saying, *Patronizing prick!*

"I'll come see you again this evening, when you're in your new room," the doctor said to Diana.

Did Zeeland wink at Diana just then? Coot was almost sure he did, and he didn't like it.

Turning to Helen and Coot, Dr. Zeeland said, "I may not see you two again until tomorrow. Goodbye now."

"Goodbye." Coot managed not to add, *And good riddance!*

"You'd better get some lunch before the cafeteria closes," Coot said to Helen.

"Right. You two will be okay, I'm sure."

"Of course, Mom! Enjoy your lunch."

After Helen was out of earshot, Coot said, "So, how are you doing, really? I expect you didn't want to upset your mother by being completely honest."

"I'm still pretty sore. The morphine helps. I'm using it less now than yesterday."

"That's good. You're really very lucky to be alive, you know. I was going crazy on Monday, not knowing whether you were alive or dead. Tens of thousands of people were killed and many more were injured."

"How horrible!"

"Yes."

They lapsed into silence for a minute or two.

"So, how do you like your doctors?"

"They're good. They make me feel I'm going to be okay."

"Zeeland likes you."

"Don't be silly!"

"Doctors think they're the gods of the hospital. They like it when patients agree."

"Now you're being paranoid."

"You better be on your guard. You're at their mercy."

"So far they've treated me very well. They saved my life."

"That's their job. It's what comes next that concerns me."

Diana grimaced, then pushed the button for more morphine.

"Mmm, that's better. No worries for me."

Diana closed her eyes. Coot sat in the single chair and waited for her to wake up again. Diana was still asleep when Helen returned.

"How's our girl doing?"

"She said she's using less morphine than yesterday."

"Yes, that's what she told me, too. It's a good sign."

"Now that you're here, I should go try to get some more work done. Our president didn't want me to leave Washington. I promised him I'd work remotely."

"Go find a quiet place, then. I'll call you if there's an emergency."

Coot managed to locate an unused classroom and was soon reading the e-mail that had collected in his Inbox since the morning. He was relieved at Ben's delight that he would represent S.A.F.E. on the WETA panel that night, but Ben still wanted Coot's article on the dangers of nuclear weapons done by morning. In the next two hours Coot was able to finish the article, which he e-mailed to Ben and Joe. The rest of the afternoon he spent reading various websites for reaction to the attack on New York. The *New York Times* and several other New York publications' websites were still not operational, but he had plenty to read from Washington and several other cities. Most editorial writers seemed to think that a forceful response to the attack was required, but they did not agree on whom to attack or with what to attack. The lack of a consensus would buy some time for the Administration to develop an appropriate response. It would be interesting to see what the other panelists have to say in a few hours.

About 5:30 Helen called to say that they were moving Diana out of the I.C.U., so Coot packed up his laptop and got back to Diana's room just as Nurse Reynolds was rolling her bed out the door.

"Wow! Look at you — Cleopatra in a hospital bed."

Diana grinned at Coot. "I bet she didn't have a morphine pump!"

"Probably not."

Helen and Coot followed Diana and her bed to the new room, whose window looked out over the Meadowlands. Nurse Reynolds moved Diana's bed into the spot nearer the door in the semi-private room.

"There you go. All set. Comfy?" said the nurse. "With any luck, you'll be out of here in a few days."

"Thanks for all your help, Nurse Reynolds," said Diana.

"Yes, thanks!" said Helen.

"You're very welcome," said Nurse Reynolds, as she left the room.

Another patient, a middle-aged woman with bushy eyebrows and a prominent nose, was already in the bed next to the window. Both her arms were in casts held aloft by cables, and her head was bandaged. She studied each of the three new arrivals in turn, then focussed on Diana.

"It'll be nice to have some company again," she said. "You look pretty healthy — for a sick person. Don't go dying on me like the last one did, you hear?"

"I'll do my best to stick around long enough to walk out on you," said Diana, rising to the challenge.

"I kin tell we're gonna git along jus' fine," the woman said. "I'm Mary. Mary Butrell. What the hell I had to get myself into this mess for, I'll never know. First trip from West Virginia to the Big Apple, and it's gotta be the day they let the lunatics out of the asylum."

"They weren't lunatics," said Coot.

"And what do you know about 'em, you old coot?" said Mary.

Diana laughed, then whimpered as her injured abdomen sent a distress signal to her brain. Coot glared at Mary.

"More than I'd like to, Mary Contrary."

"How'd you know my nickname, hon?"

"How'd *you* know *mine*?"

"Please, can we have a truce?" said Helen, looking around in bewilderment at the three verbal jousters. "Mary, I'm Helen Munson and your new roommate is my daughter, Diana. This is our friend, Coot Jenkins," she concluded, gesturing toward Coot.

"Coot?" cackled Mary. "Really?"

"It's a long story," said Coot, acknowledging to himself that it was actually a pretty short tale.

"Well, *I* ain't goin' nowhere. Let's hear it!"

"I'll give you the abridged version. When I was eleven, I was small for my age, so the kids at my new school started calling me 'Cootie'. My Little League coach shortened it to 'Coot'. Unfortunately, the name stuck."

"You didn't finish explaining," said Diana, with a mischievous grin. "You forgot the 'Old' part."

"Let's hear about the old part from the old fart," said Mary.

"Really now, Mary," said Helen.

"The kids in my neighborhood call me 'Old Coot'."

"Hah! Smart-ass little buggers, ain't they?"

"You could say that," said Coot, thinking to himself, *This woman is insane!*

"I just did say that, moron."

A younger woman with a striking resemblance to Mary entered the room, nodded to the new arrivals, and hurried to Mary's bedside.

"Mom, I just spoke with Dr. Flaherty. He's ordered another CT scan to see whether they missed something the first time. A nurse should be here soon to take you to radiology."

"Not another trip to radiology! They're gonna cook my insides before they're through with me. I'll have a brain like boiled eggplant."

"Nonsense, Mom!" The woman turned toward the others in the room and said, "Hi. I'm Sandra, Mary's daughter." Looking at Diana, she said, "Welcome to your new home away from home. As you may have gathered, the conversation here can be a bit, uh, strange."

"What's that supposed to mean, Sandra? Gimme a break! They

got me strung up like a puppet so I can't even pick my nose or scratch my ass. You expect me to just lie here and take it?"

"Just try to be calm, Mom. You want to get well, don't you?"

"Of course I want to git well, you nincompoop!"

Before long a nurse came and wheeled Mary's bed into the corridor. Mary's voice, making profane observations and giving directions, gradually grew fainter, until it could not be distinguished in the general noise of the floor.

Mary's daughter looked out the window for a moment, then turned back and said, "Mom's not acting like herself. Dr. Flaherty said that head injuries can sometimes cause people to say and do strange things. I hope she didn't embarrass you."

Helen introduced herself, Diana, and Coot to Sandra. The four talked about the attack and its effect on the New York metro area. Sandra lived in Brooklyn and commuted into the city for work. She had been urging her mother to visit for years. At last Mary had agreed to come. She took a bus to Washington, stayed overnight with friends, and then took the same train as Diana.

"I feel so bad about talking her into coming up here and then having this happen!" Sandra said, her eyes filling with tears.

"There's no way you could have known there'd be an attack," said Coot. "You can't live your life paralyzed by fear of what some random terrorist will do. There are a lot more likely dangers, such as ... such as auto accidents."

Dr. Zeeland appeared in the doorway. "I hate to break up the party, but I need to check on Miss Munson, now that she's settled in her new room." He walked to Diana's bedside. "How are you feeling?"

"Better than yesterday."

"Very good! Let me have a look at your arm." He held the cast in one hand and Diana's hand in the other.

Coot felt his face redden slightly. Did Zeeland stroke her hand with his thumb?

"Good color in your hand, so the circulation is fine. Now your leg...Foot looks good. Is the numbness from the epidural gone?"

"Yes."

"Are you still requiring the morphine for pain?"

"Yes, but not as often."

"Okay, then. I'll come back and see you in a few hours."

"Thanks for all the attention. With the good care I've gotten from you and Dr. Murray, I hope to get well and get out of here soon."

"But not too soon. We've got to make sure you're well on the road to recovery before we discharge you."

Dr. Zeeland left the room. Sandra looked at Diana and said, "Lucky you — he's cute." Diana smiled.

"Let's hope he's as competent as he is good-looking," said Coot.

"I'm sure he's very good," said Helen.

"Well, I've got to get some supper and get on over to Newark for the panel discussion," said Coot. "Helen, can you get a cab back to the hotel tonight?"

"That shouldn't be a problem," said Helen.

"I can give you a ride," said Sandra. "We'll both have to be out of here by eight."

Coot left the room, caught the elevator to the lobby, found his car, and was soon back in his room at the hotel. He changed into more formal clothes for the panel, got back into his car, and began the drive to Newark. He stopped for a burger along the way, and by 8:00 was at the Robert Treat Hotel, location of the WNJN studio.

Once inside the building, Coot found his way to the WNJN facilities. He crossed the lobby and introduced himself to the receptionist seated at a desk facing the main doors.

"Oh, yes, Mr. Jenkins, please have a seat. I'll tell Melba you're here."

Soon a tall, elegant woman entered the lobby through a door to the left, spoke to the receptionist, and then approached Coot.

"Hello, Mr. Jenkins. I'm Melba Carter, the local producer for tonight's panel discussion. Please come with me."

Coot followed Ms. Carter into an L-shaped corridor lined with dressing rooms. They passed through the Green Room and into the studio.

Ms. Carter pointed to two chairs placed next to a small table. "This is where you and Mr. Pepys will be sitting."

"Beau Pepys?"

"That's right. He should be here soon. In the meantime we'll get you made up and miked."

Once those necessities had been taken care of, Coot took a seat in the Green Room and waited for Beau Pepys to arrive.

A few minutes later Melba Carter ushered a short, balding man in a slightly rumpled blue suit into the room.

"I believe you two know each other."

"Yes, indeed. Coot, good to see you again."

"You, too, Beau."

"I'll be back for you in about fifteen minutes, gentlemen," said Ms. Carter, and she left.

Coot and Beau chatted for a while, catching up with each other, as old friends love to do.

"After what happened in New York," said Beau, "I'm surprised to see you in the area."

"A friend of mine was injured as her train pulled into Penn Station, so I came up to see her. Where were you when it happened?"

"On the downtown Lexington Avenue subway. We had just pulled into the 110th Street station when there was a muffled rumble and the train jerked like it had been hit hard in the front. Then it started shaking like it was in a high wind. People on the platform were blown off their feet. I suppose the overpressure from the explosion entered Grand Central Station and was guided by the tunnels to much greater distances than in the open air."

"Were you hurt?"

"Just a bump on my head where I hit a pole. Many people in my car were thrown from their seats but no one was badly injured."

"You were lucky. My friend's arm and leg were broken and her spleen was ruptured. She was in intensive care for a couple of days."

"I'm sorry to hear that. Say, Coot, why do you suppose they picked us for this panel?"

"Funny names again?"

"Hah! Maybe so."

Melba Carter returned and took them back to the studio. Coot and Beau sat in their assigned seats and followed instructions for testing their microphones. On a large monitor they could see the panelists in the Washington studio.

At precisely 9 P.M. the moderator in Washington, Bill Moore, began the show.

"Good evening. As part of our coverage of the terrorist attack on New York City, WETA is presenting a panel discussion tonight. Our panelists will describe what happened, why it happened, and what responses should be considered. With me here in Washington are Meghan McMurtry from the Washington Post and John Samuels from the Heritage Foundation. Joining us from Newark, New Jersey, are Coot Jenkins from Scientists Against Future Extinction and Beau Pepys from the Council on Foreign Relations. Let's get started."

"Beau, I understand that you were in New York at the moment of the explosion. What was it like?"

Beau repeated the same description that he had given Coot.

"Meghan, can you give us a summary of the effects of the attack, in terms of casualties and physical damage?"

McMurtry offered the same estimates that Coot had been finding online.

"Where did the wounded go for treatment?"

"Most of them were not treated. How could they be? Manhattan was in chaos. The streets near the blast were impassable. Farther away they were jammed with people trying to get away from midtown. Ambulances sat in traffic, their sirens wailing. The tunnels and bridges were parking lots. Paramedics pushed gurneys along crowded sidewalks toward hospital emergency rooms. The subways shuttled back and forth, ambulances on rails. Helicopters swarmed the skies over Manhattan but there were few places at ground level to land, so they could only transport a few of the most seriously injured. The hospitals in Manhattan that were still functioning were not as overwhelmed as you would have expected, due to the inability of many injured people to reach them."

"I have something to add to that," said Coot. "The Amtrak tunnel leading west from Penn Station was undamaged. Once debris was cleared from the open area across 9th Avenue from the post office, New Jersey Transit commuter trains were able to move the wounded to the Secaucus station, from which ambulances took them to various hospitals in the area."

"What many of our viewers want to know is, why did this happen? Who would want to kill so many innocent people? Why couldn't our government protect New York? John, what can you tell us?"

"The short answer is that the world contains thousands of nuclear weapons and millions of angry people. A few of those angry people got hold of a few of those nuclear weapons. Britain was able to thwart its attackers. India and the U.S. were not. As Coot pointed out in his debate with Larry Limbick, we needed to improve the odds of success. On Monday we ran out of luck."

"So you think it was just bad luck that we got attacked?"

"Not *just* bad luck. There are too many nuclear weapons in the world. Obviously some of them need to be stored more securely. There are too many unresolved problems, such as in the Middle East, and too many lawless areas, such as northwest Pakistan. The unresolved problems lead to anger. The lawless areas allow angry people to organize themselves and plan attacks. The immense number of weapons increases the probability that some weapons will be stored insecurely, stolen by criminal gangs, and sold to potential attackers."

"What can we do to improve our chances of avoiding future disasters? Coot?"

"The easiest steps involve the weapons themselves. The Comprehensive Nuclear-Test-Ban Treaty, the Nuclear Non-Proliferation Treaty, and the various strategic arms reduction treaties were important accomplishments, although enforcement has been an issue. To reduce tactical nuclear devices, we need a T.A.R.T. to go with the S.T.A.R.T."

"Beau, what would you add to Coot's list?"

"Securing existing nuclear weapons and fissile materials is also very important."

"John?"

"I agree with Coot and Beau, but I would include the necessity of working to resolve the regional problems that drive much of the anger that terrorists channel. This is the hardest aspect of dealing with nuclear terrorism. While we're working on these problems, we also need to ensure the rule of law everywhere. Failed states like Somalia provide safe havens for terrorists."

"Meghan, you've learned more about the actual device that exploded. Tell us about that."

"According to the people I've talked with at Defense, Energy, and Homeland Security, the device was an atomic land mine with a yield of about a hundred tons of TNT. That's less than one per cent as powerful as the atomic bombs that were dropped on Hiroshima and Nagasaki by the U.S. during World War II. Furthermore, the effects of the blast were not as widespread as they might have been, since the device exploded at ground level on 34th Street, right in front of the Empire State Building."

"The U.S. Army's Small Atomic Demolition Munition had a variable yield, from ten tons up to one kiloton," said Samuels. "I wonder why Mushrooms chose such low yields for the two explosions so far."

"Regardless of their motivation, the Mushrooms video said the next explosion will be ten times more powerful," said Coot. "That's what frightens me."

"How could an atomic land mine have been smuggled into New York City?" Moore asked.

"There are many possibilities," said Coot. "The weapon that John mentioned weighed only 150 pounds, so the stolen device could have been carried into Manhattan by truck, van, boat, car, or even by a very strong individual. To escape detection the terrorists could have put extra lead shielding around it, so probably it was brought in by truck."

"It's also possible that people were bribed not to inspect the vehicle with the device," said Samuels.

"Do the authorities know whether this was a suicide attack?" asked Moore.

"My sources think probably not, for two reasons," said McMurtry. "First, there was no need for a suicide attack, since the device was probably designed for soldiers to position, set a timer, and leave quickly. Second, the guys who carried out this operation were highly skilled and therefore too valuable to sacrifice unless absolutely necessary."

"What can be done to prevent another attack by the Mushrooms group that has claimed responsibility for the attack? John?"

"Nothing we can do will make us completely secure."

"Sorry! I mean, how can we move the odds in our favor?"

"In the short run, the only things we can do are reduce the number of targets and increase efforts to find the terrorists. Homeland Security has already raised the threat level to Red. Federal, state, and local law enforcement are all on alert. Special response teams have been mobilized. Security has been increased around nuclear power plants. The Statue of Liberty is closed. Streets have been blocked off near important government buildings."

"What are the authorities doing to find the guys who set off the device on Monday? Maybe the same guys are planning another attack!"

"The F.B.I. is looking for the perpetrators," said Beau. "Given the chaos in Manhattan after the attack and the diversity of the population in the city, it would have been very difficult to develop leads. Still, they must be trying. Perhaps someone overheard them saying something. Perhaps someone will notice something strange in their behavior."

"Wouldn't it improve the odds of capturing them if the F.B.I. issued a special plea for information, with suggestions of things to look for?"

"Maybe, but that tactic could backfire if it led to thousands of useless leads. It might be better to rely on citizens' common sense as to what's unusual or suspicious."

"What do we know about Mushrooms?"

"Not much," said Coot. "What worries me is that they may have two or three more nuclear devices." Coot realized too late that he had revealed too much. Jill Meecham would be furious.

"Mushrooms has been vague about how many nuclear weapons they have," said Samuels. "To the best of my knowledge no government has claimed to know how many devices Mushrooms has."

"Coot, how sure are you about the number of weapons?" asked

Moore.

Coot decided instantly that it would be better to seem stupid than knowledgable on this. "I'm not sure. I heard an estimate somewhere."

"Where?" asked Samuels.

"Yes, where?" asked McMurtry.

"I don't remember," said Coot. He hated looking as if he didn't know what he was talking about.

"Intelligence is never 100% reliable," said Beau. "Even if there were a report of a precise number, we couldn't be sure it was correct."

Coot tried hard to participate in the rest of the program, despite his acute embarrassment at having let slip such important information and then having to play the fool to minimize the damage. He felt relieved when Bill Moore concluded the discussion, saying "We've come to the end of our time tonight. Thanks to Meghan and John here in Washington and to Coot and Beau in Newark for a very illuminating discussion. Good night."

Coot and Beau removed their microphones and laid them on the table, then stood up. Coot extended his hand to Beau.

"Thanks for rescuing me there at the end, Beau."

"No problem. It was so unlike you not to be sure of your source."

The two men left the studio together and walked toward the parking lot.

"The past few days have been difficult," said Coot. "For some reason I thought that the number of weapons Mushrooms had was public knowledge."

"So, how did you find out about the number and source of the weapons?"

"A little bird told me."

"Alright, I won't press you. Like I said, the report may not be reliable anyway."

"Right. Well, it was good to see you again, Beau. I'm glad you escaped injury in the attack."

"Good to see you, too, Coot. Have a safe trip back to D.C."

Once back in his room at the Crowne Plaza, Coot went through his usual nighttime preparations. It was too late to call Helen, so he crawled into bed. Unable to fall asleep, he stared at the ceiling. He hoped he hadn't screwed up too badly by divulging the number of weapons — or by looking like an idiot!

"The doctors seemed pleased with Diana's progress," Helen told Coot as they ate breakfast in the hotel's restaurant Thursday morning. "Dr. Murray said she can go home on Sunday if she continues to improve at this rate."

"That's great news! Will you be going back to D.C. with her?"

"Yes. I can stay with her for a few days, until she feels she can manage on her own."

"Will you two fly back, or would you like to ride with me?"

"With you, if that's not too much trouble."

"Trouble? Are you kidding? I'd be delighted."

"We watched your panel discussion on the TV in Diana's room last night."

"I'm sorry to hear that. I got myself into a bit of trouble from which there was no escape except to look like a fool."

"You didn't look like a fool!"

"You're too generous."

Since visiting hours began at 2 P.M. and were limited to one person at a time, Coot and Helen agreed that they would have lunch at 1 and that Helen would see Diana first, for half an hour.

Coot spent the morning reviewing what the staff back in Washington had produced the previous three days: position papers, articles for magazines, op-eds for newspapers, and even a video, the fruit of Emily and Joe's collaboration.The attack had galvanized them as nothing else had in all the years Coot had worked at S.A.F.E.

Mid-morning, Coot got an e-mail from Ben: "Call me." This was ominous. Coot was sure Ben was not pleased with his performance in the panel discussion. He phoned Ben right away.

"I expected a stronger showing from you, Coot. You're one of my top people, but you seemed unsure of yourself. What happened?"

"I can't go into details on the phone, Ben. With all that's been going on, I thought that certain facts were public that weren't. I had to choose between looking stupid and giving credence to sensitive information. You saw the result."

"Yes, unfortunately I did. I would like to get the full story from you in person. When will you be back in the office?"

"Monday morning."

"Alright. By the way, how's Diana Munson doing?"

"Very well. I'll be driving Diana and her mother back to D.C. on Sunday."

"That's good news. By the way, I've seen the feedback you've been providing the staff, as well as your own papers. It looks like working remotely has been a success, if we ignore last night."

"Thanks, Ben."

"See you Monday, then. Ciao."

Ben had been gentler than Coot had feared.

After lunch, Coot drove Helen to Meadowlands. She went directly to Diana's room. Coot was unable to find an empty room in which to work. Even the classroom in which he had worked on Wednesday was now being used for patients in queue for permanent rooms. The waiting rooms were full as well, so Coot left the hospital and went back to his car, where he managed to get connected to the Internet. He did not have time to do more than read a few e-mail messages and check some news sites before it was time to visit Diana.

Coot waited outside Diana's room until Helen noticed him. She said her goodbyes to Diana and joined Coot in the corridor.

"She's feeling better today. Less pain, less morphine, more alert."

"Good. Why don't you come back in half an hour? I really should be working today, and you're her mom, after all."

"Okay. See you then."

Helen left and Coot entered the room. Diana smiled at him.

"Hi, Coot. Thanks for coming. I know you must have a lot of work to do."

"I didn't drive hundreds of miles to sit in my hotel room. I'd much rather visit with you than pound away on my laptop."

Mary looked up from her bed by the window. A nasty grin broke out on her weathered face.

"Well, look who's here — Mr. I-don't-know-what-I'm-talking-about himself!"

"Mary, that's so unfair! Coot is an expert in his field."

"Well, he sure didn't look like it last night!"

"Mary's right, Diana. I didn't do a very good job. I wish I could explain to you what happened, but that would just compound the problem, especially given present company."

"What's that supposed to mean, you retarded old codger?"

"Mrs. Butrell, what in the world are you going on about?" Dr. Zeeland asked as he entered the room.

Zeeland was just the guy that Coot did not want to see, much less be humiliated in front of.

"Bozo here was on TV last night, talking about the attack. I thought I'd learn something. What a disappointment! He couldn't even explain how he knew how many nukes the terrorists had. I think he was just trying to sound impressive, but when the others asked him to explain himself, he couldn't do it."

Coot felt a strong urge to strangle the old woman.

Dr. Zeeland turned his attention to Coot. "You know how many weapons the terrorists have?"

"Not for sure. I can't go into it."

"Ha! He's bluffing now! Trying to wiggle out of admitting he's a moron."

Coot smiled. This was great. Why didn't he realize it sooner? "Mary, you're amazing. I hope everyone who saw the panel discussion last night was as perceptive as you."

"Don't you patronize me, you big buffoon."

"I'm not patronizing you. I'm truly glad that you're convinced I'm an idiot."

"That doesn't make any sense at all!"

"If I weren't such a moron, I might be able to explain it to you."

"Well, I'm confused now, too," said Dr. Zeeland.

"Me, too," said Diana.

Zeeland looked at her and smiled broadly. "I almost forgot why I came in here. How are you today, Diana?"

"Diana" — he called her "Diana"! Coot's jealousy flared up once again.

"Much better, Dr. Zeeland," said Diana. "Dr. Murray says I can go home on Sunday."

"Ah, well, if Dr. Murray says you're good to go, I guess I'll have to let you."

"Poor Ralph," said Mary. "He was just getting up the courage to come on to the young honey when she announced she's leaving him."

Coot's appreciation of Mary Butrell's quirkiness increased by an order of magnitude.

The doctor spun around and glared at Mary for a moment. His face reddened and remained flushed even after his features relaxed.

"Mrs. Butrell, your injuries may be more serious than we thought. I had hoped that you would be getting over such wild talk by now. We may need to get you back to radiology for some more pictures."

"Don't bother threatening me, sonny boy! It won't work. I know a masher when I see one."

Dr. Zeeland hastened to Mary's side of the room and pulled the curtains closed around her bed.

"What the hell are you doing, you quack? Nurse! Nurse!"

"Sometimes it helps to reduce the amount of visual stimulation a head-injury patient gets," he whispered to Diana and Coot.

Coot was grinning. "We got fired at with both barrels there, didn't we, Dr. Zeeland?"

"Yeah. A good example to use when arguing for a private room."

Mary's mutterings became softer and less frequent. Zeeland's trick seemed to have worked.

Dr. Zeeland finished examining Diana's arm and leg — as well as he could with them in their casts — and left. Mary was snoring loudly behind her curtain. Coot approached Diana's bedside and grasped her right hand.

"It's great to see you're healing so well. On Sunday I'll be driving you and your mom back to D.C. How long will she be able to stay with you?"

"At least a week. Maybe longer. She wants to be sure I can take care of myself."

"You'll probably be taking care of her by the end of the first week."

"I wish!" Diana squeezed Coot's hand. "I'm sorry Mary was so rough on you. I could tell you were uncomfortable last night, but I was surprised when you seemed unable to remember where you'd heard the estimate. That didn't seem at all like you — the man who had handled Larry Limbick so well."

"I guess Mary Contrary was cackling the whole time."

"Don't worry about her. She's not in her right mind."

"Her only problem is that she speaks the truth, no matter how uncomfortable it makes others."

"You did remember how you learned the estimate, didn't you?"

"Of course, but it was important not to admit how much I knew or from whom I'd learned it."

"It must have been difficult for you to play dumb like that."

"Yeah. Ben Barker wasn't impressed, either."

"You'll just have to explain to him what happened. Then he'll be impressed with how well you covered up your mistake."

"Is there an award for best performance as a dumb-ass in a supporting-national-security role?"

"Sure. You might win a Nukey for it."

Coot laughed. That was a pun worthy of Frannie.

"What are you laughing about?" Coot's response had awoken the sleeping dragon.

"Nothing, Mary. Go back to sleep," said Coot.

"Like hell I will. And draw back this damn curtain, will you?"

Before Coot could react, Helen poked her head in the door. "My turn!"

* * *

"What the fuck are we waiting for?" Mitch Chambers had been getting more and more impatient all week. Why weren't George and the other Mushrooms willing to act? They knew what they had to do, but their analysis was backwards. They wanted to see evidence of insurrection *before* they attacked again. Why couldn't they understand that their own bold action was the necessary *trigger* of the insurrection? The masses were timid. They needed strong leadership. They needed repeated encouragement. They needed another attack to convince them that insurrection could succeed.

"Calm down, Mitch," said George. This was the same response that George always gave Mitch. How infuriating!

"We have the most powerful weapon of any revolutionary group in the entire history of the human race, and you guys just want to sit around in a fucking *warehouse* and pretend someone else has to take the initiative? You're drivinge me crazy!"

Jamie Saunders laughed. "You were already crazy before all this, Mitch."

Jamie always lit Mitch's fuse. The fucking bull dyke. Of course she could break him in two like a match stick if she wanted to. Maybe that's why she felt it was safe to insult him at every opportunity. With her physique, why wasn't she bolder? She had the body of an NFL lineman but the soul of a ballerina. She wasn't a bull dyke at all, but more like a cow, content to stand around and chew her cud. And insult Mitch. Damn her!

"It's just been four days since the New York op," said Doug Lloyd. "It takes time for people to come together, realize they have a common cause, and act."

"How long are you willing to wait?" Mitch asked, looking at Doug with annoyance. "Another week? A month?"

"We need to pay attention to what people are doing out there," said George. "Give them a chance to organize and act."

More temporizing from George. How could a man bold enough to go halfway around the world to buy nuclear weapons suddenly be so timid?

"What makes you think they *will* organize and act?" Mitch countered.

"People know that institutions are run *by* the people at the top *for* the people at the top," said George. "We just have to encourage them."

"If we keep blowing things up, they may think we're just a bunch of psychos," said Jamie. "Of course, in your case they would be right."

Mitch opened his mouth, ready to snarl a rebuttal, when the last silent Mushroom spoke.

"Jamie's right," said Bennie. "About the effect of explosions too close together, I mean," he added.

Mitch stood up, his fists clenched in frustration. "Alright, alright. We'll wait, but we're making a big mistake." He left the group and found privacy in the small bathroom. He lowered his trousers and boxers and sat down. He closed his eyes. Anger flooded his consciousness. He felt helpless. He had felt helpless before, and he didn't like it. Jamie made him feel helpless. He didn't like her. Suddenly he remembered his father's coming, naked and aroused, into the bathroom when he was sitting on the toilet as a kid. Forcing Mitch to give him the stimulation he craved. Forcing Mitch to swallow, when his every reflex was to gag. His eyes sprang open. The memory was too awful. No wonder he was so angry, so willing to lash out, to hurt people. How many fathers out there were like his father, an abuser and a drunk? He would like to kill all of them with one blow.

* * *

Sunday morning Coot and Helen went to Diana's room to help her get ready to leave.

"Are you cleared for discharge?" asked Helen.

"Yes. Both Dr. Murray and Dr. Zeeland said I could go home."

"That's terrific!" said Coot.

"No, it's not!" bellowed Mary. "I'm gonna miss the little twit."

"Twit?" said Helen. "Why would you call her a twit if you're going to miss her?"

"I don't know," said Mary. "It just came out."

"Watch your mouth, Mary, or I'll pull that curtain shut," said Coot.

"You do that and I'll ... I'll ... I don't know what I'll do. I'm so confused."

"Mary," said Diana gently, "don't you remember that Dr. Flaherty told you that you'll be confused sometimes as the swelling goes down? Part of you is getting back to normal but another part still wants to say inappropriate things."

"I guess so. Thanks for reminding me. You're a real sweetheart."

"I'm sorry I threatened to close your curtain, Mary. It's great that you're getting better."

"Thanks, Coot Jenkins. You're more of a gentleman than I thought."

"I brought you some new clothes," Helen said to Diana. "Your old ones were ruined. Would you like some help getting dressed?"

"Sure."

"I'll wait outside," said Coot.

When Coot was allowed back into the room, Diana was sitting in a wheelchair. Her left arm in its cast was protruding from her sleeveless white blouse. Her left leg, also still in a cast, was sticking straight out from her long plaid skirt. Other than that, she looked normal. Helen had brushed her hair and even helped her with a little makeup.

Coot gathered a few things from Diana's bedside table. One item was a sheet of paper with the barely-legible words "Ralph Zeeland", along with an email address and a phone number.

"What's this about, Diana?" said Coot. "Won't you have another doctor in Washington to follow up with?"

"Of course. Ralph just wants me to let him know how I'm doing."

"Ralph" now, was it? Too bad Mary was getting back to normal — Coot could use her help in nipping this hospital romance in the bud.

"All set?" asked Helen.

"Yes," said Diana. "Goodbye, Mary. You're the most entertaining roommate I've ever had. If you continue to improve as fast as you've been doing, you'll be back home soon."

"Goodbye, hon. Thanks for puttin' up with me."

"No problem. I understand what you've been through."

Coot pushed Diana's wheelchair out of the room, while Helen carried a pair of crutches. They thanked the nurses they met on the way to the elevators.

Coot left Helen and Diana in the lobby while he went to get the car. In a few minutes Diana was belted into position in the back seat, her left leg stretching across to the other door.

"It's lucky you're not any taller — you barely fit as it is," said Helen, as she got into the front passenger's seat.

Coot returned the wheelchair. That done, he took his seat behind the steering wheel. Soon they were back on the Turnpike, heading south.

"It's very odd not to see the Empire State Building on the New York skyline," said Helen. "That's my earliest memory from trips to

New York as a child."

"Mine, too," said Diana. "That building symbolized the city like nothing else."

"And its destruction is the latest proof of the need to rid the world of such weapons," said Coot.

No one said anything for a long time.

"Please come in, Coot, and shut the door," Ben Barker said, looking up from his desk. Ben was not smiling.

"I guess you want the full story of what happened during the panel discussion last Wednesday."

"Yes."

"Toward the end of the discussion Bill Moore asked what we knew about Mushrooms. I should have kept my mouth shut. Instead, I mentioned that they might have two or three more nuclear devices."

"'You don't normally just blurt things out, do you?"

"No, of course not. I don't know. Maybe I just wanted people to understand the seriousness of the situation. Anyway, I realized immediately that the numbers, which I had deduced from a Pakistani intelligence report, had not yet been made public. I felt I had no choice but to make it look like I'd just pulled that number out of my ass."

"But did you have to look like such a complete amateur?"

"Can you think of a better way to destroy the apparent accuracy of the number?"

"Well, no — that was *your* job."

"I did the best I could, on the spur of the moment. I'm sorry if that wasn't good enough for you."

"I expected better of you, that's all."

"That makes two of us."

"Okay, enough of that. How's Diana Munson doing?"

"She's back in her apartment. Her mother's staying with her for a while. Having an arm and a leg in casts makes ordinary tasks much more difficult."

"She's lucky to be alive. Many people weren't so fortunate. Give her my best, will you?"

"Sure. Thanks. I'll be in my office if you need me."

Back at his desk, Coot went through the paper mail that had accumulated while he was in New Jersey. The mechanical act of sorting was as much as he could do, after the embarrassing encounter with his boss. He cursed under his breath. Why had he messed up so badly? The thought that he might not be as sharp as he used to be and no longer able to think quickly on his feet galled him.

Since the Mushrooms' entry into Britain had been thwarted by Euro Securité guards, Coot had been wondering about the firm's continuing to milk its capture of the Mushrooms team for publicity. Their ads kept trumpeting Euro Securité's ability to protect the people of the UK, in contrast to the Indian and American governments' inability to thwart attacks on *their* soil. The tone of the ads was very negative about government in general, almost as if they had been written by the anarchists whose attack the company had thwarted. This tone seemed odd to Coot. Usually the security companies tried hard to market their services *to* governments and therefore were loathe to criticize them. The goal of such ads must be to goad the general population into demanding protection by private security firms, Euro Securité in particular.

Another question troubled Coot: why did Myron Pepsey sell the Empire State Building just before it was attacked? Coot was not the only one wondering about the sale. A reporter at the opening of the Myron Pepsey Center for Alzheimer's Research at Johns Hopkins had asked Pepsey why he had sold the building at such an advantageous time. Pepsey said that a couple of months earlier he'd received an alarming report that an unknown group of terrorists was hoping to attack the Empire State Building within a few months. Pepsey said he had immediately begun planning to sell the building and had finally found a buyer. He claimed that it was just coincidental that the closing occurred just a few days before the attack. Coot was particularly interested in the source of the report Pepsey had cited but could not find any further references to it. Jill Meecham said there were unsubstantiated reports like that coming into the C.I.A. all the time.

Coot decided to learn more about the various flavors of anarchism. He had focussed on insurrectionary anarchists up till now because that was what Mushrooms seemed to be. One type that caught his eye was anarcho-capitalism, which included the belief that governments' protective, regulatory, and legal functions could be performed instead by private companies. So, Coot wondered, who owns Euro Securité?

Despite his best efforts, Coot was able to learn only that Euro Securité was owned by EuroKapital, a private equity firm, whose investors were not required by law to be made public, no matter how large their holdings were. Coot poked around various financial and security services websites, but he found no information about EuroKapital. He sent email to a few friends in the financial and security industries. He left phone messages for others. He even mentioned his interest in EuroKapital to Jill, but she had no information on the firm's investors.

Coot and his colleagues at S.A.F.E. continued to press the case for the gradual elimination of existing tactical and strategic nuclear weapons, as well as the rapid securing of all fissile materials worldwide. Several mainstream publications, including *Atlantic, Popular Science,* and *Rolling Stone*, agreed to publish their articles, and their videos were beginning to appear on various Internet sites.

Ben seemed happy with the progress his staff had made in executing Coot's plan. Coot noted especially one e-mail message from the S.A.F.E. leader that read, "It looks like our efforts are beginning to pay off, both in old and new media. Thanks to you all for a job well done. Keep up the good work." Maybe Ben had forgiven him for the gaffe during the panel discussion after all. Now Coot could relax and focus all his energies on putting together the pieces of the Mushrooms puzzle.

* * *

Over a week had passed since the Mushrooms had attacked New York City, yet no signs of insurrection had appeared. George Boyd was the last holdout against taking further action. At last he realized that doing nothing would produce nothing, that insurrection required further initiative by the Mushrooms. Not setting off another nuclear explosion, like Mitch wanted, but something more directly motivational.

After breakfast that morning, George proposed another video that would give viewers a stark choice: rise up against the institutions that dominate their lives or face another, more destructive attack somewhere in the country. The others agreed. They spent the rest of the day arguing about the wording, but finally agreed on text to send to VI.

* * *

Coot received a most welcome phone call late Thursday afternoon: his piano had been repaired. He arranged for it to be delivered on Friday. That evening he called Diana about breakfast on Saturday — and to tell her the piano would be ready for them to use afterwards.

"Oh, Coot," said Diana, "It's really great that your piano has been restored, but I've already got plans for Saturday. Ralph is going to be in Washington for a conference next week, so he decided to come down for the weekend and I agreed to go to the National Zoo with him on Saturday."

Coot cursed to himself, then said, "Are you sure you're up for hobbling around on that leg all day? That seems like an odd sort of activity for an orthopedist to propose."

"Don't be absurd, Coot. I'll use a wheelchair. Besides, Ralph would not have suggested it if he thought it would hurt me."

"So, have you and Ralph been in touch since you left the hospital?"

"We've talked on the phone some."

"What do you see in him, anyway?"

"He's nice, he's intelligent, *and* he plays the violin. Besides, he saved my life."

"And now he wants something in return."

"I think you're jealous, Coot Jenkins!"

"Jealous? Of course I'm jealous! You know how I feel about you. I thought you cared a bit for me."

"I do care about you, Coot. You know I do. I also appreciate all you did for Mom and me after the attack."

"Do you still want to avoid a serious relationship, or is that concern out the window — with *Ralph*?"

Diana did not respond for several seconds. At last she said, "Mom and I have talked about that a lot. She feels that I am giving up all hope for happiness by avoiding involvement with a man."

"I agree with Helen. Do you?"

"I don't know. I'm still thinking about it."

"You're a terrific person, Diana. Give somebody a chance to share your life, for however long that will be — even if it's not me. Every relationship has risks, you know. Just look at what happened to Frannie."

"I know, Coot. You're really brave to be willing to face that kind of loss again. I don't want to risk hurting you more than I already have."

"Does Ralph know about your aversion to having a serious relationship?"

"Not yet. If he seems to want to be more than just friends, I'll tell him about my condition."

"*If? If?* I've seen how he looks at you, how he holds your hand. It's too late for *if*, Diana. You should tell him right away."

"Maybe you're right. It just seems so ... *awkward*. He hasn't really declared his feelings for me."

"That should make it easier. Say you're telling him because he's a doctor and you think he would be interested."

"Good idea."

"You might want to find out first what his expectations are, in terms of having a family. Just so you know he's not adjusting what he tells you because of your condition."

"You seem so cynical about Ralph, Coot."

"I'm just being careful. In negotiating I have learned to be cautious about revealing information too soon, if I want to know what the other party really thinks."

Coot entered Snuffy's alone that Saturday, except for his copy of the *Washington Post*.

"Where's Diana?" Snuffy wanted to know right away. "I kinda like her."

"That makes two of us. She's going to the zoo with a friend

today."

"Male or female?"

"Male."

"Too bad. I guess it's too much to hope for that a lion or tiger will reach out and grab him."

"Yeah. The National Zoo is too well designed for that to happen."

"You want your regular table anyway?"

"Sure, why not? I'll have a quick bite to eat and be on my way. Gotta practice my piano. It was returned just yesterday."

"So it's as good as new, in spite of the fire?"

"Seems to be."

"That's great to hear. Say, when are those guys going on trial?"

"I haven't heard a thing."

"They should lock 'em up and throw away the key. They coulda killed ya!"

"Tell me about it."

Snuffy gave Coot a menu and hurried away to deal with later arrivals. Coot gave his order to the waitress. As she walked away, he began reading his paper while sipping the coffee she had poured for him.

"Excuse me — aren't you Mr. Jenkins?"

Coot looked up. The woman looked vaguely familiar. "Yes, I'm Coot Jenkins. Haven't we met?"

"I'm Stella Preger. You saved my little boy from choking here a few weeks ago. That's him over there," she said, pointing to a table full of kids. They were all talking among themselves and looking at him. "I just wanted to thank you again for what you did."

"I was glad to help, Mrs. Preger. How are you doing?"

"It's *Ms.* Preger now. I'm divorcing Melvin. You saw how angry he could get. I was always scared of him. Not just for me, but for the kids."

"From what I've experienced at Melvin's hands, I think you're doing the right thing. I may have to testify against him, you know, if the case ever goes to trial."

"Just tell what happened. They should put the bum away for a long, long time! Anyway, I won't bother you no more. Have a nice day, Mr. Jenkins."

"You, too, Ms. Preger, and good luck to you and your kids."

The waitress brought Coot's breakfast: a Southwestern Omelet — the same dish he had recommended to Diana. *Diana!* Coot ate the omelet, finished his coffee, took care of the financial necessities, and headed back to his house. At least Coot could take this opportunity to practice.

Sunday morning Coot met Roger and Jack for their weekly run, which they had postponed for a day because Jack had a family event to attend.

"Damn, it's windy!" said Roger, as the trio started out.

"At least it'll be at our backs later," said Jack.

"I was hoping the wind would be at my back with Diana," said Coot.

"Aha! I thought you seemed...more interested in her...than you were admitting!" said Roger, already getting a bit out of breath.

"You went to New Jersey...to make sure she was okay," said Jack. "You even chauffeured...her mother around...and drove them both...back to D.C....for God's sake....Sounds like the wind's...at your back to me!"

"There's just one problem....One of her doctors...took a liking to her....A guy named Ralph Zeeland....They've been chatting on the phone....It's bugging the shit out of me."

"Let me guess — this guy is young...and single...and rich," said Roger.

"He's about her age,...I suppose....He didn't have...a wedding ring."

"That's not a sure sign...he's single, though," said Jack.

"He's a resident...in orthopedics."

"If he's not rich," said Roger, "he will be."

"Does Diana like him?" asked Jack.

"Well enough...to go to the zoo...with him yesterday."

"That's not good," said Roger. "All those monkeys...having sex...could give him ideas."

"I don't think...he needs the monkeys...for that," said Coot.

"What else...has she told you...about him?" asked Jack.

"She said,...'He's nice, he's intelligent,...*and* he plays the violin.'"

"You do pretty well...on two of those measures," said Roger.

"But I don't...play the piano...very well."

"That gives her...a chance to teach you," said Jack. "She may like that role."

"Maybe."

"Otherwise, she may feel...she has little to offer you...the famous...nonproliferation expert,...the TV star, etc., etc."

"She did seem to enjoy...giving me lessons."

"Has her attitude...toward you...changed since Zeeland appeared?" asked Jack.

"No. She still seems...to care for me."

"That's good."

"I got along great...with her mom."

"Don't underestimate...the importance of impressing Mom."

"So, tell me...why you're worried...about Zeeland," said Roger. "Other than...his future income stream."

"The guy saved her life, Roger!...How can I compete with that?...And, he's her age!"

"In the end, it comes down...to whether she likes you...or him better," said Jack.

"Yeah, and I don't feel like...I've got any control...over that....Sort of like...I've worked on nonproliferation...for twenty-five years...and was unable...to prevent a group...like Mushrooms...from getting a bunch...of nuclear weapons."

"Now you're sounding...defeatist, Coot," said Jack. "Don't go there."

"Yeah, Coot," said Roger. "You've got a lot to offer."

"Diana's decision...will have everything...to do with...how you treat her."

"Makes sense," said Roger.

"One more thing:...don't criticize Zeeland...to Diana," said Jack. "It'll just make you look...weak or even desperate."

"Yeah," said Roger. "Women aren't impressed...by weakness — unless they want...to wear the pants...in the family."

The three friends ran to the end of their route, then headed home, the wind at their backs. They agreed to run again on Wednesday, in preparation for a road race the next weekend.

* * *

"Hey, Coot, you'd better come watch this!" Joe Giancola called on Monday morning from his office across the hall from Coot. Joe, due to his role as S.A.F.E.'s publicist, had multiple TV screens arrayed across one wall of his office. Coot hurried over to see what had piqued Joe's interest.

Joe's sound system was switched to the CNN feed. The anchor was explaining that the network was about to broadcast a recorded announcement that VI had sent to media outlets around the world. "The next voice you hear will be that of a spokesman for Mushrooms."

The group's familiar avatar appeared, its features as bland and expressionless as always. Its computer-generated voice was calm, but its message was ominous.

"Two weeks have passed since I last spoke to you. We had hoped that with more time you Americans would begin to see that it was in your best interest to join the insurrection, to overthrow the institutions that oppress you and others around the world. We confess ourselves disappointed. You are still in thrall to your oppressors. You even identify with them, not realizing that you are their tools and their victims. We have placed another nuclear device in another great American city. The institutions that you serve cannot protect you. You must stand up to them to save yourselves. Join us! Organize yourselves! Time is running out."

CNN of course had its usual panel of talking heads to analyze the latest message. What could they say? Coot and Joe listened to their commentary for a while.

"The intelligence agencies have still not tracked down these guys," said one panelist. "This is a colossal failure, much worse than before 9/11."

"Maybe they're bluffing."

"I don't think so."

"Right, and remember that fellow Jenkins who said they had two or three nuclear devices?"

Joe glanced at Coot, who was flushed with embarrassment at having his gaffe mentioned on national television. "They won't let you forget about it, will they?"

"I guess not."

"Has the Administration released a statement?" said Joe.

"Not yet. I'm sure they will."

"Do these guys actually think the American people are going to join them? I mean, really. Who would follow a bunch of psychotic anarchists?"

"The number of computer security breaches has increased each of the last seven weeks. Maybe some American or other hackers *are* joining the 'insurrection.'"

"Or maybe it's just VI."

Coot and Joe resumed listening to the discussion on CNN. A legal scholar on the panel said, "Congress used its constitutional authority in 1807 to pass the Insurrection Act, giving the president the power to employ the armed forces for law enforcement within the United States in case of an insurrection. Some National Guard units trained in counter-terrorism have already been mobilized."

A representative from the A.C.L.U. said, "There is already increased pressure on civil liberties, especially the rights guaranteed by the Fourth and Fifth Amendments. The prohibitions against unreasonable search and seizure and against self-incrimination have already been largely ignored in cases of suspected terrorism since the attack on the Empire State Building. There are reports from around the country of Guard units entering people's homes and confiscating computer equipment. The Guard says the searches are justified by tips received on the Homeland Security hotline. This is getting ugly."

The CNN anchor broke into the discussion. "The president is about to make a statement from the Oval Office. We go there live now."

The president was seated behind the large, ornately-carved desk given by Queen Victoria to president Rutherford B. Hayes. The picture switched to a close-up of the president. The skin under his eyes was even darker than usual, and no amount of makeup could hide his weariness.

"My fellow Americans, as you know, a small group of anarchists, Mushrooms, has already attacked New York with a nuclear device and is now threatening a similar attack against another of our cities. The F.B.I. has proof that a related group, Viral Infection, is behind some of the recent attacks on government computer systems. You can be sure that your government is taking all possible measures to find and stop these terrorists. For that is what they are. Terrorists. They're not fighting for you, as they claim. They certainly were not fighting for the thirty thousand people they killed in New York or the hundred thousand they injured there.

"Many people have called, written, and e-mailed the White House to ask how they can help to capture these terrorists before they strike again. Today I am announcing Ferret, a new program that gives you the tools to do just that. With Ferret, you can notify Homeland Security of suspicious activity in your neighborhood or place of business. If your tip leads to the capture of the Mushrooms or their weapons, you will receive a ten million dollar reward. To participate in Ferret, you must register at www.ferret.gov. You'll need a valid government-issued ID such as a driver's license or passport to do so. If you don't have access to the Internet, you can get help registering at any school, library, police station, or government office. You must provide proof of your identity, just as you would to board an airplane. There will be a severe penalty for providing false information at this critical time.

"Some people will criticize Ferret for creating a nation of spies. I understand their concern, but I believe we have no choice. We must enlist the help of everyone in our great country to prevent further harm to the land we love so dearly. I thank you for your attention and for your help. God bless you, and God bless the United States of America."

The talking heads on CNN resumed their chatter. Joe silenced his sound system.

"Whaddya think, Coot?"

"I think Mushrooms and their allies are going for broke. Ferret's ten million dollar reward is going to get a lot of people's attention. I hope it works. There are bound to be a lot of false accusations, even attempts to frame people by registering them and giving false information."

"I wonder how many 'The bomb is definitely there' reports Homeland Security will get."

"Not so many that they obscure the one we're looking for, I hope!"

Coot called Diana the Monday night after her trip to the zoo with Zeeland. Talking about the trip with her would be easier on the phone.

"Hello?"

"Hi, Diana, it's Coot. How are you?"

"Fine. Just a little tired. How are you?"

"Fine. Would you like to have breakfast at Snuffy's tomorrow? As a makeup for missing it last Saturday/"

"I suppose so, if we can be done by 8:30. I have a lot of catching up to do at work."

"How did your adventure with Zeeland go?"

"We had a good time. Ralph's very sweet."

"Did you tell him about your condition?"

"Yes."

"So, how did he take it?"

"He was very distressed. He's going to look through the literature to find out the current state of medical knowledge on the subject."

"Did you first uncover his expectations in terms of having a family?"

"I did take your advice on that. He said he wanted to settle down with someone someday and have a couple of kids, maybe more."

"Did he change his tune when he heard your news?"

"He said there were a lot of ways to have a family. In fact, he reminded me of you, the way you look for alternatives when your first choice is not obtainable."

"A smart guy, Zeeland."

"I don't know what you fellows see in me."

"How about intelligence, kindness, beauty, charm, talent? — I could go on. In fact, I should add bravery to the list."

"Now you're embarrassing me."

"Sorry — I was just being honest."

"You do know how to make someone feel special, Coot. I just wish you would relax a little about Ralph. You're always driving past your own headlights, and now you're driving past his!"

Coot laughed. "Diana, you're wonderful! Now why don't you get some sleep? You've had a difficult time. I'll pick you up at 7 tomorrow morning for breakfast at Sniffany's."

"Sleep's a good idea. See you tomorrow.."

"Well, hello! It's good to see you two in here again!" said Snuffy, smiling warmly as Coot and Diana entered the diner. "Usual table?"

"Sure, Snuffy," said Coot.

Diana frowned briefly, then nodded to Snuffy, who came out from behind the cash register to escort them to their table.

"Right this way," said Snuffy, still smiling.

"Listen, Coot," said Diana, as they climbed into Coot's car after leaving the diner. "What's given Snuffy the idea that we're a couple?"

"Huh?"

"You heard the way he greeted us — as if he expected us to be together. What have you told him — about us?"

"I might never have seen you again if it hadn't been for Snuffy. I asked him if he'd ever seen a pretty young woman wearing a Collaboration Software T-shirt."

"And?"

"And I asked him to call me if you came into the diner."

"You sneak!"

"I used to be a Ranger, remember? Old habits die hard."

"So, that day you walked into the diner and saw me, you'd been tipped off I was there?"

"Right. Are you sorry?"

"No, of course not. I just don't like your scheming behind my back — and I don't like people expecting things I'm not comfortable with."

"Such as our being a couple."

"Yes. I'm sorry, Coot. I've thought about this a lot. Your friendship has meant a lot to me. I like you, I really do, but you want more from me than I can give you."

They sat in silence in the car, which Coot had not bothered to start.

"You don't feel attracted to me romantically at all?" he asked her.

"I've avoided any thoughts of romance with you. I don't want to hurt you.."

"You said you've 'avoided' thoughts of romance. Perhaps you're in denial about your true feelings toward me."

"Don't give yourself false hope, Coot."

"I'm not sure my hope *is* false, Diana. Maybe *you* should see Dr. Rosen."

"Maybe *you* should take me home now."

"What about my lesson and your playing on Saturday?"

"I don't think we should see each other for breakfast or for music anymore, Coot. I'm really sorry it's come to this. I think we're even on lessons and practice time. Please take me home."

Coot started the Camry. They drove in silence back to Diana's apartment. She got out of the car, then turned to face him. Her eyes were red. "If you ever think we can be just friends, give me a call. I'd like us to be friends, Coot."

Coot sat, stunned, as he watched her hurry toward her building and quickly disappear inside. Another disaster he had failed to prevent.

Coot sat in the old Barcalounger in his living room, brooding. The same question kept recurring in his mind: What had he done wrong? As late afternoon faded to evening outside, his thoughts descended from gloomy to morose. Diana said he wanted something from her that she couldn't give. It had been just a few hours since she ended their relationship. He needed some comfort. He resisted opening another bottle of wine. He didn't want to make himself sick — not after all the Chinese take-out food he had eaten. The large, soft arms of the recliner and some Bach playing on the stereo had made him feel better after Frannie died. Somehow their magic had worn off. He closed his eyes and tried to focus on the Bach.

A knock on the door woke Coot. Blinded by light streaming in from an east-facing window, he struggled to his feet and nearly fell out of his chair.

"Coming!" Who the devil would stop by so early? What time was it, anyway? He glanced at his watch.

"What the hell happened to you, Coot? You look like shit!" said Roger. Jack was standing behind Roger. Both men were dressed for running. Coot had forgotten about the mid-week run they had agreed on the previous Sunday.

"Sorry, guys. Come on in. I'll be ready in a minute."

Roger and Jack found seats in the living room. They looked around at the mess Coot had failed to clean up before falling asleep in his chair.

"Party-of-one last night?" asked Jack.

Coot did not reply, but scooped up the empty wine bottle and food containers, dumped them in the kitchen, and hurried to his bedroom. Having closed the door, he unbuttoned his shirt and tossed it aside, then unzipped his pants and sent them and his underwear flying to join the shirt. He put on his running shorts and a t-shirt, laced up his running shoes, and rushed back to the living room. "Let's go!"

The three runners had barely gotten into the park when Roger said, "So, Coot,...why were you sleeping...in your chair?...Has something happened...with Diana?...Is she engaged...to Doc What's-his-name?"

"Might as well be," said Coot. He described his conversation with Diana after breakfast the previous day.

Jack said, "Sounds like it's time...for you to back off...a bit, Coot....Give Diana some time...to sort out her feelings."

"She doesn't admit...to having any feelings...to sort out....She's been trying...to avoid...romantic feelings for me...all along."

"That doesn't mean...she's been successful."

"She said...not to give myself...false hope."

"Maybe that's part...of her denial."

"Maybe she needs...to see you...in a new light," interjected Roger. "The Coot she knows...has been sort of a brotherly...or fatherly protector."

"What am I supposed...to do about that?" said Coot.

"It was just a thought," said Roger.

Not a thought that Coot felt he could do anything about, though he wished it were possible.

CHAPTER 9

Events on the Ground

Two weeks after the attack in New York, the Mushrooms' luck changed: PATH officials found a surveillance video transmitted from the 33rd Street PATH station that showed a few seconds of a large woman climbing the stairs with a huge backpack just minutes before the blast that destroyed the Empire State Building. A retired Army colonel claimed on Fox News that the backpack was large enough to contain the Army's most portable nuclear device, the Small Atomic Demolition Munition, or S.A.D.M. He also mentioned that during the Iraq War the Special Forces joked that they should "S.A.D.M. Hussein."

George and the other Mushrooms were sitting around the little TV discussing the news. Empty soda cans and bags that once contained chips overflowed the 55-gallon drum they were using for trash.

"Somebody's gonna recognize Jamie for sure," said Mitch. "Her size was great when we needed someone to carry the A.D.M., but now it makes her easy to identify."

"PATH security needed two weeks to find something suspicious in that surveillance video," said Bennie. "Jamie's appearance is not that unusual. The authorities just got lucky.",

Jamie spoke up. "With that video out there, I bet the Special Forces guys I worked with will I.D. me in no time. Maybe they already have."

"That wouldn't be good," said George. "It would make finding you — and us — a lot easier."

"For starters, they'll be able to publicize a much better picture of you," said Doug.

The identification of Jamie herself was not their only worry. The Mushrooms had always known that a chain of identifications posed a possible threat to them. Now, George imagined that a video from the Newport station might link Jamie and perhaps Mitch to him and his van. Their whole plan could unravel if the van's progress from New Jersey to Illinois was discovered. Someone might have seen such a van pull into the warehouse. Maybe Mitch was right. Maybe they should attack without evidence of a growing insurrection.

* * *

Jamie was worried about what would happen to Sabrina, once the feds figured out that the woman with the backpack was Jamie. She and Sabrina had kept their relationship an open secret, in that a few of their friends in Seattle knew they were lovers but most of their straight acquaintances and their colleagues at work did not. This secrecy would protect Sabrina for a few days, but it was just a matter of time before the F.B.I. connected her and Jamie. Jamie hoped that they wouldn't treat her roughly or violate her privacy by leaking her identity to the media. She was completely innocent.

Outing Sabrina was not Jamie's only concern. Like most Americans by this time, Sabrina must have seen the video. Unlike them, she would have realized who the woman was. She would know that Jamie was suspected of bringing down the Empire State Building and killing thousands of people. How upset, how disappointed, how angry Sabrina must be with her now! Jamie loved Sabrina more than any other woman she had ever been with. She could not bear the thought that Sabrina would abandon her now. She had to talk with Sabrina.

Sabrina never answered calls from numbers that she did not recognize, so Jamie would have to use her own phone, despite Mitch's warning not to use cell phones. She walked casually to the restroom farthest from the television that the other Mushrooms were watching for further news about the nationwide hunt for them. She locked the door behind her. She put the battery back into her cell phone. She dialed Sabrina's number.

One ring. Two rings. Then... "Jamie! What the fuck have you done?"

Jamie had never heard Sabrina so angry, not even when California had passed the infamous Proposition 8 that limited marriage to heterosexual couples.

"Sabrina, listen for a minute, okay?"

"How could you possibly justify such a horror?"

"I know you're upset, but..."

"Upset? Upset?" Sabrina screamed. "Of course I'm upset. I just learned I'm in love with a homicidal maniac!"

"I love you, too, baby," Jamie reassured her. "I want the world to be a better place for us."

"And you think killing all those people will help? That's crazy!"

"Voting for change hasn't gotten us very far, has it?" Jamie asked. "Insurrection is the only way."

"Nobody's going to join an insurrection led by mass murderers. Have you been watching the news lately? People just want you dead."

"We'll force people to make a choice," said Jamie. "Would they rather throw off their oppressors or face another attack?"

"People are more afraid of you Mushrooms than of any institution, Jamie. You'd better face reality before you have any more blood on your hands."

"And what do *you* think I should do?" Jamie was getting annoyed at Sabrina's complete lack of sympathy. Hadn't they agreed on the corruption of institutions?

"Give yourself up and convince the other Mushrooms to do the same."

"We'd be dead meat. After the insurrection, we'll be heroes."

"Jamie, listen to me: there's not going to *be* an insurrection. You've got to find a way out of this mess."

"There's no way to back out now, Sabrina. We have to go forward."

"No, you don't! Just refuse to cooperate anymore."

"What good would that do?" said Jamie. "They'd just go ahead without me. Arming an A.D.M.'s not hard."

"You could turn them in," said Sabrina.

"You know I'd never betray my friends," Jamie said, insulted that her lover would suggest such a thing.

"Killing a lot of innocent people is far worse than betraying their would-be killers," said Sabrina.

"Are they so innocent?" asked Jamie.

"What *are* you talking about?"

"They *elect* the people who give the orders. They *choose* to work at oppressive corporations," said Jamie. "C'mon, Sabrina, we've talked about this a lot."

"Yes, but they don't deserve to *die* for that!"

"No? They support wars to protect corporate profits, but they let millions of children die every year from disease and hunger. "

"You really don't have much regard for your fellow citizens, do you?" said Sabrina.

"About as much as they have for the victims of the system they support," said Jamie. "You know, unlike some, I don't enjoy killing people."

"Oh? A lot of good *that* fine sentiment did."

"You're wrong. I wanted to make the explosion as small as possible but had to compromise with the others."

"That's something to tell the judge, if you live through this."

"Yeah. Anyway, I just wanted to warn you that the feds will eventually connect you to me."

"Yeah. I figured that out pretty quickly."

"Do what you have to do, Sabrina, but remember...I love you."

"In spite of everything, I love you, too, Jamie, and I don't want to lose you. Think about..."

Jamie heard Mitch's voice calling her. "Someone's coming. I gotta go. Love you." She disconnected quickly, removed the battery from her phone, and flushed the toilet.

* * *

Sabrina Jones was afraid. Afraid of what would happen to her beloved Jamie. Afraid of how she herself would be involved in the unfolding catastrophe. Should she get Jamie's location from the tracker program and inform the F.B.I.?

Sabrina certainly did not want to be responsible for the deaths of thousands more people. Yet she did not want to be responsible for

Jamie's death at the hands of the F.B.I., either. What if they attacked the Mushrooms' hideout like they had attacked the Branch Davidians near Waco, Texas?

Sabrina opened the tracker software on her computer and clicked on the View Log button. Something was wrong. The latest date for which the tracker app had reported Jamie's phone's location was three days earlier. She had noticed that, for the past couple of days, there had been no updates from the app, but she'd assumed that was because the phone's position had not changed. Now there was a report, but it just said *acquiring satellites*.

She vaguely remembered reading in the tracker app's online manual that if the phone's batteries were removed, the phone's GPS might lose the satellite location data it had collected and would have to start from scratch, a process that could take fifteen minutes. They had only talked a few minutes, so the GPS had not had enough time to complete its startup. Sabrina could not be sure that Jamie was still in Elk Grove Village.

Just in case she was, Sabrina wrote down the coordinates of the tracker app's last report on a scrap of paper, which she hid between pages 192 and 193 in *The Joy of Cooking* in her kitchen. She wanted to keep the tracker program running and writing its log file, so that she would know where Sabrina was, but she was worried that it could be used by the feds to hunt down Jamie like an animal and kill her. She was sure the F.B.I. would find her soon. She would have no choice but to provide her evidence.

Perhaps she did have a choice, or at least a way to delay their attack on Jamie. She created a new encrypted area on her computer's hard drive, stopped the tracker program, copied its log file into the encrypted area, re-configured the tracker program to use the encrypted area for its log, and re-started the program. Her backup program was already configured to ignore log files. Should she erase the original log file? She had the same bits stored in the encrypted area, so she would not be destroying any information. Impulsively, desperately trying to protect Jamie without putting herself into legal jeopardy, she moved the log to the trash and emptied the trash securely.

Because of these actions, the feds could not force her to divulge

Jamie's location simply by confiscating her computer. They would have to get a court order not only to take her computer but also to force her to divulge the password for the encrypted area. Now she had to decide how much to cooperate with the authorities who were pursuing Jamie with the relentlessness of bloodhounds.

Well before six o'clock the morning after Jamie's call, Sabrina woke up, worrying about what to do with the information she had hidden about Jamie's last known location. She got out of bed, pulled on a turquoise housecoat over her lilac pajamas, and went into the kitchen to make some coffee. She glanced at the shelf holding her cookbooks and wondered whether she should contact the F.B.I. Could she trust them?

Coffee mug in hand, she wandered into the living room and peeked out the drapes. She had known they would eventually come, but now, sooner than she had expected, they were here. She watched them pull up in their black sedan in front of her apartment. As they got out of their car, she could see that the driver was a short, wiry, brown-skinned man and that his passenger was a tall, muscular, blond fellow. Both were dressed in black suits, white shirts, and black ties, life imitating art. The two men strode quickly toward the front door of the building and disappeared from sight.

Sabrina rushed back to her computer, stopped the tracker program, and unmounted the encrypted area from the computer's file system. Now Jamie's precise location was protected by strong encryption and *The Joy of Cooking*.

Sabrina went back into the living room just as the intercom buzzed. She pushed the Talk button. "Hello?"

"F.B.I., Ms. Jones. We need to talk with you."

She tried to pat her hair into place as she buzzed them into the building. She opened her front door at their knock and let them in. She felt underdressed and overwhelmed, trapped in a strange mix of *The Matrix* and *Men in Black*. This could not be good.

The shorter man introduced himself as Agent Rodriguez, the taller one as Agent Wozek. How much did they already know? Surely they must have found the records of Jamie's calls to her, including the one from the previous day. Sabrina asked them to sit down on the sofa and she took a seat in an arm chair.

Wozek reminded her that it was a felony to lie to a federal agent, then asked her what her relationship was to Jamie Saunders.

Sabrina was in a daze. What point was there in trying to protect Jamie now? She said that they had been friends for about a year.

Rodriguez asked whether she had seen the surveillance video of a large woman with a backpack. She admitted that she had seen it. He asked whether she recognized the woman. She said she did.

"Who is she?" he asked.

"You already know, or you wouldn't be here," Sabrina said, her eyes filling with tears. Her unspoken thought: *God, I wish it wasn't her!*

"Talking about Jamie Saunders may be difficult for you, Ms. Jones, but we need to find her, to prevent her from possibly killing many more people than died in New York."

"What if she was brainwashed or hypnotized or drugged or something?" said Sabrina. "What if it was just a coincidence that she was near the Empire State Building that day?"

"We must find her to understand whether she was involved and, if so, under what circumstances," said Rodriguez.

"Where is Jamie Saunders now?" Wozek interjected.

"I'm not sure," she said truthfully, stunned into answering by Wozek's aggressive manner.

"You're not sure?" the agent replied. "Where do you think she is?"

"The last I knew," Sabrina said, pausing, then continuing, "she was in Elk Grove Village, but that was a few days ago."

"How did you know her location? Did she tell you?" asked Rodriguez.

"Not exactly," said Sabrina.

"Meaning?" pressed the agent.

"Meaning I had loaded a tracker app on her phone and it reported she was there. But that was several days ago. I don't know where she is now."

"We think she's still there," said Wozek. "Please show us the app's report."

"I'd rather not."

"Why not?"

"Because I'm afraid...I'm afraid you're going to kill her, and I don't want to help you do it."

Sabrina saw Wozek's jaw muscles tighten momentarily.

Taking a paper from his jacket pocket and unfolding it, Wozek said, "This search warrant entitles us to confiscate your computer and any other material at this location that's relevant to our investigation."

"That won't do you any good," said Sabrina. "The tracker log's encrypted."

"The warrant specifically mentions cryptographic keys," said Wozek.

"I don't believe that's constitutional," said Sabrina. "I want my attorney."

The agents looked at each other. Rodriguez spoke next.

"Ms. Jones, we need your help. There may not be much time to prevent a horrible catastrophe, on the scale of New York, or worse. Do you remember anything from the report?"

"You won't kill her, will you?" she asked, her voice trembling.

"What happens will depend on her and the other Mushrooms," said Rodriguez. "The Bureau will make every effort to take her into custody without bloodshed."

Sabrina's defensiveness softened a bit at Rodriguez's reminder of the Mushrooms' threat and his reassurance, although she was still worried about revealing her friend's exact location. She sat in silence, her eyes on the floor, half hoping she would wake up from this nightmare.

"By not cooperating you'll only delay, not prevent, our finding her," said Wozek. "We know the cell tower that her call to you went through, so it's just a matter of time before we track her down."

"You make her sound like some kind of animal," Sabrina said, her eyes flashing at Wozek. "She's a human being. She's my friend."

"Don't let a poor choice of words keep you from helping us prevent an enormous human tragedy, Ms. Jones," said Rodriguez, glancing at Wozek. "Where, exactly, is Jamie Saunders?"

"I wrote down the coordinates of her location," said Sabrina at last, her will to resist overcome by the realization that she could not protect Jamie for long.

"Please show us," said Rodriguez.

Sabrina got up from her chair, went into the kitchen, and retrieved *The Joy of Cooking*. As she returned to the living room, she opened the book to page 192, fished out the paper with the coordinates, and handed it to Agent Rodriguez. Tears once again filled her eyes.

Rodriquez gave the paper to Agent Wozek, who took it with him out of the apartment.

Rodriguez had a few more questions for Sabrina, but she sensed that he already had what he had come for: Jamie's location. The agent secured her cell phone and computer. She still refused to give him the password for the encrypted area that contained the tracker program's log of Jamie's locations.

When the two men were gone, Sabrina collapsed onto the sofa. She buried her face in her hands, shaking with sobs. What would happen to Jamie now?

* * *

Coot had barely gotten settled in his office Wednesday morning when his phone rang. He put down the coffee he had been sipping and picked up the handset.

"Hi, Coot. It's Jill. We've had a breakthrough in identifying the female suspect in the New York bombing."

"That's great! Who is she?"

"Ex-Army. I don't want to jump the gun on Homeland Security's announcement. Just be sure to be looking at a news channel around ten o'clock this morning."

"That surveillance video was found last week," said Coot. "What took so long?"

"The Army identified her almost right away," said Jill. "They involved the F.B.I. immediately. The Bureau wanted to investigate quietly before going public."

"Of course. Has the Bureau made any progress?"

"I can't discuss it any further. Just don't miss the news at ten."

Coot alerted Ben about the new development, and Ben called a meeting of the entire staff to watch the announcement.

Just before ten Coot took a seat in the front of the conference room. The large video projection screen was showing a CNN reporter standing in the briefing room at the Department of Homeland Security. The reporter sat down as the Secretary himself walked to the podium.

The S.A.F.E. conference room grew quiet as the Secretary began to speak.

"Good morning. Let me cut to the chase: we need your help in the hunt for the Mushrooms. Our best lead is the image of a young woman found in a surveillance video taken just before the attack in New York. We now know who she is: Jamie Saunders, a former soldier dishonorably discharged from the U.S. Army and an expert in the kind of weapon that destroyed the Empire State Building. The video showed Ms. Saunders carrying a backpack large enough for such a weapon. Stopping these murderers may depend on finding Ms. Saunders — and finding her quickly. If you have seen this woman," he said, pointing to a picture of a tall, husky woman on the easel beside the podium, "please call the number on your screen. The safety of our country depends on stopping the Mushrooms!"

The Secretary then took questions, but had no additional information for the reporters. Ben stood up at the front of the room and held up his hand for silence. The room became quiet.

"The Secretary's announcement is welcome, of course, but our job is to convince our fellow citizens of the need to abolish nuclear weapons altogether. Unless you've seen Jamie Saunders, I want you to get back to work on implementing your part of our plan."

* * *

"Goddamn it, Jamie!" Mitch shouted, as he jumped up from watching CNN. "We're fucked now!"

"Easy, Mitch," said George. "What's the matter?"

"Come look at this!"

The Mushrooms all gathered around the small television set. The Secretary of Homeland Security was announcing that they had identified Jamie from the PATH surveillance video found a couple of days earlier.

"Oh, shit!" said Jamie, slamming her large fist on the table at which she had been sitting.

"They have her photo, fingerprints, height, weight, expertise in A.D.M.s, everything," said Doug.

Sure enough, a moment later CNN displayed a picture of Jamie in her Army uniform, captioned "Suspect is Nuke Expert."

Groans of dismay erupted from the anarchists. Jamie bowed her head in apparent resignation, as if she had been expecting this development. Mitch was pacing like a caged tiger, throwing his hands up, then bringing them down with fists clenched. Only George seemed to take the new information in stride.

"We have two problems," said George. "First, can they connect Jamie with any of us, and second, can they trace Jamie or anyone linked to her to this location?"

"The surveillance videos may tie Mitch to Jamie," said Bennie.

"And Mitch and Jamie to the van and maybe George," said Doug.

"What if someone remembers seeing Jamie on the trip from Maine to New Jersey?" said Mitch. "They might find her on surveillance tapes of their own."

"And then they might link you and Doug to Jamie as well," said George, his forehead wrinkled and his eyebrows knotted.

"I'm really sorry, guys," said Jamie. "This is all my fault."

"You're damned right it is!" screamed Mitch, his fists clenched.

"Back off, Mitch," said George. "We're all in this together, as we've always been."

Mitch quieted down, but kept pacing around, gesturing and grumbling.

"As long as they can't trace the van here," continued George, "we should be safe."

"Provided we don't run out of food," said Bennie. "How long will our supplies last?"

"About two months," said Doug. "Longer, if we ration them."

"Let's attack now," barked Mitch. "What are we waiting for?"

"We haven't had a chance to look around the target like we did in New York," said George. "Where should we deploy the A.D.M.?"

"Forget the careful planning, George," said Mitch. "This has to be a quick and dirty operation."

"What do you mean?" asked George.

"Bennie and Jamie take the bomb in one van. They get as close to the Willis Tower as they can. Jamie sets the timer. They get out of their van and into ours, and we take off."

"Yeah, we've got to use the vans," said Doug, "and hope we have enough time to escape the effects of the blast."

"I can set the yield to ten tons," said Jamie. "Then we won't have to get so far away to be safe."

"But our target would escape damage if the cops had five minutes to move the device after they found it," said George. "Tipton wouldn't like that."

"Fuck Tipton!" said Mitch. "He bought A.D.M.s, not our lives."

"I didn't sign up for a suicide mission," said Bennie.

"Me neither," said Doug.

"We don't have any good choices," said George, "since we have to attack the Willis Tower."

"Can we get in touch with Tipton through Anthony?" said Doug. "Maybe he would give us another target."

"No phone use!" Mitch reminded the other Mushrooms. "The N.S.A., whatever its legal restrictions, can filter any calls we make out of the billions of calls made everyday."

"How are we ever going to get out of this mess?" asked Bennie. "There's no insurrection. There's no sure way to destroy the target. The blast may kill us if we succeed. Tipton may kill us if we fail. We're totally screwed."

No one disagreed with Bennie's description of their situation.

Quiet spread over the Mushrooms like a fog rolling in from Lake Michigan. One by one they drifted away from the TV, till only George was left to stare at Jamie's image whenever CNN chose to remind its viewers of Public Enemy Number One.

* * *

F.B.I. Special Agent Jason Maxwell and his team of anti-terrorism marksmen and demolitions experts had been deployed in Elk Grove Village ever since the Bureau had learned Jamie Saunders' identity and detected her cell phone call to her friend Sabrina Jones. Maxwell knew that Agents Rodriguez and Wozek from the Seattle office were interviewing Jones that morning, hoping to learn more exactly where Saunders was hiding. He soon had the answer, as Wozek had called in the coordinates that Jones had supplied. Now it was time to move.

Agent Maxwell gathered his team together, both the F.B.I. members and an Army specialist in atomic demolition munitions.

"Great news! The Seattle office has found Jamie Saunders' exact location from her friend's tracking program."

He gave the team the address of a warehouse on Pratt Boulevard, not far from where the team was waiting. The assembled agents gave a loud cheer. Several shouted "Let's get her!"

"We still don't know how many other people are with her," said Maxwell, "so we've got to assume she's not alone."

He paused and looked around at the team members. He had selected them all himself. In fact, he had mentored most of them since they joined the Bureau. He didn't like thinking about leading them into a trap or exposing them to danger unnecessarily.

"The plan is to surround them and demand their surrender," he continued. "We can't just shoot our way in because we don't know whether they've rigged an A.D.M. with some sort of dead-man switch that will detonate it if they're attacked."

"Can't we use chemicals to knock them out?" asked one agent. "Surely they must sleep at night."

"Nah, one of them is probably awake at all times," said another agent. "He'd have the dead-man switch."

"Obviously," said Maxwell, "our number one priority is to prevent the detonation of that device. And remember, there may be two nukes in there."

Maxwell gave the team detailed instructions as to where to deploy around the warehouse. He himself took a bullhorn and followed the other men out of the building. He got into his car, which his driver had just pulled up. The team drove to the area around the warehouse. The signals intelligence specialists set up listening devices, so that they could hear what the Mushrooms were saying inside the building. That would also enable them to tell how many Mushrooms were inside and perhaps how well armed they were.

Agent Maxwell turned on his bullhorn and raised it to his mouth.

* * *

George Boyd was startled by a man's voice, greatly amplified, saying, "This is the F.B.I. Leave the building with your hands up." George looked at the TV, which was showing a man with his arms raised in a deodorant commercial. No, the voice was closer and more threatening than any commercial.

Mitch came running into the room. "They've found us!" Jamie, Doug, and Bennie soon joined them.

"We've got to set off the A.D.M. now!" screamed Mitch, who was flailing his arms and jumping around like a chimp on speed.

"No more crazy talk, Mitch," said Jamie. "The rest of us want to get out of here alive."

"I sure do!" said Bennie.

Mitch was undeterred. "You're a bunch of chickenshits! I'm gonna do it."

He bolted toward the backpack with the A.D.M., but Jamie was too quick for him and quickly subdued her volatile teammate.

"Get offa me!" Mitch yelled. "Get off, you goddam dyke!"

Jamie slammed Mitch into the wall and lifted his arm behind his back. He cried out, in obvious pain.

"Calm down, Mitch," said George, worried that Mitch's panic would spread to the others. "We've got to figure out what to do, and quickly."

"I'm going to look outside to see what we're up against," said Bennie, starting toward the nearest window.

"No!" shouted Doug, grabbing Bennie's arm. "A sniper might pick you off."

Bennie stopped. "Oh, right."

George looked around at the little group. They had all hoped to fundamentally change the way society operated, and now they were surrounded, trapped like rats, at the mercy of more powerful forces. All they had was a nuclear weapon whose use would now cost them their own lives.

"Why haven't the feds already attacked us?" he asked.

"They're scared we'll set off the A.D.M.," said Jamie. She relaxed her hold on Mitch, who had quit struggling against her.

"That gives us a chance to bargain," said George, "for safe passage in exchange for the nuke."

Jamie, Doug, and Bennie agreed that negotiation was their best hope. Mitch, still visibly distraught, demanded that they detonate the A.D.M. if the feds rejected their demand to negotiate.

"How can we tell them we want to negotiate?" asked George.

"The building has a public address system," said Doug. "I'll turn it on." He left the group.

While Doug was gone, Jamie said, "Who can we negotiate with? I don't trust the F.B.I. Remember what they did to the Branch Davidians in Waco?"

"For once, Jamie's right," said Mitch. "Who can we trust?"

"There's this guy, Coot Jenkins," said George. " that I saw on TV a few weeks ago."

"*Coot*? Really?" said Bennie, grinning. "What's his specialty? Bugging?"

The others laughed, but their faces remained grim.

"Seriously," persisted George. "Jenkins used to be at Brookhaven Labs and now he's at S.A.F.E. I met him at a conference in Geneva years ago. Unlike the others, he listened to my ideas."

George looked hopefully around at the others: Mitch scowling, Jamie distracted, Bennie quizzical.

"Why should we trust him?" asked Bennie.

"I saw Jenkins talking with the Russians, the Chinese, the Indians, the Israelis."

"So?" said Bennie.

"By reputation," replied George, "he's a conciliator, trusted by all sides."

Doug returned a moment later. "All set." He handed George a cordless microphone.

"I'm going to demand to negotiate with Coot Jenkins, okay?" said George.

"Who's Coot Jenkins?" asked Doug, looking skeptically at George.

"A nonproliferation expert I met years ago," said George. "If more so-called experts were like him, I might not have become an anarchist."

"How is that good?" said Mitch, sneering.

"If institutions were not so corrupt," said George, "a lot of anarchists would have chosen easier lives."

LOOSE NUKES

"Alright," said Doug. "We're running out of time and choices. Go for it."

"But threaten to destroy Chicago if they attack us," said Mitch.

"Okay," agreed George.

"When you're done with that, try getting Michael Anthony at that number he gave you," said Jamie. "We're going to need a lot of help to get out of here."

* * *

Myron Pepsey paced across the large Persian carpet in his mahogany-paneled office. Back and forth he walked, considering various explanations for why the "censors" closed down the "production" he had financed. (He rather enjoyed thinking of his projects in terms of the theatrical metaphor that Paul Henry had come up with to disguise their conversations.) Could one of the actors have carelessly bragged about the success of the first two acts? Had someone informed the authorities what was going on under their noses? Had some government informant penetrated the cast?

The play had been going so well. What a shame it had to end prematurely. He hoped the authorities wouldn't come after him next. Could they possibly trace the production to him? To Paul Henry, possibly. Paul had put the production team together: the actors, the support crews. Could they tie Paul to him? Paul, the would-be actor, had always used aliases, and he was a conventional good-looking man, the sort who advertises men's shirts or after-shave lotion in glossy magazines. Yet there was that wart: the only distinctive thing about Paul's appearance, really.

Should he flee the country? His Gulfstream G650 was waiting at Peachtree-DeKalb Airport to whisk him away if necessary. Most of his fortune was held off-shore, but he still had billions of dollars in U.S. assets that he was loathe to abandon to the federal government.

Pepsey decided to wait a little longer to see what developed. He had hidden his involvement well.

* * *

At S.A.F.E. headquarters Coot was sitting in Joe's office with Ben, Emily, and a few other people watching the wall of monitors. The audio was from MSNBC.

"We have breaking news. The Department of Homeland Security has announced that fugitive Jamie Saunders has been located in a warehouse in Elk Grove Village, a suburb of Chicago just west of O'Hare International Airport, possibly with other Mushrooms and nuclear weapons. Everyone within five miles of the warehouse is being evacuated."

"Great!" the arms control experts in the room exclaimed as one. They began to speculate about what would happen. Would the Mushrooms give themselves up? Would they detonate a weapon?

Within minutes, several news networks were broadcasting from positions as near to the warehouse as the police would permit. The F.B.I. had just demanded the Mushrooms surrender.

"Why aren't they evacuating a wider area?" Ben asked Coot.

"If the devices the Mushrooms have are like the Army's small nukes, their maximum yield is only about a kiloton of TNT," said Coot. "Past about five miles, the main effect would be fallout. People would be better off staying indoors."

"Can you imagine the traffic jam if they tried to evacuate all of Chicago?" said Joe. "Having a nuclear weapon a few miles away must be frightening to a lot of people, but there are risks in large-scale evacuation also."

The group turned their attention back to the TV as a new voice erupted from loudspeakers on each side of the warehouse.

"This is George Boyd, speaking for the Mushrooms. If you attack, we can and will detonate another nuclear weapon, ten times as powerful as the one that destroyed the Empire State Building. You and thousands of other people will die. The fallout will contaminate much of Chicago. Do not attack."

"Why didn't they set it off when they realized they were surrounded?" asked Ben.

"They're fanatics but they're not suicidal," said Coot. "Now they're trying to save their own skins."

"There is a way to avoid disaster," Boyd continued. "We demand to negotiate with Coot Jenkins."

"What?" exclaimed everyone, turning to look at Coot. "He wants you," said Ben.

Coot felt his face flush. How could terrorists have singled him out? "This is unbelievable," he mumbled as he stood up, embarrassed. "I'd better get back to my desk. Jill Meecham will be calling soon."

Coot hurried back to his own office and closed the door. He sat down at his desk and put his head in his hands. Negotiate with terrorists? He had negotiated with government officials, but never with crazy people. He had never felt in danger from the other negotiators. Dealing with the Mushrooms would be more like going on a reconnaissance mission in the Vietnamese jungle.

Coot's musings were interrupted by his telephone's ringing. He picked up the handset before the Caller ID could be displayed.

"Mr. Jenkins? This is Phil Jacuzzi from Fox News. How does it feel..."

"Sorry, Mr. Jacuzzi, but I'm expecting another call," Coot interrupted. "Maybe later." He hung up. His phone rang again. CBS. He ignored the call, the first of several from numbers he did not recognize. The media were making it impossible for him to think. Another call was coming in. The White House! Coot picked up the phone. Jill Meecham's assistant was calling.

"Ms. Meecham would like to meet with you in her office at the White House as soon as possible. Can you make it?"

"Yes, of course."

"Good. We'll send a car for you."

Coot informed Ben of Jill's request. Events were beyond Coot's control now. The phone was ringing again. He began to feel anxious. Not another panic attack! No, he was well aware of what worried him this time.

Coot picked up his jacket and glanced briefly at his old briefcase, still bulging with notes and papers for his address to the Arms Control Association. If he survived the next few days, he would have to start over on that talk.

In the lobby, Coot met the White House driver. As they walked to the limo parked in front, reporters and cameramen swarmed around him, shoving microphones into his face and asking what it felt like to be the Mushrooms' chosen negotiating partner. "Sorry, I'm in a hurry," was all he could think of to say, as he brushed past the media horde and climbed into the waiting car. He was on his way to White House.

Jill Meecham rose from her desk as Coot entered her office.

"So, what do you know about George Boyd?" she asked.

"Just that he's one of the Mushrooms the F.B.I. has surrounded. His name does sound vaguely familiar, though."

"He seems to think you're more trustworthy than anyone in the government."

Coot laughed. "That's ridiculous."

Jill had apparently heard more from Boyd while Coot was en route to her office, for she said, "Boyd claims he met you at the Conference on Disarmament."

The shadowy image of an earnest young man began to form in Coot's mind. Had they discussed controlling fissile materials? How could a person who sought to prevent the spread of nuclear weapons have sunk so low as to actually use them, and against civilians?

"Boyd's politics must have changed considerably since then," Coot replied.

"Still, he wants to negotiate with you."

"But I can't represent the government!"

"You can if the president asks you to. I've already recommended that he appoint you, and he agreed that we're fortunate the Mushrooms have asked to negotiate with you."

"I'll do anything I can to help, but can't you find somebody better qualified?"

"You understand the technology. You've had experience in resolving conflicts."

"Yeah, but the Mushrooms are murderers. You need an expert in abnormal psychology, a S.W.A.T. hostage negotiator, or someone who's dealt with seriously disturbed people."

"Maybe so, but they're demanding to negotiate with you, Coot. Will you do it?"

Coot was willing to risk his own life. He had done that many times in Vietnam. What he feared more was that, if he failed to resolve the crisis, the lives of many other people would also be snuffed out. He was certainly not the best man for this job. Yet, because of the Mushrooms, he was the only man. He knew what his answer to Jill must be.

"Yes."

"Thanks, Coot. You're a good man," said Jill. "Hoping you'd accept, I got us some time on the president's schedule."

Jill escorted Coot to the Oval Office. The setting was familiar but being there in person felt strange, almost like an out-of-body experience. The president came out from behind his desk and extended his hand to Coot.

"Mr. Jenkins." They shook hands. "So good of you to help us deal with the situation in Chicago. Jill tells me you helped keep the Pakistanis and the Indians from each other's throats just before the Mushrooms exploded the device at Srinagar. She says that you have long been involved with nonproliferation and disarmament issues and that you met George Boyd in Geneva."

"Mr. President, I really have no recollection of meeting Boyd, although he apparently remembers me."

"If you only knew how many people I meet who say they've met me before but I don't remember them! It's embarrassing, really." The president smiled at Coot.

Coot did his best to return the smile and waited for the president to continue.

"So, here's the deal: you will enter the warehouse and meet with Boyd as my personal representative. You will find out as much as you can about him, his group, their security, and any nuclear devices. You will learn their demands but not agree to a bargain. You will offer to take their demands back to our government and to return with our answer. After leaving the warehouse you will report to me personally via secure video conference. Do you accept this assignment?"

"Certainly, Mr. President. I've been working to prevent nuclear disasters for most of my adult life. I can't stop now."

"Good. On behalf of our country and especially the people of Chicago, I thank you." Once again he extended his hand to Coot, but he did not smile this time. He looked sad, even haunted. Coot was beginning to understand the effect the office had on its occupants.

Coot and Jill returned to her office, where lunch was waiting for them. Coot's stomach was growling loudly, but it quieted down when the first spoonful of onion soup reached it.

"I'd feel better prepared if I knew more about dealing with people like the Mushrooms," said Coot.

"I've arranged for several briefings after lunch," Jill reassured him. "We'll stall Boyd, telling him that you'll arrive in Chicago this evening."

As they ate their salad, Coot and Jill went over what they knew about the Mushrooms, which was very little. The group seemed to have popped up out of nowhere. "Like a toadstool," as Coot put it, with a tight smile.

Over their dessert of pickled peaches Jill did surprise Coot with one piece of information.

"A while ago you asked me about the investors of EuroKapital. I managed to find the names of several. All were Europeans except for one: Myron Pepsey, the billionaire industrialist."

"Damn!" said Coot. "He's on S.A.F.E.'s board. God, I hope he's not involved in this."

"There's no smoking gun linking Pepsey to Mushrooms."

"Right. Just coincidences. Like his selling the Empire State Building not long before it was destroyed."

For two hours after lunch, Jill brought in various experts to prepare Coot for his assignment. He got briefings in crisis negotiation, the psychopathology of mass murderers, and even basic game theory, as well as a refresher on conflict resolution. He was glad they were preparing him to meet the challenges he would face, but the more he learned, the more potential difficulties he saw. He would be close to nuclear weapons controlled by people who had already killed tens of thousands of people. The Mushrooms might have their own internal conflicts, making the situation even more volatile and dangerous. Paranoid delusions were probably driving some of the individual Mushrooms, so they would be hard to reason with.

After the last expert had left, Jill looked at Coot for a moment, then said, "We've known each other a long time. Your recommendation helped me get my first job in the N.S.C."

"You were obviously the best candidate they were considering."

Jill smiled, but continued.

"I hate exposing you to such danger, but we don't have many options and we don't have much time. I wish we knew more about Boyd."

"Me, too."

"As soon as we have more information about him and his group, I'll let you know." She stood, walked to her desk, and returned with a satellite telephone, which she handed to Coot.

"You can use this secure phone to contact me. Just press "2" — the speed dial is already set up for you."

"Okay. Thanks." The sat phone looked like it had seen some rough service.

"I've arranged for a helicopter to take you to Andrews. I'm afraid there's no time to pack. You don't have any medication you need to take, do you?"

"Fortunately, no." He didn't mention the bottle of pills he had left in his office.

"One more thing. Have you ever flown supersonic before? Are you claustrophobic?"

"No to both. Why?"

"Since we have to get you to Chicago as quickly as possible, you'll be flying from Andrews to O'Hare in a T-38 trainer. Its top speed is Mach 1.3."

"You don't mess around, do you?"

"Not in the present circumstances, and neither should you: no talking to the press."

"Understood. What will happen once I get to O'Hare?"

"F.B.I. Special Agent Jason Maxwell will meet your flight and drive you there. You'd normally be given a wire, but that would be pointless. Boyd's group would quickly find and remove it, and Boyd might be less inclined to trust you."

Jill's intercom buzzed. She answered it, then turned to Coot.

"Let's go. The chopper's waiting."

On the South Lawn of the White House stood one of the helicopters used to transport the president.

"Marine One? For me?"

"The Marine One fleet is also used to transport Cabinet secretaries and foreign dignitaries. I'll ride with you to Andrews and make sure you get on the right aircraft."

"You're sending me to Chicago to prevent terrorists from exploding a nuclear weapon but you don't trust me to get on the right plane?"

"Just following orders, Coot."

Jill and Coot walked to the waiting helicopter, climbed the steps, and entered the cabin.

"Welcome aboard, Mrs. Meecham, Mr. Jenkins," said Marine Major Kincaid as she saluted her two passengers. "Please take a seat and buckle up. We'll be airborne shortly." As Jill and Coot sat down and fastened their seat belts, the major added, "We're flying you to Andrews in this VH-60N. It's a little faster than the big chopper." Major Kincaid went back into the cockpit, where she resumed flight preparations.

The helicopter lifted off from the South Lawn. With the Lincoln Memorial fading away to the right and the Washington Monument swinging into view as the chopper turned, Coot enjoyed a view few ordinary people had seen. As they passed north of the Capitol, Coot said, "It's hard to imagine the Mall without the Capitol."

"It wouldn't be there today, were it not for some courageous people on Flight 93."

"I've often wondered whether I would've had the courage they showed."

"You showed courage by accepting this assignment."

Ten minutes later they were on the ground at Andrews. A car was waiting for them.

"We need to get you into a flight suit, Mr. Jenkins," said the driver, an Air Force sergeant who introduced himself. "Tim McVeigh. Don't let the name fool you. I'm on your side."

After parking the car at their destination, Sgt. McVeigh escorted them to the entrance. "I'll drive you to the T-38 when you're all suited up."

"Do I look as weird as I feel?" Coot asked Jill when he returned. He was carrying a helmet and a bag.

"Mmm, impressive!" she replied. "Don't forget to change back into civilian clothes in Chicago, though. You might freak out Boyd."

In another two minutes Sgt. McVeigh had them at the waiting T-38. The pilot climbed down from the instructor's seat in the rear cockpit and walked toward them.

"Coot, this is Col. Sam Banks," said Jill. "I'm turning you over to him now."

Col. Banks helped Coot get properly seated in the front cockpit and instructed him on emergency procedures. "The cockpits are pressurized, so you won't have to use your mask unless there's a problem, which there won't be."

"Good. Say, do they usually assign a bird colonel to ferry people around the country?"

"You're a special case, Mr. Jenkins. I assigned myself to this duty. Just wanted to be part of history, I guess."

"I hope you won't be disappointed, Colonel. It's not going to be easy to turn Mission Impossible into Mission Accomplished."

"Then let's not waste time here on the ground. Time to fly!"

Coot listened to Col. Banks request permission to taxi out to the runway. Apparently they would not have to wait in line like at Dulles. Col. Banks moved the T-38 briskly into position for takeoff. The engine noise got much louder and Coot was pressed back into his seat as the T-38 accelerated down the runway. Moments later the nose of the trainer lifted off the ground and they were airborne, climbing fast into a clear blue sky. Coot's watch showed 3:58 PM.

The steep ascent was thrilling. Coot felt sheepish for the childlike grin spread across his face, but this was fun! Maybe he should have joined the Air Force instead of the Army during the Vietnam War. Then he remembered how many aircraft were lost in the course of that war and decided he'd made the right decision.

"How fast will we go?" asked Coot over the noise of the engines.

"About 800 miles per hour."

"Let me know before we break the sound barrier, okay?"

"Sure thing, but you'll hardly notice it. It's not like the old days, you know, with a lot of shaking and all."

Banks was right. Going supersonic was no big deal in the T-38. Coot was actually enjoying the ride, although he felt a little cramped in the cockpit. Looking at the ground from 40,000 feet, Coot could tell they were going almost twice as fast as the commercial aircraft he had flown in.

Events had moved so quickly since Jill's call that morning that Coot had not had a chance to consider his situation. Now that he was flying through the sky at Mach 1.2, time seemed to slow down and he finally had a chance to think about the looming encounter with George Boyd. He wished he could remember the man. Jill had not yet given him any information about Boyd. What could have turned him from a student observer of disarmament negotiations into a homicidal anarchist? What would negotiations involve? The warehouse was surrounded. Would Boyd be satisfied with safe passage out of the country for his group? What would happen to the nuclear devices? What might cause the group to detonate a device after all? What had he gotten himself into?

In Vietnam, Coot had often been in dangerous situations, yet he had felt prepared for the likely dangers. He was well-trained, very careful, and had comrades he could rely on. Now he would be alone, with little training for his assignment. He would have to be very, very careful. Coot hoped he would not panic again.

Less than an hour after takeoff, Col. Banks informed Coot that they were beginning their descent into the Chicago area. "Air Traffic Control has cleared us to fly right on in. We should be on the ground in about ten minutes."

On the ground and within the blast radius of a tactical nuclear weapon, Coot knew, although he kept that thought to himself.

The landing was smoother than Coot had expected. His watch now read 5:01 PM, which meant it was just after 4 in Chicago. Col. Banks quickly taxied the T-38 to a restricted area at O'Hare, where Coot could see a black S.U.V. that he assumed would be taking him to the warehouse. The trainer came to a halt and its engines shut down. The canopies popped open. Someone brought a ladder for him to climb down. Once on the ground, Coot removed his helmet and turned back to Col. Banks, who was still seated in the rear cockpit. "What should I do with my flight suit and helmet?"

"Keep them, in case you need to make a quick getaway!" said the colonel. "Seriously, you may need them if they want you in Washington in a hurry."

Coot thanked Col. Banks, then looked around for Special Agent Maxwell. He watched as a man walked swiftly towards him.

"Mr. Jenkins, I'm Jason Maxwell, Special Agent in charge of the F.B.I.'s counterterrorism team in Chicago." He flashed his ID, which Coot decided looked genuine. "Please come with me. I'll take you where you can change and then we'll go to the warehouse."

"Have you found out anything about George Boyd or the Mushrooms?" asked Coot as they drove off in the S.U.V.

"Nothing yet."

"I need to call Jill Meecham, if you'll excuse me," said Coot. He pressed "2" on the phone that Jill had given him and in a few seconds she answered. "I'm with Agent Maxwell and we're heading for the warehouse. Have you gotten any more information about Boyd or his group?" Coot was again disappointed by a negative answer.

"Just remember your assignment, Coot," said Jill. "Learn as much as you can about the group and their demands, then leave and report to the president."

"Okay. I'll call you just before entering the warehouse."

Coot fumed in silence as he looked out the S.U.V.'s window at the industrial area near O'Hare.

"After being fine at Mach 1.2 and 40,000 feet, I feel now like I'm flying blind," Coot said to Maxwell.

"I know what you mean. The Mushrooms group just popped up out of nowhere. The top guys in the Bureau are not happy with the counterterrorism section."

Maxwell pulled the car into a parking place behind a large vehicle that appeared to be a mobile command post.

"You can change inside," said Maxwell.

Coot followed the agent into the converted R.V. and was shown to a private area in which to change. He stripped off his flight suit and put on the clothes from his bag, then called Jill again. "I'm going to meet Boyd now. Any last-minute instructions or helpful hints?" Receiving neither, Coot went back to Maxwell. "Please keep an eye on the flight suit and helmet, would you?" He needed to imagine getting out of the situation alive, equipped for the return trip to Washington.

Maxwell nodded his assent. "Ready?"

Coot had not even thought to phone his kids. Well, they would know soon enough. He would not have wanted to worry them by saying goodbye. And then there was Diana. Would she miss him if he did not return?

"Yeah," said Coot. "I'm ready." What a liar he had become.

* * *

The distinctive ring alerted Paul Henry to a clandestine caller.

"Anthony."

"It's George. We need help."

"Your benefactor will not be happy about your failure."

"There's nothing I can do about it now."

"You still have a device. You can go out in style."

"No way! We didn't sign on to be suicide bombers."

"What do you have in mind?"

"We want you to provide an aircraft to get us out of here, in exchange for our silence about your role."

"Playing hardball, are you? Don't you know extortion is illegal?" Henry couldn't resist the irony.

"We just want to get out of the country, where we can't be extradited."

"Would you like a vacation in scenic North Korea?"

"Compared to being executed in the States, that would be great. Can you arrange a flight?"

"Yes. Consider it done."

Henry ended the call. He arranged for the North Korean airline Air Koryo to fly a Tupolev Tu-204 to O'Hare as soon as the U.S. government agreed to the Mushrooms' demand for safe passage. How could they refuse? A nuke unexploded in exchange for not prosecuting the most heinous crime in American history — seemed like a pretty good deal.

Yet Henry was worried. Very worried. The "productions" he had arranged for Myron Pepsey had never failed before. He was entering uncharted waters. Pepsey wanted to see him in his office in a few minutes. He had no choice but to show up and take his medicine.

Henry was trembling by the time he parked his car in the garage under Pepsey's office tower. He took the elevator to the top floor and walked quickly to Pepsey's suite. He used his card key to unlock the front doors. He nodded to the receptionist and hurried to the office in the east corner. Pepsey's secretary told him to go in. Myron Pepsey was standing at the window, his back to the door, apparently lost in appreciation of the fine view of Stone Mountain and its impressive carving of Confederate generals on horseback.

Without turning around, Pepsey said, "*The Lost Cause.* The specter of that defeat and subjugation has always haunted me."

"This hasn't been our best day," said Henry. "There will be no third act."

Pepsey turned from the window and sat in the big leather chair behind his desk. "Fitzgerald said there are no second acts in American lives. I suppose we should be grateful that we managed two in our production. Unfortunately, number three is beyond our grasp now."

Henry simply nodded, then looked at the floor. Would Pepsey blame him for the debacle?

"Now we need to do damage control," continued Pepsey. "The actors cast in Act Three are a problem."

"I understand," said Henry. He explained about the Air Koryo arrangement to evacuate the remaining Mushrooms.

"That may not be enough," said Pepsey. "They may write their own script from this point."

"I'll see that they don't," said Henry. He knew what Pepsey wanted him to do. He had no choice anyway: those actors were more a problem for him than for Pepsey.

"Good," said Pepsey. "I can't allow another failure by you, Paul."

Always afraid of Pepsey, Henry felt himself trembling again. Could Pepsey see his hands shaking?

"I'd better go make arrangements now," said Henry.

"Yes, you'd better," said Pepsey. "Write an alternative Act Three."

Henry left Pepsey's office and hurried back to his car. It would not be easy to arrange what needed to happen, but he had several ideas of what to do.

CHAPTER 10

The Warehouse

Maxwell drove Coot to the front entrance of the warehouse. Coot got out of the car.

"You in the car. Drive away. Now!" boomed a voice from the building's loudspeakers, startling Coot.

Maxwell complied with the instruction, slowly moving the car halfway down the block, still where Coot could see him.

"Further!" said the voice.

Coot waved at Maxwell, gesturing for him to go around the next corner. As the black sedan disappeared from Coot's view, he felt vulnerable, exposed, alone, his last connection to a normal life gone. His mouth was dry but his palms were sweating. He did not panic.

The disembodied voice said, "Hands up! Walk slowly toward the door." Coot did as he was told, until he was standing just outside the warehouse. He heard locks being opened. Then the voice said, "Come in."

Coot pulled the door open. No one was visible inside. He walked through the doorway. The door automatically closed behind him, leaving him in semi-darkness. Coot's eyes adjusted slowly to the dim light.

"Step to the middle of the room and take off your clothes." The voice was the same as before, but it came from a speaker in the low ceiling of the room he was in.

"What?" Coot said without thinking. "I thought you trusted me."

"Our motto is 'Trust but verify.' Sound familiar?"

Coot walked to the middle of the room and stripped down to his underwear and socks.

"Take off everything."

Coot finished undressing. As he stood naked beside his pile of clothes, the voice said, "Step back ten feet."

A door opened on the far side of the room. A man entered, walked to Coot's clothes, examined them, and left, taking the phone that Jill had given Coot.

The voice from the ceiling said, "Get dressed." Coot hurriedly put his clothes back on. As he finished, the door opened again and the same man came back in, holding something made of black fabric.

"Put on this hood and come with me."

Coot placed the black hood over his head and waited. He heard movement, then felt a hand on his right shoulder.

"Walk forward."

Coot did as he was told, responding occasionally to the guiding nudges of the hand. He heard a door open and was guided toward it.

"Take off the hood," said the same voice that had come out of the ceiling speaker, but now the person was just feet away.

Coot removed the hood and looked around the little room in which he found himself. A different man was sitting in one of two chairs in the room. There was a black satchel next to his chair. The fellow appeared to be about forty, short, pudgy, with thinning brown hair and glasses. Not what Coot had expected a mass murderer to look like.

"Remember me?" the man asked Coot.

"George Boyd?"

"Right you are, Coot. You don't mind if I call you 'Coot,' do you? After all, we meet as equals now. Have a seat."

Coot sat in the second chair and studied Boyd. Was he affected at all by the suffering he had inflicted? Was it possible to reach him emotionally? What had driven him to embrace anarchism? What was he willing to sacrifice to reach his goal? Coot decided at that moment that he must deal with Boyd not as the mass murderer of New York but as a potential partner in preventing deaths in Chicago. He must keep calm, be rational, engage Boyd.

"We were more equal in Geneva. At least we were on the same side then, or so I thought."

"Ah, yes, Geneva, 2004. You were one of the experts brought by Washington to brief the Conference on Disarmament session on U.S. proposals for a fissile materials cut-off treaty. I was a student observer from The University of Chicago's Committee on Security Studies. After your briefing there was a reception."

"Right." Coot did remember the reception.

"You were the only expert I met in Geneva who took my opinions seriously."

"Really? How did other people react?"

"Bored. Dismissive. Contemptuous. You, on the other hand, seemed interested in my proposal for an international bank of fissile materials that would buy up existing stocks and resell to countries for civilian purposes."

At last Coot remembered Boyd. "The International Atomic Energy Agency now runs such a bank."

"Yes, I know. Nobody at the I.A.E.A ever mentions that it was my idea."

"Does that make you angry?" Coot had to learn what motivated Boyd, what angered him, what he cared about.

"Enough of this chit-chat, Coot. We need to discuss what's going to happen. You're going to help us escape from this warehouse and get out of the country."

"And how am I going to do that?"

"You brought a sat phone with you. I assume it's for communicating with the authorities."

"Yes, before you confiscated it."

"Here's the deal: we abandon our nuclear weapon in return for safe passage."

"What would keep you from setting the device off by remote control or with a timer?"

"We could do that, of course. However, we're willing to allow verification that no device will explode after we leave."

"Good," said Coot. "How many devices *do* you have, anyway?"

"One. Now that we're negotiating its abandonment, there's no harm in telling you."

Coot had expected at least two, based on the Pakistani intelligence reports..

"Where's the other one?"

George leaned back in his chair. "What makes you think there's another one?"

Coot looked down at his hands, then back up at George. "Let's just say I have sources."

A frown flitted across George's face and disappeared. "Yet your sources didn't warn you about the Empire State Building."

"No, so I'll ask you now: What was your next target going to be?"

"The Sears Tower. Actually it's called the Willis Tower now."

"A grandiose plan," said Coot. George smiled.

"Suppose you do make a deal," Coot continued. "How can you be sure of safe passage?"

"You're going to come with us."

"As a hostage?"

"Oh, you're a notch above mere hostage. You're also our communications channel."

"How will this work, exactly?"

"We'll all drive from here to O'Hare, board a North Korean aircraft, and fly to Pyongyang. Then you'll be taken to the border with the South and released to make your way home."

Boyd reached into the satchel beside his chair and pulled out the phone that Jill had given Coot. "Here's your phone. Call your friends and make the deal."

Coot took the phone and pressed the speed dial key for Jill, as she had instructed him.

"Coot! Are you okay?" Coot heard a slight tremble of fear in her voice.

"Yes, I'm fine. Boyd wants me to offer you folks a deal."

"What sort of deal? You know the president said no negotiating, just reporting."

"What they want is safe passage out of the country, with me as hostage."

"What about the devices?"

"There's only one. The Mushrooms will let you send someone in to inspect the one here, to make sure it can't be detonated after they leave."

"How do they plan to get out of the country?"

"On a North Korean aircraft. I'll have to get details on that for you."

"Okay. Have you found out whether there are any other A.D.M.s?"

"No. Boyd deflected my question."

"Give me a few minutes to brief the president. I'll get back to you."

"Right." Coot looked at Boyd. "My contact will relay your proposal to the president. He'll decide whether to accept it."

"As if he has a choice!"

Before long the sat phone buzzed. Coot answered. "Jill?"

"The president can't let the murderers of thousands of Americans get away scot-free."

"Even if they give up the device?" The president's decision seemed more emotional than reasoned.

"Here's the deal, Coot," said Jill. "The Mushrooms surrender themselves and their weapons, in exchange for a guarantee the Administration will not seek the death penalty."

Coot relayed the new offer to Boyd.

"Is he crazy?" shouted Boyd. "Doesn't he know that we'll detonate the A.D.M. before allowing ourselves to be captured?"

Coot studied Boyd's contorted face. Was *he* crazy? Crazy enough to set off a nuclear device, killing his whole team? Probably not, but Coot wanted to avoid finding out.

"No, of course the president's not crazy. He's got a lot of factors to consider, including the public's demand for justice."

"Hah!" Boyd was pacing now, obviously distraught at the turn of events.

"Well?" said Coot. "What should I tell them?"

"Tell them we're not going to spend the rest of our lives in prison. Tell them we have a nuke and are prepared to use it."

Coot passed Boyd's threat to Jill, whose response was immediate. "We've got to assume the Mushrooms will make good on their threat. It's time to minimize the damage they can do. Get out of there now."

Coot ran his fingers through his gray hair. What could he say to help Jill convince the president and his advisors to make a deal with the Mushrooms? "Is justice for past murders worth the price of future killing?"

"It's no deal," said Jill. "Clear out."

The call over, Coot turned to Boyd. "I've been ordered to leave here immediately."

"Like hell!" said Boyd. "You're not going anywhere."

"C'mon, George," said Coot, feeling caught between forces he could not control. "You have a nuclear weapon, for God's sake. What do you need me for?"

"You still have some value as a hostage. They can't use nerve gas or set the building on fire with you inside."

"Don't be so sure about that. Better sacrifice me than let you kill thousands more people."

"Nah, they won't do that. Not yet."

"Then you'll want the Administration to know I'm still your hostage."

Boyd let Coot call Jill again. She had no guidance for him, just wished him luck and said his safety was uppermost in her mind. Except for the people of Chicago, he knew.

"Wait here," said Boyd. "I'll be back." He left the room, taking the sat phone with him.

Coot heard the door lock click. He was trapped, his anxiety increasing but not yet threatening a full-blown panic.

* * *

After making sure that Coot Jenkins could not escape, George Boyd rounded up his comrades to discuss the president's refusal of safe passage. They gathered in a small interior room with a window that looked out onto the warehouse floor. Doug and Jamie sat in folding chairs that they had brought with them. Mitch and Bennie, like George, stood.

"The stupid fucker thinks he can wait us out," said George.

"How long can we survive in here?" asked Bennie. "This warehouse was supposed to be a temporary staging area, not a long-term hideout."

"Like I told you, we have enough food and water for about two months," said Doug. "I always assumed we might be discovered."

"Good planning," said Jamie.

"What about power?" asked Mitch. "They could cut the power to the warehouse at any time."

"I brought a generator and plenty of gas," said Doug. "Don't worry about power."

"Anyway, if they were going to cut our power, they would have done it as soon as they found out we were here," said George. "Similarly for a gas attack. They're afraid we've set up some sort of dead-man switch to detonate the bomb."

"Maybe we *should* do that," said Mitch. "If we're serious about starting an insurrection, we've got to detonate that A.D.M., even if we're killed. After the revolution we'd be heroes, martyrs even." His unshaven face and maniacal glare gave him the appearance of a bomb-throwing anarchist from the early 20th Century.

"That's crazy talk!" exclaimed Jamie. "There aren't enough of us yet to sacrifice ourselves."

"I'm with Jamie," said George. "We're still too few, and we've already lost the teams going into India and Britain."

"We've got to figure a way out of here, so we can fight on," said Doug.

The group fell silent. Jamie sat with her head in her hands. Mitch paced back and forth, muttering to himself. No one offered any ideas. There was nothing for the Mushrooms to do now but wait, hoping the president would change his mind.

George decided to have another talk with Coot Jenkins. He liked and even admired Jenkins. In some weird way he still wanted the approval of the older man. George left the other Mushrooms and returned to the room in which he had sequestered his hostage.

* * *

Coot was wondering how long it would take someone in the Administration to realize they had to give the Mushrooms a way out, when the door of his small room opened and George Boyd stepped inside.

"Those morons in Washington haven't called again," said Boyd.

"Don't worry, George," said Coot. "They will."

"How can you be so sure?"

"The prevention of deaths in Chicago is more important, morally and politically, than avenging deaths in New York."

"Morally? What's that got to do with how politicians make decisions?" sneered Boyd.

Coot ignored the question and decided to learn more about Boyd. He needed to find some way out of the impasse. "So, tell me how you got from *security studies student* to *insurrectionary anarchist.*"

Boyd did not reply right away, as if disoriented by the change in topic.

"The more I saw of international institutions, especially at the U.N., the clearer it became that they were run by the people at the top for their own benefit, not to achieve their organizations' stated goals."

"Oh?" responded Coot, eager to learn about Boyd's motivations. "Can you be more specific?"

"Take the old U.N. Commission on Human Rights. Many of the countries represented on it abused human rights themselves. These countries sought membership in order to protect themselves from criticism. Why, Sudan was elected to the commission in 2004, at the same time it supported the genocide being carried out in Darfur by the Janjaweed militia."

Boyd was surprisingly well-informed. Coot returned Boyd's serve. "Yes, but in 2006 the U.N. General Assembly voted to replace the commission with a new Human Rights Council."

"Sure, but the council has many of the same problems as the commission. Even the Secretary-General has criticized it, but still not much has changed. The United States refused to participate in the council for a while."

"You picked perhaps the most glaring example to support your claims about institutions in general. What about the World Food Program? What about the I.A.E.A?"

"Yeah, they're better. Even the World Food Program has problems, though. In 2010 a Security Council report said that half of the food aid to Somalia is diverted to corrupt contractors, Islamic militants, and even local U.N. staff."

"But Somalia's a special case. It hardly has a functioning government. In fact, Somalia shows what happens when anarchy prevails. Do you really prefer Mogadishu to Chicago?"

"There might be some advantages, but we don't seek anarchy in that sense."

"Then what *are* you seeking?"

"Revolution!"

"Meaning what, exactly?"

"Meaning the overthrow of the institutions that oppress the people, self-perpetuating organizations, run for the benefit of the people at the top."

Coot had had enough experience with self-serving bureaucrats to know that there was some truth in Boyd's claims. He decided to probe Boyd further. "But almost all human activity is organized. Food production. Manufacturing. Education. Health care. At least existing institutions meet the basic needs of most people, even if your criticism is correct."

"There are two problems with existing institutions. First, they *don't* meet the needs of many people. A billion people in the world don't have enough to eat. Second, institutions oppress most of the people in them." Boyd was smirking now. He seemed more comfortable than he had when threatening death and destruction.

Coot thought of the advice he had been given in a briefing earlier that day: engage but don't challenge. So, he simply asked about the practicalities of Boyd's vision. "How will people be fed or children taught or illness cured, if you have your way?"

"Families and other local groups will organize themselves to grow food, produce goods, or provide services. They can trade the fruits of their labor among themselves, so that everyone has enough food, clothing, education, and medical care. The profits won't be siphoned off to the headquarters of multinational corporations but reinvested locally to fund improvements in the standard of living of the people."

Boyd's naiveté was astounding. The younger man seemed to want to return a world of seven billion people to forms of organization more appropriate for the societies that existed before the Industrial Revolution. Was it possible that the Mushrooms were sophisticated enough to acquire, transport, and detonate several nuclear devices, yet naive enough to believe people would destroy the institutions on which their continued health and welfare depended?

Coot had little hope of altering Boyd's world view. Still, it was worth a try, especially now that he was a prisoner and the Mushrooms were vowing to detonate a nuclear weapon mere feet away from him. "There are reasons that human life expectancy is so much greater now than it was in earlier times," Coot said. "The abundance of food provided by modern agriculture. Improvement in public health, including clean drinking water, the development of antibiotics, and the availability of medical care. Research and development by industry and academia. All of these factors involve complex, large-scale, persistent organizations. Ad hoc organizations simply could not attract the commitment of enough individuals over a long enough period of time to produce comparable results."

"You may say so, but what proof do you have?" said Boyd. "You're just a creature of the current order and you're defending that order."

"The burden of proof is on you," said Coot. "You can't expect people to abandon existing institutions from which they derive some benefit unless they can see alternatives already working."

"Modern communications and transportation systems enable far more cooperation among people world-wide than ever before. Look at the changes that have occurred in the Middle East in the past few years."

"I hope you don't think that these systems can be maintained over the long-term by ad hoc organizations. People want to know that the systems they depend on have some permanence."

"The organizations that maintain systems for the common good can persist as long as they're needed," said Boyd, "provided they're not being run for the benefit of the people at the top."

"For whose benefit is Mushrooms run?" asked Coot. Was Mushrooms being controlled or manipulated by some other entity for some other purpose?

"Isn't the answer obvious? For the benefit of those who desire a new order in the world."

"And who are they? Mushrooms members or others as well?"

"Our members and allies."

"Allies like VI, which you mentioned in your video after Srinagar?"

"Certainly."

"Do you also have financial backers?"

"Why do you care?"

"I always like to know who's paying for something in order to understand what's really going on."

"We have friends who help us."

"It must have taken a lot of money to pay for five nuclear weapons on the black market."

George appeared startled. "What makes you think we have only five?"

"The Mushrooms weren't the only ones who knew about those weapons," said Coot. "Surely you realize that information about the purchase of such weapons is itself valuable and could command a high price."

The idea that the Mushrooms had not remained hidden seemed to disturb George. He was silent.

"How many insurrectionary anarchists are rich enough to buy one weapon, let alone five?" asked Coot. "Who helped you?"

"We cooperate with anyone who shares our immediate goal."

"Like so-called anarcho-capitalists?"

"Perhaps."

"Some of them must be wealthy."

"A few."

"Did one of them finance your purchase of those devices?"

"Surely you don't expect me to answer that!" George fidgeted, a sign that Coot was onto something.

"It was worth a try."

* * *

After his talk with Coot, George returned to find his beleaguered fellow anarchists still as discouraged as ever about their situation.

"Why didn't the president agree to the deal, George?" asked Doug. "He's taking a big chance, leaving us here with a nuke."

"He thinks we'll surrender to face his phony justice, rather than detonate a bomb," interjected Mitch, still red-faced and agitated.

"Jenkins said something about the public's demand for justice," said George.

"So we need to give him reason to think that we're *not* the ones who destroyed the Empire State Building," said Doug.

"In my case, that's impossible," said Jamie. "They've got pictures of me and the backpack."

"But you're the only one they know about," said Mitch.

George, Bennie, and Doug turned to face Mitch. George realized what Mitch would say next.

"If you surrender, the rest of us might escape," Mitch continued.

"Thanks a lot, Mitch," retorted Jamie. "I always knew I could count on you."

"But Mitch is right," said Bennie. "They don't know anything about the rest of us."

"I thought we were all in this together," said Jamie angrily. "Are you going to throw me under the bus now?"

"I wish we could somehow all fight on together," said Doug, his forehead furrowed with concern, "but I don't see how we can."

The ensuing silence testified to the hopelessness of Jamie's situation.

"So, how about it, Jamie?" said Bennie. "You'd better surrender, or we're all gonna pay the price for those photos."

"This is Jamie's decision," said George. "None of us has the right to demand she sacrifice herself for us."

"Right," agreed Doug. "Jamie, you're a good friend. We couldn't have come this far without you."

Jamie sat as still as a tombstone, then slowly looked up, her eyes locking with George's.

"Mitch is right," she murmured. "There's no point in all of you going down."

George felt a wave of sympathy for his friend. His eyes tearing up, he went to the large woman's side and squeezed her shoulder. "Thanks."

Doug also walked over to Jamie and gave her an affectionate punch in the arm. Mitch just started pacing the room again.

Bennie said, "I still don't see how we can convince them we didn't do New York."

He looked around the group. No one volunteered an answer. Silence reigned, except for Mitch's occasional muttering.

Suddenly George smacked his right fist into his left palm and exclaimed, "Maybe we can use the avatar again."

"How?" said Doug. "The feds have closed down the satellite data service we were using."

Mitch said, "I was looking at that satellite phone that Jenkins brought with him. It's got a data port." The others turned to look at him. "We can hook up one of our laptops to it and use VI's comm software to send them encrypted instructions. Unless the feds thought to shut down the phone's data capability."

"Good idea, Mitch," said George. "What should the avatar say?"

"Threaten an immediate attack if they don't give us safe passage," Bennie said.

"Threatening an attack hasn't helped us so far," said Doug. "No, they've got to think we're not the guys who did New York."

After more discussion, the group settled on having the avatar say that the Mushrooms team that had destroyed the Empire State Building would launch another attack on the East Coast — unless the Midwest Mushrooms were allowed to leave the country. George drafted a script for the avatar and read it to the group. Mitch encrypted the script and prepared a program for transmitting it to VI as a quick burst that would get through before a monitor could react to the use of the sat phone's data channel. He then connected his laptop to the sat phone, turned both on, and ran the program. The team cheered when the laptop displayed VI's acknowledgement that it had received the transmission.

"Hah!" said Mitch. "Somebody at the White House made a mistake."

"Yeah," said George. "Once again, political connections trumped competence in a staffing decision."

* * *

A couple hours after Boyd had left Coot, he returned with the sat phone.

"There's a call for you."

Coot took the phone from Boyd.

"This is Coot."

Jill was calling. After making sure he was okay, she said, "Have you heard anything about other Mushrooms teams in the country?"

"No," Coot answered.

"See what you can find out and get back to me."

Coot kept the sat phone, hoping that Boyd would not demand it back. At the moment the fellow seemed to have something else on his mind as he paced back and forth in the small room.

"Any change in the president's position on safe passage?" asked Boyd.

"No mention of it," said Coot. "He would be impeached if he released terrorists with blood on their hands."

"Then why is he refusing to give *us* safe passage?" Boyd appeared frightened and uncomprehending.

"What?"

"If he wants revenge, he should go after the East Coast team." Boyd spun away from Coot and briefly hung his head, as if ashamed of betraying his comrades.

Coot's face was impassive but his mind was racing to deal with this revelation.

"Didn't your team destroy the Empire State Building?"

"Only Jamie Saunders was involved. The rest of us were too busy getting ready here in Chicago."

"How many teams do you guys have?"

"I don't know. We operate mostly independently."

"Why haven't we heard anything from the East Coast team?"

"You have. Their avatar took over several networks just after the New York bombing."

Coot was confused. "But that was the same avatar as we saw after Srinagar."

"The East Coast team has some expert graphics and AI guys," said George, smiling. "They handle Mushrooms publicity. I know that much."

"Yeah? Well, it's too bad you guys don't put your talents to better use," said Coot.

"Oh, don't be so judgmental, Coot. One day we'll be seen as the founding fathers of a more just world order."

"Not likely, George. In the end, you'll be crushed."

"We'll see about that."

"Getting back to Jamie Saunders," said Coot, " if she surrendered, the president might change his mind about safe passage."

"She's already said she'd give herself up if it meant the rest of us could escape."

The sat phone signaled an incoming call. Coot, still holding it, answered.

"Any news there?" Jill asked.

"The Mushrooms' East Coast team did New York. They're still at large, except for Jamie Saunders. She'll surrender if the others can get out."

"I'll let the president know," said Jill.

The call over, Boyd took the sat phone with him, leaving Coot by himself in the little room.

Coot went over the interaction with Boyd in his mind. Had he been telling the truth? Seemed like it. His fear of dying had apparently gotten the better of him for a brief time. He probably never thought his team would be discovered and face a choice between surrender and certain death.

A few minutes later, Boyd was back with the sat phone. He seemed calmer this time.

"Another call for you. Be careful what you say."

Again it was Jill.

"It's a deal. There's been another avatar takeover of the networks. The East Coast team that you mentioned has claimed responsibility for destroying midtown Manhattan and is threatening another attack unless we let your Mushrooms leave the country."

"Good grief!" said Coot. "They must have the fifth nuke."

"The president's under severe pressure to capture these fellows, but he doesn't want to risk the detonation of a bomb in Chicago. Since there's some doubt whether the Chicago group did New York, the president has enough of a fig leaf for granting safe passage to everyone but Saunders. He isn't happy about allowing a North Korean aircraft into U.S. airspace, though. It'll have to be a civilian plane."

"Let me check." Coot, relieved that a way out of the impasse had been found, explained the president's requirement to Boyd.

"We've already arranged for an Air Koryo Tupolev Tu-204 to fly here," said Boyd. "It will need to refuel en route, both ways. We propose it do so in Anchorage."

Coot relayed this information to Jill. She agreed, but stipulated that the refueling would be done at Anchorage's Ted Stevens International Airport, not at Elmendorf Air Force Base. The military did not want North Koreans getting close to such a sensitive installation. In fact, the Tupolev would have two military jets as escorts while in U.S. airspace.

"And one more thing," she added. "We want Jamie Saunders in custody before anything else happens."

The call over, Coot handed the phone to Boyd. "They want Jamie Saunders to surrender immediately."

* * *

Jamie was sitting with the others watching television coverage of their predicament when George came in. She could tell by the way he avoided looking at her that she was in trouble.

"Did you get a deal?" Mitch asked.

"Yes — but Jamie must surrender immediately." George glanced at Jamie, then looked away.

Mitch, Doug, and Bennie groaned, but Jamie just sighed.

"Just what I expected," she said. "I'll get my stuff."

"Jamie, I can't thank you enough for helping us out of this mess," said George. Doug and Bennie echoed George's declaration. The three men each gave Jamie a hug. All but Mitch.

"Mitch, aren't you even going to say goodbye to Jamie?" said George.

Mitch looked up at George, then at Jamie. "You used your phone, didn't you?"

"What?" said Jamie.

"You know what I mean," said Mitch, glaring at her. "I've been thinking about how they found us here. You used your phone to call Sabrina, didn't you?"

Jamie turned red. She had wondered whether they would blame her. Now she would find out. "Yes," she whispered.

"You stupid fucking dyke!" Mitch screamed. "You knew they would identify you from the video, find out your cell phone, and trace any calls you made."

"That's why I called Sabrina before they figured out who I was," said Jamie.

"Before they *announced* they'd figured it out," said Mitch. "You shouldn't have been using your phone at all."

"I guess not," said Jamie, tears forming quickly. The realization that she's brought the power of the U.S. government down on them all was hard to bear.

"Let me see that phone," said Mitch. "And the battery."

What could Jamie do but give it to him? Mitch took the phone, inserted the battery, pressed a few buttons, and looked up at Jamie with a satisfied look on his face.

"There's a tracker app on this phone," he said.

"What do you mean?" said Jamie. "There's lots of stuff on it. Sabrina gave it to me."

"Sabrina! I should have known!" roared Mitch, his face as red as Jamie's. This phone's been reporting your location whenever its battery was in!"

"Oh, God!" said Jamie. "I had no idea." Sabrina had not trusted her after all. Jamie was devastated. Worse, she had stupidly used her phone, leading to the Mushrooms' being surrounded and their mission aborted. She felt more ashamed of herself than she had of her father, the Ponzi schemer. Her world was coming apart: her family, her career, her love life, the insurrection. All in pieces. She wanted to kill herself, but that would be a coward's way out. Jamie was no coward. No, she would protect the comrades with whom she had hoped to change the world, the comrades whom she had unwittingly betrayed. To save them, she would surrender herself.

Jamie gathered her few possessions, but not her sniper's rifle. The feds would shoot her for sure if she emerged from the warehouse carrying that. She opened the door through which they had admitted Coot Jenkins just a few hours earlier. She tossed out the bag with her belonging, raised her hands, and stepped into sunlight for the first time since she'd left New Jersey.

A man in a dark jacket with a bullhorn was speaking to her,

telling her to walk toward him. In a daze, she complied with his instruction. When she reached the man with the bullhorn, another man appeared, handcuffed her, and put her into the back seat of a car. She vowed to stick to the story that she was the only one of the Mushrooms who took part in the attack in New York. Protecting her friends was the least she could do, after stupidly giving away their location.

* * *

With Boyd gone, Coot was free to consider his situation without distractions. A glance at his watch told him it was 6 P.M. back east, 5 P.M. in Chicago. He set the second clock on his watch to 5 P.M. and made it the displayed clock. Getting the Tupolev to Chicago was going to take many hours. He figured it was about 4000 miles from Pyongyang to Anchorage and about 3000 miles from Anchorage to Chicago. Assuming the jet could cruise at about 500 miles per hour, he estimated it would arrive at O'Hare in about 14 hours. That seemed like a long time to wait, especially with a couple of nuclear weapons lurking nearby.

Coot was getting hungry. What kind of crap would he have to eat? What about sleeping arrangements? Enough of trivial considerations.

What about Boyd's unwillingness to discuss how Mushrooms had been able to purchase multiple atomic demolition munitions? The Mushrooms' ability to arrange for a North Korean airliner to fly to the U.S. to pick up Boyd, Coot, and some other people indicated that one or more people with pretty deep pockets were backing the Mushrooms. But who? The North Koreans? No, they were too authoritarian to cooperate with anarchists. Some anarcho-capitalist? That seemed more likely. Coot decided to investigate this possibility when he was done with his current mission for the president. Assuming he survived.

Coot had avoided considering that he might be killed or injured while trying to prevent the Mushrooms from detonating the fourth nuke. Instead he had concentrated on dealing with the events of the day as they unfolded, and on executing the mission that the president had given him. Now, there was nothing more he could do for hours, and other concerns intruded on his analytical mind. The

Mushrooms's plan for escaping to North Korea had seemed relatively low-risk at first, but something could go wrong. The pressure on the president to capture the destroyers of the Empire State Building and the killers of thousands of New Yorkers must be intense. What if the president changed his mind and ordered the F.B.I. to attempt to take out the Mushrooms as they boarded the North Korean plane at O'Hare? A team of snipers could pick off Mushrooms while they were moving from their vehicle to the aircraft. Surely Boyd and the others must be thinking about this possibility, too. How might they deter such an attack?

Around 7 P.M. one of the Mushrooms came into the little room with a tray of food for Coot: canned tuna and baked beans, both cold; stale saltines; a paper cup full of water. Coot thanked the fellow for the food, despite his distaste for it. The food on the Air Koryo jet would surely be better than this! Nevertheless Coot consumed the small meal quickly, since he had not eaten anything in the eight hours following lunch with Jill.

His hunger temporarily satisfied, Coot's attention shifted to other needs, and to Diana. She had broken off their relationship just yesterday. They has not spoken since then. The ten-year-old boy in Coot wondered whether his role in preventing the detonation of another device would cause Diana to see him in a new way. More heroic. More desirable. He tried to think about something else, anything else. Where would he sleep? What would he sleep on? Yet he could not forget Diana. Memories of their time together kept intruding. Getting stuck with her in the elevator. How clichéd was that? Breakfasts at Snuffy's. It's only breakfast, she'd said, but was it? Playing the piano for her and listening to her play Bach so marvelously. Her confession of her illness. Her attacking Limbick. How sweet she was, and how fierce! Missing her after the destruction of the Empire State Building. Watching her recover from her injuries. Worrying about her and Zeeland. Was that romance, if it was a romance, really over? Diana's decision to end their relationship. Would she even be sorry if he died here in this miserable warehouse? Of course she would! He must survive this ordeal, must have another chance with her.

Coot, agitated, found himself pacing around his little prison, back and forth, around in a circle, clockwise, counterclockwise, his path, like his thoughts, stuck in the same repetitive patterns. He was rescued from obsessing by the arrival of a cot and an old blanket. They were dirty and stained, but still better than the floor for getting some rest. With the prospect of actually lying down and relaxing before him, Coot realized how tired he was. It was 11:39 back east. Would he ever see his home again?

The warehouse was a little chilly, so he lay down on the cot with his clothes on, pulled the blanket up to his chin, and closed his eyes. He had learned to sleep while on reconnaissance patrols in the Vietnamese jungle, trusting his men to protect him. Now he was alone, behind enemy lines, with no one to keep watch. He could not protect himself, even if he were awake. He gave himself up to sleep, not trusting he would be safe but merely hoping so.

"Get up!"

The command seemed odd to Coot. No one had told him to wake up in a very long time, and the voice was low and gruff and urgent, not like his mother's or Frannie's at all. Coot struggled to escape from the deep sleep that he had needed so much. Slowly he realized where he was, and why. He opened his eyes and glanced at his watch. 6:03 A.M.

A man he had not seen before was standing next to his cot, holding a black satchel like the one Boyd had carried. He was short, thin, and unshaven, with a wild aura that suggested he knew how to kill a lot of people in a hurry. He looked as if his next move would be to grab Coot by the arm and force him up. Coot pre-empted that indignity by getting to his feet and stretching.

"Who are you?" Coot asked the man.

"Mitch." The man's terse speech and gruff tone reinforced Coot's first impression that Mitch was a dangerous man. No one had made Coot feel so threatened since a Viet Cong patrol had come within two meters of his hiding place in the jungle near the Ho Chi Minh Trail.

Mitch opened his satchel and pulled out what Coot recognized as the sort of vest used by suicide bombers. Not only was it laden with explosives, but it also had a small box with an antenna mounted in the center of the back.

"What's that for?" Coot asked, his voice rising in alarm.

"Our protection. Now turn around and stick out your arms behind you."

Coot hesitated. The vest look deadly. Coot had worked with explosives in Vietnam and knew well how easily a devastating accident could happen.

"How does my wearing a suicide vest protect you?" he asked.

"We each have a dead man's switch. If one of us is shot, his switch will detonate the explosives in the vest."

"But if one of you is even wounded, all of you will die."

"Your side won't sacrifice you to get us. Now turn around."

Coot did as Mitch instructed. He shivered as Mitch slid the vest over his arms, pulled it up over his shoulders, and secured the vest around Coot's back and chest. Two locks prevented Coot from removing the vest himself. He felt trapped and vulnerable. He needed to understand Mitch's motivation.

"Why do you have a vest like this handy," probed Coot, "when you have nuclear weapons?"

"Quiet," said Mitch. "You talk too much."

"Seems like underkill," retorted Coot, smiling to himself.

"I thought about bombing the Chicago Board of Trade," said Mitch, "before we got the nukes."

"A suicide attack against capitalism? The vest is a sort of *memento mori*, then," said Coot.

"Just shut up," said Mitch, scowling at Coot. "I don't need some show-off geek wising off to me."

Despite his weak position, Coot determined to stand up for himself. His reliable stomach growled loudly, giving him his cue. "Don't I get breakfast today?" he asked. "Even a condemned man gets his last meal."

"You can starve, for all I care," said Mitch. "My job was just to get you into the vest."

Coot heard the door open and looked around. Boyd entered.

"Shouldn't I explain your plan with the vest to my contact? You do want your plan to work, don't you?" Coot asked Boyd.

"That's why I brought your sat phone along this morning. Here, tell them you'll be leaving in an armored S.U.V. with four others. Tell them you'll be wearing an explosive vest and we'll all have dead man's switches. Tell them that, if we're injured or lose consciousness, you'll surely die."

Coot took the phone from Boyd and pressed "2" to dial Jill. She answered almost immediately.

"Coot! How are you?" Jill's voice betrayed the great stress she was under.

"I'm wearing an explosive vest."

"What's that about?"

"The Mushrooms all have dead man's switches. Make sure Maxwell's people don't attack the escape vehicle or we'll all be blown to bits."

"I'll contact him when we're done. When will you be leaving for O'Hare?"

Coot checked with Boyd, then spoke again to Jill. "As soon as the aircraft has been refueled."

"Not long, then. The North Korean plane has landed at O'Hare and is being refueled now."

"So everything's going according to the agreement?"

"Not quite. In Anchorage our people boarded the Tupolev and found a dozen North Korean soldiers. They're now off the plane and in custody. Only the captain, the first officer, two relief pilots, and a flight attendant are still on the aircraft."

"Why the soldiers?"

"No idea. They're being questioned now. I'll let you know if I find out anything."

"Okay. Something's going on that we don't understand."

"Maybe," said Jill. "One more thing: Sam Bartleson from Los Alamos arrived in Chicago this morning. He's en route to the warehouse now to inspect the A.D.M. We're going to hold the Mushrooms in the building until Sam certifies that the devices cannot be detonated once they've left. And that they're not taking an A.D.M. with them."

Coot relayed this information to Boyd.

"Tell her that Bartleson should come by himself to the same door you did. His vehicle must be out of sight before he can enter."

Coot described these requirements to Jill.

"Okay. Is there anything else..." Jill's question was cut short.

"That's enough talking for now," said Boyd, as Mitch jerked the sat phone from Coot's hand.

Another ten minutes elapsed. Coot heard the muffled sound of a vehicle approaching, then instructions being given to Bartleson and his driver, and finally the diminishing rumble of a vehicle moving further and further away. Somewhere a door opened. Coot wondered if he would be able to meet Bartleson before leaving the warehouse with Boyd and the others. He imagined the group strip-searching Bartleson and confiscating any equipment he'd brought. A few minutes later the door in Coot's room opened and Boyd entered with a man whom Coot guessed to be Bartleson. He was fifty-ish, short, and slender, with skin the milky brown color of a latte. His black plastic-frame glasses and darting eyes gave Coot the impression of someone accustomed to dealing with arcane matters far from public view.

"You must be Sam Bartleson," Coot said, smiling grimly at the new arrival.

"Uh, yes," said Bartleson. "And you're Coot Jenkins?"

"Right. Be careful: my new outfit may not tolerate a sudden impact."

"I'd rather be wearing that than babysitting an A.D.M.!" replied Bartleson.

"I hear you."

"When can I inspect the device?" Bartleson asked Boyd.

"Right now. Do your thing quickly, so we can all get out of here."

Boyd and Bartleson left the room. Coot sat down in a chair, being careful to avoid hitting the vest on the back or arms.

About 45 minutes later Boyd returned. "Let's get into the S.U.V.," he said.

Coot assumed this meant that Bartleson had convinced himself that it was safe for the gang to leave and that he had communicated his findings to the appropriate authorities. Coot was nervous about moving around in the explosive vest, worried that he would bump into something and set it off. Boyd led him to an area of the warehouse that he had not seen before. A black Chevrolet

Suburban was parked in a service bay, separated from the outside by a garage-style door. Bright halogen lights shone overhead, bathing the area in a cold light that reminded Coot of a morgue. Several men were already in the S.U.V. but its engine was off. Sam Bartleson was standing near the S.U.V.

"No nukes on board," said Bartleson.

The right rear door of the Suburban opened. Boyd said, "Get in, but be careful. We don't want any accidents."

Coot climbed past Mitch and sat in the middle seat in the middle row of the eight-passenger Suburban. Jamie Saunders was not with them. She must have surrendered already. He could see that each of the men next to him had a little box with a single large red button on top. . They were not yet pressing their buttons: the dead man system was not yet armed.

"Listen up, guys," said Boyd. "Here's how we're going to get on that plane safely. Mitch is going to arm the dead man system. We'll have 30 seconds to press and hold our buttons. If anyone fails to do so, the system will disarm itself and we'll have to start over. Once the system is armed, if anybody releases his button, he'll have 10 seconds to press it again, or the explosives will detonate. Any questions?" The other men seemed satisfied with Boyd's explanation, so he turned to Mitch and said, "Arm the system."

Mitch reached behind Coot with a key. Coot heard the key slide into something and then he heard a soft beeping. "System armed, George," Mitch said. "Press your buttons, guys."

Coot saw Mitch, Boyd, and the driver press their buttons. Half a minute later he heard the beeping increase its tempo, and Mitch confirmed that the system was armed. *And dangerous*, thought Coot.

"All right, then. Let's roll!" Boyd said, as he used a remote control to open the service bay door. The driver started the engine of the Suburban, eased the large S.U.V. out of the service bay, and turned left into the service road next to the warehouse. At Pratt he turned east. Coot noticed that another black Suburban had pulled in behind them and another soon moved into position in front.

"Who's our escort?" Coot asked.

"F.B.I.," answered Boyd. "We worked out a route with them."

The convoy turned south on Elmhurst, which became York, and then made a left onto Irving Park, which followed the southern boundary of the airport. The lead vehicle turned into the O'Hare Cargo Area Road and the other two S.U.V.s followed. The guards at the service entrance seemed to be expecting them. They were not airport employees but National Guard troops. The arrival of nuclear terrorists under F.B.I. escort required military security at O'Hare.

The three vehicles followed Cargo Area Road north until they reached a parking area on their left with dozens of trailers lined up in rows. They threaded their way along the edge of the asphalt until they reached a large building, more trailers, and several cargo planes. A single large Russian Tupolev aircraft with Air Koryo markings was parked at the northern edge of the concrete, surrounded by more black S.U.V.s with flashing lights. The convoy left the asphalt through a gap between storage boxes of some sort and headed across the concrete toward the waiting Korean plane.

"Now for the moment of truth," said Boyd.

"Keep your fingers on those buttons, fellas!" said Coot, to general grunts of agreement.

The convoy reached the Tupolev and halted. Agents with their guns drawn got out of the leading and trailing S.U.V.s and formed a double line from the middle S.U.V. to the stairs leading up to the passenger door of the Tupolev.

"Let's go," said Boyd. "I'll lead the way. Bennie will go next. Coot, you'll go between Mitch and Doug. Doug is the guy to your left." Boyd opened his door and climbed out. Bennie turned out to be the driver. He and the others followed Boyd's example and exited the vehicle.

Coot's heart was pounding, his pulse rapid. Except for the panic attacks, he had never felt so nervous in his life. He walked behind Doug and ahead of Mitch, between the lines of agents, toward the stairs to the plane.

"Good luck, Coot!" said Agent Maxwell, as Coot passed him.

"Thanks!" said Coot, half smiling at Maxwell's kind attempt to bolster his morale.

"God, how I'd love to shoot those bastards!" Coot heard someone say, as he mounted the steps leading into the Tupolev.

"You do that and we're all dead, including your guy," muttered one of the Mushrooms behind Coot.

Coot and the Mushrooms entered the Tupolev through the front left cabin door, between the cockpit and the business class area. Coot had to stoop to avoid hitting his head on the door frame. A female flight attendant closed the cabin door behind them. Looking through the open cockpit door, Coot saw two pilots preparing for takeoff. Seated in the wide seats of the first row were two more Korean men whose uniforms indicated they were the relief pilots Jill had mentioned. All the window shades had been pulled down in an obvious attempt to prevent snipers from being able to spot targets inside the plane.

"Let's all sit further back," said Boyd, "so we can be together."

"Shit, George," said Mitch, "This is going to be a long flight. How about we bump the flyboys to the economy seats?"

"In an emergency," said Coot, "it would be better for the relief pilots to be nearest the cockpit."

"I agree." Doug's support was welcome to Coot. He seemed almost too reasonable to be an anarcho-terrorist.

The group moved into the economy section of the cabin. Boyd directed Coot to sit on the left in row 6. Mitch sat on the right side of the same row and Bennie in row 7, just behind Coot. No one sat in front of Coot, but Doug sat in row 5, ahead of Mitch. Boyd himself sat behind Bennie in row 8. They all still had their fingers on their buttons. Coot was surrounded.

"Hey, George, when can we let go of these buttons?" asked Bennie.

"As soon as we're airborne and Mitch has disarmed the system. In case our friends outside can hear everything we say in here, we'll keep Coot in his favorite garment and we'll keep our fingers on our red buttons. And let's keep the talking to a minimum."

The flight attendant's voice erupted from the cabin speakers, instructing them to fasten their seat belts. The four Mushrooms and Coot obeyed her instruction. Suddenly Coot heard the beeping from his vest's electronics get louder and faster--and the sound of something hitting the carpeted floor of the cabin and bouncing around. A male voice behind him said, "Oh, shit!"

Mitch jumped up and yelled, "Just press the button again, Bennie! Quick!" He fumbled in his pocket for the key to the detonator.

"I can't!" said Bennie. "The damn box fell on the floor and bounced under the seat somewhere. I've got to find it first."

"Well, hurry!" said Mitch, as he inserted his key into the detonator. "I don't want to turn the system off while we're still on the ground." A couple of seconds later the beeping from the vest returned to its normal tempo and loudness. Mitch removed the key and returned to his seat. "Bennie, you gotta be more careful."

Bennie glared at Mitch but did not say anything.

Coot appreciated the irony of mass murderers escaping from the feds, only to die because of their own ineptness.

George appeared at Coot's row with the sat phone. "It's for you. Make it quick."

Coot took the phone. "Coot here."

"Is everything going according to plan?" Jill asked.

"So far, so good. I'm still wearing the vest and my buddies are still keeping us all from being blown to bits, although we did have one scare when..."

Boyd grabbed the phone back from Coot. "That's enough. They know you're safe and they can't attack us without killing you." He went back to his seat, on the left side three rows behind Coot.

Ten minutes later the aircraft began to taxi toward the main runways at O'Hare. At the world's busiest airport, there was no queue of other planes waiting to get airborne ahead of them. Flashing lights were everywhere. The captain announced that the flight attendant should be seated for takeoff. A minute more, and the Tupolev was in the air, headed for Anchorage, accompanied by a pair of F-22 interceptors.

Once the fasten seatbelt signs had gone off, Boyd reminded Mitch to disarm the vest and take it off Coot. Mitch crossed the aisle and stood over Coot.

"Get up," he ordered.

Coot had overheard Boyd's instructions to Mitch and complied quickly, not wanting to challenge the volatile fellow.

Mitch turned off the dead man's switch system with his key, unlocked the fasteners of the vest itself, and took it off.

"Thanks," said Coot, trying to appease Mitch, who seemed as explosive as the vest he had just removed.

"Don't get too used to the feeling. I'll put it back on you before we land in Anchorage," said Mitch. "Okay, guys," he yelled to the others, "let go of your buttons but keep them handy. You'll need them again in about five and a half hours."

Coot sat back down and refastened his seatbelt. He was surprised when the flight attendant brought breakfast to the group of fellow travelers. He had not had a Korean breakfast since a meeting in Seoul a dozen years earlier. He enjoyed the kimchi, a spicy pickled cabbage that is the national dish of Korea, and even managed to eat the vegetable soup, despite its fishy broth. Some of the Mushrooms were grumbling about their meals, however. Coot heard several mentions of "eggs and bacon" and "toast and jam." Pretty provincial, for a bunch of international terrorists.

As Coot stood up to go to the lavatory, Bennie said, "Where do you think you're going?"

"Nature calls," said Coot. The sudden increase in tension heightened the urgency he felt from his bladder and his bowels.

"Okay," said Bennie, who got up and followed him.

When Coot tried to close the door for some privacy, Bennie said, "Leave the door open."

"You can at least turn your back or look away," said Coot. "How weird do you want this trip to get?" He dropped his trousers and sat on the toilet. "Are you Bennie?"

"Yeah. So what?"

"So you nearly got all of us killed this morning. That was pretty scary!"

"It turned out all right. Just finish your business, there, okay?"

"I'm working on it. What's your role in Mushrooms?"

"We're not supposed to talk with you."

"For an anarchist, George seems to impose a lot of rules."

"Not really. Today's different."

"You got that right." Coot paused, then decided to take another stab at getting information about his captors. "I guess Mitch is an expert in electronics. What's your specialty? George didn't bring you along just for the ride."

"Mechanics." Bennie looked up the aisle, as if worried that Boyd would notice he was talking with Coot.

"How did you guys find five Soviet A.D.M.s?"

"We managed."

"I bet they weren't cheap."

Bennie did not respond.

Pursuing the cost of the weapons, Coot said, "Mushrooms must have had to come up with millions."

Again Bennie remained silent. Coot needed to make him lower his guard.

"Mitch was nasty to you back there. Is he always like that?"

"Pretty much."

"None of the Mushrooms looks wealthy. You guys must have had help."

"Some rich guy, I think."

"Just one?"

Bennie reverted to his silent mode, but his revelation jogged Coot's brain into putting a few pieces together. "You ever hear of Myron Pepsey?"

Again Bennie said nothing.

"Never mind," Coot said. "Anyway, I'm done here."

Coot returned to his seat, brooding about what Bennie had divulged—and refused to divulge. Could Pepsey, a S.A.F.E. board member, be behind the whole business? The idea seemed preposterous, but the coincidences were piling up. Pepsey, unlike Boyd, wouldn't want a general insurrection, just an attempt to foment one, with lots of destruction to get people agitated, ready to embrace an extreme solution. His solution. The takeover of all protective services by EuroSécurité and other private security companies would profit Pepsey and fit into the larger anarcho-capitalist agenda of replacing the state entirely by a collection of competing private firms.

Another idea struck Coot during the long flight to Anchorage. What if Pepsey tipped off EuroSécurité to expect a team from

Mushrooms would try to enter the U.K. through the Chunnel? That would make Pepsey's firm look more capable than the Indian and later the American governments at protecting their people from nuclear terrorism.

How to get Boyd to confirm Pepsey's involvement? The story that the A.D.M.'s radiation was insufficiently shielded was dubious to begin with, given the technical sophistication of the Mushrooms. Surely Boyd must wonder about that aspect of the story as well. That flicker of doubt might be fanned into a flame of accusation, if Coot could somehow make Boyd suspicious of Pepsey's motives.

Before long, Coot noticed that Boyd had left his seat, almost certainly to visit the lavatory. He waited until he heard the door open a second time, then got up and headed for the toilet himself.

"Hey!" said Bennie, half rising from his seat.

"I'll handle it, Bennie," said Boyd, gesturing to Bennie to sit back down. Coot and Boyd met at row 29.

"Got a minute, George?" Coot asked. "Something occurred to me that I think you should know."

"Okay. A minute," said Boyd.

Coot sat down in the last row. Boyd hesitated a moment, then followed Coot's lead.

"You guys seem pretty sophisticated technically," said Coot, leaning slightly toward Boyd so that the other man could hear him over the roar of the plane's engines.

"Yeah. So?"

"Press reports said the A.D.M. your Chunnel team was carrying was inadequately shielded to prevent detection. Doesn't that seem odd to you?"

"Yeah. Something else must have gone wrong."

"Could the team have been betrayed?"

"Not likely. We've kept our activities completely secret for years."

"Somebody on the inside may have given EuroSécurité enough information to spot your team."

"Nah. Our people are completely committed to our goals and our plan for achieving them."

It was time to play the Pepsey card. Coot turned to face Boyd more directly.

"Do you know who owns EuroSécurité?"

"A private equity firm. Something like Euro Capital," offered Boyd.

"Yes, EuroKapital. Do you know who EuroKapital's investors are?"

"No. Do you?"

"I know one," said Coot. "Myron Pepsey. Ever hear of him?"

"Yes. A successful businessman. Very wealthy."

"I've been wondering how Mushrooms managed to pay for five Soviet A.D.M.s. You must've had an angel investor. That person would've known your plans and could've passed on information about them to EuroSécurité, if doing so would serve a larger purpose."

"I don't believe our 'investor' had any 'larger purpose' than inciting insurrection."

"Oh? Suppose he didn't have any confidence that your plan would succeed in getting people to overthrow their governments. Suppose he believed that several successful attacks would cause people to lose confidence in their governments' ability to protect them. Suppose he believed that people would demand his company's protective services if he could demonstrate that private security *could* protect better than their government."

"So, you're suggesting that our funder is Myron Pepsey?"

"Yes." Accusing Pepsey, a S.A.F.E. board member, pained Coot.

"Also, that he supported us in order to destroy people's confidence in government protection?"

"Uh-huh."

"And that his financial interest in the private security industry caused him to betray our U.K. team?"

"That's right."

"Sorry to disappoint you. I've never dealt with him."

"Of course he would've acted through an intermediary. If you tell me who, I may be able to find out whether he's Pepsey's agent."

"How?"

"The full resources of the U.S. government are just a sat phone call away."

"All right. I'll trust you on this. Everything else in our deal stays the same. You're still our hostage. We're still going to Pyongyang."

"Of course."

"I dealt with Michael Anthony."

Boyd's reference to John Beresford Tipton's agent on an old TV series struck Coot as frivolous. "This is no time for joking, George."

"It's no joke, Coot. That's the name he gave me, and he did come through with a lot of money."

"Okay. If you'll give me the sat phone, I'll see what I can find out."

Boyd retrieved the phone and handed it to Coot. Jill answered after two rings.

"Coot?"

"Yes, Jill. I'm glad I caught you. Listen. I need you to find out whether a man using the name 'Michael Anthony' works for Myron Pepsey."

"The name may be an alias. Can't you give me more to go on?"

Coot relayed Jill's request to Boyd, who provided age, height, weight, voice, eye color, and skin tone estimates. Boyd also mentioned a large wart that Anthony had on the left side of his face about an inch in front of his ear lobe. Coot passed Boyd's description on to Jill.

"Okay. I'll see what I can find out. You do realize it may take a good while to follow this lead, don't you?"

"Just get back to me as quickly as you can."

"Will do. How are you faring, Coot?"

"Pretty well, actually. At least I don't have to wear the vest again until we reach Anchorage."

"That's enough," said Boyd, as he pulled the phone out of Coot's hand and ended the call. "Get back to your seat. I'll come get you if she calls back."

Coot, annoyed at Boyd's commanding tone but not wanting to press his luck, returned to his seat, pleased at how well his probing had gone, despite Boyd's skepticism and reluctance to cooperate.

At noon Central Time the flight attendant brought lunch to her passengers. She said the single dish was bibimbap, which Coot had had once before, on his return flight from the conference in Seoul. Coot's large bowl had a layer of white rice at the bottom. Sautéed and seasoned cucumbers, zucchini, bean sprouts, and some other vegetables that Coot did not recognize came next. Finally there was a fried egg and some thinly-sliced marinated beef on top. Coot knew from his previous experience with bibimbap to mix the food before eating it. Once again he heard grumbling about the food from the non-cosmopolitan terrorists, but he thought the food was quite tasty. Not bad, if it turned out to be his last meal.

While waiting for more information about Michael Anthony, Coot began to think about Diana again, just as he had the night before. Surely she must know by now that he was the Mushrooms' hostage. His kids must know, too — and fear for his safety.

About an hour before the scheduled landing in Anchorage, Boyd showed up at Coot's seat. "Your lady friend is on the phone. Come on back here." He led Coot to the rear of the aircraft and handed him the sat phone.

"Jill?" he said.

"Yes, Coot. Everything still okay?"

"Yes."

"Good. Here's what I found from talking with my contacts at C.I.A. and the Bureau. 'Michael Anthony' is an alias used by Paul Henry, an attorney who sometimes represents Pepsey. Boyd's description, including the wart, matches the descriptions provided by agents who have met Henry. I have considerable confidence that Boyd's contact was indeed Paul Henry and that we have a definite tie to Myron Pepsey."

"Thanks, Jill. I'd better go."

Still holding the sat phone, Coot turned to Boyd. "Anthony is Pepsey's man, all right. His real name is Paul Henry."

Boyd's face flushed and he clenched his teeth, then said, "Why should I believe you? This could all be a trick to get us to surrender."

"What kind of proof would satisfy you?" asked Coot. "We don't have a lot of time."

"How about a picture of Pepsey and Henry together?" suggested Boyd.

"This phone doesn't have a screen," said Coot.

"No, but if it has a data port," said Boyd, "we can connect Mitch's laptop to it."

Coot turned the phone over in his hand. On the left side was a jack labeled *DATA*. "Looks like we're in business."

Coot called Jill again and told her what he needed to convince Boyd of Pepsey's and Henry's involvement. Half an hour later, she called back to give Coot the link to a picture the F.B.I. had put up on a publicly-accessible website. Coot wrote the link on an airsick bag and handed it to Boyd.

"You'd better hope this picture proves Anthony is Pepsey's man," said Boyd. "We don't like being deceived."

"Don't worry about me, George. You should be worrying about yourselves. Your U.K. team has already been betrayed. If Pepsey thinks that you can tie him to the attacks, he will certainly try to kill you. There's even a chance that, once our fighter escort drops off, this aircraft will be attacked. If I were you, I wouldn't leave Anchorage. In return for your testimony, you might be given immunity from prosecution or be allowed to plead guilty to a lesser crime."

"I've got to talk this over with the other guys."

"Sure." Coot went back to his seat and waited for George and the others to make up their minds.

CHAPTER 11

Crucial Decisions

Holding the airsick bag tightly in his hand, George followed Coot back up the aisle. After making sure Coot was back in his seat, George turned to Mitch, who was sleeping across the aisle from Coot. He tapped Mitch on the shoulder.

"What the fuck, George?" Mitch growled. "Let me get some sleep, will ya?"

"Listen, Mitch," said George, "I need you to hook up your laptop to the sat phone again and let me have a look at this link."

"Why?" demanded Mitch, scowling.

"You'll see soon enough. Let's not waste time arguing."

Mitch continued to grumble but got his laptop from the overhead bin and connected it to the satellite phone, just as he had done to upload the fake claim of responsibility for the New York attack. Soon a picture of two men, one bearded, one clean-shaven, appeared on the laptop's screen.

"Goddamn," said George. "It's Anthony, all right."

"Goddamn!" shouted Mitch, his face reddening, his fists clenching. "This fuck-up is all your fault, George."

"Blaming me isn't going to help, Mitch," said George, more calmly than he felt. "We need to figure out what to do now."

George collected the team for a conference in the rear of the aircraft. Mitch stood in the aisle, fidgeting, while Doug and Bennie took seats. George stood facing them, the three men with whom he had worked for years to plan the attacks, acquire the weapons, and carry out the operations on U.S. soil.

"What's going on, George?" asked Doug.

"We have a problem," George began.

"What, exile in North Korea?" said Bennie.

"Worse," said George. "We may not even get there." He recoiled at the thought that he may have led the Mushrooms into a trap.

"We've been betrayed," Mitch snarled.

"Yes," said George, his head bowed in shame.

"Who's the traitor?" asked Doug, his voice uncharacteristically harsh.

"Michael Anthony," said George, "and Tipton."

"Why do you think so?" persisted Doug.

George showed the picture of Henry and Pepsey to Doug and Bennie. He explained the true identities of their benefactor and his agent, then laid out the case that Coot had built for him, including the involvement of Pepsey in EuroSécurité.

"This explains how the U.K. team got busted," concluded George.

"But who knew about the U.K. team's planned entry?" asked Bennie.

"Just that team and us," said Doug. "Right, George?"

"I'm afraid not," said George, his face reddening as he realized the significance of what he was about to say. "Anthony, uh, Paul Henry knew."

"What?" screamed Mitch. "George, you're a fucking idiot!" He lunged at George, who backed away as Doug and Bennie restrained Mitch.

"Calm down, Mitch," said Doug. Turning to George, he asked, "Why did you trust Henry?"

"We needed money to carry out our plan, and Henry wouldn't supply it unless I agreed to keep him informed."

"Didn't you ask why he was willing to help us?"

"Of course, but Henry just said he had generous and sympathetic friends."

"Some friends!" said Bennie, a scowl on his face, his hands clenched into fists.

"You stupid fuck," growled Mitch. "You shoulda found out more."

"I tried to, but Henry refused to say anything," said George.

"Without that money," said Doug, "we'd've had no chance to buy the A.D.M.s and our plans would've gone nowhere."

"Yeah," said Bennie. "Who knows when we would've found another source of A.D.M.s?"

"I had no idea of Pepsey's involvement, or of his business interests," said George, "until Coot told me just now."

"Why trust Coot?" Doug persisted. "He's working for the feds."

"He's offered us the only explanation we have for the failure of the U.K. team," replied George.

"Let's suppose Coot is telling the truth about Henry and Pepsey," said Doug. "Why did you call us together? What's the problem?"

"Put yourself in Myron Pepsey's shoes," said George.

"I dunno, George. I've never worn alligator or rattlesnake before," said Bennie, to general laughter.

"I mean," said George, "here we are, on our way to North Korea, with knowledge that could lead the feds back to Henry and then to Pepsey himself."

"You're implying Pepsey may want us dead," said Doug.

"Pepsey and Henry," said George, pleased that Doug, at least, was coming to the right conclusion.

"The fuckers probably planned all along to have us killed after the U.S. operations," said Mitch, slamming his fist into a seat back.

"So what do we do?" said Bennie. "If we surrender, we'll go to prison, or worse."

"Yeah. They'll fry us," said Mitch.

"What about a plea bargain?" asked Bennie.

"Only George could testify against Henry," said Doug. "The rest of us have no leverage."

"So we have to choose between certain imprisonment and probable assassination?" said Bennie.

"Looks like it."

Silence spread over the group. The others looked at George.

"What are *you* going to do, George?" Mitch's tone was suspicious, accusatory.

George had not realized until challenged just what he wanted to do.

"I'm going to testify against Henry and Pepsey," he said.

"Abandoning us and saving your own skin, huh?" Mitch said, his face contorted with suppressed rage.

"Lighten up, Mitch," said Doug. "Let's hear what George has to say." Bennie murmured his agreement.

"It really pisses me off that they've used us to enrich themselves," said George. "We're trying to start insurrections against people like them."

"They sold us out," said Bennie, "the bastards!"

"You guys understand why I gotta take them down, don't you?" said George, looking at Doug and Bennie.

"Sure," said Doug. "You're the only one who can."

Relief swept over George. Doug was the most thoughtful of the other Mushrooms. His support counted for a lot.

Mitch was more difficult to convince. "So you're gonna get off in Anchorage," he snarled, "and let us risk Pepsey's vengeance by ourselves?"

"What else can I do?" said George. "You think I wanted it to work out this way?"

"Hang on, guys," said Doug. "The feds don't know that George is the only one who can finger Henry. Maybe we can all get immunity."

"It's worth a try," said Bennie.

"I'll have Coot propose this to his contact," said George.

The others agreed with the plan, although Mitch grumbled about not being able to trust the authorities to keep their word.

* * *

After the meeting broke up, George got Coot and took him to the rear of the plane again.

"We've decided you're right about Pepsey."

"That's smart."

"Suppose we agree to testify against Pepsey and Henry. Would the Justice Department give us immunity from prosecution?"

"I can't answer that question, but it's worth asking Justice. Do you have an attorney?"

"No, and no time to find one."

"Okay. If you'll give me the sat phone, I'll see what I can do for you."

George retrieved the phone and Coot once again called Jill. He explained George's proposal. Jill agreed to ask the Attorney

General directly about granting the Mushrooms immunity in exchange for their testimony against Pepsey and Henry.

Jill had still not called back when the Tupolev began its descent into the Anchorage airport. Mitch brought the explosive-laden vest and strapped Coot into it again. Beads of sweat formed on his forehead and crept down his face. One accidental bump against someone or some thing might detonate the vest. Mitch made sure everyone had his button ready, then armed the vest. It was soon beeping like it did before when all the buttons had been pressed.

At 2:15 P.M. Central Time the aircraft touched down in Anchorage, taxied to an isolated part of the airport for refueling, and was immediately surrounded by cars with flashing lights. Coot set his watch to read the current Alaska Time of 11:15 AM. Less than five minutes later, George brought Coot the sat phone. Jill had the Attorney General's answer: no immunity but no death penalty.

"That's bullshit!" said George when Coot gave him the news. "They expect us to give up our escape plan in exchange for life in prison?"

"Looks like it," said Coot.

"Then the original plan is still in effect. We'll finish refueling and head for Pyongyang."

Coot told Jill of George's decision. "I'm still worried about an attack on this aircraft once we leave U.S. airspace," Coot said. "I don't understand how the A.G. can turn down a chance to prosecute Pepsey. His wealth enabled him to turn a bunch of idealistic anarchists into a potent force for killing thousands of people. Surely you folks in Washington can come up with a better plan."

"I understand and share your concerns, Coot. I'm really worried about you. I'm doing everything I can think of to get you out of this alive."

"Thanks, Jill," said Coot. "I know you're doing the best you can."

"You'll be glad to hear that your plane will be over U.S. territory for at least three hours," said Jill. "The flight plan has you flying along the Aleutian Islands chain. Your fighter escort will be with you that whole time. You'd better take off soon, though. A massive storm is heading your way. Oh, I almost forgot to tell you — Diana wishes you good luck."

Diana! Coot thought. *Does she care what happens to me?* Still basking in the glow of Diana's good wish, he handed the phone back to George.

In another ten minutes the Tupolev was climbing back into the deep blue Alaskan sky. Mitch came over to Coot's seat, disarmed the vest, and removed it. "Thanks!" said Coot. "That thing makes me nervous." Mitch glared at Coot and did not reply.

Something else made Coot nervous: if Pepsey had paid for the Soviet A.D.M.s, then he probably had also paid for the use of the Tupolev. As soon as the aircraft left U.S. airspace, they would be completely at his mercy. The pilots might divert the flight to some secret landing strip where both terrorists and hostage would be killed.

An hour and a half into the flight Jill called again. "Better news this time, Coot. The F.B.I. learned from Jamie Saunders that she couldn't testify to direct contact with Paul Henry. To catch the biggest fish, the A.G. realized, he needed the testimony of the other Mushrooms. Of course, the country is in an uproar over their escape, so his flexibility is limited by the politics of the situation. Here's his offer: Boyd and the others will be prosecuted only on federal conspiracy and weapons charges in exchange for their testimony against Pepsey and Henry. There will be significant prison time, but at least they'll be safe from retaliation by Pepsey."

Coot explained the new offer to George, then said, "You have two choices: being hunted down by Pepsey or spending a few years in prison. If Pepsey paid for this plane, you're in more danger than you realize. How do you know where the pilots will fly you, once we leave U.S. airspace?"

Once again George gathered his team to discuss their options. Coot overheard snatches of their conversation.

"We're fucked, man, we're totally fucked!"

"We're going to be on the run from Pepsey for the rest of our lives."

"Cooperating with the feds is the only way we can protect ourselves."

When the gang had finished their meeting, George took Coot

once again to the rear of the aircraft. He had the sat phone with him. "We've decided to cooperate," he told Coot. "I'll tell the captain to take us back to Anchorage."

"Smart," said Coot, relieved that at last the Mushrooms were beginning to behave rationally.

Boyd went to the front of the cabin and spoke to the flight attendant. She picked up the cabin phone, said a few words, paused, then said something to George, who seemed to respond angrily. In a moment he was back with Coot. "They refuse to return. They say they have orders to fly us to Pyongyang."

"This confirms my theory that Pepsey is calling the shots here," said Coot. "I'll call Washington and let them know that you decided to cooperate and that the flight crew is refusing to go back to Anchorage."

"Wait. We have weapons. We could storm the cockpit," said Boyd softly.

"The crew may also be armed."

"We're risking our lives whether we fly to Pyongyang or try to seize control of the plane."

"True. What weapons do you have?"

"A couple of 9mm Glocks."

Mitch, Bennie, and Doug joined Coot and Boyd. The flight attendant was still at the front of the aircraft.

"Guns won't be enough," said Mitch. "I can rig explosives from the vest to destroy the door lock."

"Too risky," said Coot. "An explosion would blow open the body of the aircraft."

"And we'd all be killed," said Boyd.

Coot thought wryly that once again George Boyd and he were on the same side.

"Maybe if we threaten to use explosives, they'll be more cooperative," suggested Doug.

"It's worth a try," said George. "We'll grab the flight attendant first. With the right skill set, she could be dangerous."

The action, when it began, happened quickly. George, followed by Bennie, went to the front of the cabin and pulled a Glock on the flight attendant. She raised her hands and snarled something in

Korean. Bennie wagged the other Glock at the two relief pilots, who remained seated. George picked up the phone the flight attendant had used to talk with the pilots and said slowly, in English, "We have explosives and weapons. Open the cockpit door, or we will blow it open." After waiting a moment, George repeated the threat, but still no reply.

"They're not cooperating," George, turning around, reported to the others. He, Bennie, the two relief pilots, and the woman walked back to the galley.

"We'll soon be out of U.S. airspace," said Coot, "and unprotected from whatever Pepsey has planned for us."

Mitch said, "I'll rig up a charge from the vest on the cockpit door."

"How much damage will one charge do?" asked George.

"Enough," replied Mitch, his eyes gleaming with excitement.

"Too much," said Coot, aware that the flight attendant was listening. "Don't risk it!"

"You shut up," snapped Mitch.

"Please." The flight attendant startled Coot by her sudden intrusion into the conversation. "Let me try again." George handed the cabin phone to her. She spoke in rapid Korean, paused as if waiting for a reply, then smiled for an instant and handed the phone back to George. "The captain has changed his mind, but he says that the weather all along the coast is bad. Fairbanks looks okay. We need permission to land there."

George turned to Coot. "Can we get that?"

"Give me the sat phone. I'll check."

* * *

Diana was sitting next to Jill in the White House Situation Room when Coot called. She was attending meetings on the hostage crisis because, according to Jamie Saunders, the VI hacker group facilitated Mushrooms communications.

"The Mushrooms have changed their minds," Jill reported. "They wanted to return to Anchorage, but a big storm has closed the airport." She turned to the Air Force liaison. "How about Fairbanks, General McComb?"

Brigadier General Stanley McComb glanced at the topographical map of Alaska on the large video monitor. The Tupolev's position was updated on the screen every minute. Satellite imagery of the weather in Alaska was also superimposed on the map.

"As you can see, Mrs. Meecham," the general began, sounding like a patient but paternalistic teacher, "Fairbanks is north and a little east of Anchorage, and quite a ways inland." He pulled a laser pointer from his pocket and lit up Fairbanks. "They'd have to fly over the coastal Chugach Mountains" — another flourish with the pointer— "and then the Alaska Range further north. It's doable, provided the storm doesn't move east too fast."

"But look, Stan," said the Army's Bradley Baxter, "heading north, they'd have to fly within 60 miles of Greely. I don't like letting a North Korean aircraft get anywhere near there."

"Our Raptors can keep them well away from your interceptors, Brad," replied McComb.

"How have those aircraft done in bad weather?" Baxter's smile was almost a smirk, Diana noticed. Inter-service rivalry was usually fun to watch, but not now. Not when Coot was on a plane needing to land safely in bad weather.

"So what's your recommendation, gentlemen?" asked Jill.

* * *

George handed the sat phone to Coot again. Jill was back with an answer.

"Landing in Fairbanks is okay, but the plane absolutely must stay well away from Fort Greely, especially with tensions still so high with North Korea."

"Understood." Coot was well aware that Fort Greely housed the anti-ballistic missile interceptors and radar systems that protected the U.S. mainland against I.C.B.M.s. Disabling the interceptors at Greely would expose the U.S. to North Korean blackmail.

"The Tupolev must follow a route due north to Fairbanks," Jill continued. "We understand that some deviation may be required because of local weather. Two F-22s will be escorting the aircraft at all times."

"Thanks, Jill."

"One final thing. The F.B.I. is going to arrest Myron Pepsey and Paul Henry." Jill wished Coot well and disconnected.

Coot explained Jill's instructions to the Mushrooms, then to the flight attendant, who spoke with the captain. Soon the plane began to bank to the left, flying east toward a path north to Fairbanks.

* * *

"Damn!" Myron Pepsey banged his fist on his desk, causing Paul Henry to jump. "They've turned around? Why?" Pepsey had not expected such a rapid deterioration in the situation.

"The captain had clear instructions to leave U.S. airspace and then divert to the island where the reception committee was waiting," said Henry, "but the Mushrooms had explosives with them."

"This isn't good. This isn't good at all," said Pepsey.

"What shall we do?" asked Henry.

"We?" said Pepsey. "You're the one in trouble, Paul. Boyd only met you."

"True, Mr. Pepsey, but I could never have come up with the funds for those weapons on my own."

"If you get out of the country, to a place without an extradition treaty with the U.S., there's no way that your personal wealth can be determined."

"But how could I?"

"I've got the Gulfstream ready and waiting at Peachtree-DeKalb. Nobody would know you were on it. You'd just...disappear."

"I'd need an income in my exile," said Henry.

"No problem. I have funds in many countries. How does half a million a year sound?"

"Very generous, Mr. Pepsey. Thank you."

"You'll have to leave right away. I mean *now*. Go straight to the airport. You know where the plane's always parked. The crew will know where to take you. The United Arab Emirates. I'm through dealing with North Korea."

"All right."

"And, Paul," said Pepsey, "if you get really anxious and need relief, try these pills. They've always helped me."

Pepsey put two small white pills into an unlabeled medicine container and handed the small bottle to Henry.

Paul Henry left. Myron Pepsey picked up the phone and called the captain of the waiting Gulfstream.

"Amir," said Pepsey, "Another trip to the U.A.E., leaving A.S.A.P. This time it's one-way, as we discussed might be required someday. You know Paul. You and he won't be coming back."

* * *

Paul Henry drove to Peachtree-DeKalb airport, being careful to observe the posted speed limits. He could not afford to be stopped by a cop. Not now. Henry entered the airport and parked in general parking, not as he usually did, in Pepsey's private area. He walked a few hundred yards to the Gulfstream, whose twin engines were already running.

Henry boarded the aircraft, giving his coat to the pretty flight attendant. He did not return her smile. He took a seat on the left side of the plane. He could have sat anywhere.

The cockpit door opened. Henry recognized Amir, the young captain that Pepsey was so fond of.

"Welcome aboard, Mr. Henry," said Amir. "We're leaving right away." He paused, apparently considering whether to ask something that was troubling him. "What's going on?"

"You don't want to know," said Henry, and turned to look out the window.

The Gulfstream began to move toward the taxiway. They would indeed be taking off immediately. The aircraft proceeded to the assigned runway, paused a moment, then began to pick up speed.

Henry caught sight of flashing red and blue lights behind them, getting closer. He could hear sirens, too, though faintly inside the luxurious cabin. The plane slowed as the engines throttled back, then turned left onto another taxiway. There were other cars with flashing lights ahead of them. The Gulfstream was being forced to a part of the airport with which Henry was not familiar. This could not be good.

Henry felt panic rising in him. He was tempted to take the pills that Myron Pepsey had given him. He should have asked what they were. What if he had a bad reaction to them? Then, despite his increasing his anxiety, one clear thought came to him: he posed a threat to Myron Pepsey. Those pills might be Pepsey's attempt to eliminate him, as he had tried to eliminate the Mushrooms, as he had sacrificed tens of thousands of New Yorkers in his mad scheme to promote his private security business. Paul Henry decided to save those pill for a better use. He had to represent his own interests now.

* * *

"Thanks, Amir," said Pepsey. "It's not your fault. We just ran out of time." He hung up the phone, cursing as he did so. Things were going from bad to worse. He hoped that Paul Henry became anxious enough to swallow those pills. Now what? He couldn't escape by air. He had a car available for such an eventuality. It was registered to a company not obviously linked to him. He would take that car and drive, with a fake passport, to Hartsfield-Jackson, Atlanta's airport and usually the busiest in the world. On the way, he would shave his beard. How he hated to do that! He'd had his beard in the passport picture removed, to facilitate such an escape. He would buy a ticket on the first available flight to the U.A.E. and wave bye-bye to his U.S. fortune and legal jeopardy.

His planning was interrupted, as men in dark suits, guns drawn, burst into his office.

What a poor performance this was! Just the same old clichéd arrest scene depicted in hundreds of cop movies. The same request for the suspect to raise his hands, the same Miranda warning, the same handcuffing, the same perp walk past stunned business associates, the same gauntlet of reporters and TV crews. Nothing new here. How boring! He deserved better treatment, an arrest fitting for all he had accomplished, worthy of his own good taste.

* * *

As the Tupolev flew over the Pacific Ocean, Bennie sat with his Glock, guarding the relief pilots and the Korean woman who was their only link with the pilots in the cockpit. The Korean woman kept her eyes on him. Bennie must have been sleepy, since every so often he would give a little jerk and his head would snap back.

"You need someone to take over guard duty?" George asked.

"Nah, I'm fine." Bennie stretched his left arm over his head while keeping his right hand with the Glock in his lap.

The plane flew on. Coot could see thunderheads rising massively to the north. Eventually the aircraft must have been due south of

Fairbanks, since it banked slowly to the left, then settled into a steady course once more. The two F-22 interceptors were still escorting them.

The Alaska coast appeared far below the Tupolev, including Prince William Sound, site of the Exxon-Valdez oil spill years earlier. Soon they would be flying over Port Valdez, the southern terminus of the Trans-Alaska pipeline. Storm clouds appeared not far to the west. They were at the mercy of the elements as well as the Koreans. The air became rougher, the further inland they flew. Outside, the thunderheads loomed ever closer.

* * *

Back in the Situation Room, Diana was sitting quietly, listening to Jill and the generals talk. She spoke up only when she had something new to add to the discussion.

"The storm system is closing in faster than we expected," the Air Force's General McComb reported to the small group gathered in the Situation Room. "They need to be farther east."

"What are the options?" asked Jill. She drummed her pen on the mahogany table. Diana knew that her boss did not like being at the mercy of uncontrollable forces like the weather.

"They could follow the Richardson Highway, or we could vector them further east and have them fly up Copper River."

"Advantages of one over the other?"

"Richardson goes all the way to Fairbanks, so it would provide a guide for the Koreans and for the escort."

Army general Baxter slapped the table. "Not that way. The Trans-Alaska Pipeline parallels the highway, so there's a risk to strategic infrastructure if they use that route."

"The Raptors can protect the pipeline." McComb waved his hand, as if swatting away Baxter's suggestion.

"Okay," said Jill. "What about Copper River?"

"It's really a massive glacier," said Diana. The generals turned toward her. "It's not as good a landmark for navigation, should they lose communications."

"Good point." General McComb's support pleased Diana, despite the unwelcome attention he paid to some of the female staff at the N.S.C. "And a rescue would be much harder on that glacier."

"Let's go with the Richardson route, then." Jill's decisiveness impressed Diana. "General McComb, please let your people know." Jill handed the sat phone to Diana. "Tell Coot about the change in plans. I have to excuse myself for a minute. Speed dial 8." She left the room quickly, her heels making quick taps on the hard floor of the hallway.

Diana suppressed a smile at the thought that even Jill needed a bio break occasionally. Feeling awkward about calling Coot after she had broken off their friendship, she pressed 8 on the phone.

The man who answered was not Coot. The next voice she heard was his.

"Hi, Jill."

"No, Coot, it's Diana." Her voice trembled slightly. "Jill had to step out and asked me to call you." She cleared her throat. "You need to go further east to avoid the storm." She explained the new route. "Tell them to follow the escort."

Hearing Coot's voice again made Diana fear more viscerally for his safety. "How are you?"

"Not too bad, considering." Coot's voice sounded more strained than she had ever heard it.

"Well, I hope..." She realized that she was talking into a dead connection and put the phone down. "I guess they don't want him talking to us."

"The bastards!" General Baxter gave the table another pounding, startling Diana and making the phone bounce.

* * *

Moments after Coot relayed the change in the flight path to the Koreans, the aircraft began to bank to the right.

"What's going on?" Mitch asked, looking quickly from George to Coot, his strident voice cutting easily through the engine noise. "I thought we were going to fly straight north."

"Looks like the weather is moving east faster than they expected," said Coot. Snowy peaks appeared far below on either side of the aircraft. "Anybody know the geography around here?"

"Yeah," said Doug. "I did some climbing in Denali a few years ago. There's mountains all over the place. We must be over the coastal range."

"Dangerous country to fly over." George grimaced, as he ran his fingers through his thinning hair.

"Not if you're high enough." Doug seemed confident, but Coot was thinking about aircraft whose pilots had keyed in the wrong altimeter setting before takeoff and ended up plowing into a hillside.

For the next ten minutes, the aircraft made several turns to the left. The snow-capped mountains beneath the aircraft gave way to a more verdant though hilly landscape. Storm clouds still loomed to the west. The Tupolev flew on, generally in a northwest direction, across the flattest terrain they had yet encountered. Coot was glad they were no longer flying over mountains but he knew that the great Alaska Range lay between them and Fairbanks.

The Mushrooms were all quietly sitting in their seats. Bennie still had charge of the Korean flight attendant and extra pilots.

* * *

"They're still following the Richardson Highway," General McComb reported. "Now passing Glennallen. If the weather holds off, they should be able to fly the 200 miles to Fairbanks in about half an hour."

"Good," said Jill. "They'll have to cross some pretty high mountains in the Alaska Range, though."

"No problem," said the general.

* * *

Coot sat looking out the left side of the aircraft. The Alaska Range stretched west and then south ahead of them, but storm clouds obscured even its tallest peaks. Something was not quite right. He listened. The noise from the right engine was decreasing. Was it just his imagination? They would need both engines to fly over the range, which included Mount McKinley. He looked back at George. "Is the right engine getting quieter?"

George did not respond right away, but turned his head and looked out the window. "Yeah. Maybe."

Doug seemed to be listening intently too. "There's definitely less noise coming from the right than from the left."

"We're losing altitude," said Mitch.

The cabin phone rang. Bennie handed it to the Korean woman.

"Find out what's going on."

Without argument, she spoke in rapid Korean to the cockpit, then disconnected. She looked worried. "We're losing power in the right engine. We can't take a chance on flying over the mountains."

"You'll need permission to deviate from the flight plan," said Coot.

"We're surrounded by mountains," said Doug, alarm in his voice. "This is bad. Can we land at an airport near here?"

"Phone home," said George, handing Coot the sat phone. "Find out if there's a way through the mountains."

* * *

Jill leaned forward at the sat phone's first ring, but Diana was closer to it. The younger woman looked at her boss for guidance. Jill gestured for Diana to answer the call.

"Coot?"

"Yeah. Our right engine is losing power."

Diana gasped. "That doesn't sound good."

"The Koreans want a new flight plan."

Diana explained the situation to Jill and the generals.

Jill turned to General McComb. "What are the alternatives?"

"They can continue to follow Richardson. It's not as direct a route, but that's the way the pipeline goes, more or less."

"Yeah, but that takes them right past Fort Greely," said General Baxter. "Something's fishy about this."

"Is there any way to verify the engine trouble is genuine?" asked Jill. She twirled a pen in her two hands, something Diana had noticed Jill did when encountering new information. She imagined Jill spinning the situation in her mind, considering it from all angles.

"Not quickly enough," said McComb. "We're gonna have to decide whether to trust them on this."

"The Koreans were on their way back to Pyongyang when they were forced to return to Alaska," said Diana. "Why suspect them of planning to attack Greely?"

"I agree," said Jill.

"Still," said Baxter, "they may seize this new opportunity."

"C'mon, Brad," said McComb, "it's just an airliner. They'd have to be on a suicide mission."

"Yes," said Jill, "there are two Raptors with them."

The thought of F-22s launching missiles at Coot's plane appalled Diana.

"We're prepared for all conceivable threats," said McComb.

"So," said Jill, the pen now stationary in her right hand, "we'll have them follow the highway past Greely and on to Fairbanks."

* * *

"Got it." Coot ended the call from Jill and told the others of the new flight plan. The flight attendant informed the cockpit of the change, never taking her eyes off Bennie.

"The F-22 on this side is wiggling his wings," said George.

"That means 'follow me,'" said Coot. "We should be banking to the right soon."

"The escort's turning," said Doug. A moment later the Tupolev turned as well and was soon flying level again.

"I still see mountains ahead," said Coot.

"I saw a break in the range before we turned," said George, "but now I just see mountains, too."

"I hope these guys know what they're doing," said Coot. "Flying a big airplane at low altitude in mountainous country is a tricky business."

Yet on they flew, the magnificent Alaskan landscape unfolding slowly beneath them.

CHAPTER 12

Surprise Attacks

"General, the attack has begun."

"Excellent!" Vice Chairman Kim nodded to his adjutant. "Keep me informed of our progress in breaking the strings of the puppet master. The puppet regime will collapse when the puppets see that their master has abandoned them."

* * *

"Holy shit!" General Baxter jumped to his feet, his eyes on the large monitor's scrolling news feed. "Those crazy bastards in Pyongyang have attacked across the D.M.Z.!" Diana, Jill, and General McComb turned toward the monitor too. Short-range missiles were falling in Seoul, Incheon, and Suwon. Tanks and armored personnel carriers were rumbling across the D.M.Z. and D.P.R.K. soldiers were pouring out of previously undiscovered tunnels. After decades of occasional incidents, a full-scale invasion by the North was underway. Fighting was heavy at several locations in the D.M.Z.

The door of the Situation Room flew open. In strode the president, the vice-president, and the national security advisor, followed by their aides. Jill, Diana, and McComb rose in deference to their leaders.

"You folks must have seen the news." The president's grim expression confirmed the report on the news feed. He turned toward Jill. "Despite the seriousness of Coot Jenkins's predicament, we need the Situation Room to manage the events in Korea."

"Understood, Mr. President." Jill picked up the sat phone. Diana was relieved that they would at least be able to communicate with Coot, even if they could not see exactly where the Tupolev was.

The monitor that had shown the position of the Air Koryo jet now showed a picture of the Korean peninsula. Blue icons showed South Korean forces, purple icons the U.N. deployments, and yellow icons the North Korean units. Red icons denoted the locations under attack by the D.P.R.K. As Diana watched, the yellow icons moved further south, with the blue and purple icons in retreat.

"We must respond to the attacks on South Korea," the president continued, "with a massive attack on the North, to eliminate their capacity to make war."

The others agree, except for the vice-president, who said, "But, Mr. President, as you know, the North now has missiles with nuclear warheads that can reach the continental U.S."

"I'm counting on our missile defense shield to intercept the few missiles that survive our counterattack," said the president.

The vice-president raised his hands in supplication. "But in the most recent tests, the shield has been only partially successful."

"If we don't defend the South now," said the president, "the Europeans, the Japanese, and the Israelis will doubt our commitment to defend them. Our alliances will unravel."

"And then everyone will want nuclear weapons," added the national security adviser.

Jill walked toward the door of the Situation Room. "Diana, Brad, Stan, let's go back to my office. Maybe we can patch the aircraft data feed into the monitor there."

* * *

Out of the corner of his eye, Coot sensed sudden movement. Turning his head, he saw the Korean woman leap onto the nodding Bennie, grab the Glock from his unresisting hand, and wrap her arm around Bennie's neck in a choke hold.

"Surrender your weapons and that vest," she ordered the Mushrooms.

"Do what she says," said Bennie, barely able to speak.

"She could be part of Pepsey's plot," said Coot.

The woman tightened her hold on Bennie's neck. He gurgled.

"Hand over your weapons now or your friend is a dead man."

George gave her the other Glock. Muttering to himself, Mitch surrendered the explosive vest. The relief pilots were grinning at their sudden rescue.

"You, get over there with your friends." She shoved Bennie roughly toward the others. "I want that satellite phone, too."

George retrieved the sat phone and handed it to her. Coot feared the consequences of Jill and the others' not knowing what had happened aboard the aircraft. Would they assume the worst and shoot down the plane?

The woman, still covering the Mushrooms and Coot with the Glock, picked up the cabin phone and barked orders to the pilots. She spoke with an authority that belied her being merely a flight attendant.

"Who *are* you?" asked Coot.

"Colonel Gwon Su-bin, Korean People's Army," answered the woman. "Now," she continued, "I have a little surprise." She looked at Mitch. "You, go into the galley and open the large cabinet. Bring back what you find there."

Mitch muttered something that Coot could not catch, but he did as he was told. In a minute he returned, struggling with a large backpack, grinning like a boy with his first present on Christmas morning.

"Oh, shit!" said George. He looked back at the woman. "How did you get that?"

"Did you really think you could smuggle a nuclear weapon into my homeland, fool?" she spat. "The Supreme Leader let your little plot develop, since he thought it would work to his advantage, but then an even better opportunity came along.".

"What do you mean?" asked George. Sweat glistened on his forehead as he struggled to deal with the new reality.

"How often would a North Korean aircraft be allowed into U.S. airspace?" She grinned as she led the Mushrooms toward understanding why their plan for the fifth nuke had failed.

"We brought your weapon with us and have been looking for a chance to deliver it." The Korean was almost gleeful as she said, "The best part is, the U.S. buffoons will blame the attack on you."

"What attack? Where?" Bennie asked, not even looking up at the woman.

"The U.S. ballistic missile defense installation at Fort Greely." The woman's chest swelled as she announced the audacious plan.

"Does that system even work?" asked Mitch.

"Well enough to handle a few missiles from North Korea," said Coot, proud of his country's defensive prowess, even though he understood that anti-ballistic missile systems tended to provide an adversary with an incentive to strike first.

"American arrogance." Her sneer conveyed more than her words.

"Don't you realize those missiles are in hardened silos?" Coot was eager to give the Koreans any reason to abort their attack.

"Certainly," she answering, smiling, "but the radars are not. They're in domes on the surface. Even a small nuclear explosion would destroy them."

"How do you know there aren't backup radars?" Coot asked, searching for some flaw in the North Koreans' plan.

"Our intelligence says none are operational." She seemed supremely confident. Even if she were wrong, the results could still be catastrophic for all involved.

"Why didn't you try to deliver it before we got to Anchorage?" Doug sounded more curious than alarmed.

"Isn't it obvious? Our approved flight path was far from Fort Greely. It would have been hard to get close enough before we were shot down."

Coot knew that their flight plan plus a quick diversion would get them close enough to Fort Greely to deliver a weapon. And there was no way to warn Jill.

"Do you think you can drop an atomic bomb and escape?" Coot was incredulous.

"Escape is not important — our mission is to serve the Supreme Leader and the Fatherland."

The woman's fanaticism frightened Coot more than the Mushrooms did. Even volatile Mitch was held in check by the others.

As the aircraft continued forward, Coot could see mountains

rising above them on either side. They seemed to have entered a pass or valley. The Tupolev was getting closer to the ground with every second. The Koreans were taking them on a one-way suicide mission. Coot felt panic rising in his body, a visceral foreboding he'd not felt since Vietnam. He fought the fear, trying to think of some way out.

* * *

A dozen stony-faced men sat around the large table at the National Defense Commission, waiting for updates on the situation in the South. Vice-Chairman Kim Dae-Hyun occupied his customary position next to the empty chair reserved for the Supreme Leader.

"Beg pardon, General. The Americans have launched scores of cruise missiles from their ships," Vice-Chairman Kim's aide whispered, bowing and backing away as he spoke, as if he would be blamed for the counterattack.

The General grunted. He did not like being wrong. He had advised the Supreme Leader that the U.S. president would not risk the destruction of even one American city by attacking the D.P.R.K. Kim knew his days, maybe even his hours in the leadership were numbered. He determined to do what he could to save his honor and his place in history.

Kim stood and surveyed the men around the table. He knew several of them wanted his job. One of them would soon have it. He cleared his throat. "The Americans have responded to our thrust by attacking our homeland. Everything we have built here will be destroyed. We will land on the trash heap of history. We must act swiftly, or our strategic assets will be lost, and with them will go our last chance to preserve our honor."

No one stood to argue with him. They had all agreed to recommend the attack, even Vice-Chairman Gong Dong-Min, despite his apprehensions concerning the effectiveness of the U.S. missile defenses.

Kim picked up the telephone that connected the conference room to the headquarters of the Strategic Rocket Forces. "Launch immediately," he barked into the handset.

Kim hoped he would live to see the missiles reach their targets. He was glad that a plan was in motion to increase the chances of their doing so.

* * *

Diana watched the technicians finish bringing up the display of the Tupolev data on the monitor in Jill's office. How fortunate that she had recommended early-on that Jill have the ability to monitor events in her own office. Jill had pulled several strings to get the equipment and network connections installed quickly.

"The Tupolev is losing altitude," General McComb observed. "They were supposed to stay at 8,000 feet."

"How high are they now?"

Jill's alarm was apparent to Diana. Would she order the Air Force to shoot down Coot's plane?

"5,000 and dropping."

Jill grabbed the sat phone, punched 8, and waited. "No answer. I don't like this. Something's happened on that plane."

"Take 'em down," said Baxter.

"I agree with Brad," said McComb. "We have very little time. We can't risk their attacking the interceptor base. Not with hostilities underway in Korea."

"No!" said Diana, thinking not just of Coot but of the Flight 93 passengers who prevented the fourth hijacked airliner from crashing into the Capitol on 9/11. "Give Coot a chance to figure something out."

Jill's phone rang. She held the phone to her ear. "God, no!" Ashen, she turned back to face the others. "North Korea has launched seven missiles toward the U.S. mainland."

"I knew something was wrong with that damned plane maneuvering ever closer to Fort Greely." Baxter's right fist, lacking a nearby table, slammed into his left palm. "Take 'em out."

"I'm sorry, Diana." Jill laid her hand on Diana's. "There's no time to lose." She stood up. "General McComb, give the order to attack."

* * *

Coot's head snapped reflexively to his left as he heard many sharp impacts and tearing metal, followed quickly by a flash of light from under the left wing of the Tupolev. The Tupolev bucked toward the left, pitched forward, and headed down rapidly. Coot's seat belt pressed hard against his thighs as he was jerked around by the stricken plane.

"They shot out the engine!" yelled Mitch.

For the first time in his ordeal that day, Coot was sure that he would not live to see another sunrise. He would never see Brad and Jeannie graduate, marry, and start families. Never again see Diana, even as a friend. He had had a good life, a good marriage, a good family. He had done good work in promoting peace and a safer world. But he wanted more of life. To rid the world of nuclear weapons. To become more than a friend to Diana.

The sound of metal on flesh. A woman's cry of pain. Coot looked around. Bennie was holding a Glock to the Korean's temple. Blood streamed from her nose and mouth.

"You bitch," Bennie shouted, "I should blow your fucking brains out." He handed the other Glock to George, who pointed it at the relief pilots.

The silence outside was broken as the right engine started again. Its malfunctioning had been a fake to force a change in course.

As the plane pulled out of its dive, Coot realized that the Raptors would surely attack the Tupolev again.

"Hurry, give me the sat phone!"

George tossed the phone to Coot, who grabbed it and punched 2.

* * *

"Coot? What the hell's going on?" Jill looked at General McComb, her eyes wide. Diana knew her boss was wondering the same things as she. Had the attack been thwarted? Could they save Coot? Jill turned on the phone's speaker.

"The fifth nuke — it's here."

"How...?" Jill's eyebrows converged, causing deep wrinkles that signaled Jill's confusion.

"The Koreans brought it with them," said Coot. "They captured a Mushrooms team trying to smuggle it into the North."

"I have worse news," said Jill. She told Coot of the North's attack on the South, the U.S. reprisal, and the seven I.C.B.M.s in flight toward the U.S.

"Shoot the damned plane down now!" yelled Baxter, turning to McComb.

"No!" Coot yelled back. "The Mushrooms have seized the A.D.M.

but they aren't doing anything with it. Give me time to negotiate with the Koreans."

"Negotiate, hell!" said Baxter.

"How much time can we give Coot?" Jill's question was directed at General McComb.

"Ten minutes, tops," he replied. "Coot, tell the Koreans to climb back to 8,000 feet. We'll get back to you with further instructions."

* * *

We've got to make them climb back up or we'll be shot down," Coot shouted back to Boyd.

"How?"

"There's only one way left," said Mitch. "Blow the cockpit door."

This time Coot did not object. Actually putting explosives on the door might convince the captain more than a mere threat to use them. Still, Mitch's enthusiasm for using explosives inside the aircraft alarmed Coot. George and the other Mushrooms had better keep Mitch under control, or they were all dead meat.

Mitch removed all but one of the explosives from the vest that Coot had worn, walked to the front of the cabin, and attached the vest with its remote control to the cockpit door.

George brought Colonel Gwon to the front of the cabin, while Bennie remained behind to guard the relief pilots. George gave Gwon the phone to the cockpit.

"Tell the captain that we're going to blow the cockpit door open unless they open it themselves," said George.

The woman, looking nervously at the makeshift bomb, spoke Korean into the phone.

"The captain says glory awaits us when we complete our mission," she reported.

"All right, then," said George. "Let's blow the door."

Coot hoped the Mushrooms were still bluffing. George was certainly playing his part well.

Mitch gave out dead man switches to George, Doug, and Bennie, then armed the vest, as he had done when Coot was wearing it. The vest began to beep rapidly.

"Hold your buttons," Mitch instructed the others, who did as they were told, and the beeping slowed.

Everyone moved toward the back of the plane.

"I'll cover the cockpit door." George pulled the Glock from his belt and pointed it toward the front of the aircraft as he backed down the aisle.

Bennie herded Gwon, the other Koreans, and Coot to the rear galley, where they were joined by Mitch, Doug, and finally George.

"How big a blast is this going to be?" asked Doug nervously. He, too, was a convincing actor — or he was genuinely worried that Mitch would actually detonate the vest.

"Big enough," growled Mitch.

"But what if it wrecks the cockpit or the fuselage?" said Doug. "Then we're all gonna die."

"It's too late to worry about that," retorted Mitch, a maniacal look on his face as he stared at the button under his thumb. "I wanna do the honors."

"No, Mitch!" yelled George. "Not yet!" Coot realized that George was no longer acting, that Mitch had taken control and was determined to detonate the explosive on the cockpit door.

"We're gonna die anyway," said Mitch, an eerie coolness in his voice. "We might as well go down fighting."

Like a priest raising the chalice during the Eucharist, Mitch lifted high his dead man switch and removed his thumb from the red button.

The vest began beeping more rapidly from the cockpit door. "Ten, nine," Mitch counted down.

Bennie rushed at Mitch, who grabbed the Glock from Bennie's hand and shot Bennie in the shoulder. Bennie screamed, as blood poured from his wound. Coot lunged to his right and caught the controller that Bennie had tossed when shot. He pressed its red button, but the rapid beeping continued from the cockpit door.

Mitch, still holding his dead man switch, backed away from the others and resumed his countdown. "Four, three, two..."

"No!" shouted the colonel.

Mitch, still covering the others with Bennie's Glock, put his thumb back on the red button and looked at the woman.

"Ready to cooperate?" he asked, as the beeping from the vest slowed again.

"I will order the captain to return to 8,000 feet." Her assertion of authority proved that her role on board the aircraft was more important than Coot had realized.

"Do it," commanded Mitch. "

As Mitch lowered the dead man switch, his finger still on the button, the erstwhile flight attendant picked up the galley phone, gave brisk instructions in Korean, and hung up. "We will fly on to Fairbanks," she reported.

"You didn't have to fucking shoot me!" Bennie snarled at Mitch. "And turn off that goddamned vest."

"Not till they open the door," said Mitch.

Doug helped Bennie to a nearby seat. "I'll get some first-aid supplies from the galley."

Coot walked back to his seat, carefully holding Bennie's dead man switch.

George hurried to the front of the cabin, pushing Colonel Gwon ahead of him. As they reached the cockpit door, it slowly swung open. George pointed his Glock at the captain and said, "Get back on course."

A faint smile crossed the captain's face as he looked at the Glock and then at George. "Very funny. This must be first time terrorists hijack own plane!" He turned back to the controls and muttered something in Korean to the first officer.

George directed the flight attendant to take a seat at the front of the first-class area and motioned for Mitch to disarm the vest.

In a few moments Coot felt the plane begin to climb again. He looked out his window and could see an F-22 leading the way.

George brought Coot the sat phone. "Here. Tell your lady friend that we're on our way to Fairbanks."

* * *

"Wonderful!" said Jill, with the sat phone once again on speaker. The generals and Diana were clustered around Jill and the phone.

"What about the nuke?" asked General Baxter. "The Mushrooms have already used one on New York. We can't trust 'em not to use this one, too."

"They're not suicidal," said Coot.

"Stay on the phone, Coot," said Jill, "until you land in Fairbanks."

"We want to know exactly what's going on on that plane," added Baxter.

CHAPTER 13

End Game

Coot sat with the phone in his lap. George did not try to retrieve it. Doug had put the A.D.M. into a seat and buckled the seatbelt tightly around it. The Mushrooms were discussing something among themselves, but Coot could not hear what they were saying over the sound of the single working jet.

Mitch's voice rose above the engine noise. "It's our last chance!"

Coot looked back toward Mitch, whose face was red, whose expression was wild, as he stood in the aisle.

"It's over, Mitch." Doug was standing next to Mitch, his hand on the disturbed man's shoulder. "Calm down. It's over."

"No!" roared Mitch. "Not when we have one left." He glanced over at the belted A.D.M. "We can set the timer and push it out a door as we go over the air base. At worst we can blow up the pipeline."

"We do that, and we can forget about plea bargaining." George had joined the two men, but faced forward. He kept glancing at the woman.

"We bargain and we lose everything we've fought for, everything we believe in."

Coot felt the weight of the sat phone in his lap and wondered whether Jill and the others could hear the Mushrooms' debate. If he raised the phone to his ear, a Mushroom might notice and confiscate it. Coot looked around for the weapons. A Glock was sticking out of the waistband of George's pants. Mitch must still have the other one.

Coot watched in horror as Mitch drew the second Glock from behind his back and aimed it at George.

"Mitch, no!" George's shout came just before a shot echoed loudly in the enclosed space. George cried out and fell to the floor, bleeding from his chest.

Doug reached for George's Glock, but Mitch shot him, too. The colonel took cover in her seat.

Mitch turned toward Coot. "You!"

Coot ducked down in his seat as Mitch's third shot whizzed over his head. He heard something heavy being dragged down the aisle toward the back of the aircraft. He peered around the edge of his seat and saw Mitch pulling the A.D.M. behind him toward the door on the right side at row 19.

George, his face contorted in pain, looked at Coot. "He's...crazy." George reached down with his left hand, struggled to pull the Glock out from his waistband, and managed to shove the gun up the aisle toward Coot. "Take... it."

Coot wasted no time in grabbing the weapon, then retreated to his sheltering seat. He could hear Mitch working to get the door open. He looked out his window, saw the mountain pass opening below. In minutes the Tupolev would be over the interceptor base at Fort Greely. He whispered into the sat phone.

"Can you hear me?"

"Yes." Jill's voice. "We heard shots."

"Mitch has shot the other Mushrooms. He's about to arm the A.D.M. and dump it out the door. We're almost to Greely."

"We've got to destroy that plane," said Baxter. "No matter who's on it."

"No!" Coot hissed into the phone. "If he has armed the weapon and it survives intact, who knows where it might explode? The interceptor base? The pipeline?"

"Then what do you suggest?" Jill's authoritative voice helped Coot control his nerves.

"George gave me his Glock. Mitch has the other one. I'll try to take him out." Coot took a deep breath. His heart was pounding. "If I fail, ..."

"You won't fail, Coot." Diana's voice was firm.

Coot hoped his tactical combat training had prepared him to win a fight with Mitch. He looked around his seat back again. Mitch was a dozen rows back, struggling with the door, apparently unable to open it with just his left hand while he kept looking up the aisle to where Coot and the Korean woman were hiding. The A.D.M. lay next to him, a symbol and an example of the evil that Coot had long sought to eliminate from the world.

Coot sprang from his seat into the aisle, bolted toward Mitch, who looked around too late to raise his weapon before Coot's single shot hit him in the chest.

Mitch crumpled to the floor, his wound bleeding profusely. He leered at Coot. "Fuck you...It's too late," he gasped. "I set...the timer." His Glock lay beside him. Coot grabbed the gun, stuck it into the back of his pants, and pulled Mitch away from the A.D.M.

Coot went to the A.D.M. and opened the control panel's cover. He found the toggle switch used to arm the device. He pulled the switch down, but it sprang back into position. Once armed, the device was bound to detonate.

The countdown timer read 6:15 and continued to tick off the seconds. He rotated the timer thumbwheel, but the display did not change. The device would explode in six minutes. Coot set the countdown timer on his watch to match the A.D.M.'s clock. He felt the same kind of nervousness that he had before going on a reconnaissance patrol in Vietnam, but it was manageable. He knew what he had to do.

The yield display showed 1.00 — the maximum yield of one kiloton of TNT. He rotated the yield thumbwheel, but the yield display did not change, either. When the A.D.M. exploded, it would damage even reinforced concrete structures within half a mile of ground zero.

Coot looked up the aisle toward where the colonel had been sitting. She wasn't there. The cockpit door was open, the pilots still at the controls, dealing with the complexities of flying a large aircraft with just a single working engine.

"Mitch is down," he barked into the sat phone, "but the A.D.M. has been armed and will detonate in less than six minutes." He wiped the sweat from his forehead with his left hand.

"Christ!" Baxter's oath hurt Coot's ear.

The Korean colonel appeared from the work area opposite the front lavatory. She had a pistol. Coot dove behind the seats near the door for cover. He hauled the A.D.M. into position to protect himself.

The woman fired once, twice at him, but the sturdy backpack and shielding of the A.D.M. took the shots. He had no time to appreciate the irony of his life's being saved by a nuclear weapon. The timer read 5:43.

He returned fire, but the woman took cover.

"You'll be at Greely in less than five minutes," said General McComb. "The pipeline's underground where you are. The area's uninhabited. Push the weapon out now."

"The stewardess is actually an army colonel, the boss here. She's got me pinned down. I can't open the door."

Coot looked over the A.D.M. in time to see his Korean adversary pop up and take aim at him. He fired two rounds at her. She screamed and shot wildly, missing Coot's head by inches. Her weapon clattered to the floor and she disappeared behind a seat.

There were shouts in Korean from the cockpit, but the woman did not reply and no one came out to investigate. The relief pilots were cowering in their seats.

His timer was down to 4:51.

"You're over exposed pipeline now," said McComb. "You have to change course. Can you get to the cockpit?"

"I think so." Coot began to creep toward the front of the aircraft. He passed the fake flight attendant, who was slumped against a seat back, lying in a pool of blood, not breathing. He would definitely be sending a case of a fine Bordeaux to Justin at Potomac Tactical Training.

"The Raptors have moved into attack position behind the Tupolev," said McComb, "in case you can't dump the bomb in time."

"We can't take a chance on losing those interceptor radars," Baxter said, "not with North Korean missiles heading our way."

"We honored our commitment to defend South Korea," said Jill, "risking the nuclear counterattack that's now underway."

Giving the order to shoot down his plane would be difficult for

Jill, Coot knew. She would want him to realize why she had to do it.

"I understand," said Coot. "Do what you have to do." He suppressed the image of Sidewinder missiles taking down the Tupolev and continued toward the cockpit. The pilots appeared to be working hard to keep the damaged aircraft in the air and on the prescribed course. "I'm just outside the cockpit door," he whispered.

"You must drop the A.D.M. in the mountains southeast of Greely, 15 nautical miles away," said Baxter. "It'll take you 3 and a half minutes to get there. Hurry!"

The timer was at 4:15.

Coot moved quickly to the cockpit door and pointed his Glock at the captain. "You want to live?" The captain spun around in his seat and the first officer turned his head to look at Coot. "The bomb is armed and will explode in four minutes. "I must push it out of the aircraft." Pointing to a low mountain range east of the aircraft, Coot gave an order that he desperately hoped would be understood and obeyed: "Fly there. Now!" The captain stared at Coot. "Now, I said, or we'll all die!" The first officer said something that Coot did not understand, but at his words the captain turned back to the controls and put the Tupolev into a steep bank to the right.

When Coot saw that the aircraft was headed in the right direction, he sprinted back to the A.D.M. The timer read 3:55. The window exit that Mitch had tried would require lifting the A.D.M., so Coot dragged the heavy backpack a few rows aft to a larger door. He stood in the narrow space normally occupied by a window seat. He wrapped his left hand around the belt from the middle seat and braced his feet on either side of the door. With his right hand, he pulled the lever and struggled to push the door to the side. It slid into the fuselage. Coot's upper body lurched forward, pushed toward the open door by the cabin air as it rushed out, drawn by the lower pressure created as the outside air blew past at 250 miles per hour. The seat belt tightened, jerking Coot's arm and shoulder, but it held firm, keeping him inside. For the moment, he was safe.

Still holding the seat belt, Coot dragged the A.D.M. toward the door. Shivering from the frigid and turbulent air near the door, he checked the timer again: 3:10. He desperately wanted to push the A.D.M. out then and there, but he resisted. When it exploded, it must do so deep in the mountains, protecting not only the people on the ground, the interceptor base, and the pipeline, but also the Tupolev.

Coot heard voices. The sat phone! He picked it up from beside the A.D.M. "We're heading east toward the mountains."

"So we see." Jill sounded pleased but not relaxed.

Coot looked at his watch. "Three minutes till this thing explodes." His heart beat rapidly in his chest. He could feel the blood pushing through his body, into his muscles, preparing them for action.

The Tupolev continued its eastward course. The cold, turbulent air near the door made Coot shiver.

Across the aisle from the open door, Mitch lay where Coot had dragged him, where he had drawn his last angry breath. Bennie, Doug, and George were still alive. Bennie and Doug seemed to be less seriously wounded than George. Doug had just a tourniquet around his right arm, but George's open shirt was soaked in blood. Doug was pressing a bandage against George's chest. Coot went to them after glancing at the timer: 2:30 left.

"George, thanks for the Glock." Coot felt a strange bond with the younger man. Such a misguided fellow, but one who at last had made the right decision when it counted most, for Coot personally and for the country.

"Mitch was always a risk," said Doug. "We needed his electronics expertise, or we wouldn't have involved him."

"You guys had better buckle up." Coot was worried about what the explosion's shock wave would do to the Tupolev and its passengers. George was in particularly bad shape, and his testimony would be required to nail Myron Pepsey.

Coot checked the timer again: two minutes to go, and 90 seconds till they were over the drop zone. He reported the condition of the four Mushrooms to Jill and the others.

"You've got to get the hell out of there after getting rid of the device," said McComb. "You'll have maybe thirty seconds to get into the shadow of the mountains. Don't look back, just in case our calculations are wrong. You should be able to get about two miles away from the explosion."

"Is that far enough to be safe?" asked Diana.

"Simulations put the overpressure at .25 p.s.i. That's enough to shatter glass," said Baxter. "It could shake the plane a lot."

One minute till detonation. Coot put down the sat phone, grasped his seat belt lifeline, and pushed the A.D.M. closer to the open door. He looked out on the snowy peaks below. When all this was over, he must come back to this beautiful country. Forty-five seconds. The mountains and valleys flew by below. One of them would soon be a melted wasteland.

"Now!" came the cry from the sat phone. "Now!" shouted Coot. He wrapped the seat belt around his left hand again, put both feet against the massive back pack, and pushed with all his strength, launching the A.D.M. out the door. He saw it tumbling briefly, and then the deadly device was gone. He used his free right hand and his remaining strength to slide the exit door shut again.

Coot raced past the injured Mushrooms and the dead Korean. He halted at the cockpit door. He'd forgotten his Glock, but then remembered the one nestled in the small of his back. He left it there. "The bomb's gone. It'll explode in 20 seconds." He waved his hands forcefully and shouted, "Go, go, go!" Even without the obvious threat of force, the captain increased the throttle of the good engine. The Tupolev banked left and accelerated away from the valley into which Coot had dropped the A.D.M. Coot sat in the nearest seat and fastened his seat belt.

Suddenly there was a flash of light that lit up the whole sky. Ten seconds later the plane was buffeted by the worst turbulence Coot had ever experienced. There was a cry of pain from behind Coot. Poor George. Then it was over. Next stop: Fairbanks.

Coot closed his eyes, took a deep breath, then exhaled forcefully. For the first time since leaving Washington, he had no immediate worries about loose nukes. Tension drained from his body. He wanted some concrete indication that he was not a disembodied spirit. His eyes still closed, he squeezed the arm rests of his seat. Their hardness reassured him that his world, his physical world, continued. Another indication: an incoming satellite call. He answered it.

"Congratulations on a great performance, Coot." Jill, now not using the speaker, sounded pleased but still very tense. "You prevented the destruction of the U.S. missile defense shield and the Trans-Alaska Pipeline. Now we must hope the shield does its job well."

"It was a close call," said Coot. "You were spared giving the order to shoot us down."

Jill did not reply. Then Diana spoke. "Coot, you were magnificent! I was so worried that you were going to be killed."

"So, we're still friends?"

"More than ever," she whispered in his ear, her voice choked with emotion.

Coot felt his face flush, heated by the rekindling of hope for a life that included Diana. He was glad for the relative privacy of satellite communications. "Life-threatening episodes are powerful wake-up calls, aren't they?"

"I'll say. I can't wait to see you when you get home."

"Likewise," said Coot. "Maybe dinner and a piano lesson?"

"Sounds great! Hurry back."

"You can count on it." For a moment, Coot felt as high as Mount McKinley, which he knew Diana would call Dinali. Then he remembered that seven nuclear-armed missiles were still racing toward his beloved country.

* * *

Jill, Diana, Baxter, and McComb returned to the Situation Room, taking the sat phone with them. The president and other officials were staring at one of the large monitors on the wall. Diana followed their gaze. Seven yellow lines had come out of North Korea and were quickly extending themselves toward North America. Seven red dots flashed in the lower forty-eight states. Diana gasped as she read the labels on the dots. Seattle. San Francisco. Los Angeles. Denver. Chicago. Detroit. St. Louis. She and Coot both had family members in those cities. Diana wondered whether their residents had been warned to take cover. Evacuation was hopeless. Better to be in a basement than in a car when a nuclear weapon exploded nearby.

As four lines reached Alaska, four blue arcs rapidly grew toward them. Diana knew that, high in the skies over Alaska, four warheads sped downward toward their targets, while four interceptors rushed toward them. A similar drama unfolded over the Pacific Ocean. The monitor showed three blue arcs reaching toward three yellow ones. One by one, six of the yellow lines went orange and six of the red dots turned a steady green, as six kinetic kill vehicles struck warheads, fragmenting them with the energy of hypersonic collisions. Shouts of triumph echoed around the room. Jill and Diana grinned broadly at each other.

Diana's joy vanished and her hand flew to her gaping mouth, as the seventh blue line vanished over Alaska and the seventh yellow line continued to grow. One warhead continued on its fateful course. The red dot labeled "St. Louis" continued to flash. Another blue arc erupted from California, as another interceptor tried to catch up to the sole surviving warhead. To Diana's eye the eighth interceptor seemed to have too much distance to cover and too little time. The endpoints of the arcs were not converging on the monitor. The St. Louis blues would likely come to have far greater poignancy than ever before.

Diana glanced at the president. Tears streamed down both his cheeks. She remembered that he had spent his childhood in St. Louis and attended Washington University there. His brothers and a sister still lived in the area. The most powerful man in the world, he was unable to prevent the destruction of his own family.

"Remind me how big their warheads are." The president kept his eyes fixed on the dot and the line.

"Eight kilotons, Mr. President," said the national security advisor.

"Ah, yes," said the president, his eyes still glued to the monitor. "Half the size of the Hiroshima bomb."

"Yes, sir."

"And how many people did that bomb kill?"

"About 150,000, sir."

"Mmm." The president bowed his head. "I guess it's time to pray."

Diana looked back at the monitor. The yellow line was almost at the red dot, the obliteration of St. Louis imminent.

Another monitor on the wall was showing CNN's coverage of the attack. After the all-clear had sounded for the six spared cities, CNN had concentrated on St. Louis. The screen was divided into quadrants. One showed the great arch and the downtown area, including the massive traffic jams at the bridges leading east across the Mississippi River. Another showed the huge Boeing Defense, Space & Security facility in Berkeley, Missouri, a suburb St. Louis. A third quadrant pictured the campus of Wash U, deserted except for a solitary bearded man holding a sign that read "The End Is Near, and We're Fucked." Talking heads occupied the fourth quadrant, but they talked in silence.

The yellow line had almost reached the red dot on the missile tracking monitor, but Diana noticed that the dot had moved about thirty miles northwest of St. Louis itself, near Grafton, Illinois. Apparently the North Korean missiles' notorious inaccuracy would spare the St. Louis metropolitan area from the worst effects of the coming blast.

A great flash appeared in each of the first three quadrants of the CNN feed. The talking heads momentarily quit jabbering.

"Oh, God," murmured the president. Others in the room were not so delicate in their oaths.

The missile monitor flashed white text near the now-steady red dot:

Yield: 7.8 KT
Longitude: 90° 30' 59.42" W
Latitude: 39° 00' 15.25" N
Altitude: 1000 ft

"Damn, that was close!" McComb waved his phone with its map app at the group. "Smack in the middle of Pere Marquette State Park."

"Let's wait for casualty reports before we celebrate," said the president. "And we have a war to prosecute."

* * *

The sat phone rang, startling Coot.

"Hi, Coot!"

Diana's excited voice made Coot's pulse race. "What's happened?"

"Six warheads were destroyed and the seventh exploded above a park northwest of St Louis."

Coot's smile widened into a toothy grin. He pumped his fist, as delighted in victory as any Super Bowl winner. "The country's dodged a lot more than a bullet."

"The blast started a big fire in the park." Diana became quieter. "We don't know how many people were killed or injured. We think the North Koreans intended to hit the big Boeing plant."

Coot thought not just about the unfortunate people in the park but about the many more who had been killed elsewhere in the world, and the millions who just moments earlier had escaped a horrible death. "Seven American cities narrowly escaping destruction, two successful terrorist attacks, and two more thwarted should convince people of the dangers of nuclear weapons anywhere in the world." His resolve grew firmer than ever, strengthened by his own brush with death. "We absolutely must get rid of them."

"You know I agree with you on that." Diana's voice was soft and soothing in Coot's ear. Just what he needed to hear after his ordeal in the sky.

The damaged Tupolev made a rough landing in Fairbanks, causing another cry of pain from George Boyd but a great sense of relief for Coot. He exhaled the breath he had held since he first saw the runway below, and grinned.

The sat phone signaled another incoming call.

"Mr. Jenkins? F.B.I. Agent Bob Winston here."

"We have two dead on board." Coot felt calm giving the body count. "One Mushroom and one Korean, plus three injured, one seriously, all Mushrooms. The four pilots are uninjured."

"We're lucky the toll wasn't higher. Much higher," said Winston. "What about the weapons and the vest?"

"I have both Glocks and the Korean woman's weapon. The vest is here somewhere."

Winston explained the plan to evacuate the Tupolev to Coot, who relayed it to the Mushrooms.

The aircraft taxied to a remote part of the airport, where it was quickly surrounded by marked and unmarked cars with flashing red and blue lights. Two ambulances were also parked nearby. This time, Coot noticed, several media trucks idled outside the ring of official cars. With the "flight attendant" dead, the first officer opened the main cabin door. A set of stairs had been moved into place and a S.W.A.T. was climbing them. Two paramedics with a stretcher waited at some distance from the aircraft.

Coot turned to George one last time. What a shame, that such a smart, knowledgeable fellow had allowed anger to dominate his life. Tens of thousands of New Yorkers had lost their lives because of George's alienation. Yet, the results could have been much worse if Boyd and the others had decided not to cooperate. Without holding out his hand, Coot simply said, "Good luck, George. With your help we'll have a reasonable chance to nail Pepsey and Henry."

A man with an assault rifle at the ready stepped into the cabin, glanced quickly around, then looked at Coot. "F.B.I., Mr. Jenkins. You okay?"

Coot nodded. More agents entered the cabin and headed up the aisle toward the cockpit, stopping to frisk the live Mushrooms and check the two bodies. One agent remained with the injured Mushrooms. She talked with them, then radioed for the paramedics to board with the stretcher. The other agents took the captain, first officer, and two relief pilots into custody.

Coot looked back at the first agent, then glanced at the pile of pistols on the seat beside him. "You'll want to take these."

The man gathered up the Glocks and Col. Gwon's pistol, then turned back to Coot. "And the vest?"

Coot pointed to a nearby seat. "Over there. You're welcome to it."

"Agent Winston is waiting for you outside, Mr. Jenkins."

Coot walked to the cabin door and stepped out into brilliant sunlight shining from the dark blue Alaskan sky. He closed his eyes and inhaled deeply the crisp Alaskan air, then relaxed and breathed out, feeling the tension of the past few weeks flow from his body. He felt lighter in spirit than he had in a long, long time.

Made in the USA
Charleston, SC
13 October 2013